SWEET CONQUEST

"We are enemies, Colonel," she said curtly. "You the conqueror, and I the prisoner. It is not a position that allows for truce."

"We are also people." He took a step toward her. "Cannot two people develop a liking for each other despite politics, Virginia?"

"If you consider you have the right to use my given name, Colonel Marshall, then I must consider that the privilege is mutual."

She had hoped to goad him again, but the colonel was a stubborn man, and there was something about her slight, determined figure, the proud set of her head, that stirred him as no woman had ever done. "My name is at your disposal. My friends call me Alex."

"And what do your prisoners call you?" Her hand was on the wooden latch of the dairy door, the knuckles white under the unnaturally fierce grip.

To her horror, a lean, strong hand closed over hers. "I do not wish to fight with you, Virginia. There are other things I would much prefer to do."

It was quite true, he realized, keeping his hand on hers, lifting her face with the other. The gray eyes widened in startled protest as his words sank in, and a tremor shook the slim frame as he placed his mouth firmly and deliberately over the full, generous one below . . .

BELOVED ENEMY

BELOVED ENEMY

JANE FEATHER

ZEBRA BOOKS
KENSINGTON PUBLISHING CORP.

ZEBRA BOOKS are published by

Kensington Publishing Corp.
850 Third Avenue
New York, NY 10022

First Printing: July, 1987
10 9 8 7 6 5 4 3 2

Printed in the United States of America

Part One

When the blast of war blows

Chapter One

They came at sunset. There were perhaps two hundred of them, the evening sun setting alight the round helmets and breastplates, turning the tips of steel pikes and halberds into glowing candles. Perhaps a third were on horseback, the remainder on foot—a silent, orderly brigade tramping across the overgrown lawns, neglected driveway, and paths that led to the house.

She stood waiting in the open front door on this warm summer evening of 1648. The house at her back was a Jacobean mansion of soft, sea-weathered stone, the classical cornices and pilasters bespeaking an age before civil war, when an English gentleman could afford to indulge his taste for the gentle arts of architecture and landscaping, and build for posterity the manor house that declared his wealth and endeavor.

The brigade drew closer, and it became clear that one man rode slightly ahead of the front ranks. Her practiced eye approved both his horse—a magnificent black charger standing maybe twenty hands—and the easy seat of the rider. The latter carried neither pike nor musket, but one gloved hand rested on the hilt of the sword at his hip, the other held the reins as loosely as if he were astride a placid mare.

The cavalcade came to a halt at the base of the shallow flight of steps leading to the front door. She remained at her post, waiting in silence. For a long moment the quiet was broken only by the whinny of a horse, the clink of a bridle as its wearer tossed a head and pawed the gravel. The ranks of men in their leathern britches, helmets, and breastplates stood at attention as the sun dipped behind the headland and vanished into Alum Bay.

As if the loss of the sun were a signal of some kind, the leading horseman declaimed: "I am come by the authority of Parliament to sequester all lands and property pertaining to · one John Redfern of this Isle of Wight, whose Malignancy to the rule of Parliament has been proven."

The figure on the steps merely inclined her head. What else was she to do? It was not as if she had an army at her back, muskets trained on the silent ranks come to wrest from her her birthright. She had a ready sense of the absurd that in happier days had landed her hip deep in childhood trouble, and now it again came most inconveniently to the fore — two-hundred armed men facing one unarmed, unprotected woman! Her lips twitched.

The man had witnessed many emotions during these years of civil war. He had seen bravado, resignation, true courage, abject terror, but never could he remember seeing laughter on the face of a Royalist when the New Model Army enforced the decrees of Parliament.

He swung from his horse and mounted the steps, drawing off his gauntlets. "Your name, mistress?"

"Is this an introduction, sir? Or simply an inquisition?"

Her eyes were gray — as cold as the Atlantic Ocean crashing against the Needle Rocks that stood guard over this stretch of water between the Isle of Wight and the English mainland. She was young — barely twenty, he decided. Tall for a woman, but her frame slender and pliant as a willow in the deep-blue kirtle of homespun linen, a white apron tied in a businesslike fashion that merely served to accentuate a waist that he could span with both hands. Her skin carried the golden bloom of summer days spent in the open air. He glanced down at her quiet hands. A slim gold band encircled her ring finger, and the hands were as brown as the small face, but there was a work-roughened quality to their skin

8

that indicated hardship.

Alex Marshall, the youngest son of the earl of Grantham, suddenly remembered his upbringing. "I am Colonel Alexander Marshall, mistress."

"That is an uncomfortably royal name for a Roundhead to carry, Colonel," she said, without immediately responding to the introduction.

Alex Marshall had few scruples when it came to pitched battle, little compunction when he fulfilled Parliament's orders and arrested the king's adherents, sequestered their estates, and disinherited their occupants. Until this moment, however, he had never felt the slightest inclination to vent frustration on a woman.

Those gray eyes mocked him as she curtsied and said, "Virginia Courtney, Colonel. I have little hospitality to offer you and . . ." She gestured at the throng. ". . . your cohorts. But what I have, I gladly extend."

Alex was conscious of two-hundred pairs of eyes at his back as he stood alone facing this extraordinary woman who made fun of him with every supple movement and every glint in her eyes. A woman who offered him hospitality as a gracious hostess extending succor to the wanderer.

"Who is here with you?" It was a harsh demand, an attempt to establish a supremacy that was usually unquestioned.

"Why, no one, Colonel. I am quite alone," she responded. "You need have no fear for your men's safety. They are not about to be attacked." The voice was dulcet, sweet in its insolent challenge.

Ginny watched him covertly. She must take care not to antagonize the conqueror too much lest she endanger others than herself. It was a fine line she must tread if she were to achieve her object. He was in his late twenties, she decided, and as personable as it was possible for anyone to be in that detestable uniform. His eyes were a mélange of greeny-brown — not true hazel, but moving in that direction; his eyebrows dark brown and most definitive. An aquiline nose stood above full lips that at this moment were set in a thin line. There was an uncompromising set to the jaw, Ginny reflected, as she wondered what color his hair would be if he ever took off that helmet. One thing she knew, it would be cropped short in the manner of all Roundheads.

"What relationship do you hold to John Redfern?"

"His daughter, sir."

"And where is your mother?"

"Dead, these six months." It was a flat statement. "My father, as I am sure you are aware, died three years ago at the Battle of Naseby."

"And your husband?" His eyes fixed on the wedding ring.

"Killed during the surrender of Oxford." It was another simple, expressionless statement.

"And where is your household, Mistress Courtney?" She was forcing this catechism from him, putting him in the position of a boorish brute dragging the catalogue of war deaths from a lone widow. The thin line of his lips tightened.

"Gone." She shrugged with an assumption of ease. "There is little purpose, Colonel, in maintaining an estate destined for the block. I have lived alone these past six months. If you doubt my word, you have only to look around." Ginny gestured to the overgrown lawns, the box hedges around the flower garden springing out of their former ornamental shapes to throw unruly sprigs into the weed-infested broad walks, destroying the neatness of the rectangles and squares that had marked her mother's beloved garden.

"There is absolutely *no one* living with you?" He stared, incredulous.

"Have I not just said so, Colonel?" A martial light appeared in the previously cold gray depths of her eyes. She was enjoying herself, Alex Marshall realized, as she stood challenging him in the face of an armed brigade.

The colonel, however, was most definitely not enjoying himself. It had been ten years since anyone had questioned his authority, either implicitly or explicitly, and it was not an experience he wished to continue — particularly when the questioner was a mere slip of a girl.

"How old are you?" he snapped.

"I do not consider that to be your affair, Colonel." Had she overplayed her hand? It was a lamentable tendency she had

10

when her blood rose in anger or when the game took precedence over the goal. Tread softly now!

She had little chance, however, to follow her own advice. The colonel spun her around and propelled her into the house away from watching eyes. The hall was large and cool, the walls elaborately paneled, the plasterwork of the ceiling ornate. A broad staircase with an intricately carved baluster led to the upper floors. But the colonel, at this point, was not interested in admiring his surroundings. "I asked you a question, Mistress Courtney, and I will have my answer."

"And if I choose not to give it to you?"

"Then you will discover, girl, that I am an uncomfortable man to challenge." He spoke very softly.

It was that soft voice that convinced Ginny, more than the hand still gripping her elbow and the exasperation in the greeny-brown eyes. Deciding that she had played with fire for as long as it was safe to do so, Ginny shrugged nonchalantly and said, "nineteen, Colonel."

"And why have you been permitted to remain here unattended?"

"In the absence of my parents and my husband, sir, there is no authority that I am prepared to acknowledge," Ginny replied coolly.

"And what of your husband's family? There must be someone who stands guardian to you. You are not yet of age."

"I did not say I had no guardian." She spoke slowly as if to a half-witted child. "I said only that there is no authority I am prepared to accept."

Taking her chin between long fingers, he tilted her face and examined it thoughtfully. It was an arresting countenance, dominated by those fine eyes, but much more youthful than he had originally perceived. "My child, I am afraid that your parents and your husband must have sadly neglected their duties. You appear remarkably undisciplined."

Virginia, her composure shattered as he paid her back in her own coin, attempted to pull herself free from his hold, but the fingers tightened on her chin. He held her thus for a

11

minute longer and then, with a satisfied chuckle, released her. "It is not pleasant, is it, Mistress Courtney, to be goaded? Come, I wish to inspect the house."

"You wish to see it first, before giving your men the freedom to pillage?" Venom coated every word as she took her revenge. The gasp of outrage this time came from the colonel. He took a step toward her, but she stood her ground, for he was not to know that her knees shook beneath her skirt.

"My men do *not* pillage," he hissed.

"Then they are the exceptions to the rule," bravely she said. "Vandal and Roundhead are held to be synonymous these days."

It was, of course, true and a fact that Colonel Marshall deeply regretted. Many beautiful houses and priceless paintings had, in the last year, fallen victim to the besieging cannon, the soldier's pike, and the burning torch. But his own men were too well disciplined, too much in awe of their colonel, who punished the slightest excess with a fearful consistency.

"You may rest assured, Mistress Courtney, that the house and its contents will suffer as little harm as is consonant with occupation," he said stiffly. "I intend to make this place my headquarters during my sojourn on the island and would be glad if you would show me what accommodations the house has to offer."

Virginia curtsied and inclined her head. "I am at your service, Colonel. There are but twelve bedrooms, counting mine own. Of course, there are the servants' quarters, but I hardly think you may house all your men there."

Alex heard the note of mockery again and fought to keep a tight rein on his temper. His moment of supremacy had not lasted long. "My men will bivouac in the gardens and the orchard."

"I do hope that they will show respect for the shrubs and the fruit trees," she murmured sweetly, turning toward the drawing room.

Alex Marshall regarded the slender straight back, the firm set of her shoulders, the arrogant tilt of her head where glossy chestnut braids formed a neat crown. Mingling with his infuriation came reluctant admiration and the most intense curiosity. What kind of woman was this, who faced adversity with a grim humor and a conquering army with a defiance laced with irony? He had the liveliest desire to find out.

Blissfully unaware that such a desire played perfectly into the hands of Virginia Courtney, he strode to the open front door and in ringing accents gave orders for the dispersal of the troops before he accompanied her on the tour of this gracious house.

Leather carpets covered the floors of the dining and drawing rooms; the stools held gold nails, and green velvet covered the few chairs reserved for the elderly and honored guests. It was a house that bespoke both the wealth and taste of a seventeenth-century English gentleman. The usual trestle table had given place to solid black oak with ornamental legs; beds and cupboards were of the same magnificently carved wood. Framed pictures hung on the oak-paneled walls, and the colonel recognized several Rubens and Van Dycks. In the deep embrasures of the windows, marble sculptures stood carefully placed to catch the eye. But the miasma of neglect hung in the still evening air, exemplified in the tarnished bronze and gold furnishings, the dust nestling in the knots of the intricate carvings, running in white lines down the folds of the velvet draperies.

"It is a little difficult for one person to maintain such a house in true order," Ginny said in inadvertent defense, dusting a small table with her apron.

"Quite so, mistress," he concurred, averting his gaze from the slight flush of discomfiture mantling the sun-browned cheeks and the sheen that obscured the clarity of her gaze.

Alex had hidden the tragedy and pathos of this war behind his vision of a land no longer ruled by the despotism of the Stuart monarchy—a land where Parliament, elected by the people, held the only definitive voice of the lawmaker. But on this summer afternoon, on this small island outpost of the greater island that was England, in the dust of a neglected manor house and the militant sparkle of a pair of gray eyes, the greater purpose became diminished, split into the atoms of its suffering human parts. This girl had lost her father in the great Battle of Naseby, three years ago, when Cromwell's New Model Army had won a decisive victory against Charles I and the royal army under the command of his nephew, Prince Rupert. The following year, she had lost her husband when the king's headquarters at Oxford had surrendered and King Charles had given himself into the hands of the Scots, no more friends of Parliament than he was. In the wake of their victory, the parliamentary armies had besieged the estates of the Cavaliers who still held out for the king; Parliament had imposed crippling fines on the Malignants—fines that had forced them to sell off vast acres of field and woodland. In extreme cases, the lands had been sequestered and the owners disinherited. This island backwater, however, had escaped for two years until the king had chosen to illuminate it with his presence. Having been handed over to Parliament by the Scots, who hoped thus to make peace, he had been seized by the army and imprisoned in Hampton Court. Charles I had listened to explosive rumblings within the army as the Radicals overcame the Moderates, and his very life had become threatened as talk of bringing him to summary justice grew stronger. In November 1647, he had escaped Hampton Court and taken sanctuary in Carisbrooke Castle on the Isle of Wight, ostensibly the guest of the governor, Colonel Hammond, who found his Royalist sympathies clashing mercilessly with an office he held by the authority of Parliament.

Alex Marshall's brigade was part of the reinforcements sent to the Isle of Wight—their task to deal harshly with the many local Royalists rallying around the king, as Royalist uprisings swept through England and Wales, bringing this, the second civil war in six years, to a land already riven and denuded by strife.

When he had come to the Redfern estate this evening, to exact Parliament's penalty, he had not expected to find only John Redfern's orphaned, widowed daughter standing between the enemy at the gate and her inheritance. It seemed

14

to make nonsense of the presence of an entire brigade, and this young, unprotected woman was making him feel like a posturing idiot.

"You will grant me sufficient time to remove my possessions from here? Or are they also sequestered, Colonel?" Ginny's heart pounded as she broached the all-important matter. Had she read him rightly in those first moments? Read correctly the paradox inherent in the ingrained authority of the commander, who could not tolerate a challenge, and the chivalry of the noble born, who would not cast out a defenseless woman. If she was right, both those facets of his personality would dictate that he keep her under his eye, at least for a short while.

She opened a heavy door onto a west-facing corner room. It was a girl-child's room with its dimity hangings to the bed and the windows. A spinning wheel stood in one corner, the hemp of flax partly spun and carded. A wooden doll, prettily dressed, sat on the window seat. A set of tortoise-shell combs lay on the dresser, and the armoire stood open to reveal her scant wardrobe.

For the moment ignoring the sarcastic question, Alex went to the casement standing open to the sea. The house stood on the cliff above Alum Bay at the westerly end of the Isle of Wight. The small cove was famous for its variegated sands — every color of the rainbow — and for its commanding position at the point where the ocean gave way to the relatively peaceful waters of the Solent. In the evening light the Needle Rocks presented a mellow nonthreatening image to those who did not know these waters. The English mainland was still just visible across the five-mile stretch of water, and the coast of France, should King Charles finally decide to make his escape complete, a day's sail across the channel.

"There is no need for you to remove your possessions, mistress, since you will continue to occupy this chamber." The colonel turned from the casement, his decision made.

Ginny frowned even as her heart leaped. She *had* read him right, but she could not allow her relief to show. Her mouth took a recalcitrant turn. "You will pardon my stupidity, sir, but I do not appear to understand you."

Alex Marshall sighed. Unless he was very much mistaken, Virginia Courtney was going to prove a most troublesome acquisition. "Then let me make myself plain, once and for all. Since you have no visible guardian and are a widowed minor, you are now a ward of Parliament."

"A prisoner?" Her eyebrows lifted. "No, Colonel. You have not the right to take noncombatants prisoner, and I have not resisted you in any fashion, so can hardly be designated a combatant."

"Very well," he said. "If that is the attitude you wish to adopt, then I am quite willing to play my own hand." Crossing the chamber, he again tilted her chin, ignoring her indignant gasp. "Mistress Courtney, with the authority invested in me by Parliament, I herewith place you under house arrest. You are the only surviving heir of the Malignant John Redfern, whose estates have been sequestered, and I deem it impolitic to allow your freedom. Your movements are restricted to the house and the immediate boundaries of the estate until such time as Parliament decrees otherwise."

Until such time as Alex Marshall decrees otherwise, Ginny amended grimly. It was exactly what she wanted, of course, but for some reason that did little to reduce her annoyance, did nothing to reduce another strange feeling that she could not identify. A feeling that seemed to have something to do with the armored body standing almost knee to knee with her, the warm strength of his fingers holding her chin, and the curious glow in the greeny-brown eyes. Her eyelashes fluttered in an attempt to conceal any revealing sparks from the intent scrutiny bent upon her upturned face. "It appears, Colonel, that I have no choice but to accept my position. It is to be hoped that your soldiers will also accept that position."

"You need have no fear, mistress." Alex, once again at a disadvantage, spoke brutally. "So long as you behave with circumspection, my men are not going to rape a woman under my protection."

"Then I must be grateful for that protection," she re-

16

sponded gently.

"Do not tempt me, Virginia!" Releasing her chin abruptly, he stepped away from her as his anger flared.

"I do not recall according you the right to use my name."

"You are not in a position to accord me any rights whatsoever. I suggest you accept that fact with all due speed before my far-from-inexhaustible patience runs out!"

It appeared to be a suitable moment to yield gracefully. The colonel was quite convinced of her reluctance to remain in the house under his protection. She had only to offer the semblance of defiance now and again to ensure that he remained so convinced. "And how is my imprisonment to be conducted, colonel? Am I considered sufficiently dangerous to be kept under guard?" It was her last challenge for the time being.

A telltale muscle twitched in the colonel's cheek. "You will restrict your movements according to my decree. Should you break parole, you will be confined within doors. It is understood?"

"Perfectly, Colonel." Ginny sketched a curtsy. There would be no need to break her parole to complete her work. Her main fear had been that she would have been turned off the estate by the occupying forces. But the closer confined she was to home, the easier it would be. Until Edmund's wound was sufficiently healed for him to make his escape. Then would she make hers, also.

"Am I to be permitted to go about my business now?" she asked demurely. "Dusk is falling, and I should shut up the chickens before the fox begins to prowl. The horses also require my attention, the cow needs milking, and I must water the vegetable garden."

"How much livestock do you have?" He frowned, forgetting his exasperation with her for the moment. The tasks she had just described were those better suited to a domestic servant than to the daughter of a lord. She would most certainly have been educated to sew and spin, to distill medicines from herbs for the use of the household, and to make the fruit syrups and wines from currant, cowslip, and elderberries. In addition she would have been taught fine cooking and the methods of curing meat for the long winter months, and of preserving herbs and fruit. But the heavy outdoor farm work was not considered a suitable occupation for a lady of the great house.

"I have kept just enough for my own purposes." She shrugged, well aware of the thoughts that had prompted his question. "Two horses, a dozen chickens, one cow, oh . . . and a pig, which I had intended to have slaughtered to supply me with meat during the winter months. A local farmer, in exchange for the use of a pasture, supplies me with grain for bread and feed for the cattle. I have been able to maintain the vegetable garden, and the orchard has borne well this year. I am in no danger of starving, Colonel, so long as my husbandry is efficient."

What an extraordinary woman she was! "You are most resourceful, Virginia. But I will have one of my men undertake those tasks for you. In exchange, you might perhaps prepare a meal for myself and my officers. We are heartily sick of campfire cooking and have plentiful supplies." He found himself offering her a smile, inviting her sympathy, then realized that it was hardly appropriate in the circumstances.

His plan did not suit Virginia at all. She needed the freedom of the garden and the stableyard, the cover of the routine business that would take her there. In her turn, she gave him a hopefully winning smile. "I will be happy to cook for you, Colonel, since I consider you to be my guests. But I would prefer to perform my own tasks in mine own fashion. I do not see what reasonable objection you might make to that."

Alex could think of none, either — except that it was not the work of a lady. But Virginia Courtney was no ordinary member of that breed, and he had, perhaps, achieved sufficient victory for this day. Anyway, that smile was quite irresistible. It started in her eyes, which crinkled at the corners in the most appealing fashion, before the full lips curved to reveal unusually fine white teeth. Her face lost all its cold-eyed irony and became that of a vibrant young woman well aware of her charms and possessed of a delicious sense of humor. Alex Marshall suddenly wished he had met her at some other time and place.

"As you wish." His voice was brusque, hiding these uncomfortable reflections. "You will be pleased to remember, however, that you now fall under my command, and as you will learn from my soldiers, I do not tolerate disobedience." Swinging on his heel, he left her bedchamber.

Ginny nodded to herself. There was little reason to doubt his statement. Her only course lay in placation and the appearance of total obedience. For as long as she was allowed to move freely around the estate, accustoming the men to her presence and the routine nature of her movements, she could continue to provide for Edmund and Peter, keeping the secret on which hung all their lives.

With swift decision, she strode from the room, along the gallery that ran three sides of the second floor overlooking the entrance hall below. She paused for a moment, hiding behind a carved pillar to look down on a lively scene. The men marching through her house for all the world as if it were their own were clearly officers, to judge by their insignia and the spurs on their booted feet that rang out on the stone-flagged floor. They appeared to be taking inventory and were doing so in a seemingly orderly fashion, their voices as educated and well modulated as their colonel's.

Of course, this civil war was not a war between classes, Ginny reflected. It was a war of political and religious convictions, and there were as many of the well-born fighting for Parliament as there were fighting for King Charles. Many of the noblest houses had been split asunder, brother against brother, father against son. Was Alex Marshall a case in point?

Ginny slipped down the backstairs that gave direct access to the kitchens. There were men here, too, but common soldiers carting supplies—sides of beef and pork that they hung in the cold, flagged pantries, sacks of flour and meal, leathern flagons of wine. Oliver Cromwell's New Model Army clearly looked after itself. Outside, the stableyard was a hive of activity as the cavalry saw to the needs of their mounts. The Redfern estate was typical of its kind and geared to the breeding and purchasing of horses. They were the only form of transport and were now beginning to replace oxen for the heavy farm work. No self-sufficient estate could afford to ignore their needs. As a result, there was ample accommodation in the now-empty barns and stables for the twenty horses of the elite cavalry.

Virginia had kept two horses: her own mare that had been her father's wedding gift, and a cart horse to pull the dray when she went to collect her payment of grain and hay. They both appeared restless at this abrupt intrusion into the quiet lives they had led for the last six months. No move, however, had been made to dispossess them of their stalls, and she fed, watered, and soothed them.

The horses were considerably more amenable than Betsy. Ginny disliked the cow intensely. She was an obstinate creature, that would kick over the pail any chance she had. But Ginny had chosen to keep her over her more docile sisters because she gave the richest milk with a heavy golden crown of cream that made excellent butter and cheese.

The cow left her pasture willingly enough and moved docilely to the barn. She needed relief, after all, and was prepared to be good until it was afforded her. Only when her swollen udders were empty did she decide to kick up her heels. Ginny sat on the three-legged stool, resting her head against the warm, heaving flank as her fingers, skillful now after months of practice, kneaded and pulled. It was hard work, but her hands had grown strong, and the milk gushed forth to fill the pail. Afterward, she would skim the cream and mix it with raw eggs — a powerful concoction for the wounded man, one that would bring the strength back to Edmund's thin body and do much to repair the loss of blood. Make him again as strong and hardy as his foes — a worthy opponent for men like Alex Marshall.

The thought rose as unbidden as the image of the broad soldier's body that had stood so close to her own. Those greeny-brown eyes hovered in her internal vision. There had been one most disconcerting moment when those eyes had softened and glowed, freed of the angry flash of his response to her deliberate sparring. Supposing she had met him five

20

years ago, before Giles Courtney had been a suitor for her hand . . . before there had been any need for sparring? But five years ago, Alex Marshall would already have declared himself for Parliament, and no Royalist maid would have captured his eye, any more than she could do so now.

"Careful now! She'll have that over." It was as if her errant thoughts had worked a magic to conjure up the reality of the image. It was the colonel's voice, the colonel's arm pushing past her to whisk away the wooden pail from beneath the cow's belly. Ginny, deep in her reverie, had missed the warning shuffle of Betsy's feet.

She looked up at him with a laughing apology, hoping that her scarlet cheeks would be explained by embarrassment at her carelessness. He had shed the breastplate, helmet, and sword, wore the simple garb of the off-duty soldier, and his eyes were alight with laughter.

"Daydreaming, Mistress Courtney?"

"I fear so, Colonel. It is not wise with one of Betsy's ilk."

"No," he agreed, considering the baleful cow. "There's a slyness in her eyes."

"Yes . . . I must thank you, sir, for your timely intervention."

"I find that I prefer your gratitude to your challenges," said the colonel, lifting the pail. "It is not that I object to the militant sparkle in your eyes, you understand. Simply that I think you look rather truer to yourself when you smile." So saying, he flicked the end of her nose with a free forefinger. Ginny's jaw dropped at this casual, almost proprietorial gesture. Out of uniform, he seemed, if it were possible, even surer of himself and his commanding control over the circumstances. She was still searching for an appropriately dignified snub when he moved to the door, saying with a laugh in his voice, "You'll be wanting this in the dairy."

Ginny found herself skipping to keep pace with him as he strode across the stableyard and into the dairy. "It is surely beneath your dignity, Colonel, to carry pails of milk?" It was a fairly lame taunt, she recognized, but the best she could do in the circumstances.

Alex, to her irritation, chose to treat it as a straightforward observation. "A good commander, Virginia, does not stand on his dignity. I cannot ask my men to do what I am not prepared to undertake myself."

"Indeed not," she muttered as he placed the pail on a slate shelf beneath a high window.

"We are in agreement, then, on something." Still smiling, he turned back to her. "Let us cry peace, Virginia." Alex, since their last encounter, had decided on a change of tactic with his new responsibility. Continual head-on skirmishes would be as exhausting as they would be counterproductive, and he had decided to try disarming the opposition.

Why not, she thought for one wild moment as the temptation to yield sang its siren song. But then she remembered the fugitives hidden in the priest's hole. How could she ever have forgotten them? Virginia Courtney was a Royalist, the orphaned daughter of a Cavalier Malignant, the widow of a man who had died, albeit reluctantly, in the king's cause. And Virginia Courtney had hidden in her occupied house two fugitive Cavaliers, and not for the first time in the last six months, either.

"We are enemies, Colonel," she said curtly. "You the conqueror, and I the prisoner. It is not a position that allows for truce."

"We are also people." Unwilling to give up too quickly, he took a step toward her. "Cannot two people develop a liking for each other despite politics?"

"I think you are being naive, Colonel." She turned away to hide the flicker of uncertainty she knew would be revealed on her face.

"Virginia . . . ?" His voice arrested her at the door, and with great reluctance she paused, keeping her back to him.

"If you consider you have the right to use *my* given name, Colonel Marshall, then I must consider that the privilege is mutual."

She had hoped to goad him again, to return the relationship to the simple black and white of opponents, but the colonel was a stubborn man, and there was something about the slight, determined figure, the proud set of her head, that stirred him as no woman had ever done. "My name is at your disposal, mistress. My friends call me Alex."

"And what do your prisoners call you?" Her hand was on the wooden latch of the dairy door, the knuckles white under the unnaturally fierce grip.

"This is something of a unique situation for me." She heard the measured reply and, to her mesmerized horror, saw a lean brown hand close over hers, felt the warmth and the strength. "I understand your difficulty," the voice resumed in the same even tone. "But if I do not fight with you, then you will find it difficult to engage in battle yourself. I do not wish to fight with you, Virginia. As it happens, I find that there are other things I would much prefer to do."

It was quite true, he realized, keeping his hand on hers, lifting her face with his other. The gray eyes widened in startled protest as his words sank in, and a tremor shook the slim frame as he placed his mouth firmly and deliberately over the full, generous one below. For an instant, her eyes closed, her lips parted; then she broke free with a violence unwarranted by the gentle hold and banged the door shut behind her. Alex was left staring into the middle distance, his lips warm with the memory of hers, as he wondered what sorcery had entered his orderly, self-determined existence that hitherto had allowed no room for impulse.

Ginny fled to the henhouse, where she herded the chickens inside and collected the eggs, the routine activity of scolding and chasing inane birds somewhat soothing. What had just happened? An almost complete stranger had kissed her. She knew about the scandalously loose morality that had been the norm at court before the war. Edmund had told her when he had returned home after his first visit. He had reveled in every one of her shocked gasps, had answered every eager question with his newly acquired sophistication and the knowledge of his two years' seniority over his erstwhile playmate. Alex Marshall had presumably been an habitué of the court in the old days. While she did not know his lineage, he bore himself with the breeding of the courtier, and young men of his kind were presented, as Edmund had been, by the age of sixteen. Had he assumed, because she was a widow and a noblewoman, that she would understand the game? Would share his sophistication? And she could hardly believe she had responded. For one breathless, terrifying moment her body had fired in a manner she had never before experienced; her lips had softened and parted; she had leaned against him, her eyes closing . . . .

Ginny dropped an egg on the brick floor of the henhouse. It splattered in golden and white reproof, and the hens cackled in mockery. She gathered the remaining eggs in the skirt of her apron and made her way back to the house. She had an immensely difficult task to complete, and she would complete it, consigning the aberrant response to the man, her captor, Alex Marshall, colonel in the New Model Army, to the cess pit where it belonged.

Ginny took pleasure from the vulgarity of her thought as she entered the empty pantry. She took a loaf of bread, apples from the dry store, a round of cheese, and a slab of bacon, placing them carefully in a deep wicker basket that she then covered with a piece of sacking. The basket was heavy, but she would have to swing it as nonchalantly as if it were empty. When she returned, the basket would innocently contain produce from the vegetable garden and orchard. But her heart beat uncomfortably fast when she reentered the kitchen where a soldier in a leathern apron was mixing cornmush in a huge cauldron simmering over the vast range.

"Ah, Mistress Courtney." The colonel appeared in the kitchen door. Ginny's hand tightened on the handle of the basket. Supposing he should offer to carry it for her? The sweat of fear trickled down her back.

"You were looking for me, Colonel? As you see, I am still here, in obedience to your command."

To her relief, the sardonic note rang true and clear, and she saw the humor leave his face to be replaced with an angry glower. There were at least half a dozen soldiers in the kitchen to overhear the insolent challenge in her tone, and the colonel could not, on this occasion, allow it to pass.

"You would be well advised to remain so." He clipped his words and then strode out of the kitchen into the main part of the house.

"Eh, mistress, if you'll accept a word of advice, you'd best watch your step with the colonel. He's a fair man, but a hard one if he's crossed." The advice came from the soldier in the leathern apron, his face as brown and wrinkled as a pickled walnut.

Ginny shrugged with an assumption of insouciance. "Should he come inquiring for me, you may tell him that I am gone to pick vegetables and fruit for his dinner. He should not take objection to such an innocent activity." She went back into the yard and made her way toward the vegetable plot where she remained for a few minutes, desultorily picking beans.

There was no one in sight; the barn hid the vegetable plot from the stableyard and from the ground-floor windows at the back of the house. She would have to take the risk that no one was watching from an upstairs window to see her saunter casually from the garden in the direction of the west side of the house. Except for Ginny's corner casement, the wall here was windowless, facing as it did the Atlantic Ocean from where the winter gales roared viciously, battering against the wind-pitted stone. There was no garden on this extremity either, just the springy turf of the headland stretching to the cliff top. Once there, one would need to know exactly where the door was to identify, in the seemingly haphazard cracks of the stonework, the three lines that formed the rectangle. The spring lock was cunningly concealed beneath the moss clinging to the base of the wall. One minute a small figure in a blue kirtle stood against the wall of the house, and the next it had disappeared with all the speed and dexterity of an illusionist.

The air was cold and musty, the stone steps narrow and steep, and it was as black as pitch. But Ginny knew the way too well to need light, although she never made the journey without fear, however hard she tried to rationalize. There were no skeletons, no hobgoblins, no monstrous spiders and gigantic rats waiting to leap out at her; and she was no longer the petrified nine year old that Edmund had lured into the secret passage and then abandoned. By the time he had come back for her, she had been hysterical and inconsolable, and it was only loyalty to her beloved playmate that kept her silent in the face of adult questioning. She had had her reward for the remainder of that summer. Edmund had been her willing, grateful slave and never once told her she was only a stupid girl and she couldn't go birds' nesting or rock climbing, or any of the other infinitely exciting pursuits that seemed to fall most unfairly to the lot of the male gender.

Ginny smiled to herself as the memories chased away her fear, and she felt her way up the steps. She had received a goodly number of switchings that summer for neglecting her household duties, until John Redfern had told his distraught wife to allow the child a few months of freedom. She had a lifetime of duty ahead of her . . .

A glimmer of light appeared above, and Ginny paused to catch her breath. The basket seemed much heavier now, and the climb was steep. The faint glow, she knew, came from a single tallow candle, and the light reassured her not only of the journey's end but of the well-being of the fugitives.

"Ginny?" It was barely a whisper.

"Yes." She climbed the last few steps and emerged into the small round chamber.

Edmund struggled up from his pallet, his face even more ashen than she had expected.

"Are you worse?" Ginny took the three paces necessary to reach him, panic flickering in her eyes.

"No, no," he reassured her. "Better. But what is happening? Peter and I have been desperate for news. They have come?"

"They have come," she affirmed it simply and turned to the other man. Like the wounded Edmund he was unshaven, the long wavy hair of the Cavalier unkempt.

It had been ten days since Edmund Verney and Peter Ashley had taken refuge in the priest's hole, following the example of a dozen others in the preceding months. Last November, they had come with the king to Carisbrooke Castle and for four months had played the role of king's courtier, helping to maintain the myth that Charles I was no prisoner, simply a king indulging his divine right to do as he pleased—a myth that Parliament had been prepared to indulge until war had begun again on the mainland, and the likes of Alex Marshall had been sent to the island to make manifest the king's imprisonment. There had been skirmishes between the local Royalists and Parliament's reinforcements, and Edmund, Ginny's hotheaded cousin, who had never learned to recognize trouble unless it came with the force of a sledgehammer, had put aside the role of courtier and ventured forth to wage battle against those whom he still considered to be rebels. He had sent at least two to their deaths in a scrap at Newport before the sword point had slipped through his shoulder.

There was no safety then in Carisbrooke for the wounded murderer of Parliament's men. Colonel Hammond could not afford to antagonize Parliament by providing protection, and the king, himself, was powerless. Edmund, with Peter's help, by night and by stealth, had made the journey from Newport to Alum Bay—not a long journey if one was not bleeding from a deep wound, and if one was not being hunted. They had evaded the hunters to find spurious safety with a nineteen-year-old widow who, day by day, awaited the arrival of the occupying forces—an arrival that would put an end to her "safe" house and the runs she made in the small sailboat, ferrying fugitives across the Solent to a place where they could prepare themselves to fight another day.

"Peter, I have brought enough food for several days; there is no knowing when I may be able to return. There are about two-hundred men. The officers have occupied the house, and the men are setting up camp in the orchard and gardens."

"But what of you?" Edmund demanded, wincing as his sudden anxious movement sent pain shooting through his bandaged shoulder.

"I am under house arrest." Ginny dropped to her knees beside the pallet and began to unwrap the blood-stiffened bandages. "The colonel appears to have some strangely cavalier notions about the propriety of sending a recalcitrant widowed minor to seek her fortune." She gave Edmund her usual mischievous grin as she made her tone light and teasing. "I am become, I am reliably informed, a ward of Parliament. Is it not absurd?"

Edmund managed a wan smile that did little to hide the pain in his eyes as she eased the dressing from the ugly shoulder wound. Ginny sniffed the torn, reddened skin carefully and then signed with relief. "It is still clean; there are no signs of malignancy, thanks be, and it is healing well. I was unable to bring a fresh poultice but will try to leave one beneath the elder bush outside in the morning, and milk and eggs. You have sufficient water, Peter?"

"At the moment." The young man indicated the keg in the corner of the room. "Now Edmund's fever has abated he needs less, and I can manage with little."

Ginny frowned. "Bringing water presents more difficulties than food. I would not care to explain to Colonel Marshall why I choose to carry pails of water to the cliff head."

"Marshall?" Peter stared at her. "Alex Marshall?"

"Why, yes. Do you know him?"

"We were at Oxford together. He is the youngest son of the earl of Grantham. There was a time when we were close friends . . . " Peter's whisper faded. "He was a powerful friend and, I fancy, will be as powerful an opponent."

Ginny frowned. "What else do you know of him, Peter? Did he once play at court as scandalously as the rest of you?" She smiled in the hope that the question would thus seem joking and disinterested.

"Not Alex Marshall," Peter declared. "He has always been a career soldier with leanings toward the Puritan. He and Prince Rupert were close, though — both mad for soldiering and both brilliant commanders — until this damnable war happened, and Alex, for reasons of his own, joined the rebels. It nearly killed his father, and his mother died soon after, of a broken heart, it is said. The earl has disowned him, and his brothers are sworn to vengeance."

Ginny shuddered as she filled in the details this succinct word picture gave of a devastating family schism. What kind of man was it, who could split his family asunder for the sake of a political ideal? Who could forsake all the traditional loyalties to king and kin?

"He is not a man to be trifled with." Peter tuned uncannily into her thoughts. "He is a man of rigid principles and has always been held in both fear and respect by friends and foes alike. His loyalty is to his country, first and foremost. He was always in favor of reform, of a reduction in the king's power. When he came out against the king, there was little surprise."

"We leave here tonight." Edmund spoke with more strength than he had evinced in the last week. "You stand in sufficient danger already, Ginny. If you are caught harboring wanted men, then you will lose your head."

"Oh, stuff!" She tore a sheet of fresh linen and began to rebandage the wound. "It is quite perfect. Who is to suspect two fugitive Cavaliers of hiding in the midst of the lion's den? You could not be safer and will suffer only boredom and inactivity until you are able to travel. In the meantime, I will make myself an obedient prisoner of the colonel's, and his cohorts will become accustomed to my presence and will cease to notice me. The sailboat is well hidden in the cave, and when you are well enough to sail for the mainland, we shall contrive our escape."

"Edmund is right," Peter said heavily. "You must no longer bring us supplies, not when a brigade of Roundheads swarms over the estate. We will make our escape this night."

"Now you are being absurd. Apart from the fact that Edmund is weak and in pain, I do not know the routine of the camp yet. We must wait for the moment when the tide is right and we are least likely to be observed. Otherwise, we shall all lose our heads."

"But the risk you take . . . " It was the last objection — they were all well aware of the sense of her statement.

"It is less than attempting to escape tonight. We must be patient."

"There seems little option." Peter sighed. "But I cannot like it."

"We are not in a position to like or dislike anything," Ginny retorted tartly and then apologized for her sharpness. The prisoners would be in torment, cabined in the semi-darkness of this tiny chamber with no activity to take their minds from their lonely danger, and no facilities but the wooden pail that Peter emptied each night under cover of darkness. "I must go before my absence is remarked. Be patient, Edmund, for just a little longer. I know it is not your greatest virtue, but I fear it is one you must learn to practice." She smiled a reassurance that she didn't feel and prayed that Edmund, who knew her so well, would not see through the facade. The son of John Redfern's widowed sister, he had grown up with the Redferns, providing Ginny with the sibling she had never had, and the brotherly companionship of one who was not a brother, and with whom, therefore, she could share so many growing pains.

She left the way she had come, opening the stone door a crack, peering around to ascertain that the coast was clear before slipping out into the dusk. Rather than return immediately to the vegetable garden, Ginny strolled casually to the orchard. If anyone had noticed her leaving the garden earlier, she could say that she had decided to pick fruit first. No one would think that it had taken her about twenty minutes to walk the quarter mile to the orchard.

The orchard seethed with life as the men set up their bivouacs and lit the braziers that would cook their evening meal. They had for the most part discarded their breastplates and helmets and sat amidst their tents polishing armor, joking and talking, taking their ease on this warm summer evening in the peaceful surroundings where no pitched battle threatened for the morrow.

Ginny moved amongst them, picking fruit from the lowest branches. No one spoke to her, but they stared as if she were some kind of misshapen exhibit in a traveling circus. Women were a luxury. The colonel permitted no camp followers, and excursions into the local towns were strictly regulated, doled out like spoonful of medicine to purge the unruly body. The men grumbled at the strictness of the regime and compared their lives with those of their colleagues in brigades where the command was lax. But even as they complained, they knew that their colonel was as careful of their lives as he was of their morals. In battle he was always at their head, never threw them into futile engagements, thought more of strategy than vainglory, and they were well fed and as rested as it was possible for an army on the move to be.

The word had gone around that the colonel had placed the mistress of the manor under house arrest and she was to be accorded all due respect. If discovered attempting to leave the immediate boundaries of the house and garden, she was to be prevented with courtesy and escorted to the colonel. These orders, however, did not alleviate the lustful stirrings at the sight of that svelte body, the firm high breasts pressing against the bodice of her gown as she reached up for a succulent piece of fruit, or the delineation of her hips as she bent to pick up a windfall.

Ginny was acutely uncomfortable and decided that she would avoid the orchard in future. Those stripping eyes made her feel like a coquettish wanton, deliberately tantalizing those who could not take advantage of her apparently freely offered charms. If it were not for the protection of Alex Marshall, she would not have left the orchard unmolested, of that Ginny was convinced as she walked away, fighting the urge to run.

Chapter Two

The stableyard was now quiet, the horses bedded down and their attendants gathered in a companionable group by the barn, wooden spoons scraping the tin porringers clean, the contents of pewter tankards disappearing down thirsty throats.

The kitchen was deserted. Ginny laid the basket of produce on the table and worried about the task she had agreed to perform. How many officers did the colonel command? And what in the world was she to serve them in the short time available? He had spoken of plentiful supplies, and she had seen evidence of that earlier. At least the range was lit, although it made the kitchen unpleasantly warm. Well, first she must discover how many she was to cook for. With a purposeful tilt of her head, Ginny went in search of the colonel.

The house carried a strange atmosphere. After the emptiness of the last six months, it hummed with habitation; but it was an alien presence — a hostile army interested only in possession. The house was merely an object to be taken, no longer the home of a loving family but the sequestered property of a Malignant.

Ginny was the stranger now, a prisoner in what had been

her home until her marriage four years ago. For two years she had lived on the Courtney estate in Dorset until Giles had finally been unable to resist his family's pressure to declare himself for the king. After the news of his death, the year following her father's, Ginny had left the narrow, restrictive environment of the Courtneys and returned thankfully to assume the role of dutiful daughter to her ailing mother. It was a role she infinitely preferred to that of widowed daughter-in-law paying obeisance to the vicious tongue of her husband's mother and the vituperative malice of her sisters-in-law. Just after her mother's death, Ginny had discovered a young man hiding in the orchard — the son of one of the local Royalists who had fallen foul of Parliament's men. His house had been sacked, the estate pillaged, and all male members of the family arrested and sent to Winchester jail for summary trial and execution. Only the sixteen year old had escaped. It had been deepest midwinter, and the snows had lain thick. Ginny had hidden the fugitive in the priest's hole and two nights later sailed him to the mainland. It had been an horrendous trip, not only because of the winter seas that made Fiddler's Race, ripping parallel to the shore of the island, an even wilder current than usual, but also because of the armed fortress of Hurst Castle, standing on its spit, protruding from the mainland to guard Southampton and the Solent from invasion from France. Keyhaven was the nearest and safest landfall to Alum Bay, but it lay behind Hurst Castle, which commanded, also, the Keyhaven River. Ginny had been forced to sail diagonally across the Solent, to avoid the castle and land at Beaulieu. On her return, she had dismissed her household, unwilling to implicate them in her chosen form of war work, and had set up her safe house for those on the island who wished to join with the Royalists on the mainland. The ferries that had previously run from the mainland to Cowes, Yarmouth, and Ryde had been stopped by Governor Hammond when King Charles had first sought his protection. Then Ginny had established her own ferry service, and word had spread rapidly. She had hidden them in the priest's hole until tide and weather conditions made the winter journey possible, and then delivered them to Beaulieu.

But she could no longer perform that role, and she would throw in her lot with Edmund and Peter. It had been agreed among them while they awaited the occupying force that would come to the Redfern estate as surely as it had done to all the others. And when this war was settled, one way or the other, she and Edmund would marry.

Once, when he was seven and she was five, they had plighted their troth. Then, of course, they had both grown up, and John Redfern had given his daughter to Giles Courtney. She had detested the man from the first, but her mother had forcefully reminded her that at least he was personable and young — a mere five and twenty. She could have found herself affianced to a man twice his age, had her father so decreed. It was a simple fact of life, and Ginny had bowed her head to the yoke, until civil war had burst upon the land.

Now she had neither husband nor inheritance, and her fate rested entirely in the hands of Colonel Alexander Marshall — rested there until Edmund was well again. She had no one now, except Edmund, to whom she was tied by the love and loyalty of friendship, as was he to her. There was no passion in their love, but they loved with the depths of indissoluble friendship, and after a passionless, loveless, friendless marriage, life with Edmund would be both a heaven and a haven. And the last years had brought enough unwanted passion in both their lives to last an eternity . . . hadn't it?

She heard the colonel's voice coming from the dining room, and memories of that moment in the dairy, when she had felt something previously unimaginable, rolled over her in an inexorable tide. Had that extraordinary sense of compulsion, of inevitability, been passion? The undeniable desire of a particular woman for a particular man — a desire that subsumed all differences and could be slaked only be consummation?

No! The man was her captor, her enemy, one who was as responsible for the death of her father and the wounding of her dearest friend as if he himself had wielded the sword.

She raised her hand to knock upon the oak door. But why should she? This was *her* house, and they were her guests. No one else might perceive the situation in that fashion, but Virginia Courtney, née Redfern, most certainly did. She opened the door.

There were twelve men in her dining room, standing around the table, examining an enormous map. They all turned at the sound of the opening door, and the surprise on their faces was politely extinguished.

"Good evening, gentlemen." Virginia dropped a curtsy. "You will forgive my intrusion, but I was unsure how many I am expected to prepare dinner for." Her eyes slipped past those of their commanding officer.

"There is no expectation, mistress." The colonel's voice was low. "If you find yourself unequal to the task, we shall dine in our accustomed fashion."

"Pray do not concern yourself, sir. I am quite equal to the task." The door closed again on the crisp statement, and Alex, with a muttered excuse, strode after her.

"Virginia!"

She stopped at the kitchen door. "Yes, Colonel."

"I thought you had agreed to use my name."

"I do not remember such an agreement, sir." She went into the kitchen, and the colonel followed.

"I think that perhaps you do," he said, watching as she rolled up her sleeves and threw flour on the pine table in preparation for pastry making.

"I remember that you took shameless advantage of a defenseless prisoner," she declared, filling a bowl with water from the brass jug.

"If that was indeed the case, Mistress Courtney, then I can only apologize."

"Do you doubt it?" Her hands moved automatically, crumbling butter into the flour. If she concentrated on the task in hand, then maybe her racing blood would slow and he would leave her. She would make a meat pie, her thoughts rattled on. There were beef and kidneys aplenty, and she had picked a basket of mushrooms this morning . . . this morning before this double invasion had occurred,

35

an invasion not only of her freedom, but of some part of her own self—a part she never before had had occasion to acknowledge.

She received no verbal answer, simply warm hands on her shoulders, turning her to face him. Their eyes fused, and the reality of the kitchen, the sparking range, the murmur of voices in the stableyard became simply a part of the background of a tapestry where they stood embroidered in the forefront, held forever until the embroiderer completed the picture. And then the embroiderer chose to complete the picture. Alex's head bent, the full lips captured hers. Without volition, her mouth opened to receive the exploring tongue that danced against the whorls and contours of her cheeks, fenced with her own that was suddenly muscular and knowing and explored in turn deep within the warm, velvety cave of his mouth.

Ginny felt her nipples peak, hard and burning against the linen of her bodice, and the most peculiar weakness in her loins. With an incoherent, panic-stricken mumble, she fought the hands that had released her shoulders and now grasped her hips, holding her against the heat of a pulsing, rising shaft. It was a sensation she knew well. How many nights, in the years of her marriage, had she felt Giles's readiness, the hands impatiently spreading her thighs so that her own unprepared body was laid ready to receive the invasion? But this was quite different. She could feel the moistness as her body prepared itself of its own accord, drowning out all logic and reason.

"No!" She turned back to the flour-coated table, her hands shaking. "You want my body as well as my inheritance and my freedom, Colonel? It is a curious code of honor that allows for the ravishment of a helpless widow—prisoner though she may be."

Alex went white. "That was no ravishment, mistress. I have never kissed a more willing woman. Widowhood has clearly left you with some unfulfilled needs."

They were trading cruel insult for cruel insult in a blind reaction to a torrent of emotions neither of them had expected or could explain.

"How dare you?" Ginny whirled, fury at a taunt that touched the mainspring of her panic, drowning her fear.

With great deliberation he laid a hand on her breast where the nipple still rose hard against the lacing of her bodice. A sardonic eyebrow quirked, a smile played over the full lips as she stood frozen under that hypnotic touch. Then with a mocking bow, he removed his hand and strode from the kitchen.

Ginny stood for a long moment, stunned, her pulses racing as the color came and went in her face. Just whom had she been trying to fool with that little speech? Just whom had she been trying to fool with her earlier thoughts of the peace and comfort of a passionless marriage? She was nineteen years old and, until this moment, had never truly understood the meaning of the word "passion." With an incoherent mutter, half-sob, half-profanity, Ginny fled the house, crossed the yard at a run, heedless of the curious glances from the men, and headed for the cliff top. A narrow, slippery path of colored sand led down to the beach. It was a path more suited to a goat than a human, but Ginny had been climbing it since she was a toddler. As children, she and Edmund had slid down it on their backsides in a hair raising tangle of limbs, much to the detriment of their clothing; not even the certain knowledge of the punishment that would follow if they were caught had proved sufficient deterrent.

But those days were long past, and now Ginny scrambled down with a modicum of dignity, placing her feet sideways to prevent slipping. The small beach was deserted under the blackening sky where the evening star threw its nightly message of reassurance to the dark side of the earth. The sea came gently into the sheltered cove, lapping the sand with a soft sibilant sigh.

Ginny thought of the fourteen-foot sailboat hidden on its runners in the cave beneath the cliff. It would be an easy matter to drag it to the shore, hoist the sail, and be off, away from the turbulence of the last few hours. But the boat was the only form of escape for Edmund and Peter, as well as for herself. She had no choice but to endure until the time and tide were right and she had sufficient information to plan their escape carefully.

Endure what? Ginny sat on a rock and gazed out to sea, allowing the elemental patience of its rhythmic swells to seep into her and restore her own calm. She must, for her friends' sake, endure an imprisonment, the terms of which were hardly arduous. No, that was not the problem. She had never been one to flee from reality, and now she hauled the monster from its depths and faced it with a clear-eyed glare.

Marriage to Giles Courtney had been a walking nightmare — a life sentence of captivity made intolerable by the jealous resentment of his mother and sisters who regarded the young bride of the only male heir as an interloper. Ginny, the only child of an indulgent father and a frail mother, had scrambled through her first fifteen years, more at home behind the tiller of a sailboat than in the distillery or at the spinning wheel, although she had been scolded and chastised into the proper education of a lord's daughter who would one day manage her own great house.

Giles Courtney, on the surface, had had little to complain of in his fifteen-year-old bride. She was attractive, wealthy, and well versed in her duties. She was also, however, indecorously independent, and Giles, accustomed to women who spoke to their menfolk only when spoken to, had suffered acute embarrassment when he had brought his bride, supposedly in triumph, to Courtney Manor.

Ginny, in spite of her intense dislike of this man with his pompous bearing and sense of self-consequence, and of her dismay at finding herself away from her beloved Isle of Wight, landlocked on a stifling mainland, had tried to be open and friendly to his family. She had realized soon enough that open friendliness was considered undisciplined discourtesy. Lady Courtney had ruled the female members of the household with a matriarch's iron fist, and her son's bride had been expected to obey orders and to keep silent. She had been accorded less consideration than her husband's unmarried sisters, and Giles, accustomed to the worshiping care of his womenfolk — a care that kept him, all unrecognizing, in total submission — had offered her no support.

He had been a clumsy inexperienced lover . . . Lover? Ginny laughed mirthlessly as she sat on her rock. If there had been any of loving in that hasty satisfaction of his need, she had missed it. It had been a sordid, sweaty business of grunts and discomfort as her unprepared body received the invasion. Sometimes she had prayed that she would conceive and for nine months be free of the nightly rape. Giles would never have endangered his heir, and if she had carried his child, then her position in the household would surely have changed. But mostly the thought had filled her with revulsion, and she had accepted the monthly bleedings with relief, although her continued barrenness had brought her yet more unkindness from her inlaws. But how could one possible bear in love the child of a man one despised?

In that entire year, Giles had kissed her perhaps a dozen times — a perfunctory peck before he had pushed her night-gown to her waist. Soon he had ignored even such minor acknowledgments of her emotional presence in the body that he had used as if it were no more than the chamber pot beneath the bed. In childhood she and Edmund kissed occasionally as the hormones of puberty had burgeoned, but they had been experimenting as children did, keeping close the guilty secrets of their growing bodies and turbulent emotions.

But when Alex Marshall had kissed her, something had happened that bore no relation to her previous experiences. Her body had responded of its own accord, every nerve seeming to flicker in expectation of stimulation — whether of pain or joy, it mattered not. And it had been joy. Yet she knew almost nothing of the man himself, only what she had gleaned from Peter and deduced for herself. A man of unremitting purpose, steadfast and determined. What then had happened to him, to cause him to break every rule in his book, to consort with a prisoner and an enemy who held principles and beliefs abhorrent to him?

Ginny sat on her rock, thinking her thoughts as dusk became full night, and she could now only hear the sea curling onto the sand and retreating with a wet slurp. Clouds obscured the wedge of the three-quarter moon and the stars. She could smell the threat of the impending summer storm in the strengthening wind, hear it in the crash of a breaker on the Needle Rocks. The colonel's men would have a miserable time of it in their tents in the orchard.

Lightning forked in the sky, and automatically Ginny counted the seconds until the thunderclap. The storm was about five miles away. It was time she returned to the house. The colonel and his officers had presumably provided themselves with dinner in the absence of their cook, and an apple and a piece of cheese would satisfy her own meager appetite.

As she made her way across the soft sand to the steep path, Ginny glanced upward. The entire cliff top was ablaze with the light of flickering torches. She had been so lost in her melancholy, her back to the house, she had not thought to look in that direction. Had they discovered Edmund and Peter? Her heart pounded sickeningly, sweat misting her brow as she stumbled up the path, slipping and sliding as her usual expertise vanished under the sway of panic.

It was a ten-minute climb, and caution reasserted itself as she reached the top. She had no desire to draw attention to the path, which was well hidden except from the eyes of those who knew where to look. Ginny clung to a scrubby bush beneath the overhang until certain that the lights were not trained in the immediate vicinity. Then she hauled herself onto the springy turf and lay still, flat on her stomach, for a breathless moment. Voices reached her from the surrounding gardens, but there were no sounds close to. She got to her feet and, crouching low, ran across the wind swept headland as the first drops of rain heralded the storm. A quick glance reassured her that the door to the priest's hole remained invisible and unviolated.

Nearing the stableyard, Ginny slowed, brushed down her skirts, and sauntered across, headed for the open kitchen door outlined by the golden light of oil lamps. The yard, for some reason, was deserted, the men presumably engaged in whatever curious nighttime exercise their colonel had commanded. Perhaps this happened every night — some ritual maneuver designated to keep an army not facing immediate battle on its toes. Peter had said that Alex Marshall was a brilliant commander, one who knew how to stimulate morale and maintain his troops in perfect condition.

The kitchen was as empty as the yard, although the trestle table held the remnants of a cold meal of bread, meat, and cheese. Ginny grabbed an apple and a pear from the basket, cut a wedge of cheese, and slipped silently up the backstairs to her own chamber. The door stood open onto the corridor. Surely she had closed it when she had left earlier? She remembered doing so as an automatic declaration of her ownership of one portion of this occupied house.

Locking the door behind her, Ginny heaved a sigh of relief. This room at least was her own, held the familiar possessions of her childhood and youth, offered her peace and privacy from whatever went on elsewhere. It had always been thus — a haven where she could kick and stamp at unjust restrictions; could weep away the sorrow and hurt of childish punishments; could create a magical universe whose contours and rules might be changed at will, in whatever direction the creator's fantasy took them; could brood with delicious mystery on the workings of her body.

Lightning forking into the sea lit the room for a moment, and the crash of thunder followed instantly. The storm was directly overhead, and Ginny ran to close the casements as the rain tipped from the sky. Instinctively, she offered the prayer for those facing the storm on the seas. A child of the sea, she treated the water with all the healthy respect of one well versed in its sudden treachery.

The sound of raised male voices downstairs exploded through the house, and without knowing quite why she did so, Ginny tore off her clothes, dropping them in a careless heap beside the window as she dragged her nightgown over her head, and leaped into bed, ignoring the fact that she had neither brushed her hair nor washed her hands where the sandy grime of the cliff path clung beneath her fingernails. Her impromptu supper lay neglected on the broad window sill.

Booted feet clattered on the stairs, along the corridor, and stopped outside her door. The handle turned and met the

41

resistance of the iron key. There was a tentative knock, an unfamiliar voice. "Mistress Courtney?"

Ginny stared into the darkness mitigated by her accustomed eyes. Should she acknowledge the call or pretend to be asleep? The latter, she decided. It would involve her in fewer explanations, and she need both peace and privacy at this moment. The peace and privacy that might restore her accustomed sense of control over her destiny, her accustomed composure, and put thoughts of Alex Marshall into perspective so that she could concentrate on her plans for escape, could stop thinking wild, unbidden thoughts of passion, and could think instead of a calm, orderly future — once this messy present was behind her.

She remained silent and heard the sound of booted feet retreating along the corridor. A bugle call sounded from somewhere in the grounds — probably signaling the end of the exercise. There was a strange quiet in the house now. Not the silence of isolation to which she had become accustomed, but the brooding quiet that came when a large group of people ceased all activity, waiting. Waiting for what? Ginny's heart began to pound, and only the thought of her locked door provided comfort as she lay, aching with the fatigue that went beyond tiredness and denied the respite of sleep.

Downstairs in the dining room, Alex heard his aide-de-camp, young Diccon Maulfrey, tell him that he rather thought Mistress Courtney was abed and asleep. The fresh-faced, twenty-year-old lieutenant made his report to a blank-eyed commander, who merely nodded and dismissed him curtly. Alex felt a fool. Virginia's disappearance had created a panic-stricken frenzy that had somehow blotted out all his calm reason. He had taken her prisoner on a curious whim, nettled by her sharpness, by the cold mocking satire and the fearlessness of her challenge. And by something else, too. By his admiration for her, by the overwhelming sense that she was like no other woman he had ever met, by the feeling that he could not cast upon the world, alone and friendless, a woman who was both defenseless and courageous. So he had assumed responsibility for

Virginia Courtney and in the doing had discovered something else again—a yearning that the soldier, intent on principle and purpose, had never before allowed to intrude. He was as experienced in the ways of the world and the needs of the body as any of his peers, took his release whenever and wherever the opportunity arose, but he had always been capable of controlling his body's urgencies, to live for as long as need be without women. Now, in a few short hours, he had lost all caution, all sense, his careful purpose buffeted to the breaking point by a young woman with a tongue like a bee sting. An enemy who, even as she mocked him, even as she fought herself, yielded to the same power that consumed him.

He stood at the diamond-paned casement, staring out at the lashing rain, hearing the wind's howl, feeling its breath whistling through the cracks of the window frame. His men had searched the house and the estate, and they had not found her. She had, therefore, broken her parole. She was a ward of Parliament's representative. He must behave now in a manner consonant with that position. Only then could he recover his operational error and prove, both to himself and to the men under his command, that this night's frantic search had had a serious wartime purpose, had had nothing to do with the need of a tortured would-be lover to find an errant would-be mistress.

Alex stalked to the door. "Diccon?"

The lieutenant appeared immediately.

"Have sentries posted at all outside doors. In future, Mistress Courtney is not to be permitted to leave the house from sundown to sunup. If she attempts to break the curfew, then she is to be brought to me."

Diccon saluted and went to fulfill his instructions. His colonel was not one to tolerate infraction, and if the lady of the manor had defied an order, then she would be no more spared the consequences than any other under his command.

Alex eventually went upstairs. The house was now still, men and officers dismissed to their quarters. Outside Virginia's door he paused. How did he know with such cer-

43

tainty that she was not asleep? She had a right to know of the curfew, he reasoned. If she did not, it could cause her embarrassment on the morrow. He tapped gently at the door. "Virginia, I must speak with you."

Ginny heard the soft voice, the discreet knock, and realized that it was for this that she had been waiting. Her voice quavered in response. "What is it you wish to say to me, Colonel?"

"Open the door," he replied. "I do not wish to wake the house by shouting through a yard of oak."

She slipped from the bed, deep in the knowledge of inevitability, and drew her wrapper around her before turning the iron key.

Alex stepped into the room. He had intended to deliver his message on the threshold—hadn't he?—but, instead, found himself closing the door quietly behind him. She stepped back, her eyes frightened, except that they carried the same tormenting yearning as his own. Perhaps that was why she was afraid. He was, himself.

"Where have you been? My men have been searching the island for you."

"For me!" Ginny sought safety in her tongue. "I had assumed, Colonel, by all the activity, that you have found a nest of Cavaliers under a gooseberry bush."

Alex struck a flint against the tinder box and lit the candle standing on the mantelpiece. "You have sand between your toes," he remarked, and she remembered his statement in the dairy—that if he refused to fight, she would be unable to do so. "They are very pretty toes," he continued with a curious frown, "even dirty as they are."

"I went to the beach." What sort of a conversation was this? Was she defending her dirty feet or answering her captor's inquiry?

"The beach is not contained within the boundaries of the estate, Virginia. You violated your parole."

"I did not think of it in that way. The beach and the cove have always been mine. I have sailed the bay since I could walk." Even as she made the explanation, Ginny realized how much she might have revealed. She had told this man she was a sailor. It would take little deduction on his part to

44

conclude her most logical means of escape.

But instead Alex moved toward her, took her hands. "What else can you do, my indomitable little shrew of the sandy toes, besides battle the invader and the seas?"

Ginny thought of a passionless lifetime, a lifetime of duty. She had but to speak the word, and this man would leave her, leave her to live that life, when the world settled, never to have known the glory. In this time of schism why should she be bound by a self-imposed discipline that had never been the courtly norm before civil war? She had done her duty, married her father's choice, taken her place amongst hostile in-laws — done everything except produce the heir. Why should she not, just once, allow her mind and body the freedom they craved? All the customary bonds and rules of society were fragmented. She was no maid, and who would ever know, besides themselves, that Ginny Courtney and Alex Marshall had, once upon a mad time, enjoyed each other?

Even as she thought she still had a choice, his hands left hers to slide around her back, and her skin burned beneath his touch. The iron bands of a courage that had kept her in antagonism melted in the forge of a white-hot lucidity — the absolute knowledge that she wanted this, that if she did not take it now, it would be lost to her forever.

"Oh, sweet Ginny," he whispered against her hair. "This is lunacy, but I am moon-mad, bewitched. Tell me that it is the same for you."

"It is the same."

His tongue ran gently across her lips, probed the corners of her mouth, tasting her sweetness. "I cannot imagine why you should taste of honey and not of vinegar." He chuckled, sliding his hands down to cup her buttocks. Ginny shuddered at the shocking intimacy. Only Giles had ever put his hands there and then only to shift her into the position that suited him, or to grip with bruising fingers as he expended himself. This was a totally different touch — a hungry touch of passion that nevertheless acknowledged her and her right to feel and fulfill her own passion.

Alex half-lifted her as he moved backward to the bed. Ginny's eyes were closed as she floated in the ether of pure sensation. Her brain no longer held the reins of control, and her body seemed as formless as mercury. She fell back on the bed, and he came with her, still locked against her mouth as his hands now moved urgently over her breasts, lifting the aching nipples with the heel of his palm. Ginny moaned, twisting her body, covered only by the thin layer of cotton, beneath the contours and promontories delineated by the leather and linen garb of the soldier above. Her own hands seemed to know instinctively what they were to do and where they were to put themselves, unbuttoning his shirt, curling in the wiry chest hair, slipping to the muscled back and then down beneath the belt of his leathern britches.

Alex raised his head, looking down at her as if seeing her for the first time — her reddened lips, swollen under his kisses, her limbs sprawled in wanton abandon, her erect nipples, dark splodges against her nightgown. Passion and longing filled the gray eyes that seemed to contain her soul, and the invitation was both an offer and an imperative. How could he refuse either? His mouth returned to hers.

She yielded her body, then, to the hands that stroked even as they held her fast. He moved his mouth from hers only long enough to cast aside the wrapper, raising her body as he drew her nightgown over her head. As she trembled in her nakedness, he whispered to her, soothing and stroking, and told her how beautiful her body was, how strong and clean were her limbs, how translucent her skin. She had never before shown herself naked to a man; Giles had preferred darkness for coupling. But under the words of praise, she lay, bold and proud, feeling herself as flawless as this lover was telling her she was. When his hands parted her thighs in magical exploration, she heard herself beg for gentleness and understanding, whisper that she had never known loving, only invasion, and the green-brown eyes lifted for a minute to glow their promise. She lay watching as he undressed, revealing the soldier's body, hard of muscle and sinew, a lean, long fighting machine that bore a thin, white scar slash across a thigh, another drawn fine over his rib cage. He came to her, gentling her with hands and mouth as her body quivered in a confusion of panic, anticipated pain, and the white-hot brand of desire. And the panic went, the memory scars of pain healed beneath his touch, and there was only the fierce wanting and an explosion of exquisite joy.

When he left her, it was far, far too soon, but the hard edges of reality were stiffening the malleable wax of the dream. The lover was soldier again, commander of a brigade, and he could not afford to be found in the chamber of his prisoner. Before he left, he remembered to tell her of the curfew, and even though he kissed her in apology, the words made clear again the truth of their relative positions.

Ginny, in the light of the flickering candle as the storm raged against her casement, attempted to quieten the storm boiling within her, and to douse the light that for a magical time had moved from a flicker to a full clear glow. Whatever it was that had happened, be it love or lust, it could not be allowed to interfere in her future — a future that could not contain a Roundhead colonel. She had known from the beginning of the madness that it could only be an ephemeral moment, the last chance, the one and only chance she would ever have in a lifetime of duty. She must leave the island tomorrow, she and Edmund and Peter, fasten again the shackles of duty and loyalty, and keep the glorious lunacy of this night in the secret embers of her soul.

She found she had no desire to sleep and sat at her window, keeping watch as the storm died and the first faint glimmers of a sunless dawn turned the night's darkness to a gray heaviness. A bugle call pierced the air with its insistence, and the house came to life around her. There was an urgency in the hurrying feet, the sharp commands, the snap of irritation, and she heard Alex's voice, cool but commanding. The storm had been all that she had expected, and the men camped in the orchard had had a wretched time of it as the rain bucketed, running in torrents under, over, and between the flimsy tents. The wind had howled, tearing at the pegs, and the lazy and inexperienced had lived with the consequences as their fragile shelters had flown with the gusts. The campsite was in chaos, and Ginny listened to the sudden silence in the house as the entire brigade, from the colonel down, pitched in to restore order.

So fate had played into her hands. The house was deserted, the colonel and his men in the orchard, and the tide would be full in Alum Bay at eight o'clock. Ginny dressed rapidly and slipped from the room. She went directly to the still room, where she stood for a moment, allowing the silence to seep into her pores, her ears pricked for the slightest sound. Nothing . . . except the voices carrying through the now-still air from the orchard.

Twenty minutes of careful activity produced the poultice of herbs and distilled alcohol that would keep Edmund's wound clean and aid the healing. This was one area of housewifery in which Ginny excelled, simply because it fascinated her. There were few of the common, and no-so-common ailments, that she did not know how to cure or at least ease. She had spent much of her childhood gathering simples in the company of the old women of the island, learning the art of healing.

The poultice went into a wicker basket covered by a checkered napkin, together with a plentiful supply of fresh bandages, and Ginny crept downstairs to the dining room. The wall panel sprung open as her foot pressed the requisite floorboard, and she was inside, the concealed door closing behind her as her knowing fingers found the catch. She remembered the story of how her grandfather had summoned locksmiths from London to achieve this marvel. Since Henry VIII's reformation, when Catholic priests had found refuge in the secret passages and chambers of the houses of their sympathizers, most newly built houses of the nobility contained in their plans some such hiding place. Her father's father, with a fascination for all things mechanical, had constructed his own, utilizing every device known to the age. John Redfern, in his turn, had kept the mechanism well oiled, although the priest's hole and the secret passageway had, in his lifetime, only been used in play by his tomboy daughter and her equally mischievous cousin.

It was ten shallow steps to the stone chamber, and she whistled softly to reassure the captives that the intruder was not be feared.

"What do you do, coming from the house?" Edmund was on his feet, still shaky, but his color was better, although, like Peter, his complexion carried the waxen tinge of long days away from fresh air and light.

"How strong do you feel?" she asked, setting down her burden. She explained her plan rapidly, even as she encouraged Edmund back to the pallet and swiftly applied the poultice to a wound that was much less red and swollen. She changed the bandage, nodding with satisfaction. "There is no seepage of fluid, Edmund. If you avoid wetting the bandage on the crossing, then it will not need to be changed for several days."

"How am I to manage the cliff path, Ginny, with only one hand?"

"On your backside, as we used to do." She fashioned a sling from the napkin, securing his arm against his chest. "You will go between us, but you must not attempt to use this arm."

"You were always overfond of giving orders," Edmund grumbled, even as his eyes shone with the prospect of activity and release.

"Indeed." She grinned through her tiredness and the desolation she could not admit, even to herself. "And on this occasion, my friend, you will obey."

Edmund tugged one of the long braids that now hung down her back. "I will, general, because I must. But when this is over, we will refashion things, will we not?"

She smiled because she could not answer the question that referred to their agreed future. "Come, I will go first and spy out the land. My presence on the cliff top will require little explanation if there are watchers."

They followed her down the steps that for once held no terrors for her. What power did ghostly imaginings have over the reality of the executioner's axe, the pile of straw, stained by the severed head? That would be their fate. There could be no other if they were discovered, unless it was the hangman's noose in Winchester jail.

She cracked open the heavy stone door at the stairs' foot,

listened, and heard only voices carrying faintly from a distance. They would surely not guard the cliffs or keep a watch on the blank side of the house that faced only the unfriendly sea? The expanse of springy turf stretched to the cliff edge, offering no shelter, only the possibility of a headlong dash. But there was no one in sight, no patrolling soldier with pike and musket.

" 'If it were done when 'tis done, then 'twere well it were done quickly.' " She shot a smile over her shoulder, and Edmund again pulled a braid.

"Ginny was always more inclined to mind our tutor than I, Peter." He was doing his part, no wounded passenger but a whole man, not one weakened by loss of blood and captivity, a man undaunted by the prospect of the open cliff top and the goat's trail on slippery sand leading to an unknown, battlestrewn future.

She heard his resolution, and it stiffened her own. "You must run. We cannot help you until we reach the path."

"I know it. I have strength enough."

Ginny ran then, crouching low as if she could thus be invisible on the wind-swept headland, paying no heed to the two behind her, knowing that she could not afford to slow her pace. She was the hare to their hounds, and they could keep her pace . . . *would* keep her pace until it was possible to hide beneath the cliff overhang and regather strength.

The path was there, invisible to all but the accustomed eye. For others there was simply the sea stretching to a horizon, broken only by the Needle Rocks. Ginny paused for the barest second to hitch her skirt into her belt. She kicked off her sandals and tucked them also into the belt, leaving her legs bare from the knee down. Peter and Edmund were behind her as she slipped over the cliff, her feet seeking purchase in the sand. She grasped the tendril of a scrubby bush with her uppermost left hand, steadied herself, and reached with her right to help Edmund who sat down abruptly, his slithering fall prevented only by her feet barricading the path. She moved down in the ungainly manner of a crab, allowing Edmund to slide the few feet necessary to give Peter room to come over the cliff and onto the path.

Edmund's face was sheened with the sweat of pain and effort, his breathing labored. Peter, unwounded but affected by the days of fearful inactivity, also needed time to recoup. They could afford a few moments, and Ginny stood sideways on the path, her bare feet gripping the sand as she listened for the hue and cry that would tell them they had been spotted. There was nothing but the call of the gulls.

"You can manage with one hand, Edmund," she whispered, again with that reassuring, teasing smile. "For this once, you need have no fear of returning to the house with torn britches."

"Maybe not, but I have no desire to face the world with a scraped and ill-covered posterior," he retorted. "I shall contrive, never fear, if you will but move yourself."

Ginny went down the incline backward, one hand on Edmund's ankle to control the speel of his descent, as Peter crouched above, protecting the injured shoulder as best he could. When they reached the cove, Edmund's color had changed to an alarming waxen yellow, and the eyes that had been bright before were now dull in the aftermath of the first battle won. Ginny reached for his wrist to feel his pulse that was rapid, but not dangerously so.

"You must rest in the cave whilst Peter and I launch the dinghy."

The cave was cool and damp beneath the cliffs, and the sailboat on a wheeled trailer offered mute salvation. Edmund sank into a corner, his back against a rock. "Help me," Ginny said to Peter. "I am able to do it alone, but it will be faster with two."

Peter, who knew nothing about such things, followed her instructions, lending his weight as she swung the trailer around so the dinghy's bow faced the sea. They ran across the sand, hauling the trailer behind them, and at the shoreline, she swung it again, pushing both trailer and boat, stern first, into the shallows.

"Take this back to the cave, and fetch Edmund." It was a terse instruction that Peter Ashley obeyed because Virginia Courtney knew what she was doing. Knee deep now in the water, she was unfastening the boat from the trailer, pushing the dinghy free as Peter dragged the trailer clear. She then held the boat's painter and tossed her sandals over the bow into the boat.

Peter ran the now-light burden to the cave, shoved it to the back, and helped Edmund to his feet. "She was always thus," Edmund said with a gasp of effort. "No tree was too high, no cliff too steep for Ginny."

Peter smiled grimly, supporting the wounded man around the waist. "In this matter of sailing, my friend, I am glad to yield authority to one who knows. I do not care for the sea."

Alex, order restored in the orchard, searched the house. She had disappeared again, and this time he must find her himself. He longed to see her, ached to whisper in her ear his delight in that mole she had, high on the inside of her right thigh, the bruise, like a ripe plum, on her hip. Had she acquired it thumping open the door of barn or dairy when her hands were full? He wanted to know.

She would be on the beach, of course. She had told him last night that that was her special place.

Alex strolled across the cliff top, hiding his eagerness beneath the commander's swagger. Halfway down the broad path to Alum Bay, the only path that he was aware of, he saw her. She was not alone as she pulled a boat on a wheeled trailer to the water's edge. Alex began to run in the same blind panic that had informed his search of the preceding night. He could not lose her, now that he had found her, whatever Royalist treachery she was engaged in. Royalist it most certainly was, to judge by the long hair and broad sash of the man helping her. Alex saw her swing the boat into the sea with all the expertise of one well versed in these matters, saw the man run up the beach with the trailer until he was lost to sight. Alex's feet pounded on the path, and he was thankful for the light clothes that he wore, the lack of armor that made it easy for his fit body to eat up the yards. The long, broad path descended diagonally to the beach, and when he reached the bottom, he was hidden from the shoreline by an outcrop of rock at the water's edge at the extremity of the cove.

He saw the man reappear, together with another whose arm was in a sling and who staggered like one whose strength was at a low ebb. Ginny was holding the boat in the shallows, up to her knees in the water, and as the two men drew close, she pulled the dinghy back to the shore. He heard her voice, clear in the sea air. "You must remove your boots if you do not wish to land with wet feet."

The two men did so, the able helping the injured. They handed them to her, and she tossed them into the dinghy to join her own before stretching her free hand to steady the men as they clambered aboard.

She would not go with them, would she? Not after last night? But he saw her hitch herself over the stern, hoist the gaff-rigged sail that stood crosswise to the mast. She held the boat into the wind as the uninjured man followed her instructions and dropped the rudder into the slots and secured the pin.

Alex ran across the beach then, and as he did so, the man stood up, rocking the frail craft, a flintlock pistol in his hand.

Ginny saw Alex a second after Peter, the second necessary for the pistol to appear.

"You cannot!" She struck his wrist with all the force of which she was capable. "He is unarmed, Peter."

For an instant the tableau remained immobile. The dinghy held into the wind by a slim brown hand on the tiller, the sails flapping uselessly until the hands would draw tight the sheets, push the tiller to the right, and so catch the wind; an unarmed man on the beach, his body targeted by the cumbersome barrel of the pistol; two men in the boat, one crouched by the mast, incapable of action, the other holding the weapon that wavered and then dropped.

Alex moved to the shoreline where the waves lapped an inch from his boots. "Peter Ashley," he said quietly. "It has been a long time since last we met."

"I could have wished it had been a different time," Peter replied.

"I, also." Alex looked at Ginny but spoke to Peter. "You may go in peace and in the memory of our past friendship, but Mistress Courtney remains here."

"No, Ginny!" But even as her cousin struggled to his knees on this cry of protest, she had swung herself over the stern.

"It is right thus, Edmund. One day I will explain to you why. For now, you must accept the fact. Peter, you must take the tiller."

"I know nothing of sailing." He looked at her, aghast and frightened, and the man on the beach watched and listened.

"Edmund will guide you. You can run before the wind out of the bay. You have only to move the tiller to the right if you wish to turn to the left for the wind, and similarly the other way. It is not difficult, and if Edmund turns to face the sail, he will be able to instruct you."

Edmund swiveled around, his back against the thwart, a haunted, desperate expression on his face as he realized how helpless he was to gainsay her. She spoke to him in a low whisper that excluded the others. "Fiddler's Race is not at present running too fast between here and Yarmouth, so you should cross it before then. Make for the Beaulieu River, avoiding Hurst. Beaulieu has always been safe, and you will find friends at Buckler's Hard."

"And you?"

"This is what I want. There is not time to explain all, but we will meet again, my friend. God go with you."

"And with you, Cousin." Edmund turned his head to lock eyes with Alex Marshall, as if to imprint him on his memory. "If I were able to defend you, I would do so."

"I know, but there is no need for defense. I will be no unwilling hostage, Edmund."

"You had always a recklessness in you, Ginny. I know not why you are doing this, but I will accept the fact out of necessity. When I am able, I will find you again."

She brushed his lips with hers. The waves slapped gently against her calves as she pushed the boat out. "You must drop the centerboard, Peter, as soon as you are clear of the sandbank. Edmund will tell you when." The dinghy's sail caught the wind. Her dinghy, her only way to evade destiny, skipped across the calm waters of the bay.

She turned to the man standing waiting for her on the beach. He crooked an imperative finger, and she waded to the shore, to face and make sense of an unforeseen fate.

Chapter Three

"You were leaving me?"

"Yes."

"Why?"

"Because I thought I must. Because last night had no place, no grounding in the reality we both have to live. I am a Royalist and will do all I can to further the king's cause. You are a Parliamentarian, a Roundhead, and will do all you can to further your own cause."

"Then we must be both lovers and enemies," Alex stated softly, watching the sailboat that had now neared the point of the headland. "It will, on occasion, be a little uncomfortable for both of us, but you remain a ward of Parliament, and after this day's work I will keep a close guard of you."

"And I will evade that guard, as and when I may." Were they, with these half-threats, half-promises, laying the groundwork for a relationship that must encompass both that of lovers and of prisoner and captor?

"I do not doubt it," he replied matter-of-factly. "I knew you were resourceful, but I had not realized to what extent. Shall we return to the house? I wish to know who was the man you kissed, where they have been hidden, what it was you said to him at the last, and what other subversion you have been engaged in."

"I will not tell you."

"You will eventually." He spoke with calm certainty, looking down at her, his expression perfectly composed. "You are a veritable gypsy . . . Ginny. Is that not what those you kiss, call you?"

"It is what my friends call me." She returned his gaze steadfastly.

He smiled slightly. "I wonder then what I should call you, my lover and my enemy, my raggle-taggle gypsy of the bare brown legs and sandy feet and filthy hands."

Ginny inadvertently dropped her eyes to her hands. They were indeed filthy, and she knew not how to answer his question, or even whether he required an answer.

"Unhitch your skirt," he instructed in the same even tone. "You cannot appear thus in front of my men."

Ginny flushed and obeyed, for once at a loss for words. His calmness in the face of what had just happened filled her with unease rather than reassurance. The certainty of his statement that she would eventually tell him what he wanted to know sent pinpricks of fear down her spine, and she shivered in the warm overcast morning. What did he intend to do with her now that he knew what she was? Certainly not the passive victim of a war in which she played no part, but an active participant in the enemy cause, one who, for six months, had been responsible for ensuring the safety and escape of wanted men.

"Come," he repeated. "It is time to make an end of this — or, perhaps, a beginning."

Ginny turned and walked across the beach toward the cliff path. Alex, after a moment of surprise, ran after her. "Where the devil do you think you're going?"

"To the house," she replied. "As you commanded." She gestured to the path, and Alex stared in astonishment upward at the sheer cliff. "Up *there*?"

She shrugged. "I have always done so. It is the shortest route."

"For a goat, maybe," Alex declared. "No wonder you are always so dirty! Well, I do not aspire to mountain climbing. We will use the human path." So saying, he took her hand and marched off across the beach. Ginny was obliged to run to keep up with the length and rapidity of his stride that did not shorten or slow as he mounted the incline. When she stumbled, he jerked her forward impatiently, for all the world like an irate parent with a recalcitrant toddler at hand.

They reached the cliff top, and Ginny blanched at the picture they would present as he hauled her across the stableyard and into the house.

"Please," she begged. "Can we not walk in a more dignified fashion?"

He stopped and looked down at her. "So, the raggle-taggle gypsy does have a care for appearances."

"It is not necessary to drag me behind you. I am coming as fast as I am able." Some of the old fire appeared in her eyes and received a faint glint of humor in response, and the release of her hand.

"Take my arm, then, mistress mine, and we will proceed in as stately a fashion as your bare feet will allow."

With a courtly mocking bow, he offered his arm and, having no choice, Ginny gritted her teeth and played along with the farce. They sauntered across the stableyard, the colonel responding punctiliously to the salutes of the soldiers whose eyes seemed to Ginny to be riveted on her feet, her sandy kirtle, the dirt-encrusted nails of her hand resting on her escort's crisp linen shirt sleeve, her hair disheveled by running and scrambling. She wanted to weep with mortification and nearly did so when the colonel stopped in the hall to answer some question of a middle-aged major, and when she attempted to move away, up the stairs to her own sanctuary, he told her, in the tone of voice he reserved for erring ensigns, to remain where she was.

She stood rigidly at his side, staring at the thick surface of dust on an oak bench beside the front door. It was where her father had been used to sit when his soiled boots were removed. He had had a passion for cleanliness, loved the gleam of wood and the shine of pewter and copper. Not even his adored daughter had escaped censure when he discovered her muddied and in torn clothing. What would he think now of his beloved house occupied by booted soldiers? Of his dust-laden, tarnished possessions? Of his daughter who had betrayed the king's cause, the cause John Redfern had died for, by yielding to a body and a compulsion she had been unable to resist? Who stood now, a gypsy wanton, a prisoner possessed by a man who was the captor of her spirit, her body, and her person?

Alex concluded his conversation and ushered her into the dining room where he closed the door firmly.

"Was it necessary to humiliate me in that manner?" Ginny whirled on him, too angry now to be frightened.

"That rather depends on what one considers necessary," he said evenly, picking up the sheaf of papers on the refectory table. "I have suffered considerable humiliation at your hands this day. It seemed not unreasonable to exact a small penalty." He frowned as he scanned one of the papers, continuing almost absently, "I also wished to make clear to you that you remain under my command. Since you have warned me that you will do all you may to evade your position as a ward of Parliament, I deemed it necessary to show you the nature of my authority." He strode to the door. "Diccon?" The aide-de-camp appeared and saluted smartly. "The messenger who brought the letter from Governor Hammond, is he still here?"

"Yes, Colonel. He is in the kitchen. I thought you might wish to speak with him."

"You thought well, Diccon. Send him to me."

"If you will excuse me, Colonel, I shall go to my chamber," Ginny said stiffly, moving to the door in the wake of the lieutenant.

"No, I do not excuse you." He replaced the papers on his desk. "We shall both remain in this room until you give me the information I require." He looked at her directly. "I am sorry, but this is wartime. You may terminate whatever inconvenience and discomfort you will suffer any time you choose. I wish to know the identity of the wounded man, how he became so, where they have been hiding, and what instructions you gave him. Then you will tell me what else you have been doing in the past six months."

"Why must you know?" Ginny felt the cold sweat of despair. "You must have seen us from the cliff path. You had time enough to call for reinforcements; yet you let them go."

"Yes," he agreed. "I let them go because of you. Had I called for reinforcements, you and they would be on your way to Winchester, and there would be nothing I could do to save you. The methods employed there to extract information from a prisoner are considerably less subtle than any I might use. Your friends would have heard you scream, as you would have heard them. And afterward, when you had given your interrogators all you knew, and much that you didn't in order to escape the pain, when you desired only death, they would have hanged you."

"You have seen this?" She gazed in horror.

"Yes, I have seen it. And because I have, I would not condemn you to such a fate in spite of your treachery."

There was a sharp rap on the door, and Ginny sat on the window seat, cold, hungry, exhausted, and devastated by the brutality of the truths she had just been given. She had been aware of those truths in the furthest reaches of her mind, but they were not things one allowed oneself to think about. Alex had forced her to think of them, to feel and to smell the degradation of inflicted pain, to hear the mewling cries from the broken body, to know the coarse prick of the noose around her neck.

But she could not tell him, could not betray Edmund and all those others on the island who had assisted fugitives in the past. Alex had let Edmund and Peter go because of her, but Edmund Verney was a wanted man, and there would be nothing to prevent Alex sending a messenger to alert the mainland forces. Wounded, her cousin would not be able to make much speed, and if they knew where to begin their search . . . And what havoc would Parliament's forces wreak amongst the peaceful inhabitants of Buckler's Hard? The fisherfolk and farmers who had offered succor to those she had delivered.

The long morning wore on. Alex talked with the messenger from Governor Hammond, he conferred with his officers, wrote reports, the quill pen scratching on the parchment; all the while he ignored the figure on the window seat. Once he left the room, and a soldier came in, wooden-faced, to stand before the closed door. On the colonel's return, the soldier departed. When she could hold out no longer, Ginny asked, in a low, hesitant voice, to visit the privy. Alex merely nodded and summoned the same soldier to accompany her. The eyes of both officers and men slid past her as she made the return journey with her stolid, silent guard, studiously ignored her presence when they came into the dining room to do business with the colonel. At noon, Alex was brought a bowl of soup, a trencher of bread with a slab of cheese and a mug of ale.

Ginny had not broken her fast this day, and then, as she watched him eat, tears pricking behind her eyes, she realized that she had taken no food since noon yesterday. Last night's supper presumably still lay neglected in her chamber, because last night something had happened that made thought of food an irrelevancy. And sleep, also. Now she was tired to the point of death. She shifted on the hard, ungiving oak of the narrow window seat as her thigh muscles cramped. She needed to lie down. There was only the floor, but it would do. Sliding down, Ginny curled her body tightly, pillowing her head on her hands.

"No, Ginny. You may not sleep unless you do so on the window seat." Alex bent over her, lifting her to her feet. His voice seemed incongruously gentle to her bewildered, desperate senses, but there was no mistaking the implacable note. "I wish this to be over soon," he said quietly, holding her as she sagged against him. "When you have told me, you shall bathe, sleep, and eat, and you and I will begin anew, knowing who and what we are."

The thought was seductive, almost irresistible. Edmund's name rose to her lips, and then the image of Winchester jail dried her mouth. She sat again upon the window seat, her head drooping on her chest as she dozed fitfully throughout an interminable afternoon when the nausea of hunger churned in her belly and she hardly knew whether she was awake or asleep. The single note of a bugle hammering insistently, repetitively, created images of battlefields strewn with the broken bodies of the dead and wounded, and she walked amongst them, looking . . . always looking for someone. Her father? . . . Edmund? But she was not searching among the flotsam of the king's dead, but through that of Parliament, Oliver Cromwell's men . . .

She awoke from her trance with a cry of terror as a hand touched her shoulder, and she found herself looking into the eyes of the man she had been seeking. It was full night outside, she saw through the window at her back.

"Sweet Ginny, you must tell me." He spoke softly, urgently. "I cannot bear to see you thus, but I must know. I will promise to keep his identity a secret, will keep the knowledge of their escape to myself, but this is war, my love. I have to know how you have done this thing, and how often, and I have to block further escapes. You have nothing to lose by telling me, since you are no longer in a position to continue this work. But others may try, and all unknowing, they will run their heads into a noose if it is not made clear from the outset that escape from the island is now impossible. If I know the details, I will make the warning manifest. No one will suffer from what you tell me, unless they choose to ignore the warning."

"You would make a traitor of me?" The tears flowed now, hot and fast, and he held and soothed her.

"No traitor, Ginny, but a pragmatist, one who recognizes the appropriate moment to yield. You will cause no deaths or hardship by telling me, I give you my word. I will simply place guards obtrusively at all points on the island where a boat might slip away, and alert the mainland forces to do the same. You know the places, do you not?"

She nodded through her tears, grateful for the kerchief that wiped her eyes, the strong arm around her shoulders, the broad chest that received her head. Pathetically grateful for the comfort that followed acute discomfort, for the attention that followed blind, cruel indifference. She had heard tell of skillful interrogators, those who waited for the breaking point and then offered succor, support, and understanding. Alex had used those techniques, playing on the weakness of her nerve-strung, sleep-deprived body, her exhausted emotions, her hunger, and her fear, before offering her both excuse and rationale to give him what he wanted.

Even as she despised herself and hated him, Ginny heard her voice stumbling over the answers to his questions. Then he left her for a moment, to give a series of crisp orders, before coming back to hold her again, as she wept in shame at her weakness. Later he carried her upstairs to her chamber, where a steaming tub, floating with fragrant herbs, stood before a fire, newly kindled in the grate. There was food and wine on the corner table.

"I would stay with you, if it were possible," he said, setting her on her feet, steadying her with one hand. "But you must see to your own comfort tonight, and tomorrow, when you are rested, we will talk again."

"You promise that no harm will come to Edmund?" Ginny moved away from the steadying hand to find her own grounding on her own still-bare feet.

"Have I not said so?" He smiled sadly. "You hate me, now, Ginny, as you hate yourself. But I will keep my word; and tomorrow, when we talk, you will understand why this was necessary, and why you took the only option you had."

The door closed behind him, and the iron key turned in the lock. She was a prisoner in her own room, and the man who held the key to the door also held the key to her soul.

She bathed and washed her hair, ate a little of the food, but found, strangely, that she was no longer hungry. The bread and meat stuck in her throat, and the wine sickened her stomach. She crawled into bed and lay shivering, although the room was warmed and comforted by the soft glow of the fire that had always been an incredible luxury even in the depths of winter. Only when she was sick had her mother had the fire kindled, and as a result, Ginny always associated the cheerful crackle with the gently soothing care of her mother and her nurse, with feeling pleasurably helpless and weak. She felt both those things now, but the sensation was not pleasurable.

Sleep rescued her from the lash of her self-disgust, and for twelve hours she was dreamlessly unconscious, waking yet again to the note of the bugle, to a bright, clear rain-washed morning, to the sound of male voices and the tramp of feet. Edmund and Peter would be safe now, if Alex had kept his word. With luck and good friends, they would be on their way to join the main Royalist force in Surrey. Activity and a sense of purpose would do more for Edmund's health and well-being than any sickroom care she could provide. He was young and strong, and the wound healing well. So long as it did not reopen, he should be able to use the arm again in a week or so. Would he blame her for her betrayal? Would others see her confession as treachery? Could she have held out longer? Would a few more hours have made any difference? She knew that eventually Alex would have wrested the answers from her. She had not the physical strength to resist such deprivation indefinitely. And, while Alex's feelings for her would not allow him to sentence her to the torturers in Winchester jail, his ruthless single-minded devotion to duty and principle would have allowed him to offer her no quarter, either.

There was a rap at the door, and the voice that she now recognized as belonging to the young man Diccon called. "Mistress Courtney?"

64

"Yes," she answered, unafraid that he would open the door. Only Alex would assume the right to enter her chamber, and he would not accord that right to anyone else.

"I am to escort you to the colonel," Diccon said. "When you are ready."

"Then you must wait a few minutes." Ginny slipped to the floor, drawing her nightgown over her head. Her eye fell on the tray of barely touched food, and she realized that she was ravenously, healthily hungry, that she was clean and well rested, that the sun was shining, that Edmund and Peter had escaped, and that Alex Marshall awaited her belowstairs.

She was nineteen years old, an insignificant cog in the machinery of this war-torn world. What had happened between herself and Alex yesterday was an incident of war, simply that. In all such incidents, there had to be both loser and victor. She had lost on that occasion, but because of the strange magic that existed between them, the victor had promised not to take full advantage of his victory. There would be no repercussions, and the only name she had given him had been Edmund's. All the others, if they now acted with circumspection, would be safe. Ginny, herself, now knew the enemy in the person of her lover, as did he know the both in her. It would be a curious, dangerous game that they played from now on, but it carried the inevitability of destiny.

Ginny dressed herself with care, determined that there would be no further observations of the "gypsy" kind. She put on her best gown — a soft apple green with lace edging to the shoulders and low-cut bosom, where the creamy swell of her breasts rose delicately amidst the lace. The color brought out the rich chestnut highlights in the hair that hung, long and shining with cleanliness, to the small of her back. This morning she did not braid it, but secured it behind her ears with the tortoise-shell combs that had been her mother's. She slipped into the soft kid slippers that, like the gown, were worn only for special occasions. Such occasions had been few and far between in the last five years, but if ever there were a moment for finery, it was now, when she stood on the brink of an exciting, uncertain fate.

"I am ready, Diccon." She used his name unconsciously; it was one she had heard so many times during the lonely hours on the window seat that it came naturally to her lips. The key turned, and the door swung open. The lieutenant's eyes widened as he took in her appearance, so vastly different from the working attire she had worn when first they had come to the house, and even more so from her bedraggled state of yesterday.

She smiled at him and dropped a small, polite curtsy. Diccon blushed and stood aside as she went past him with a satisfying rustle of her skirts. She smiled a greeting to those she met along the gallery and on the stairs, and it was returned instantly. Suddenly these men seemed no longer the faceless captors of her house, members of a brutal invading army. There were people with their own joys and sorrows, their anxieties about loved ones left behind while they went to war, their terrors at the prospect of violent death or wounding, of the surgeon's knife in the field hospital, of gangrene and typhus.

Alex paced the dining room, waiting for her. How would she be? Mutely hostile in closed-face defiance? Wretched with shame and despair at her breaking? Sharp-tongued and cold-eyed with that bitter irony he had first seen? Any or all of them? Damn this war that had made beasts of them all, that had turned the peaceful peasantry into savages who raped and pillaged, tortured and killed indiscriminately and in vengeance. Civilization had regressed two hundred years in the last five, and no one regretted that fact more than Alex Marshall. And no one felt more passionately that the end must justify the means.

"Good morrow, Colonel." Her voice was light, the gray eyes smiled, and for an instant he stood stunned. He had seen her beauty from the first, responded to it from the first, had for a few short hours known it in the fullest sense. He had seen her energy, her ability to forget herself and her appearance in the fierce pursuit of purpose. And he had seen her exhausted, crushed, and broken. But until this moment, he had never seen the Lady Virginia Courtney. She swept him a curtsy, perfect in its depth, and he found himself bowing with the meticulous formality of the court.

The dining room door closed behind Diccon, and they were alone in a silence that coiled and wreathed around the tumult of their past dealings, and prepared for the future.

"Are you well?" Alex broke the silence at last, taking her hands, lifting them to his lips to kiss the work-roughened fingers.

"Yes, I am well," she replied honestly. "But devilishly hungry." The refectory table carried the remains of breakfast — a soldier's breakfast of sirloin, fat bacon, coddled eggs, and wheaten bread. A jug of ale stood amidst the wooden platters, knives, and pewter tankards that bore witness to the number of men who had broken their fast.

"What may I serve you?" Alex asked courteously, taking a knife to the sirloin, eyebrows lifted to punctuate the question.

"Everything," she replied, drawing a stool to the table, keeping her back to the window seat, that mute reminder of yesterday's agonies.

"When you have finished," Alex said slowly, "I wish you to show me the priest's hole and the secret passage."

"Why?" It wouldn't matter to show him now, since she could no longer use it, but by the same token, it should not matter to him either.

"I am afraid, Virginia, that I cannot allow you to have secret knowledge of a way out of this house. I cannot take the risk that you might use that knowledge."

Such a thought had not occurred to her, but she remembered how yesterday, on the beach, she had told him she would evade his guard if she could, to continue subversion as and when the opportunity arose. It was an understanding that lay beneath whatever turns their relationship might now take.

"And if I refuse?" She spread thick golden butter on the rough bread, watching the sunlight dance over the smooth black wood of the table.

"Then my men will find it."

Virginia looked around the room, imagining it in ruins, the rich paneling prised from the walls by pikes, the glowing floors torn up, the delicate moldings smashed. Only if there were still someone hidden in the priest's hole, would she allow her father's house to be destroyed, even if that house no longer belonged to her.

"Would you sack the house?" she asked quietly, knowing he would answer her truly, just as she knew what that truth would be.

There was pain in his eyes, but he still said, "I will do whatever is necessary to bring this war to a speedy conclusion. There has already been too much blood to have scruples about shedding more. To run shy at this point will make futile the sacrifices of those who have already given their lives."

"But you did not send me to Winchester jail."

"No." Alex swatted a fly buzzing at the bacon. "I love you, and I will keep you from harm insofar as I am able. But because I now know who and what you are, I will prevent you from causing harm to mine own cause."

"That is a fearsome responsibility you undertake," she said thoughtfully. "To keep safe the lover whilst circumventing the enemy, when the two persons are contained in one body."

"We shall see whether it is a task to which I am equal," he replied. "We understand each other, you and I?" His eyebrows lifted again.

"Yes." She looked at him fearlessly. "Lovers and foes until . . ."

"Until the conflict is resolved."

"Death resolves many conflicts."

"And it may well resolve this one, but I will pray for a happier conclusion, Ginny."

"I also." She stood up. "Come, I will show you the priest's

68

hole. The mechanism is most ingenious." She struck a flint and lit a candle. "There is no light," she explained, "and I have always been afeard of the passage, ever since Edmund locked me in one afternoon because he wished to hunt hare with the village boys and my presence would have been an embarrassment."

Alex thought of the wounded man in the boat, the man she had kissed, her cousin with whom she had grown to maturity, and he envied Edmund Verney who had known her in her growing, had teased her, and found her a nuisance.

"I hope he was well thrashed for his unkindness," Alex remarked, following her into the cold darkness.

"No." Ginny chuckled, shielding the candle that flickered as she pressed the catch to close the panel behind them. "I did not betray him."

Her voice faltered, and Alex stated flatly, "You have never done so. If Edmund Verney comes to harm, it will be through nothing that you have revealed."

Ginny did not respond as she reached the small chamber. She held the candle high, revealing the stone walls, the blood-stained pallet, the wooden pail.

The air was dank and fetid, and Alex could not help his recoil. Better to die in battle, surely, than to cower like rats in this wretched hole? But then he had never been faced with such a dilemma. He had never been hunted, and the battles he had fought he had won.

"We should remove this. It makes the air foul." He picked up the pail, his voice brisk and matter-of-fact.

Ginny nodded and led the way down the cold steps to the outside door.

They stood in the cool, clear morning, where the sea air was sharply fresh. Ginny breathed deeply of ozone, lifted her face to the breeze.

Alex emptied the pail around the elder bush. "Do you care to ride?"

"Of all things." She smiled. "But I am not dressed for it."

"Anymore than you are dressed for scrambling through secret passages," he teased, removing a cobweb from her hair. "You did not think to change your dress, and your slippers are soiled."

"We were talking of serious matters, and I forgot such mundane considerations," Ginny offered.

"And how often do you remember them?" His eyes danced.

"Rarely," Ginny admitted ruefully. "I was always the despair of my mother."

"I can imagine." Alex gave a shout of laughter. "A disobedient, stubborn, little gypsy, I'll lay odds." Then his laughter died, and he cupped her face. "You are not so very different now, and, for my sins, I would not have you otherwise."

"I am neither disobedient nor stubborn," she said softly, "since there is no one who has the right to command my obedience."

His eyes darkened. "It is not necessary to repeat that we are in opposition. I understand that fact, but I was talking of the lover, not of the enemy."

"It will not always be easy to separate the two." Even as she said this, her arms went around his neck, her body reaching against his length, feeling the warmth of the skin beneath his shirt. It was she who kissed him, this time, her hand palming his scalp as she pulled his head down, standing on tiptoe to assert the equality of love.

When they drew apart, Alex touched her swollen lips. "For this day, we are simply lovers. There will be no words of enmity between us. We will talk and exchange histories, and you will show me this island that you love so dearly."

"Very well," Ginny agreed, turning back to the secret door that still stood open behind them. "Do we return as we came to the further detriment of my gown? Or shall we surprise your men by reappearing like ghosts in the yard?"

"We will return the way we came," Alex replied smartly. "A few more cobwebs will make little difference, and I have no desire to traipse around the house."

Once again in the dining room, the panel shut tight behind them, Alex blew out the candle. "Put on your riding habit, Mistress Courtney. We shall go exploring."

The promise contained in the statement made her toes curl in the kid slippers. There would be time and opportunity enough for enmity in the days ahead, when the Roundhead colonel and his Royalist prisoner clashed as they surely would. But today was for loving. "I will meet you at the stables," she murmured.

"In ten minutes, then. There is much that we must learn about each other, Ginny."

He touched her lips with a long forefinger, and she ran from the room, hugging the promise, remembering belatedly to slow her pace and compose her features in an expression more befitting the captive lady of the manor.

Chapter Four

Hair braided and in riding habit, Ginny was in the stableyard ten minutes later, a cloak thrown over her arm because the wind came briskly from the sea. A soldier, iron-gray hair cropped close to a round, bullet-shaped head, was saddling the magnificent black charger on which Alex Marshall had ridden to take possession of so much more than the Redfern lands and property.

"This is a fine animal," she said, running her hand down the velvety nose. The charger whickered with pleasure and nuzzled her palm with rubbery lips.

"Aye, mistress," the soldier agreed, "pure Arabian and steady as a rock on a battlefield."

"What name does he carry?"

"Bucephalus," he answered.

"Bucephalus!" Ginny swallowed her disbelief. So had Alexander the Great named his horse. Surely Alex didn't see himself as the warrior emperor? Choking back the bubble of mirth, she went into the stable to bring out her own high-stepping, neat-boned mare. Jen sniffed the wind eagerly, and the sinews of her neck rippled at the prospect of exercise.

"Ah, you are before me, Mistress Courtney." Alex's voice came from behind, and to hide her pleasure in the sound, Ginny buried her face in the mare's warm neck, inhaling the rich scent of horseflesh.

"Saddle Mistress Courtney's horse, Jed," Alex instructed briskly, taking Bucephalus' reins. Jed grinned cheerfully.

"No, there is no need. I am quite able to saddle my own horse," Ginny said automatically.

"That is not in question. See to it, Jed."

"Yes, Colonel." Jed saluted and went to the stable for tack.

Alex turned to Ginny, his voice low and clipped. "You may offer your challenges and contradictions as often as you please when we are in private, but you will not do so in front of my men."

Ginny opened her mouth to protest that she had no such intention and then, as Jed appeared, closed her lips tightly, turning to take the bridle from the soldier, as Alex swung himself onto his horse.

Jed gave her a leg up, adjusting the stirrup leathers, and tightened the girth. Horses and riders clopped across the yard.

Ginny was angry at a rebuke that had had no justification. Alex, judging by his continued silence, was also clearly annoyed. "I had not the intention of offending the emperor's self-consequence," she declared.

"What the devil is that supposed to mean?" He frowned at her.

"Why, simply that a Bucephalus can only be ridden by the warrior emperor," she returned sweetly, pressing her heels into Jen's flanks, encouraging the mare from trot to canter, and then to full gallop.

Alex, after an instant of stunned incredulity, put Bucephalus to the gallop and thundered after her. The mare's stride could not outpace the charger, and once alongside, Alex leaned over and seized the reins at the bit, pulling Jen to a halt.

"For your information," he stated, "the horse was a present from my father when I attained my majority. He was named when I received him, and I could not, without wounding my father, change it."

"Oh." Ginny looked fixedly at the sea. "In that case I will apologize for drawing the conclusions that I did, but you gave me good reason to do so. I was not deliberately countermanding your orders, and were you a little less sensitive to supposed challenges, you would have realized that."

There was a long silence as Alex continued to maintain his hold on Jen's bridle. Then he said, "It is a little difficult to explain, Ginny, since you have not until now experienced military life, but there is a rigidity that you must learn to live with. My orders and my statements may not be questioned in public. If I allow anyone to do so, then I am diminished in the eyes of my men, who rely absolutely on my command for their safety. The brigade has to operate as one man in obedience to one mind—mine. Only thus can they be efficient, and only in efficiency can they be as safe as it is possible to be in wartime."

"But I am not a member of your brigade."

Alex sighed. "This was supposed to be a day without enmity, but perhaps this should be said at the outset. You are, in the eyes of my men, as much subject to their commander as they are. Do not question my authority in public, Ginny. We shall neither of us enjoy the consequences."

"And if I accept that you have authority over the prisoner-enemy, do you accept that you have none over the lover?"

There was a long silence, while gray eyes remained locked with the green-brown ones. "That is another issue for another day," Alex said at last. "But you must remember that I have assumed responsibility for your safety and will take what measures are necessary to ensure that safety." He released Jen's bridle. "Did you not promise to show me this island?"

He was right, that was a battle to be fought another day. Again Ginny took him by surprise. She was off across the springy turf, calling over her shoulder, "Let the emperor's steed match the lady's mare, Colonel." A fieldstone wall marked the boundary of Squire Elmhurst's estate, and Ginny set her horse to the jump, sailing over with Alex, on his magnificent beast, a hair's-breadth behind.

Bucephalus overtook Jen within seconds of touching ground and thundered ahead, eating up the coarse ground of the field beneath four pounding hooves. Eventually, Alex checked his mount and waited for Ginny, who came up beside him, laughing exultantly with the spirit of the chase, her cheeks glowing and eyes sparkling.

Alex wondered how this woman in a few short hours had destroyed his calm purpose, was now exposing him to the danger of taking risks with a career and a duty that had always been all and sufficient. She was not beautiful — too tall, brown-skinned, and bold-eyed — but there was something about that erect carriage, the heavy coils of chestnut hair that required no sun to bring out the luster, the direct clarity of the gray eyes that transcended conventional beauty.

"I appear to have lost that race." She laughed, throwing back her head in pure enjoyment. "Let us see if you will win the next, emperor on an emperor's steed." She turned her horse down a steep but broad path to a wide sandy beach. "Have you ever galloped through the waves, Alex? It is one of the great pleasures in life for both man and beast."

She rode Jen into the waves, automatically hitching her skirt to her knees as she had been used to do in the old days with Edmund.

Alex watched and smiled. "We will try to match you, my raggle-taggle gypsy."

She was off in the instant, Jen skipping through the waves with all the delicacy of a dancer as Bucephalus, heavier and unaccustomed to such terrain, floundered as he struggled to keep his footing. Both horses and riders were soaked when the mad water gallop ended and Ginny turned her mount onto the beach. "You forfeit the race, I think," she called over her shoulder, slowing her horse as excitement danced in her veins. Bucephalus, now freed from the constraints of unfamiliar water, thundered across the firm sand, and Jen skittered in surprise, catching Ginny unawares so that she tumbled from Jen's back in a whirl of sea-wet skirts to land with an undignified thump on the sand.

Alex was off his horse in the instant. "Are you hurt?" Anxiety rang in his voice, showed dark in his eyes.

"Only my dignity." Ginny laughed and gave him her

hands to haul her upright. "Pride comes before a fall, as I recall."

"I think that tumble lost you the race," he said softly, his hands cupping her face, turning it this way and that as if he were examining a rare piece of china. Ginny seemed to lose herself in his eyes, huge and glowing with that warm light as he smiled down at her. She began to tremble like an aspen leaf in the wind.

"What forfeit must I pay?" she heard herself whisper, although she knew the answer well enough.

"No forfeit," he replied. "I will take only what I know you give willingly. You are made for loving, Ginny." The kiss was gentle at first as he ran the tip of his tongue over her lips, darted between them to withdraw instantly at the moment her mouth opened in hunger to receive him. Still holding her face, he tantalized her thus for an aching eternity as her body quivered with that now-familiar yearning. But at last he yielded to her soft moaning pleas and plundered her mouth with a rapacious tongue, and she met thrust for thrust, reaching against his body, heedless of pride or of modesty as she pressed herself to the hard warm throbbing against her thighs.

"I want you," Alex said, drawing back to look into her eyes. "And I would have you, Ginny, here on the beach where the gulls call and the waves fall. *Here,* my sea sprite."

"And I would have you," she replied. "Here on the sand."

His fingers worked in the heavy coils of her hair, releasing it from constraint to fall in a shining cascade down her back. "I will do all I may to please you." Holding her with one hand, he twitched the cloak from the mare's saddle while Jen stood patiently beside Bucephalus on the sand.

Ginny found herself swung upward as one arm caught her behind the knees, the other grasped her strongly across her back. She reached her own arms to encircle his neck, drawing his head down to renew the interrupted kiss, as cold and clear as before in the certainty that this was as right as it was inevitable — reckless though it was.

Alex strode with her across the beach to the shelter of the cliff. He set her gently on her feet before tossing her cloak onto the sand.

Controlling his impatience, he unlaced the strings of her bodice, and Ginny stood still, trembling like a small wild animal facing the fox.

"Do not be afraid," he whispered, sliding the neck of her habit off her shoulders. "You know I will not hurt you."

"I am not afraid," she replied simply, "unless it be of the power of my wanting."

A wash of tenderness flooded him, controlled him as he cupped her breasts. "I also am afraid of that power, my love," he whispered. "Let me love you, sweet, and allow your body to feel and do what it must."

His words again caressed, gentled as his touch aroused. The habit slipped to her ankles leaving her clad only in her cotton drawers and a thin chemise, the low scalloped neckline doing little to cover her breasts that he now drew from their hiding place, bending his head to take the upstanding nipples in his mouth. Ginny arched backward, thrusting her breasts against his warm hands and the flicking tongue that lifted the aching engorged nipples, teasing as it stroked.

"Let us rid you of these last obstructions," Alex said, his lips moving upward to kiss the point where her neck met her shoulders. The simple tie of the chemise parted at her back, and then she stood, naked under the bright sky on the deserted beach.

Alex touched her as she stood before him, touched her in wonder, turned her and ran his hands down her back, over her bottom, down her thighs. And when he had finished this exploration, he drew her down to the velvet bed of her cloak. When she reached for him, he whispered to her to lie still and accept the pleasuring; there was time enough later for reciprocation, and she lay back, glorying in a passivity that by its giving was not truly passive. She had lain as immobile and without feeling as a tree beneath Giles, but he had needed only to take, and it had mattered not to him that what he took was not freely given, was simply an obedience to a loathsome conjugal duty.

Alex kissed the fast-beating pulse at her throat, raised each wrist in turn to press his lips against the matching pulse, before moving down her body, a finger playing in the shell of her navel as his eyes held hers. Her body stirred beneath his touch, and he ran a long, lazy caress from hip to ankle, still watching her eyes that held only a dreamy joy as she shifted with languid pleasure.

He parted her thighs, and Ginny gasped, her eyes sparkling not with fear but with excitement. His fingers pit-patted across the sensitive satin of the inner skin before moving higher. All the while he watched her face, holding his own rising excitation in check, wanting to ensure that he was truly pleasuring her.

Ginny moaned softly as a strange tightness grew in her belly — grew and coiled beneath the questing fingers that had found what they sought. She opened like a flower under the morning sun, and the gentle probing became insistent. How was he able to create this wonder? The thought came and went as she felt a presence inside her, moving with the same speed as the fingers outside, and then the coil tightened beyond bearing and burst apart. She heard her own sobbing cry from somewhere outside herself as the muscles of her thighs and buttocks squeezed around the magic of his fingers, and then released to leave her pulsing and heavy with relaxation.

Alex kissed her, his mouth hard as his own need became imperative. He stripped off his clothes and moved over her as he slid his hands beneath her hips, lifting her to meet him. Ginny cried out as he entered her, the exultant cry that he remembered she had quenched before, when there were people who might hear, and her legs curled around him, drawing him deep against the cleft of her body.

She was a woman made for loving, Alex thought again, made for the giving and receiving. As he moved within, Ginny moaned, thrashing wildly beneath him, her heels pressing into his buttocks demanding her own fulfillment as she promised his. Her eyes were open, locked with his, and he saw the wonderful flash of surprise as exquisite pleasure overpowered her, the incredible translucence of her skin as she gazed at him in bewildered wonder, cried out again, and held him tight as his own completion throbbed within the tight chamber of her being.

Ginny lay crushed beneath his weight, his fast-beating heart pulsing in rhythm with her own, their skins blended in the salt mist of ecstacy. With a reluctant groan, Alex rolled off her and, propping himself on one elbow, examined her face. The shy smile she gave him increased the radiance of her skin, the residue of wonder lurking still in the gray eyes.

"I do not think," he said softly, "that I have ever had such a loving."

"Since I have never experienced loving, I have nothing to compare it with." She was teasing him, and he chuckled.

"That, Mistress Courtney, deserves a dunking."

Ginny squealed as he sprang to his feet with a resurgence of energy and hauled her upright, bending to put his shoulder against her stomach as he tossed her over and ran with her to the sea.

"Don't!" she yelped as he made to throw her backward into the waves. "I do not wish for my hair to become all salty. It is but newly washed."

Alex laughed, standing waist high in the cold Atlantic. "Hold it up, then, because you're going in." He slid her down the length of his body, and she gasped as the water shivered her midriff.

"It's freezing, Alex!" Her teeth chattered, and then she felt his hands parting her thighs beneath the waves, cleansing her skin of the residue of their passion with seductive strokes that made her shiver with something other than cold. Alex grinned wickedly, turning her round to run his fingers in an intimate knowing caress down the cleft of her buttocks.

"Off you go, now. I'm going to swim. This water's too cold for standing still." A playful smack accompanied the instruction, and Ginny leaped through the water, holding her hair high until she reached the shallows. She turned to watch him as he cleaved the water with a powerful overarm, the auburn head a dark splodge against the gray-green sea. Ginny contemplated taking her revenge by drying herself on his shirt and then decided that he had not deserved such treatment. Instead, she rubbed herself dry vigorously with her chemise — the one garment she could do without on the way home. Her habit was wet from the mad ride, though, and sandy from her fall, and without a comb and the wooden pins that Alex had removed, there was little she could do about her hair.

Ginny slipped into her drawers and surprised herself by an involuntary giggle, something she hadn't done in years, but the thought of riding through the camp in her disheveled condition was somehow deliciously funny. And then the laughter died abruptly. It mattered not a whit if the whole world knew of her shocking conduct. She had nothing to lose except a reputation that now seemed quite irrelevant. Suddenly she wrapped her arms across her breasts in an unconsciously protective movement. She did have something else to lose—the man, Alex Marshall, and all that went with the love and passion of man for woman and woman for man. But how could she not lose it? There was no place in wartime for the consummated desire between a colonel in Cromwell's New Model Army and the daughter of a Malignant. No place for more than the ephemeral joy between two people opposed in every way but that of bodily fit and contour.

"Ow!" Deep in her reverie, she hadn't heard Alex creep up the sand behind her. He caught her around the waist and lifted her off her feet, her bare back pressed against his cold wet chest. "Put me down!" Her legs flailed indignantly. "You've made me all wet again."

"It was quite irresistible." He laughed, setting her on her feet. "The sight of you in nothing but your drawers, with your hair hanging down your back, staring into space on a deserted beach. What were you thinking?"

"Nothing at all," she declared, "except how wonderful I feel."

"I'm not sure I believe you," Alex said quietly, "but I will do so for the moment because I must."

"The colonel must return to his troops," Ginny said, accepting his statement thankfully, handing him her chemise. "Use this to dry yourself."

Alex frowned but said nothing as he dried himself roughly and dressed.

80

Ginny shook the sand from her cloak before throwing the garment around her shoulders and tucking her hair beneath the hood. "How much of a wanton do I look?" she asked with a tiny smile that did little to dispel the strain that, while it took nothing away from the glory they had shared, cast a shadow over the present and the nebulous future.

"If you remain swathed, you will pass muster," Alex said, tipping her chin to drop a kiss on her nose. If she would play the game, then would he also. "The only difficulty I see is how to hide one soaked undergarment from sharp eyes." He wrung out the sodden shift with a frown of mock puzzlement.

"I will conceal it beneath my cloak, together with the rest of the evidence of my abandonment." She laughed lightly. "Let us put gloom behind us for the moment, and I will guarantee to race you back with cunning rather than speed."

She caught Jen's reins, hitched her skirts over one arm, and put a foot in the stirrup. "Help me up, Colonel."

Alex boosted her into the saddle with one hand under her bottom. "You were quite capable of remounting unaided," he told her when she made laughing protestation at this undignified helping hand.

"Maybe so, sir," Ginny rejoined. "But you could at least have made a pretense of chivalry."

"And forgo such an opportunity?" he questioned, one eyebrow raised quizzically.

Ginny laughed. "I will be first in the stableyard, Alex," She was away before he had mounted Bucephalus. Alex thundered after her, but by the time he had reached the cliff top both Ginny and her mount had vanished. Obviously she knew a shortcut, and Alex resigned himself to following the path he knew.

She was waiting for him in the field adjoining the Redfern estate, and said slyly, "It occurred to me that if I appeared without you, your men might think that I had given you the slip, and then their commanding officer might be obliged to demonstrate that his prisoner had broken her parole and must face the consequences."

Alex scratched his nose, frowning thoughtfully. "I hate to

disappoint you, chicken, but that is another of your challenges I intend to refuse."

"Spoilsport," she threw at him, encouraging Jen into a trot.

They reached the stableyard in sober decorum, to be met by an anxious Diccon, who handed Alex a folded paper. The aide-de-camp was clearly controlling his excitement only by the most supreme effort.

Alex read the missive, and the frown that Ginny now knew so well drew the thick eyebrows in a bridge over his nose. "When did this arrive?"

"Two hours ago, sir," Diccon responded.

Two hours ago, when Parliament's colonel was making love to the enemy on a deserted beach. Ginny could hear Alex's thought as clearly as if he had spoken it.

Alex swung from his horse and helped Ginny from hers. His face was tight and closed, his hands impersonal. "I fear, Mistress Courtney, that you must repair to your chamber. I regret the necessity to confine you behind a locked door, but I have much to do and cannot spare a man to guard you."

"And if I give you my word that a guard will not be necessary?"

Alex hesitated, raising his eyebrows. He could not ask her directly, in the seething stableyard, if she was telling him that for this moment she would not use her freedom and the absence of observation for her own purposes.

"Have you ever had reason to doubt my word?" she asked softly.

"No." Alex shook his head. "But if you ever give me cause to do so . . . ."

"There is no need for threats."

"Very well. But stay close to the house." A gleam appeared in the green-brown eyes, and his voice dropped. "I may have a need to lay hands on you."

"I shall not stray, Colonel," Ginny murmured, lowering her own gaze to hide the responsive spark.

Alex strode off without a further word to her, throwing orders at Diccon, who followed his colonel like an eager puppy.

Ginny had no idea what had been in the message, but she found herself in the midst of what, at first, appeared to be a maelstrom of confusion and then, once she could make sense of the parts, became a hurried but orderly business of departure. The bugle called incessantly, the orchard campsite was dismantled, horses were saddled, supplies loaded onto carts. Soldiers and officers scurried around her, commands were shouted and obeyed. No one appeared to notice her as she watched, listened, and formed her own impression of the efficiency of Alex Marshall's brigade.

It was late afternoon when a young ensign appeared at her elbow. "The colonel wishes to see you, Mistress Courtney."

She nodded. "Is he in the dining room?"

"Yes, mistress."

"Then I have no need of escort." She said it gently but nonetheless forcefully, and the youngster shuffled awkwardly.

Ginny crossed the hall where the oak floors bore the tracks of muddy boots, but where no signs of the usual devastation of occupation were visible. The invaders were clearly moving out; so what plans had been made for Parliament's ward?

Alex was alone in the dining room, but his sword was at his hip, gauntlets in hand, breastplate and helmet in place. He was every inch the soldier and none of the lover. "I must drill the brigade," he told her without preamble. "While I do so, you will pack those possessions you may carry easily on the journey to London."

"I go to London as a prisoner?" She looked at him across the dining room, once again his adversary, proud and challenging, the gray eyes cool.

"As a ward of Parliament and my personal responsibility," Alex replied, almost with detachment. "You are a most resourceful Royalist rebel, Mistress Courtney, but your subversion will now cease. I will not hand you over to the proper authorities, but I *will* assume responsibility for your conduct myself, until such time as it is safe to let you loose again. The Scottish army has crossed the border, and

Cromwell is preparing for a forced march to meet them. I am ordered to join with the main force at London, there to await further instruction. You will accompany us."

"I was under the impression, Colonel, that you did not permit camp followers." As she goaded him, with that insolent little smile that so infuriated him, it was as if the time on the beach had never been, as if time had telescoped and they were back at the beginning again.

"This is the way it is to be, then, between us?" he asked, slapping the leather gauntlets against his palm. "You will not accept your position gracefully?"

"Prisoner of a conquering army is not an easy position to accept, gracefully or otherwise," she countered. "Have we not agreed that we are enemies? You will have your work cut out, sir, to keep me from my duty."

A tiny smile touched his lips as she delivered the bold challenge. "Doubtless I shall, Ginny, but I shall do so, nevertheless. Now, make all speed. We leave for Newport within the hour, and take ferry for Southampton with the dawn tide."

Her commanding officer had spoken, and what choice did she have anyway? She could perhaps slip from the estate during the drill and take shelter with friends on the island. But she could not get far in an hour, and Alex would not rest until he found her, and when he did, her freedom would be even more severely curtailed. Besides, there was little she could do on the island, without her house, now that Parliament's net had closed. And she could find no pleasure at all in the prospect of being without Alex, even when they were in antagonism. No, better to fall in with his plan for the moment, at least it would mean no immediate separation, and who could tell what opportunities might come her way to further her own cause?

An hour later, she was again mounted, the mare standing in the late afternoon sunlight on the driveway before the house. The silent ranks of men stared rigidly ahead, their officers as still and quiet as they, when heavy wooden planks were nailed across John Redfern's door, sealing it as Parliament's property until such time as it should come beneath the auctioneer's hammer, to belong to a faithful adherent of Parliament's cause. Ginny blinked back her tears, as she looked at her home for the last time. Alex was beside her, but she could not bear to look at him as he waited for his orders to be fulfilled. Then the task was completed. The bugle called, a parade ground voice barked a command, and the brigade wheeled to begin the march back to war.

Chapter Five

They rode at the head of the ranks of marching men along the fragrant country lanes where wildflowers and herbs stimulated by the warmth of the early evening sun threw out their mingled scents, and flocks of cawing crows arced above the pine trees before settling in chattering groups for the night.

The messenger, appearing suddenly, galloping toward them, his body crouched low over the saddle as an indication of his urgency, bore the insignia of Colonel Hammond. "*Now* what triviality's exercising Hammond?" Alex muttered, and Ginny shot him a surprised, sideways look. He had spoken with a degree of irritation that seemed to indicate a familiar exasperation with the governor of Carisbrooke Castle, the man who was, to all intents and purposes, the king's jailer.

"Colonel Marshall?" The messenger saluted smartly, reining in his mount with an abrupt tug that was quite unnecessary unless one wished to imply extraordinary haste.

"The very same, Ensign." Alex returned the salute without checking his horse. "You have a message from Carisbrooke?"

The ensign was obliged to turn his horse in the narrow lane as the cavalcade proceeded calmly on its way. Ginny felt sorry for the young man, struggling to complete the awkward maneuver whilst keeping pace with the front riders. Any self-consequence he might have felt in his mission had certainly been punctured by the colonel, and Ginny wondered why it should have pleased Alex to take out his exasperation at Colonel Hammond on this fresh-faced innocent. But then there was a great deal that she did not yet know about Alex Marshall.

"Your message, Ensign?" Alex inquired, eyebrows quirked, once the youngster was facing the same way as the rest of them.

"Colonel Hammond wishes to speak with you urgently, sir, before you leave the island."

"On what business?"

"I do not know, Colonel." The messenger flushed as if he were in some way responsible for his lack of knowledge. "But the governor is much concerned and says that he must consult with you before you take ferry at Newport."

They rode in silence for a moment, Alex frowning into the middle distance, allowing the suspense to develop. He could not possibly refuse the governor's request, Ginny thought, feeling curiously relaxed and detached as her body moved easily in the saddle. But this hesitation was definitely part of some game, some politicking perhaps. Isolated as she had been, she knew little of what went on elsewhere on the island, only what snippets were brought by fugitives to her safe house. Edmund and Peter had had little to add, in spite of their residence in the castle. The king held court, rode, and hunted apparently at will; tennis courts and bowling greens were kept in immaculate condition for his use; his entourage dined lavishly on twenty courses every afternoon. Carisbrooke Castle could have been St. James's Palace or Hampton Court, except for the whispers, and the comings and goings of closed-face Roundhead soldiery.

"Major Bonham?" Alex's crisp voice broke the quiet. "You will command the brigade from here to Newport, supervise the embarkation. I will rejoin you by the morning tide."

The major acknowledged receipt of the order with no apparent surprise. "Do you go alone, Colonel?"

"No." Alex turned sideways in his saddle. "Diccon, you will accompany me. I would have Jed, also. He is riding with the spare horses at the rear. Fetch him."

"And what of Parliament's ward?" Ginny mused softly. "Is she to fend for herself overnight?"

"I beg your pardon, Mistress Courtney. Did you say something?" Alex smiled down at her. If she thought he had forgotten her in the past distracting moments, the look in his eyes rapidly corrected the impression.

She shrugged with an appearance of nonchalance. "Nothing of any importance, sir. Am I also to continue to Newport?"

"Eventually," he said. "I'll not lay the responsibility of watching you on Major Bonham; he has enough to do. You will come with me to Carisbrooke where Lady Hammond will have a care for you until morning."

Ginny felt a thrill of excitement. She was to pass the night under the same roof as her king. Maybe, if she played her hand well, she might be granted an audience, and maybe, just maybe, there would be a task for her, something that could be accomplished by one marching with Cromwell's army.

Jed appeared on a sturdy cob, batman and mount looking stolidly comfortable with each other, as if they had both just been plucked from some accustomed peacetime activity in field or yard — as, when this war started, they probably had, Ginny reflected. The four of them, with the messenger in tow, increased their speed, leaving the orderly ranks of the brigade behind as they made their way to Carisbrooke.

The gray stone castle was a familiar enough sight to Ginny, as it was to all the islanders, but there had been little need to garrison the castle in peacetime, and she had not seen it in recent months, so was unprepared for the signs of fortification on the ramparts, the abundance of armed guards, the closed drawbridge and portcullis. The drawbridge was lowered and the portcullis raised rapidly, however, when Colonel Marshall was identified, and they passed through into the first inner courtyard where Govenor Hammond, a harassed-looking gentleman with worried eyes, stood waiting to greet them.

"My thanks, Colonel Marshall, for coming so promptly," he said with a short bow. "We have uncovered another escape plot, more elaborate than the others. I do not know how I am to deal with the situation. I am both jailer and host to His Majesty, and it is a damnable position. Parliament has offered no guidance as to how I am to comport myself and—"

"Just a minute, Hammond!" Alex interrupted the governor sharply. "I would prefer to discuss this when we are without an audience."

The governor seemed to see Ginny for the first time, and his eyes widened even as he recollected himself and his surroundings. The courtyard, crowded with the king's courtiers and Parliament's soldiers, was not the place to pour forth his woes, and the gray eyes of the young woman so peculiarly accompanying Colonel Marshall held the most candid curiosity. He coughed apologetically and looked at his visitor for enlightenment.

"Mistress Virginia Courtney," Alex said. "She is the orphaned daughter of John Redfern, and widow of Giles Courtney of the Dorsetshire Courtneys."

The governor bowed. "In happier times, I was acquainted with your father, mistress. He was a brave gentleman."

"Thank you," Ginny responded politely. There was little else to be said. Governor Hammond, however, still looked as if he did not fully understand matters, and Alex seemed to be taking a malicious pleasure in teasing him by withholding further explanation. Ginny wanted to laugh. The governor was so obviously nonplussed by the presence of a bona fide Cavalier at the side of one of Parliament's most dedicated adherents.

"Is Lady Hammond in residence?" Alex inquired, swinging off Bucephalus and handing the reins to Jed. "I should be grateful if she would have charge of Mistress Courtney until morning." Reaching up, he took Ginny by the waist and lifted her down in a thoroughly matter-of-fact fashion, as if there were no unusual intimacy in the gesture.

"She will be delighted, I'm sure," the governor said, looking even more bewildered. "Does Mistress Courtney accompany you to Newport, then?"

"And beyond," Alex replied blandly, and Ginny had to turn away to hide her laughter.

"Allow me to escort you to my lady, mistress." Giving up all hope of receiving further enlightenment, the governor bowed courteously, indicating with an elaborate flourish of his broad, feathered hat that she should precede him through an arched gateway across the courtyard.

"I will pay my respects, also," Alex said with an easy smile, following them.

They discovered the governor's wife surrounded by her ladies in a long gallery in the castle's west wing. Ginny found herself subjected to a distinctly shrewd appraisal as she made her curtsy. "And why does Mistress Courtney accompany you, Colonel Marshall?" Lady Hammond demanded directly, clearly not suffering from her husband's reticence. "A brigade on the move is no place for a young gentlewoman. If she has no family, you had best leave her here with me."

Now what, Ginny thought. Clearly it was not a decision in which she was considered entitled to participate. The opinion of young women as to their fate was rarely sought, as she knew from bitter experience, and the discussion between Alex and Lady Hammond would continue above her head. It would be interesting, however, to see how he dealt with what was such an obviously appropriate proposal.

"Mistress Courtney is a ward of Parliament, lady," Alex was saying smoothly. "Your offer is most kind, but I am afraid I cannot accept it. She has been engaged very successfully in activities to aid the rebels these last six months, and I cannot risk leaving her on the island. I am taking her to London where Cromwell may decide her fate."

"Indeed." Lady Hammond regarded the tall young woman thoughtfully. Her eyes were lowered demurely, as was right and proper in front of her elders, but there was something about her carriage that implied such respectful decorum might not be habitual. "Well, the decision is yours, of course, Colonel. If she is such a threat to Parliament's cause, perhaps she should be held in one of the chambers near the guardhouse until you have completed your business with my husband."

"I am confident, lady, that your supervision will be more than adequate," Alex replied. "She should not, however, be permitted to go outside unattended." So saying, he bowed punctiliously to Lady Hammond, inclined his head to Ginny with a murmured, "Mistress Courtney," and left the gallery with the governor.

"So, child, you have been aiding the rebels," Lady Hammond said. "You must tell us how. We are well accustomed to intrigue within these walls, indeed we are plagued by it, but hear little of what goes on elsewhere." She gestured toward a low stool, seating herself on an armless chair, arranging her copious skirts around her.

"I have done little, lady," Ginny demurred. She had nothing to lose by recounting the truth of her adventures up to the arrival of Colonel Marshall. The women in this room were all in an ambiguous position, Royalist by inclination, Roundhead by circumstance, and even if one of them was inclined to betray her, there was no longer any secret to disclose; however, she could not help feeling reluctant to reveal her harum-scarum existence in this excessively proper company.

"I do not think Colonel Marshall would have made a prisoner of you, assumed responsibility for you, were your activities insignificant," Lady Hammond said, a touch of acerbity in her tone. "That gentleman is not inclined to waste either time or energy. If I judge your story to be of sufficient interest, the governor will ask the king to grant you an audience. He is in sore need of a little encouraging diversion after the failure of his latest plot."

"I would be deeply honored, lady," Ginny said, meeting Lady Hammond's gaze directly for the first time. Lady Hammond looked into the clear gray eyes and nodded. As she had expected, there was more to this young woman than was initially apparent. Perhaps Alexander Marshall was also aware of that. It was impossible to imagine, of course, that a man of such rigid principle and devotion to duty could be sidetracked by an unusually spirited girl. That she was most unusual, Lady Hammond became absolutely convinced as Ginny told her story to a rapt audience.

"His Majesty will be glad to hear that Edmund Verney and Peter Ashley made their escape," Lady Hammond said briskly as the tale came to an end. "We will request an audience for you, after dinner."

During dinner, Ginny had ample opportunity to observe King Charles since he sat with his favored courtiers and the Hammonds on a raised dais at the head of the two long tables that ran down the grand hall on either side. A periwigged footman stood behind the king's chair, his sole purpose, as far as Ginny could see, being to hold the monarch's gloves while he ate. The meal was preceded by a lengthy reading of the Liturgy, at the king's insistence, Ginny's neighbor whispered disconsolately to her. It mattered not how hungry they were, or how late the meal if the king had been out hunting, his devotion insisted that the religious exercise be completed. Once they had sat down, conversation, in spite of the quantities of good Rhenish wine, seemed subdued, and of Colonel Marshall and his aide-de-camp, Diccon Maulfrey, there was no sign. But then it would hardly be appropriate for the king's avowed enemies to break bread with him. Ginny could not help wishing, as course followed course and the meal stretched into infinity, that she also was dining in private, preferably in the sole company of Alex. . . .

A polite question from her neighbor brought her out of the somewhat uninhibited and rather more than pleasant reverie inspired by this thought. Her cheeks warmed slightly as she fought for composure and returned a vague response, conscious of the elegance of her interlocutor's gown compared with her own riding habit, which, while it was both well cut and serviceable, could hardly be compared with the ruched silks and rich laces bedecking those around her. The apple-green gown that she had worn for Alex that morning—was it only this morning?—was in her baggage traveling with the supplies at the rear of the brigade. It had not occurred to her that she would require more formal attire on this short visit to the court at Carisbrooke. The men were as splendidly dressed as their ladies, their wide sleeves slashed with silk, their coats laid with broad plate silver-lace, their hair, beneath broad cockaded hats, elaborately curled to their lace-trimmed shoulders. And no one was more magnificent than King Charles.

Ginny found herself silently comparing the richness around her with the simplicity of the Roundhead garb. Alex, in the soldier's leather and linen, the auburn hair cropped to his ears, bare-headed unless in armor, seemed somehow worthier of respect, more dignified than these peacocks who were behaving against all the evidence as if nothing had happened to disturb the even tenor and absolute permanence of their pleasure-seeking, self-satisfied lives. Throughout the land, chaos and anarchy reigned, as the king's followers rose again in his cause, rose against an army now well equipped and highly disciplined. Scattered and without leadership, the Royalist rebels had not a chance against such an opposition; yet around this dinner table, those for whom they were prepared to die acted as if nothing existed outside the quiet, orderly world of the court.

Not until after dinner, when she was presented to King Charles, did she realize this judgment had been, at least in some cases, overly harsh.

It was with fast beating heart that Ginny accompanied the

governor into a richly furnished, round chamber in the east turret. It was King Charles's private sanctum where he received only those to whom he chose to grant special audience, and Ginny had been made fully aware by Lady Hammond of the honor about to be done her, and to whom she owed gratitude for arranging it. Charles was now forty-eight years old, and a bitter, disillusioned man still believing in his divine right to rule his people as he saw fit, still sorrowful rather than angry that his subjects chose to defy God and His laws by challenging the authority of His representative. Had Ginny felt the slightest doubt as to her fealty, once in the royal presence it would have disappeared instantly. The king's deportment could only be described as majestic, and it would have been impossible to approach him with less than the utmost respect and reverence.

She sank to one knee in a deep curtsy when the governor presented her as the daughter of John Redfern. It came as no surprise to Ginny that the family tie would be viewed with more respect than her Courtney connection. Her husband's hesitation to declare himself for the king in the early years of the war had been conspicuous. Her father, on the other hand, had been at the king's side from the beginning until his own death.

"Pray rise, Mistress Courtney." The king spoke in a soft, pleasant voice, bending to take her hand and draw her to her feet. "Your father was a dear and true friend. We miss him sorely."

"I also, sire," Ginny replied with simple truth.

"I understand you share our present fate," King Charles went on with a whimsical little smile. "Prisoner of Parliament."

"Ward of Parliament is how my position is described, sire," Ginny replied. "But in truth I think the difference is purely semantic. My freedom is curtailed in either instance."

"That is certainly true of ourself, is not, Hammond?" The king directed a sardonic smile at the luckless governor who knew not how to answer him. "You may leave us to talk with

94

Mistress Courtney." The king dismissed Hammond with a careless wave, then turned to Ginny. "I do still have *that* freedom, mistress — the right to the company I choose. You have news of two of our friends, I understand." He sat on a silk-covered chair and looked up at Ginny expectantly.

Ginny, standing before him, told of her safe house, the priest's hole, the runs she had made with fugitives to the mainland, and finally of the escape of Edmund and Peter. "They were beyond the headland when Colonel Marshall appeared on the beach," she explained mendaciously, "so he was unable to prevent their flight. They should have landed safely at Buckler's Hard before the Roundhead forces on the mainland could be alerted." It was a pity she could not tell the truth that would present Alex in a kindlier light, but to do that she would have to reveal so much more.

King Charles said nothing immediately, and the silence stretched in the candle-lit room. Ginny looked beyond his shoulder, out at the dark night filling the round casement. She was tired. It had been a long day, and if they were to reach Newport to catch the morning tide, they would have to be up before dawn.

"You have much courage, mistress." The king spoke, his voice now heavy. "There are many like you, all over my country, doing what they can, whilst I am immured here, unable to offer even verbal support. They entrap my messengers, foil my every plan. I do not think I shall ever leave this island except in death."

"Do not say so, sire." In spite of her weariness, Ginny could not help responding to the dull note of resigned despair in the king's voice. "As you say, there are many working in your cause."

"But they need encouragement, and I am unable to get even a word of it out of this prison."

"Will you entrust me with your message, Your Majesty?" Ginny spoke without reflection, there was no need of it. She had hoped for an opportunity to be of use, a task to perform that would give her the satisfaction of circumventing Parlia-

95

ment's colonel even as she remained his prisoner, and this was perfect. "Since my departure from the Isle of Wight is at Parliament's order, I shall certainly be able to carry your message to the mainland. Once there, I shall be traveling as freely to London under Parliament's protection as any Roundhead. No one will suspect a prisoner of using her captivity as cover for subversion." She smiled, the gray eyes danced as the plan took shape. She had sworn to Alex that she would do all she could in the king's cause, and this was even better than she could have hoped.

"And if you are discovered, child?"

Ginny shrugged. "I will take my chance, sire."

The king frowned. "I have known Alexander Marshall since he was a youth. He and my nephew, Rupert, were close friends and shared much in happier days. He is as dedicated to his principles as he is ruthless in their execution. I would not have you fall foul of him."

Ginny shivered. The king talked of Alex in the same tone and much the same words as Peter Ashley had done, and her own experience gave her little reason to doubt either of their statements. But there was the magic between herself and the colonel that had saved her from Parliament's vengeance once; she would have to trust that it would do so again should she in truth fall foul of him. "I will take my chance, sire," she repeated quietly, "and will be deeply honored to serve you."

"How will you accomplish this?" The king, having made token protest, seemed to accept her statement as both natural and expected. He rose and went over to a square oak table beneath the window on which stood an inkstand, quills, and parchment.

"I cannot say exactly." Ginny watched as he seated himself and began to write. "It will depend on my gaining speech with people in the countryside, to discover the position of Royalist bands. Once I have found out their whereabouts, seeking them out will depend on opportunity and circumstance. I do not yet know how closely guarded I shall be on the march. I can only say, Your Majesty, that I will do all in my power."

"Yes, of course." He sanded the sheet of parchment before reaching for the candle, holding it so that a blob of melted wax dripped on the sheet. He pressed his heavy, intricately carved signet ring into the wax, then nodded with satisfaction. "This document is simply to establish your credentials as my messenger. Should it be discovered, there will be no information of any importance to be found."

Ginny nodded, folded the sheet, and placed it in the deep pocket of her habit. She would find some place for it amongst her baggage when they rejoined the brigade. "And your message, sire?"

"Simply one of encouragement. You will speak directly for me, saying that they fight in God's army for a righteous cause and their king stands beside them in spirit." He paused. "You will say, also, that we will not desert them. The stories that we are planning flight to France are a loathsome fabrication designed to cause them to lose heart. We are no cowards, and will never betray our servants. The message is clear?"

"Perfectly, sire." Ginny curtsied, taking the hand outstretched toward her, pressing her lips to the royal ring.

"If you are discovered, you will not hesitate to disclose this message to your inquisitors. Nothing will be gained by your suffering unduly."

Ginny swallowed, her mouth drying at his words, the thought of Winchester jail rising vividly to mind. Perhaps Alex would not save her a second time.

Finally dismissed, she left the royal presence, past the armed guards standing at ease outside the door to his sanctum, making manifest the true nature of the king's imprisonment. It was late in the evening, and there were few people in the stone-walled corridors as she made her way toward the bedchamber she was to share with one of Lady Hammond's daughters. Rounding a corner, she saw him, perched negligently on the stone sill of a deep window embrasure, hands thrust into the pockets of his britches. Her heart did a flip-flop behind her ribs. The dark corridor was deserted, and he didn't move as she approached slowly. Even as her skin rippled in delicious anticipation, the letter deep in her pocket seemed to glow through the stuff of her habit, burning against her thigh, declaring its presence to the enemy. If only she could bid him good-night and pass on. But she reached him and stopped as involuntarily as if he had barred her path.

"You have been with the king?" Alex said quietly, for the moment keeping his hands in his pockets.

"Yes," Ginny agreed, forcing herself to meet his eye with bold candor. "The governor was good enough to request an audience for me — for my father's sake, you understand?"

Alex reached out a hand, lazily almost, but when he took her chin, holding her upturned face steady for his scrutiny, there was nothing casual or indolent about the pressure of his fingers, or about the sharpness of the green-brown eyes. "Plotting already, my little rebel?" he asked gently.

"I do not know why you should think that!" Ginny snapped, taking refuge in anger. "What possible opportunity could there be here? I do not think I am capable single-handedly of spiriting His Majesty out from under his guards. Do you, Colonel?"

Alex laughed. "No, I do not think that even you are capable of accomplishing that."

"You have perhaps forgotten that I consider the king to be my ruler, one to whom I owe allegiance, as my father did before me. *I* am not engaged in treachery against the lawful king—"

"Careful, Virginia!" Alex interrupted, his voice ominously soft. "Do not push me too far."

"Well, I do not understand why I should be accused of plotting, when the king has simply done me the honor of receiving me. It is an opportunity I thought never to have had, and I do not see why you should spoil it for me." The note of hurt petulance was feigned, but it convinced Alex.

His eyes softened, and a long finger ran over her lips.

"I crave pardon, Ginny." Maintaining his hold on her chin, his free hand moved up to palm her scalp. She quivered, even as her tongue peeked in invitation from between her lips. Alex's eyes narrowed. "Brazen minx," he whispered. "If you do that again, I'll not be responsible for the consequences."

Ginny felt the strangest surge of power prickling along her spine, mingling with the imperative wanting that was now become familiar. Deliberately, she ran her tongue over her lips, her eyes bold, taunting him with the sensual invitation that he had no way of accepting, here in a quiet corridor of Carisbrooke Castle.

"Sometimes, I fear that I shall rue the day I rode to John Redfern's house," Alex groaned, yielding to the temptation he could not seem to resist. His mouth covered hers, but Ginny, suddenly the aggressor, pushed with her own tongue deep within the warm cave of his mouth. Wickedly, her hands ran down his back. One hand pressed urgently into the taut buttocks, while the other slid round his body to enclose the hard evidence of his arousal. He moaned against her mouth, and that wonderful sense of power again flooded her. Her captor he may be, the arbiter of her movements he may be, but in this business she too could assert mastery. Except, as she reached against his length, felt the moist heat of her body, the tremors in her limbs, Ginny sensed her control slipping away, the need for their union all encompassing in its immediacy.

"In the name of the good God, stop!" Alex dragged himself upright, placing his hands on her shoulders, holding her away from him as he shook her slightly, almost in desperation. "What are you trying to do to me?" His eyes darted down the corridor. "You are a sorceress and a wanton, Virginia Courtney, and you would ruin us both."

"And am I not already ruined?" she asked, only half playing, but touching his face. "Mistress of the enemy with no ravishment as excuse? How long will your men believe in my virtue, Alex?"

"God's life, Virginia! But you know how to say the wrong thing at the wrong time!" Alex hissed, keeping his voice low with an effort, but ever mindful of the public corridor. "Get yourself to bed. We leave before cockcrow." Turning her with rough haste, he pushed her down the corridor away from him, then stood watching as she walked with that wonderful erect carriage, head held proudly. She was right, of course. In the long run, his own reputation would not suffer from this alliance — mesalliance? So long as she did not harm Parliament's cause or lead him to neglect his duty, he could take whatever mistress he chose without censure, drawing only the slightest comment. Even the fact that she was his prisoner would be condoned with a knowing chuckle.

Virginia's position would be very different unless she maintained that she had been forced, raped by her captor, and held against her will. Knowing her as he thought he did, she would not stoop to such artifice, would instead hold boldly to the truth. And the truth would indeed ruin her.

Chapter Six

Ginny crept into the darkened bedchamber assigned to her, listening to the deep breathing of Amelia Hammond coming from behind the drawn curtains of the high feather bed. She had not intended to upset Alex by stating the truth in that half-joking fashion. It was not a truth that disturbed her in the slightest. Orphaned and friendless, what did she have to lose by being known as the colonel's mistress? Since planning for the future was a futile exercise when one could not count upon living beyond the next day, worrying about it was equally so. She would take her chance and live one day at a time, accepting the rough with the smooth. And if the time ever came again when one could contemplate a future, then it could not possibly be worse than the one that had awaited her, bound by indissoluble ties to Giles Courtney.

Stripped to her shift, she climbed onto the high mattress, careful not to disturb her sleeping bedfellow. In spite of her fatigue, her body was restless — restless because it was unsatisfied, she decided ruefully. Those few moments in the corridor had set off the chain reaction of a passion that demanded consummation. Presumably it was the same for Alex, bedded somewhere in this castle. It would be easy enough for him to obtain release though, Ginny reflected disconsolately, throwing herself onto her stomach. There were always women to be found, ready and willing in exchange for a few coins to . . .

The hand on her shoulder seemed to wake her before she had even fallen asleep. "It is time to rise, mistress." The serving wench placed a ewer, from which rose a comforting wisp of steam, on the dresser beside the window. "You are to break your fast in the small parlor by the east door." She left a candle burning on the mantel before departing as softly as she had come.

Yawning, Ginny slid to the floor. There was not even a streak of gray in the sky, and Amelia Hammond barely stirred as Ginny washed gratefully and dressed again in her riding habit. In her befuddled, sleep-soaked state, it seemed as if she had only just taken it off. She braided her hair as best she could in the dim light of the single candle, which she then took with her as she let herself out of the chamber. However sleepy some of its inhabitants, the castle was very much awake at this unearthly hour. Soldiers strode purposefully across the courtyards, servants scurried through the corridors, and Ginny found one willing to direct her to the breakfast parlor.

Alex and Diccon were there, examining a map. The aide-de-camp was standing by the table, gnawing on a chop; Alex, perched casually on the corner of the table, was gesturing with a pewter tankard as he cut a wedge of cheese from an enormous round. They both looked up as she entered, and Diccon mumbled an embarrassed greeting through a mouthful of meat, wiping his greasy hand hastily on his britches.

"Good morning, Virginia." Alex looked, to Ginny's jaundiced eye, as if he had passed a long and peaceful night. His eyes were bright, complexion fresh, clothing as neat and tidy as always. "You slept soundly, I trust."

"Not long enough," Ginny returned, a slight edge in her voice. She had been somewhat unsure as to how she would greet him after last night's abrupt departure, but annoyance and fatigue seemed to be providing the answer.

"You will feel stronger when you have broken your fast," Alex replied in soothing tones that irritated her even further.

"It is too early to eat." Ginny filled a tankard with ale from the jug on the laden table. "Pray do not let me disturb you. You were clearly engaged on some vital military matter."

"Are you always so ill-tempered in the morning?" Alex inquired, spreading golden butter thickly on a slice of wheaten bread. "You are making poor Diccon feel most awkward. I am sure he thinks he is in some way responsible. Eat this."

Ginny, feeling a little ashamed of herself, took the bread and butter and smiled at the aide-de-camp who did, indeed, look rather uncomfortable. "Do not mind me, Diccon. I did not sleep soundly or long enough last night, a fact for which you can hardly be held accountable." The lieutenant offered her a radiant smile and his eyes glowed. Ginny blinked. Such a simple apology surely did not deserve quite such a degree of warmth? Alex, interpreting the smile correctly, gave an internal sigh. Life was already sufficiently complicated without young Diccon being smitten with a case of calf love.

"If you have breakfasted sufficiently, Lieutenant, would you make sure Jed and the horses are ready and waiting at the gatehouse? We take horse in ten minutes."

Diccon flushed as he recollected himself, saluted smartly, and left the room.

"I do hope you will become accustomed to early rising," Alex murmured. "Being subjected to a fit of the sullens every morning will prove tedious, I fear."

"I do not object to rising early, if I gain my bed equally early," Ginny retorted. "And you are entirely responsible for my disturbed night."

"How so?" he inquired with more than casual interest.

Ginny bit her lip crossly. She had not meant to refer to the wretched tossings and turnings of deprivation, or to her dismal reflection that Alex would not be obliged to suffer in that manner. "I meant nothing." She took a gulp of ale.

"You *did* mean something," Alex insisted. "You cannot make such an accusation without explaining it."

"Oh, do not make me say it," Ginny begged. "It is so mortifying."

Alex chuckled. "Shall I guess?" Reaching for her hands,

he drew her between his knees. "You were, perhaps, eager for love?"

"And you were not, I suppose," Ginny mumbled, feeling his knees pressing her thighs warmly through the material of her habit. "Or if you were, there was always something you could do about it."

"Like what?" His eyebrows lifted. "You are not, I trust, going to say something very shocking."

"Like kitchen maids," Ginny snapped, pulling at her hands.

Alex disconcertingly burst out laughing. "Kitchen maids! You ridiculous girl! If it wasn't funny, it would be insulting. I'm not some rutting stud, whatever you might think."

"Oh, do let me go." She pulled at her hands again. "I do not see why you should mock me."

"You deserve it for making such an outrageous suggestion. What would you say if I suggested you could always go down to the barracks to relieve your needs? It comes to the same thing."

"It does *not*!" Ginny protested. "But I do not wish to talk of it anymore. I have not yet finished my breakfast."

"Then you had better do so with all speed." He opened his knees before releasing her hands. "At some point, Ginny, we must talk of what you said last night." He spoke seriously. "I beg your pardon for being so brusque. I should not have packed you off to bed quite so abruptly, but I found the truth somewhat unpalatable."

"I do not," she said quietly. "It is a fact I am happy to live with. I do not care if the whole world knows of it."

"You are speaking without due thought," Alex said with a sigh.

Ginny spun round on him, saying fiercely, "It is *my* fate, Colonel, and I will embrace it as I choose. You have a care for your reputation and your career, and leave me to manage my own."

Alex inhaled sharply, and that telltale muscle twitched in his cheek. "You are going to have to learn not to talk to me in that fashion, Virginia. Unfortunately, I do not have the time to teach you at the moment. Finish your meal and be at the gatehouse in five minutes." Swinging on his heel, he marched from the room, leaving the door open.

Ginny felt the prick of tears behind her eyes. She had been outrageously rude in the face of his apology and genuine concern about a matter that did involve them both, and the irritability of fatigue was poor excuse. She simply wanted him to accept that the opinion of the world was of no importance to her and, while they need not flaunt their relationship, Alex need not exercise an unnecessarily chivalrous restraint that would deprive them of something that fate could wrench from them at any moment anyway.

Abandoning the breakfast table, she made her way to the gatehouse where Alex, Jed, and Diccon waited, already mounted. Diccon swung to the ground the minute she appeared, ready to assist her to mount Jen. In her anxiety to avoid the colonel's eye, she smiled her thanks rather more warmly than the help warranted, and was both comforted and amply rewarded by the lieutenant's glowing response. To Alex, it looked as if she were deliberately encouraging his aide-de-camp, and his lips tightened. There was nothing he could say or do at this point, however. Diccon was behaving in a perfectly appropriate fashion, for all that he looked like a soulful puppy, and Virginia had only smiled after all.

Dawn was breaking as the silent group clattered through the arched gateway, over the drawbridge, and onto the road to Newport, leaving at their backs the sorrowful image of Carisbrooke Castle and its royal prisoner. An hour later, they rode into Newport, the main town on the Isle of Wight. Even at this early hour, the prosperous market town was bustling as storekeepers raised their shutters and inn servants hurried through the paved streets. The air was laden with the mingled smells of fish, tanning, and hops from the breweries, fisheries, and leather manufacturers who made up the town's main industries and accounted for much of its prosperity.

Visits to Newport during her childhood had always been a great treat for Ginny, particularly when she was allowed to accompany her father about his business, or when he sat as magistrate at the assizes. The town seemed little different now, the older buildings, half-timbered and plaster-fronted, standing side by side with the newer ones of brick and timber. But where once there had been only farmers, goodwives going about their household business, fishermen, and storekeepers, there were now soldiers. Tankards in hand, they lounged outside the inns. Officers strode down the streets, spurs clinking. Ginny waited for some sign from the slovenly looking soldiers that they acknowledged their officers but saw none, just as the officers appeared not to notice the slouching men.

Alex gave vent to a disgusted exclamation as a foot soldier reeled against the wall, then spat in the gutter. "Have they no pride? No discipline?" Spurring his horse, he descended on the knot of tavern leaners who jumped to alarmed attention as Bucephalus reared over them. They were subjected to a blistering tirade from the colonel, who told them in fearsome detail what their fate would be were they under his command, then ordered them back to their brigade. Grim-faced, he returned to his own companions. "If I had time to find their officers, this town would jump," he declared furiously. "How can we expect to win a war when there is no pride in the uniform, no cohesion, no sense of self-respect? I'd like to have every man jack of them under my command for twenty-four hours!"

Ginny glanced at Jed and Diccon. They seemed quite unperturbed by their colonel's vehemence, in fact were nodding in agreement. She herself, while she had known this side of Alex existed, found herself fervently hoping that she would not have to witness such a display again. And, even more fervently, that *she* should never find herself on the receiving end. It was hard, though, to avoid making the mental comparison between the men in the streets and what she had seen of Alex's brigade, where the men stood tall and proud, went about their work with smooth efficiency, snapped to attention at the mere glimpse of an officer. If it took that scalding tongue to turn them into the effective, single-minded fighting machine that would ensure their safety inasfar as it was possible, what right had she to question his methods?

On reaching the quay, they found Major Bonham, calm, complacent even, Ginny thought, surveying the flat-bottomed ferries where the horses were tethered in rows, each one attended by a foot soldier. The remainder of the brigade were embarked on similar craft, clearly at ease, until a bugle called at the sight of their commander and the loose ranks became stiff columns. Alex acknowledged the salute. "Stand them at ease for the crossing, Major." He dismounted, reaching up to lift Ginny from the mare the instant before Diccon offered his hand. "Jed will see to your horse. Come." His palm was in the small of her back, the pressure gentle but firm as he moved her toward the ferry where stood his officers.

Ginny resigned herself to being hurried along in this proprietorial manner. That he was still annoyed with her, she was in no doubt. She could almost feel the coolness radiating from his hand.

On reaching the edge of the quay, however, she twitched away from his guidance, catching up her skirts and springing nimbly across the yawning gap between the quay and the ferry. Alex, in spite of his annoyance, could not help a tiny smile at this renewed evidence of her ease with all things nautical. She shook out her skirts and went over to the port rail from where she could watch her beloved Isle of Wight recede in the morning mists. If the mists cleared rapidly, once they were well out into the Solent, she would be able to see the house that was no longer her home, standing on the cliff top above Alum Bay. Perhaps such an indulgence would not be wise. To break down, here amongst these men, was unthinkable. One should look forward, after all, not back. But she could not move as the anchor chains rattled, the mooring ropes were tossed into the ferry, and the wind caught the broad sail as the helmsman swung the wheel. The ferry moved out into the Solent on the swelling tide, and Ginny rested her chin on her elbows propped on the rail.

"I could not leave you behind, Ginny." Alex spoke softly, suddenly behind her, touching her shoulder in brief comfort. "Even had I the inclination to lose you, my duty

107

demands that I keep you under my guard. You understand that, do you not?"

She nodded and sniffed, feeling in her pocket for her handkerchief. Her fingers closed over the king's document, and with the feel of the stiff parchment her tears dried. What right had she to lament the loss of her home when the king had lost his freedom and so many had lost their lives in the cause? And besides, would she not rather be here, locked in passion and conflict with the man who aroused her to such peaks of glory, offered such an expanse of wonder to be explored.

With a decisive movement, she turned from the rail. "I have done with grieving, sir."

Alex looked at her, a frown in his eyes, then inclined his head in brief acknowledgment. As he began to move away, she said softly, "I crave pardon for my earlier discourtesy. It was inexcusable."

"Yes," he said thoughtfully. "It was. You will be wise to ensure that it does not happen again. But I will pardon you, on this occasion."

And for that small mercy, Ginny supposed, she should be grateful.

It was mid morning when the procession of ferries turned into Lymington estuary. The river was as busy as always with small craft plying backward and forward between the flat marshes on either side. As the leading ferry approached the cobbled quay, men and boys, clustering around the bollards and leaning against the low stone wall, leaped forward to receive the mooring ropes thrown from the ferry by a sinewy ferryman whose bare torso was burned a deep mahogany. The helpers on the shore would expect to be paid, and Ginny wondered whether Cromwell's army did pay for such services rendered, or whether they came under the heading of expected loyalty to Parliament. The ferries were all docked side by side, and the complicated process of disembarkation began.

Jed came over to Ginny. "Colonel wants you to stay on board, mistress, until the brigade's reformed."

"Why?" She frowned in puzzlement. "I can wait on the

108

quay."

Jed shuffled his feet on the wooden deck. "I think as 'ow Colonel feels you'll be safer here, beggin' your pardon."

"I will not be able to run, you mean." She shrugged easily. "I do not think I would get very far, do you, Jed?"

"Not if Colonel doesn't want you to," Jed concurred. "Doesn't want you to try, though. Could be awkward."

Ginny had little difficulty believing this laconic statement and settled down on a coil of rope to watch the disembarkation. It could have been chaos with the horses, unnerved by the voyage, stamping and tossing their heads, the two hundred men milling around unloading the carts of supplies; instead, everyone seemed to know exactly what they were to do, officers were everywhere, playing as active a part as their men, and Alex, Ginny decided, seemed to have the gift of being in ten places at once. She watched him closely, noticing how he never seemed to be interfering, was not averse to putting his shoulder beneath a particularly awkward bundle, how the men joked and laughed around him. Yet she knew the awe bordering on fear in which they held him.

The sun was warm, the ferry rocked gently on its mooring, the ropes creaked with the sound that to Ginny was as soporific as a lullaby. Her eyes drooped as a wondrous lethargy spread through her. She curled up on the coil of rope, pillowing her head on her hand, inhaling the sun-soaked fragrance of the wooden deck, the faint oily smell of the rope, the salt-fish river marsh smell.

Colonel Marshall's brigade formed up in orderly ranks on the quay, cavalry at their head, baggage carts neatly loaded at the rear. The sight seemed to please their commander since, after roll call and inspection, an hour's liberty was announced. A low cheer rose from the ranks at the prospect of the freedom to roam the street of Lymington town. An hour was not long, but if the wenches were willing and the ale strong, much could be accomplished.

Alex turned with his officers toward the Ship Inn on the quay. "Fetch Mistress Courtney, Diccon, will you? She will be as much in need of refreshment as the rest of us, I daresay." He shook his head with a slight smile as Diccon, transparently eager, set off back to the ferry. It was probably best to let him work out his own problems. Keeping him away from Ginny would most likely only exacerbate his tendre; besides she would be more than capable of dealing with any inappropriate behavior on the part of the lieutenant without the colonel's interference.

The taproom was crowded, but the landlord was more than willing to supply a private parlor abovestairs for Parliament's officers. Apart from anything else, he didn't want any trouble, and there were many of his regulars who wouldn't take kindly to drinking in the company of Roundheads. Ale, bread, meat, cheese, and fruit were brought and, to the landlord's relief, promptly paid for. One could never be too sure these days whether what was provided would be considered a contribution to the army's well-being.

Alex went over to the tiny, diamond-paned window looking down on the quay. Diccon was loping across toward the inn, and he was alone. Alex's back stiffened. She could not possibly have managed to evade Jed's eye on the ferry. But if she had, in the melee on the quay, she could easily have slipped away. Controlling his impatience, he forced himself to wait until Diccon bounded into the room.

"*Where* is Mistress Courtney, Lieutenant?" he demanded softly.

Diccon looked stricken. "It's—it's rather awkward, Colonel, you see she . . ."

"She what, Lieutenant Maulfrey?" There was total silence in the dim, heavily paneled room as Diccon struggled for words to express his embarrassment, having no idea what it was that the colonel suspected.

"She's—well—asleep, Colonel," he stammered. "I—I did not know whether to wake her or not. She looked so peaceful, you see, and—and she did say this morning that she had not slept well last night. Shall—shall I go back and wake her?"

Alex visibly relaxed, and the rest of the men followed suit. "No, Diccon. We will leave her for a little while; then I will go myself, since she must eat before we move on."

Half an hour later, he stood looking down at the sleeping figure. He could quite see Diccon's difficulty; Ginny did look entrancingly peaceful. He wanted to stroke the curve of her cheek, slip his little finger between those full, slightly parted lips, tantalizing her with his touch. As he watched, she rolled over onto her back, flinging one arm carelessly above her head, the movement lifting the generous roundness of her breasts beneath the laced bodice. His body stirred in inconvenient response. Jed, sitting on an upturned pail splicing rope, coughed and gave his colonel a shrewd, appraising look.

Alex grinned faintly. Jed had had a care for him since he was first out of short coats, and there was little that he missed. "There doesn't seem much I can do about it, I fear," he said. "I appear to be bewitched."

"Aye, Colonel," Jed agreed placidly. "It'll all come out in the wash eventually, the way things do."

That was always Jed's philosophy. Things untangled themselves in the end, so there was no point fretting. Alex dropped on one knee beside the sleeping Ginny. "Wake up, sweetheart," he said softly, shaking her shoulder.

Ginny's eyes shot open, then she smiled dreamily. "You have walked out of my dreams, or it is that you walked into them? One or the other."

"Either way, I am content to have it so," he replied, taking her hands and pulling her upright. "You must eat and drink now. We march until sundown."

"And then?" Ginny knuckled the sleep from her eyes, adjusted her bodice, tucked away errant strands of chestnut hair.

"Then we make camp," he said.

"I have always wanted to sleep in a tent," Ginny remarked.

Alex laughed. "I hate to disappoint you, chicken, but you will not be sleeping in any tent. You will be billeted with my officers and myself in the village, preferably in a chamber above the ground floor with a key that I may turn."

Ginny shrugged with an assumption of nonchalance at this reaffirmation of her prisoner status. It was something she must learn to handle with dignity since the reminders

111

would be constant and she was not prepared to lose face in front of the brigade by showing that it bothered her. If she gave Alex her word that she would make no attempt at subversion, he would probably relax his guard, but she could not do that, not when she carried the king's document in her pocket, not when she would be looking always for an opportunity to pass on her message.

They went into the inn where Ginny ate and drank with some enthusiasm. It was the first time she had been in such close quarters with the men whose life she would share over the next weeks, and it became clear to her that they did not know how to treat her, whether to acknowledge her presence or ignore her. The presence of a woman was obviously constraining, and several ribald jokes ended abruptly in a cacophony of coughing and shuffled boots as they remembered she was there.

"Alex, this is going to be impossible," she whispered unhappily, scrambling unaided onto Jen's back. "They do not know where to look, and neither do I."

"They will become accustomed to you," he said calmly, "if you behave naturally. The one thing you will not do under any circumstance is to go near the men. While you were on your own property, your position was clear. But when we are on the road, I cannot vouch for your safety if you wander amongst them. They may well consider it an invitation. You understand me?"

"I cannot imagine why I should want to wander amongst them," Ginny retorted, nettled at such an assumption. She remembered vividly that time in the orchard when she had felt like a teasing wanton offering forbidden fruit, and had absolutely no intention of exposing herself to such an uncomfortable experience a second time.

"Just so long as you understand," he said. "I do not wish to restrict your movements more than you make necessary, so will give you the freedom of the officer's billet and the surrounding area. But that is all."

"You need have no fear I shall forget my captive state," Ginny said, chewing her lip. "I do not know why you cannot say these things without sounding as if you are giving me orders."

"Would you have me mask the truth then?" he inquired, and Ginny had the unmistakable impression that something was amusing him. It was grossly unfair of him to laugh at her when he had the upper hand so definitely.

"There are times when I dislike you intensely," she declared with some feeling. Nudging Jen into a trot, she pulled ahead of Alex, deciding that she preferred her own company. She was not alone for long, however, as Diccon Maulfrey drew rein alongside her.

"May I ride with you, mistress?" He gave her a shy smile.

"But of course. Why do you not call me Ginny? Since I have been calling you Diccon with lamentable freedom since yesterday."

"I should be honored." He flushed with pleasure, and Ginny began to feel a great deal better. With him at least, she could have a conversation that would not deteriorate into a series of commands and implied threats.

"How long have you been with Colonel Marshall's brigade?" she asked, swishing at the hedgerows with her riding crop.

"Since I joined the army, last August," Diccon supplied eagerly. "It is quite the best brigade in the entire army and is known as such. The colonel is without doubt the most successful and respected commander."

"Apart from General Cromwell," Ginny murmured gently.

"I do not know," Diccon said seriously. "There are many who say they would prefer to serve under Colonel Marshall, notwithstanding. He does not take unnecessary risks, you understand."

"That is indeed a recommendation in battle," Ginny agreed with a laugh, then reined in her mare as her eye caught something in the field beside the road. "Now that is a piece of luck. I have been searching for camomile for several days. I must gather some. My supplies are short."

Before the bewildered Diccon could make head or tail of this sudden speech, she had knotted the reins on the mare's neck, slipped to the roadway, and was striding with energetic determination into the bordering field, her skirts swishing around her ankles.

"What the deuce?" Alex thundered up beside Diccon.

"Something about camomile, sir," the lieutenant said in a bemused tone.

"Camomile?" Alex scratched his chin, shaking his head in a gesture of defeat. "Major Bonham, halt the march. Mistress Courtney, it seems, has decided to pick flowers, and we cannot leave her behind."

The major's lips twitched as he turned to give the order, and there was open merriment on the faces of the other officers. Within the ranks of marching men there was only speculation as to what had caused this sudden halt.

Ginny came back to her horse, smiling with pure satisfaction. "That is a great stroke of fortune," she informed all and sundry. "Camomile is hard to find, but its soothing properties when given in a warm draft cannot be equaled. It is also an excellent purge — not too rigorous, you understand." She tied the bunch of herbs into her kerchief, inserting it carefully into the pocket of her habit. "Oh," she said, suddenly becoming aware of the stillness around her. "Did I cause you to stop?"

"You did," Alex concurred. "Is this passion for picking wildflowers absolutely imperative?"

"Strictly speaking it is not a flower." Ginny swung herself onto Jen again, her tone of voice frankly informative. "It is a most valuable simple. No one skilled in medicine can be without it."

"You are expert in these matters?" Alex signaled for the march to begin again as he asked the question.

"I have some small skill." Ginny shrugged with dismissive modesty. "I have been interested since I was a child and am told I possess some of the qualities of the healer."

"I see." Alex looked thoughtful. "There is no end, it would seem, to your talents. I would just ask that when next you see some valuable addition to your medicine basket, you would give us a little warning before you leap from your horse."

Ginny looked at him and saw that he was smiling. As indeed was everyone, very much as if they had just found

114

the last few minutes enormously amusing. Why that should be, she could not imagine, but then she was not able to share their sense of the absurdity of one lone woman halting with impunity the progress of Alexander Marshall's brigade in order to gather herbs by the roadside.

It was eight o'clock and almost dark when the brigade reached the village of Romsey. They had been on the road for six hours, and Ginny was beginning to feel as if her rear was cemented to Jen's saddle. Waking up in Carisbrooke Castle this morning seemed as if it had happened two days ago. She staggered slightly as her feet touched ground again, and Alex steadied her with an anxious hand.

"Are you all right?"

"I think so." She grimaced. "It is just that my behind is numb."

He grinned and whispered, "You need a good rubdown. I'll see if it can be arranged later."

"Hush!" she hissed, as the little prickles of anticipation ran down her spine.

Alex composed his features and said in his customary brisk tones that could be heard by all, "You may walk around a little with Jed; it will help the stiffness. I must arrange for the billeting. When I have done so, you will be able to rest." So saying, he strode off with Diccon in attendance toward the timber-beamed, thatch-roofed inn across the village green.

The customary orderly bustle began around them as she and Jed strolled companionably around the village, Ginny arching her back every now and again against her hands to relieve the aching muscles. There were eyes everywhere, peering out of the small cottage windows and from behind doors opened a crack. Children, bolder than their elders, appeared in the narrow lanes, gazing with frank curiosity, running excitedly to the village green when the bugle sounded.

"Do they see friend or foe?" Ginny mused aloud as a front door clicked shut at their passing.

"Depends." Jed shrugged. "There'll be some for the king and some for Parliament, like always."

"And under the same roof, too." Ginny looked at him, eyebrows raised. "That is the case with the colonel's family, I understand."

"Aye." There was silence. Obviously Jed did not care to discuss his colonel's private affairs, and Ginny could only respect his reticence.

They came back to the green to find it transformed. It was now an encampment where the glow of braziers and the smell of roasting meat indicated that the men had wasted little time in seeing to their needs. Ginny sniffed hungrily. "Why are they not billeted in the cottages, Jed? It is usually done, is it not?"

Jed grunted scornfully. "Colonel won't have it. Makes 'em soft, and the result's always the same, slackness and loss of discipline. Living in the open keeps 'em fit, away from pestilence."

Ginny nodded her comprehension. There was certainly truth in the latter statement. In the crowded cottages where sanitation was poor, if not nonexistent, disease could run like wildfire. It was much better to be out in the fresh air.

At this point, they were hailed by Diccon, who had shed his uniform and was looking very cheerful. "Billets are ready," he announced. "There's stabling for the horses at the inn, Jed. Colonel says to find your own billet there. I'm to escort Mistress Courtney inside."

"Are you all quartered in the inn?" Ginny inquired as they went through the narrow door into a small flagged hallway from which a stone passageway ran to the rear of what struck her as a rather cramped building.

"Oh, no, mistress." Diccon blushed. "I—I mean, Ginny. Just the colonel, yourself, Major Bonham, and me. The major and I are to be bedfellows, and I understand you're to share with the landlady's niece."

"And who does Colonel Marshall bundle with?" Ginny inquired sweetly.

"Why, no one." Diccon seemed positively shocked at the very idea. "The other officers are billeted in cottages around the village."

"I see."

They turned into a tiny parlor where a pink-cheeked serving girl was setting platters and cutlery on a round table beneath the window. Alex stood beside the empty grate, a cup in hand. "Ah, there you are. You will take a cup of wine, and then Sally here will show you to your chamber where you may remove your dirt before supper. Diccon, you are dismissed until then."

Ginny accepted the wine and took a long gulp, finding it instantly restorative. She waited until Sally had followed Diccon out of the room before saying, "I do not care to share beds with strangers. I would prefer to share yours."

"Do not be foolish, chicken. You know that is impossible. I am sorry the accommodations are so cramped here; we will hope to do better in our future resting places."

"It is not impossible. I have already told you I do not care what people may say; and who would censure you? Envy you, maybe, but neither your officers nor your men would question your actions. Do not tell me they do not find women as and when they may."

"That, Virginia, is very different," Alex stated. "Of course they do. But I will not flaunt you as my mistress."

"Then I shall flaunt myself," Ginny declared, "until you realize how ridiculously prudish you are being."

Alex's eyes narrowed, and he put his cup on the table with a snap. "Are you threatening me, Virginia?"

"Well, I fail to see why you should have the monopoly on threats," she countered, although she felt just a little uneasy.

Alex sucked in his lower lip while regarding her thoughtfully. She had issued a most definite challenge, and she was so damnably desirable with that tip-tilted chin jutting its defiance, the fearless gray eyes where passion lurked, the rise and fall under her swift breath of that magnificent bosom.

"Let us not quarrel about this," he said eventually, his tone conciliatory. "It is a ridiculous bone of contention. We will compromise. You will not live openly as my mistress, but we will not concern ourselves if the truth is suspected. Discretion can do neither of us any harm."

Ginny had to acknowledge he was right, in fact had

117

regretted her challenge the minute the words were out of her mouth. She didn't particularly want to exhibit herself as a whore, indeed was not entirely sure how one would go about it. "Well, what is to be done about sharing with the landlady's niece?" She reverted to the original complaint.

"I am certain she is a sound sleeper." His eyes twinkled mischievously. "She will not know whether you are there or not. Are we agreed, my raggle-taggle gypsy?"

Ginny nodded, lips pursed in satisfaction. "Agreed, sir."

Chapter Seven

Half an hour before dawn, Alex woke as he had told himself he would the instant before falling asleep. Ginny, warm and naked, was somehow tangled up with him. He smiled to himself in the darkness as he gently lifted one soft round arm from its resting place across his throat. His hand brushed against her breast as he returned the arm to its own body, and she moaned in sleep, pressing herself against him, as wonderfully lascivious in her dreams as she was in her waking state. A wisp of chestnut hair tickled his nose, and softly he propped himself on one elbow, drawing the sheet away from her, unable to resist the temptation to look at her for a moment when her body, uninhabited by that swift, challenging personality, lay vulnerable and open to his gaze.

Her skin glimmered whitely in the gloom before dawn, stretched smoothly over the clean, graceful lines of her limbs, the generous curves of breast and hip. Those curves had surprised him at first; when she was dressed they were masked by her height. Naked, that deep firm bosom was magnificent, those sweet pink nipples so wonderfully responsible to the merest whisper of a touch. It was impossible to look at her without touching, and with a small sigh of resignation he bent his head, flicking her breast with his tongue. She stirred, whimpered, but kept her eyes tight shut even as her nipples peaked, small and hard, beneath the

119

moist caress.

His hand stroked languidly down the long length from waist to ankle, tracing the indentations, cupping the curves, and he felt her body come vibrantly aware against him, her skin dancing beneath his fingers. His loins throbbed with pleasurable urgency, and he drew her leg over his hip, slipping his hand between her opened thighs to touch her in the ways he knew would bring her to his own point of readiness.

Ginny gave herself up to the almost hypnotic sensation, her body still deeply relaxed in the aftermath of a sleep not yet dissipated. Her head was buried in the crook of his shoulder as Alex held her sideways against his body, his other hand now grasping her behind the bent knee flung across his hip, drawing her even closer as he entered her with one smooth movement. Ginny sighed in soft satisfaction at the wonderful sense of completion she felt with his presence, moving in gentle rhythm within. She felt the finale creeping up on her like a thief in the night, tried to resist it, to prolong the ecstacy of the orchestration, but it happened anyway, without cymbals and drums this time, rather a soft, lyrical coda of flute and violin.

"Good morning, my little gypsy," Alex whispered, kissing the corner of her mouth as he left her body. "You must return to your own bed, sweeting." Even as he said this, the piercing, insistent alarm of the cock sounded, followed on the instant by others as barnyards and chicken coops acknowledged the new day.

Ginny groaned but did not argue. Struggling into a sitting position, she swung her legs over the edge of the bed, feeling for her discarded nightgown. "If anyone sees me in the passage, they will think I have been to the house of easement," she said practically, dropping the garment over her head.

"Hurry then. Jed will be here in a minute with my shaving water." He gave the long burnished tresses a quick tug as she stood up, then sprang energetically out of bed

120

himself, striding to the door. He lifted the latch carefully, then peered out into the corridor, beckoning to her over his shoulder. Ginny slipped past him, but not before she had run a distinctly familiar hand between his thighs. "Shameless hussy!" Alex accused her on a soft choke of laughter. "Get along with you, before I throw caution to the winds and have you again."

"Promises, promises," Ginny murmured, then leaped away from him as his palm swung.

She regained her own chamber just as her bedfellow awoke. The girl seemed too befuddled, however, to register more than that Ginny had apparently risen before her. She offered to fetch water for Ginny, an offer that Ginny gratefully accepted, and, having dressed, left Ginny in a dreamy contemplation of the past night.

The bugle sounded reveille, and Ginny went to the casement looking out over the village green. The encampment seemed to come instantly alert with voices calling cheerfully and men scurrying around fastening on armor, eating and drinking on the move. The inn was now fully awake also, and Ginny heard Alex's voice crisply engaged in conversation with Major Bonham. There came a loud knock at her door. "Mistress Courtney? Are you awake?"

Ginny grinned, calling back, "I am, Colonel. It would be hard to continue sleeping in such a hub of activity."

"We leave within the hour, so make haste and break your fast." The sound of retreating footsteps reached her, and braiding her hair swiftly, she grabbed her hat, crop, and gloves as she left the room and made her way downstairs to the parlor where she had dined last night in the company of the colonel, the major, and the lieutenant.

This morning, however, it was empty, although the table showed evidence of having been raided fairly thoroughly. She made an adequate meal of bread and a boiled egg washed down with buttermilk, then, realizing that there was neither sight nor sound of Alex, his officers, or Jed, who appeared to be her unofficial guard, she made her way down

121

the passage into the kitchen.

"Good morrow, goodwife," she greeted the plump figure of the landlady politely.

The woman straightened from the fire where she was setting a cauldron of water to boil and turned to Ginny, her heat-flushed face startled. "What can I do for you, mistress?"

Ginny looked around cautiously. Still no sign of anyone who should not hear what she had to say. She came further into the room. "We are come from the Isle of Wight," she said casually. The landlady's expression did not change, although she stood still, wiping her hands on her apron. "The king is held there," Ginny said, watching closely.

"God rest his soul," the goodwife said stolidly.

"I was taken prisoner on the island," Ginny went on. "My father's estate sequestered."

Still there was no response. The landlady, of course, would be afraid of treachery, afraid that the woman who rode with Parliament's army was out to trap her into some form of rebellion, unless she happened to be a staunch supporter of Parliament, in which case Ginny was taking the risk of betrayal. But somehow she didn't think so. Time was too short for pussyfooting. She must take the risk.

"I met with the king, and I bear his message for those fighting for him." Thank God she had been right. The woman's face broke into a beam.

"There's plenty in these parts who'd be glad to receive it," she said in a low voice.

"Will you tell me where I may find them?"

The goodwife hesitated. "How can I know you are to be trusted?"

Ginny looked around her again. She could hear voices in the stableyard beyond the kitchen door, but none in the inn behind her. Her tongue ran over suddenly dry lips as she stepped close to the landlady, drawing the king's document out of her pocket.

The woman stared in awed reverence at the king's seal.

"Mistress Courtney . . . Ginny?" Diccon's voice sounded

from the passage, and Ginny thrust the parchment back in her pocket, turning toward the door with a bright smile.

"In the kitchen, Diccon."

"I was afraid I had lost you," Diccon said naively, appearing in the doorway. "Jed is ready to take your baggage back with the supplies. May he fetch it from your chamber?"

"Yes, indeed," Ginny said, amazingly without a tremor in her voice. Jed appeared behind Diccon. Would either of them think anything of her being alone in the kitchen with the landlady? Think enough of it to mention it to the colonel? "The goodwife and I have been discussing the best way of preserving mushrooms," she said cheerfully. "Whether they are best dried or pickled. It is a question, I think, of what one wishes to use them for. I favor them pickled in pies, but dried if they are to be made into a compote. Do you not agree?"

Diccon and Jed looked somewhat nonplussed, not having ever before been asked for an opinion on such a matter. Ginny laughed easily. "I daresay you would not be able to tell the difference, would you?"

"Like as not, mistress," Jed agreed. "Colonel's waiting for you."

"Very well." Ginny turned back to the landlady with a tiny smile of resignation, the smallest shrug. "My thanks for your hospitality, goodwife."

The woman inclined her head, then went back to the fire where the cauldron of water was coming to a vigorous boil. Diccon motioned courteously toward the door, and Ginny preceded him out into the early morning sunshine.

Alex stood with his officers, listening attentively to a corporal, and the colonel's face was grim. He glanced over his shoulder at Ginny as she appeared in the inn door, and he frowned. It was a puzzling frown since, while it seemed to have something to do with her, it did not appear to be directed *at* her. She would have liked to have gone over to him, but something about the way they were all standing seemed to exclude her. Besides, Diccon was waiting with cupped palms to toss her up onto Jen. She accepted his help with a smile of thanks, then watched him go over to the group.

"Maybe you'd care for some greengages, mistress. It'll be a thirsty ride, I reckon." The goodwife came suddenly out of the inn, a cloth package in her hand. Walking over to Ginny, she handed it up as Ginny leaned down to receive it. There were certainly greengages nestling in the napkin, but in the moment she took it, the woman said barely audibly, "The red fox will take you to those you seek between here and London." Then she was gone back inside, leaving Ginny to puzzle over the cryptic information. Who or what was the red fox?

Alex walked over to her, his face grave. He stroked Jen's nose absently as he came straight to the point. "The ride today is going to be unpleasant, I fear."

"In what manner?" Ginny felt a flutter of apprehension as she wondered if the unpleasantness had anything to do with her.

"There has been some fighting along the road between Winchester and Newbury." He paused, frowning. "Not clean fighting, but skirmishes and reprisals. The results lie about the countryside. It will not be a pleasant sight."

"Bodies?" she heard herself ask in a small voice.

"And worse," he replied bluntly. "I would spare you if I could, but we must take the quickest route to London and it is along that way that these things lie. You will ride in the middle of us and try not to look around you. That is the best I can do for you."

"I understand." Ginny stiffened her shoulders. "I am no stranger to sickness and death, Alex."

"No, I did not suppose you were, but I would hope you were a stranger to brutality, to the savagery of revenge."

Ginny shuddered, feeling slightly sick. Alex was preparing her as plainly as he was able for the previously unimaginable, and she had heard enough stories of this war to know that he would not be exaggerating. Living on the island,

124

they had been spared the full impact of the fighting and occupation by armed forces, but she knew of the lands laid waste, the women raped and murdered, the children dying of starvation. She could find no adequate response, so remained silent.

Alex nodded, then left her to mount Bucephalus. "Sound the drums, Major. Today we will march to the rousing music of battle lest we forget why these things are happening."

At the first drum roll, the hairs on the back of her neck seemed to lift, her scalp to prickle, at the eerily stirring sound. The ranks of men seemed to stand taller, to march more briskly as if with a reaffirmation of purpose, and Ginny could only admire the commander who had his finger on the pulse of a two-hundred-man machine and knew exactly how to combat the inevitable lowering effects of the sights of war's aftermath.

They reached the walls of Winchester in three hours, seeing little evidence of war along the way. The sun was just reaching its mid-morning fullness, and Ginny looked idly up at the ramparts as they neared the gate to the city. Black carrion birds, ravens, starlings, and crows, wheeled and shrieked, and, with a jolt, she realized why. The ramparts were nauseatingly decorated with frieze of pikes, each one bearing a head. They were barely recognizable as human, the eye sockets picked clean, hair straggling dryly like baked straw. Ginny gazed in dreadful fascination. Edmund, Peter, and she herself could have been amongst that number, left as a fearful reminder of the consequences of treachery until the flesh was picked clean from the skull and only the bleached bones remained.

They passed under the thick, medieval stone archway, returning the salutes of the guards. And within the city, there was worse. In the market square there were gibbets from which hung the bodies of Royalist troopers, bodies scarcely cold.

"Why?" Ginny whispered, swallowing the bitter lump of bile that rose in her throat. "What did they do?"

Alex looked at her. "They were on the wrong side."

"That is all? You would condone this butchery for such a reason?" She stared at him, horrified. This man who had made such wondrous, tender love to her only that morning, just a few short hours ago, could treat such brutality with this callous indifference.

"No, I do not condone it," he said. "General Colney is indeed a butcher. He has not learned the principle that a little intimidation teaches better lessons than a flood. People become indifferent to punishment when there seems no justice in its administration and no way of evading it."

"So you object only to the number put to death?" she said slowly, "not to the act itself."

"It is necessary," he replied shortly. "If we are overly squeamish, this business will never be ended. The rebels must learn that they fight a lost cause, and they must pay for fighting it."

And would she also pay for fighting it, Ginny wondered. In many ways, she already had. She had lost her home, her fortune, had been thrown penniless and unprotected upon the world unless she chose to seek the protection of the Courtneys—protection that they could not deny her, except she would rather die. But that punishment was a consequence of her earlier activities and those of her father. What of her present role as king's messenger, spreading the very message that this savagery was designed to prevent, that the cause was not lost and the king still demanded their support? Yes, she would pay if she were discovered. It was the harsh reality of war.

They halted at the military barracks, and again Ginny shivered at the forbidding stone buildings, now that she had some inkling of what went on behind their walls. She found herself listening for the screams, examining the faces of those they passed for some overt signs that they had been engaged in torture and murder. How she expected such indications to manifest themselves, she did not know, and, indeed, saw nothing but stalwart yeomen going about their

126

business as placidly as if they were back in their fields.

"I have to meet with General Colney," Alex said as the cavalcade halted. "You can have no interest in making his acquaintance so—"

"On the contrary," Ginny broke in. "I have a great interest in telling him exactly what I think of his butchery."

Alex's lips twitched. "Such an indomitable little shrew you are. However, while I am sure you would be able to set him to the rightabout with very little difficulty, I think it more advisable to avoid such a confrontation. Apart from anything else, I am outranked by the general, and should he decide to take a personal interest in your fate, there is little I could do to prevent him. You understand me, I am sure."

"Yes," said Ginny in a considerably more docile tone. The message was not hard to read. "What should I do, then?"

Alex chuckled. "How remarkably obedient you are become all of a sudden."

"It is not amusing!" Ginny retorted. "How can you make a joke of such horrors?"

The laughter left his face. "You have not yet seen the worst," he warned. "And it is you who amuse me, nothing else." Ginny made no response, nothing suitable coming to mind, and Alex continued, "If you wish, you may visit the town with Jed. If you avoid the market square, I daresay there will be things to interest and amuse you."

"Are you not afraid I will evade Jed's guard?" inquired Ginny, not with any seriousness. "The streets may be crowded."

"No, I am not afraid of that," Alex replied. "It would take someone trickier than you, Mistress Courtney, to succeed in such an endeavor."

Jed heard his instructions to accompany Mistress Courtney about the town with a laconic grunt, and Ginny decided that he would probably have preferred to spend the time exchanging news with his cronies in the barracks. She could hardly blame him—accompanying some female around the city streets was a tedious alternative to ale and soldiers' talk. She, however, was fascinated, never before having been in a town as large as Winchester. The number and variety of the stores was almost bewildering, and if that was not enough, from every corner came the lilting calls of street vendors. The city's inhabitants were going about their business as placidly as if the market square were not hung about with executed Royalists, and the town garrisoned by a large Parliamentary force.

Pausing outside a pie shop, she looked hungrily at the wares displayed, the savory aromas of meat and golden pastry setting her saliva running. " 'Tis noontime, I reckon," Jed said, guessing her thoughts. "You'll be needin' nourishment." He moved into the shop.

Ginny flushed with embarrassment. "Jed, I have no coin. I am not particularly hungry."

"Colonel gave me his purse, said I was to buy whatever took your fancy," the batman replied sturdily. " 'Tis not your fault you're without monies." He bought two pies, laying two brass farthings on the counter before handing a pie to Ginny. It was hot, and steam rose from a small slit in the succulent piecrust. Ginny, deciding that further protest would be both undignified and self-defeating, sank her teeth into the pastry with a sigh of pleasure, slurping at the rich gravy before it could run down her chin. Feeling, for the moment, thoroughly contented, she strolled with Jed out of the shop, pies in hand, and when they were finished, Jed bought her gingerbread and a black-currant cordial from a street vendor. A holiday atmosphere seemed to prevail, despite everything she had seen, and they stopped to watch a dancing bear, huge, ungainly, and pathetic as it struggled around on its hind legs. Ginny laughed and clapped with the rest but decided that she preferred the jugglers, whose dexterity struck her as amazing, and she wished she had a coin to toss into the threadbare cap as it came around. But it did not seem reasonable to dispense Alex's funds in such a matter, particularly since he was not here to enjoy the entertainment himself.

They returned to the barracks to find the brigade already in formation. Jed, for the first time, allowed a flash of unease to cross his face as he looked at the colonel, already mounted. He hurried across the barrack square, Ginny following. "Beggin' your pardon, Colonel, but the time passed me by." Standing stiffly at attention, he saluted.

"Oh, it was my fault," Ginny said swiftly. "I was enjoying myself so much, I forgot all else. There were jugglers, you see."

"Yes, I do see," replied Alex with a little smile. "Put Mistress Courtney on her horse, Jed. We've twenty miles to cover between here and Newbury, and we'll not wish to make camp before then, not if all I've heard is true."

Ginny's light holiday mood dissipated at these words, and she remembered what was in store for them on the march ahead.

She would never forget the long hours of that afternoon. The drum continued to beat, but the drummer played a mournful tune as if he was unable to achieve the rousing spirits of that morning. Apart from the drum, there was only a grim silence punctuated by the tread of marching boots, the clop of hooves. There was devastation on all sides: fields laid to waste, corn and wheat ruined, orchards destroyed, cottages blackened, roofless, and in some cases still smoking. And there were the bodies, mutilated and left to lie in the ditches where flies buzzed over the dust-coated, black blood of their wounds. They hung, head downward from the trees, or stretched beside the roadside, stripped of their clothes and left for the scavenging dogs.

Ginny tried to close her eyes, hemmed in as she was in the center of the lines of officers, the burly back of Major Bonham ahead of her. But some perverse part of her nature forced her to see what man was capable of doing to man, to burn the sights like acid into her mind so that she would never forget what beasts war made of the human breed. These broken bodies no longer held allegiance to any cause; it was impossible to tell which side they had been on, in death they were indistinguishable, Cavalier from Round-head. It was certain that the flies and the dogs drew no distinction.

"Why can they not be buried?" She head her voice, startling in the silence, and realized it was the first human sound anyone had made for what seemed an eternity.

"They will be, eventually," Alex replied.

"What the dogs and the carrion birds leave," she said bitterly. "There are troops aplenty in Winchester. Why can they not be sent to bury the dead?"

"Soon it will happen," he said, as if soothing a fractious child.

The smell of corruption hung heavy in the still afternoon air, and the pie and gingerbread, eaten with such a light heart, rebelled in her belly. She pressed a hand to her mouth and prayed silently for the strength to hold on, to be spared the humiliation of vomiting in this company, but more, to be spared the need to dismount, to get down amongst the dead.

Alex looked at her, understanding and compassion in his eyes. Her face was waxen, sheened with a light film of sweat, and her shoulders sagged. How well he knew what she was going through. When he had first understood the horrors of war, he had crouched behind a hedgerow, spewing out his guts for hours, bitterly ashamed at such weakness in a man who would be a soldier. Virginia Courtney was doing better than he had done, it would seem. A grim determination radiated from the tall, slender figure, and he felt again the admiration for her that had so drawn him to the proud, fearless young woman who had challenged the conquerors with such wit and irony.

They marched the twenty miles to Newbury in five hours, the men stepping out briskly, hurrying to put death and destruction at their backs. Ginny settled eventually into a kind of trance, moving with Jen's rhythm automatically, her eyes glazed. She was not accustomed to riding as hard and long as they had done in the last two days, and on the periphery of consciousness lurked the certainty that once the ride was over, her body would take its revenge for the unusual demands made upon it. It was not that she was particularly frail, quite the opposite. Sailing, swimming, cliff climbing had made her stronger and more muscular than was customary with her sex, but prolonged riding required different muscles, and it was with overwhelming relief that she greeted the sight of the small market town nestling at the bottom of the hill.

"Are you stiff again?" Alex dismounted with enviable ease and came over to Jen where Ginny continued to sit, for the moment unable to order her muscles to make the required movements to put her on the ground.

She sighed. "I do not think I was made to be a soldier."

"It will get easier," he promised, lifting her down but holding her with a steadying arm at her waist. "Tomorrow is Sunday, a day of rest, so you will have time to recover."

"Somehow, I did not think you would acknowledge the seventh day," Ginny said, leaning against him. "Not in this urgent business of war."

"Even in war, we make time for worship," he said seriously.

Ginny looked at him in some surprise. "Are you pious, then?"

"I am no Bible thumper, if that is what you mean. But there are many who fight this war for religious reasons, and, while I am not amongst them, I will honor their beliefs." Ginny knew well to what he was referring. There were many men who feared that King Charles, at the dictate of his French wife, the unpopular, zealous Romanist Henrietta Maria, would restore the Catholic church to the land. It was this fear that, in many cases, led to the demand for the king's dethronement. Others, like Alex, fought for political reasons. "Besides," Alex went on, "worshiping together as a community is good for morale."

"Ah," Ginny said with a grin of total comprehension. "I was sure the colonel had to have a military reason also."

131

"Don't mock me," he ordered with feigned menace. "Come into the inn, now, and we shall see what quarters we can provide for you this time."

The inn was rather more spacious than the one at Romsey, and a small chamber under the eaves afforded Ginny total privacy. It was rather more primitive than those on the lower floors, but there she would have had to share again, so was well content with Goodwife Brown's offering.

"I must bathe," Ginny announced with determination. "I reek of horses and am covered in dust. May I do so unguarded, Colonel?"

Alex looked at her through narrowed eyes. She seemed to have recovered from the spiritual ill-effects of the ride. He had thought to give her more freedom during this halt, the pale, subdued creature of the afternoon hadn't looked capable of taking advantage of increased privileges. Now, he was not so sure but decided that it was a risk he could afford. His men were everywhere; she could never escape undetected. "Listen to me very carefully, Ginny. While we are quartered here, you may do as you wish so long as you do not go near the men's encampment without escort, and you do not stray too far from the immediate vicinity of the inn. If you wish to go further afield, you will ask my permission."

"And would you grant it?" In spite of her aching exhaustion, the note of challenge was still in her voice, and the gray eyes glared her refusal to accept gracefully the authority of her captor.

Alex sighed. "That would depend. But you will not venture far unescorted, I can promise you that." Suddenly, he smiled, reaching out to brush dust, which rose in a white cloud, from her shoulder. "You must definitely need a bath, my little gypsy. Maybe, when you smell sweeter, your disposition will similarly improve."

Ginny gasped indignantly, then saw the funny side and chuckled reluctantly. "You could do with one yourself, Colonel, for much the same reasons."

"The pump in the stableyard will do me quite well," he

replied cheerfully, then grinned. "Since I'll not be the only one taking advantage of the opportunity to strip off under cold water, you'd be advised to leave the stableyard out of your itinerary if you intend to go a-wandering. I don't think Diccon for one would ever recover from the embarrassment."

"Then I shall watch from abovestairs," Ginny told him with a sweet smile. "My chamber overlooks the yard, and I find the prospect of so many strong, muscular men revealed in all the glory of nature's endowments most exciting." Her eyes opened wide, and she touched her lips with her tongue.

"I cannot help feeling," Alex said thoughtfully, "that you were not whipped often enough as a child. Have a care, lest I decide to repair the omission."

"I wouldn't advise it, Colonel," she came back swiftly. "You'd have to sleep sometimes." She was gone on the instant, leaving Alex shaking his head with a rueful if appreciative smile. Virginia Courtney was utterly indomitable.

Ginny, feeling pleasantly satisfied with the outcome of that exchange, went into the kitchen in search of the innkeeper's wife. That lady was instantly responsive to Ginny's request for a bath, and a tub was filled for her before the range, a worked screen placed in front of it to allow a modicum of privacy. Ginny fetched clean clothes from her baggage and went back to the kitchen where she found only Goodwife Brown and two wenches.

"With so many chickens, goodwife, you must need to have a care for the red fox," Ginny remarked casually, beginning to unlace her bodice. Did she detect just the slightest stiffening of the woman's shoulders? Her remark could be construed as quite innocent; it was just a little peculiar to refer to the red fox, when simply fox would do as well.

"He gives us little trouble, mistress," the landlady said.

"Maybe there's some folks who'd welcome him," Ginny said. Now stripped to her shift, she went behind the screen without waiting to see what reaction the observation would cause. Better to let things lie and see if the seed would take root and sprout.

The bath was sheer heaven, and she lay in the water for a long time, listening idly to the comings and goings in the kitchen beyond the screen. One of the serving wenches appeared with a fresh jug of hot water, which she poured over Ginny, who stretched luxuriously. Somehow, the knowledge that she would not have to ride tomorrow released the aches in bones and muscles, imbued her with new energy. During this halt, she must make contact with the king's men if she was ever to fulfill her commission between here and London. Even if she could not see them for herself, she must at the very least entrust the king's message of hope and support to someone who would be able to deliver it for her. If the innkeeper's wife showed no inclination to take the bait, then she must use her freedom to roam around outside to fall into conversation with other townsfolk, some of whom would be for the king just by the law of averages.

Chapter Eight

It was amazing what clean clothes did for one's spiritual well-being, Ginny reflected, emerging from behind the screen in fresh undergarments and the blue kirtle she had worn the day Alex Marshall had ridden up to John Redfern's door. The simple gown felt wonderfully light after three days of wearing her riding habit, which latter garment was in sore need of sponging, brushing, and pressing. She could do that and wash her underclothes, and they would dry during tomorrow's day of rest.

Goodwife Brown expressing no objection, Ginny filled the washtub and settled down to her laundry.

"Have you come far, mistress?" the goodwife inquired, sitting on the long bench beside Ginny to shell peas.

"From the Isle of Wight," Ginny replied.

"How is it that you ride with Parliament's army?" The question was put with more than a hint of aggression. "Camp followers, and we've seen enough of 'em hereabouts, are not overly concerned with cleanliness."

Ginny flushed. "I am no camp follower, goodwife. I am the daughter of a Malignant, now made ward of Parliament at the colonel's orders. I ride with them as a prisoner to London." She wrung out her shift, twisting the material fiercely to remove the last drops of water.

"I meant no insult," Goodwife Brown said rather more mildly. "But you've not been ill-treated, it seems. You move without pain."

"So you think I have bought fair treatment?" Ginny shook out her stockings, thinking that if this woman knew the truth, that would indeed be the construction she would put upon the situation. And, on one level, she would not be far wrong. It was an uncomfortable reflection.

"I think nothing, mistress," the innkeeper's wife said with a tranquil smile. "I'm not one to meddle in the business of others. And I'd blame no one these days for avoiding suffering however they may. You came from Winchester?"

"Aye. 'Tis not a journey I'll forget," Ginny replied soberly. "Dogs and carrion, but no sign of a red fox."

"The fox waits for nightfall before he prowls," the woman said, picking up her bowl of peas and getting to her feet. "The washing line is behind the barn, just before the herb garden. On your way back, you could bring me some rosemary."

Thoughtfully, Ginny went outside into the evening air. The smell of cooking fires came from the fields, accompanied by voices sounding relaxed and cheerful, raised in laughter and mock anger. The prospect of a day of rest was clearly doing its work on men, fatigued and depressed by the day's long march. The fox waits for nightfall before he prowls. Was that a message? And if so, what should she do about it? Go a-prowling herself? Difficult, if not impossible at night. Alex would have guards posted around the inn, so even if she were not subjected to a curfew, she would be unable to go outside unnoticed. She must just wait and see, spending as much time as she could in the kitchen. Not even Alex would think anything of that. It would be natural enough for her to gravitate toward female company.

When she returned with the rosemary, Goodwife Brown said, "Do you sup with us, mistress?"

"No, she does not." Alex spoke suddenly from the door. "Parliament's ward sups with Parliament, goodwife. After

136

which she will immediately seek her bed. One secret of a successful compaigner, Mistress Courtney, is to seize and make the most of all opportunites offered for rest." He was holding the door for her, making it clear that Ginny was to leave the kitchen on the instant. So she had been mistaken in thinking that he would not be concerned by her continued presence in the kitchen. She should have known, of course, that he would leave nothing to chance. He must be aware that, by mixing with the common people, she would inevitably come into contact with the king's supporters, and, while he did not know that she had most urgent need for that contact, he obviously intended to keep her isolated as much as possible.

With a careless shrug, she pointedly thanked the innkeeper's wife for her cooperation in the matter of the bath and the laundry, hoping that Alex would take the point that her activities had been innocently domestic. If he did, he made no reference to it as he escorted her to the inn's parlor where the long refectory table was set for supper and all his officers awaited them.

Ginny steeled herself to an uncomfortable meal in this company, knowing that they would find her presence constraining. An officers' mess was no place for a woman, or, at least, not for a woman who had no services for sale. To her surprise, she found herself the center of attention. She sat at Alex's right hand; Diccon, as a result of an adroit maneuver, sat on her other side. The remainder of the company, from the rather austere Major Bonham down to the youngest and most insignificant ensign, seemed to vie for her attention, hanging on her every word. It took her a while to realize what was happening, until she realized that these men, so long deprived of female company of their own class, were responding to a woman as they would have done in their own dining rooms in happier times.

Ginny, who had never truly learned that a woman's place in male company was to listen, flatter, and offer only the most uncontroversial commonplace conversation, began to

137

enjoy herself. She had never been in such a situation before. At her father's table, she had been the daughter of the house, allowed an unusual amount of license certainly, but still expected to be very much subservient. At the Courtneys' table, women did not speak at all unless spoken to, and even then required the tacit permission of the matriarch to reply for themselves. Now it seemed, she could say whatever she wished and was attended to in the most flattering manner.

Alex, guessing what was going through her head, was enormously amused. The commander was also pleased at the happy effect of her company on his officers, who seemed more relaxed than they had done for quite some time. She had the good sense to avoid politics, he noticed, and she also drank very little, placing her hand over her cup when an overzealous Diccon attempted to press her to take more. Barely nineteen she might be, but that pretty head was well screwed onto those determined shoulders. She would make a most worthy wife one of these days . . . But not for the likes of Alexander Marshall who intended to play a major role in the new England, once the fighting was done with and reconstruction could begin. Such a devoted Royalist would never agree to throw in her lot with a man ambitious to share in the governing of a land without a monarch.

These dismal reflections drew his eyebrows together in a deep frown, and conversation round the table faltered. "Something troubles the colonel, it would seem," Ginny said boldly.

"I beg your pardon?" Alex looked at her sharply. "Why should you say such a thing?"

"You are frowning, sir, in a most fearsome manner," she responded, taking a tiny sip of wine. "You must know how we all tremble at the merest hint of your displeasure. It has thrown quite a pall over us, wondering, as we are, who is unlucky enough to have earned your disfavor."

There was a stunned silence as everyone waited for the colonel's blistering tongue to lash the perpetrator of this extraordinary insolence.

Alex carved a slice of sirloin from the joint in front of him, then reached for the mustard. "You, as it happens, Mistress Courtney, were the subject of my thoughts," he said eventually. "And you are right, they were not particularly pleasant reflections." Calmly, he proceeded to eat his beef, and after a minute or two conversation picked up again round the table.

"Am I not to know the content of these reflections, sir?" Ginny inquired in a quiet and most polite tone.

Alex turned sideways and examined her thoughtfully. Was mischief prompting this persistence? Did she want to provoke him to a display of anger in front of his officers? Or was it simply that natural teasing that she seemed so fond of? If that was the case, she obviously hadn't realized that teasing a colonel in front of his men was not entirely appropriate. Of course, if he pointed that out to her, she would just laugh, as he well knew, and accuse him of being pompous and overly concerned with his dignity. Perhaps he was.

"I prefer to keep them to myself for the moment," he said neutrally. "It is getting late. Do you not think it would be sensible for you to retire? You've had a long day."

"It is not good to go to bed on a full stomach" Ginny said. "I would like to have a walk first, if the colonel permits."

Alex hesitated, and Diccon said eagerly, "I would be happy to accompany Mistress Courtney, sir."

In spite of himself, Alex smiled, remembering how puppy love was by turns bewitching and heartrending. "Then do so, Diccon. But don't keep her overlong from her bed."

Ginny looked at him indignantly. "Colonel, I am quite capable of deciding for myself when to go to bed. I realize that I am your prisoner, but your authority cannot extend to such personal matters."

Alex pushed back his chair and stood up. "Come with me." Taking her by the arm, he ushered her ungently from the room, before saying with tight-lipped impatience, "I have told you once, Virginia, you may not question my authority in public. You have been taking inordinate delight in provoking me this evening, and I will not have it."

"I have offered the emperor's consequence again," she said scornfully. "If you think you have the right to tell me when to go to bed in public, I will tell you in public that you do not have that right, and if your consequence suffers as a result, then I am sorry for it."

They glared at each other in the narrow passageway, like two dogs spoiling for a fight. Then Alex sighed. "Why must we always be at odds in this childish manner?"

"It is your fault," Ginny accused him. "I have done nothing."

"Except refuse to accept your position."

"And I shall continue to do so. I should tell you, Colonel, that I am not one of your unfortunate ensigns, and you do not intimidate me in the least." Ginny punctuated this statement with a short, firm nod, ignoring the mocking voice of conscience pointing out that that was not entirely the truth.

"Then perhaps I should do something about that. It seems to me, my dear Virginia, that you stand in sore need of a little intimidation." Alex spoke with soft menace, and Ginny stepped backward involuntarily, coming up against the hard and impenetrable wall at her back. Alex stepped in front of her; he did not touch her, but he was so close, she could feel the heat of his body, the warmth of his breath on her cheek. "You are going to bed," he said. "And you are going now! I will give you just one chance to do so on your own two feet." He stood aside, motioning with his hand to the stairs.

Ginny's heart thudded in her chest, her face flushed with fury and the mortifying knowledge that she could not defy him, for to do so would only bring acute humiliation. Head high, she twitched aside her skirts and marched past him, up the stairs to the little chamber under the eaves.

Alex, instead of returning to the dining room, slammed out of the inn, furious with himself for that cheap victory

140

over a matter so trivial. She had the power to get under his skin, to nettle him so thoroughly with her damn challenges and her total disregard for his authority that he found himself behaving in a manner that made him feel simply ridiculous. Neither of them had come out of that stupid tangle with any dignity, and it had been totally unnecessary. He was going to have to learn to fight only the battles that were worth fighting.

Ginny, standing at the little casement looking down on the darkened stableyard, was having remarkably similar thoughts. Why did they behave like that? There was more than enough conflict inherent in their situation without making mountains out of molehills. It was only his authoritative manner that drove her to make those ridiculous, unnecessary challenges, and he could not really help that manner, not after so many years of command. She was going to have to learn to provoke him only when it would serve a useful purpose. Now, she was banished abovestairs without having had the opportunity to talk with the landlady again. If she had simply laughed at Alex's injunction and gone for a walk with Diccon, it would have been easy enough to find an excuse to visit the kitchen without him. The aide-de-camp didn't strike her as at all suspicious by nature.

Disconsolately, Ginny prepared for bed with little hope of sleeping. It was a warm night, and the heat hung heavy in the airless little room. Perhaps this was another mistake, and she should have accepted the shared bed downstairs. If she and Alex hadn't squabbled, she probably would not have been sleeping in it anyway . . .

The scratching at her door was so faint that for a moment she was not certain she had heard anything. But it came again, unmistakably. Slipping to the floor, she crept across the room, and lifted the heavy wooden latch to open the door a crack. Goodwife Brown stood outside, a finger to her lips. Silently, Ginny pulled the door wide, and the woman slipped inside.

141

" 'Tis madness," she whispered, "under their very noses, but when the world's gone stark staring mad, what's to be done? I had thought you would return to the kitchen before retiring."

"I had intended doing so," Ginny replied, with a rueful smile, "but fell foul of the colonel and found myself banished."

The innkeeper's wife nodded, then went over to the casement and stood against the wall, peering down. "There are guards at every door," she muttered, then suddenly swung round on Ginny. "What business do you have with the red fox?"

"A message from the king," Ginny said succinctly. "The innkeeper's wife in Romsey told me to seek out the red fox. He will help me deliver it."

"Aye." Goodwife Brown nodded again. "You have more than your word, mistress?"

Ginny went over to the roll of baggage, felt through it, and drew out King Charles's document. The goodwife received it with the same reverence as the landlady at Romsey. "The red fox will bear your message. You cannot go yourself. If you escape, there will be reprisals, and we'll not be responsible for causing the suffering of others."

"You think Colonel Marshall would punish the town if I were found to be gone?" Ginny frowned, certain that the woman was wrong.

"Why should he be any different from any of the others? We'd all be questioned, at the very least."

That much Ginny could believe. "How, then, am I to give the king's message to the red fox?"

"Tomorrow, at church. When you receive the Host. If you follow the sidesman, it will be arranged that you are without escort at the communion rail." The goodwife went to the door, then froze, her hand on the latch, at the sound of booted feet on the wooden attic stairs.

"The colonel," Ginny breathed, knowing that tread full well. Her eyes darted around the room, confirming what she already knew. There was no possible hiding place in the sparsely furnished chamber. They would have to bluff it out. "My thanks, goodwife," she said loudly, as the footsteps halted outside the door. "You have been most kind."

Goodwife Brown, catching on rapidly, opened the door, saying over her shoulder, "It was nothing, mistress. I am glad to hear that you are not indisposed. Oh, Colonel. I beg pardon, I'm sure." She looked credibly startled at the broad figure standing with one hand raised, clearly about to knock on the door. Before Alex could say anything, however, she had hurried past him and was moving down the stairs with a light speed that seemed incongruous with her ample girth.

Alex stepped into the room. "What business did the goodwife have with you?"

"She very kindly came to inquire after me, wondering if mayhap I was indisposed, having retired so soon after supper. You understand?" Somehow, she managed to sound still aggrieved, turning back to the tumbled bed where the twisted sheets bore ample witness to her tossings and turnings.

To her inexpressible relief, the explanation seemed to satisfy him. "It is as hot as Hades in here," Alex observed. "If you are still desirous of taking the night air, I will accompany you."

"But I have my nightgown on," Ginny protested, even as she recognized the olive branch.

"That is easily remedied." Alex smiled, catching her hands and drawing her against him. "It is simply removed." His fingers undid the ribbon at the neck, before he caught up the skirt of the gown, lifting it up her body with slow deliberation. "Mmm," he murmured appreciatively, tossing the garment onto the bed. "I fancy a different form of exercise, I think."

"It is too hot," she whispered in faint protest.

"Will you defy me again, little rebel?" His hands slipped to cup her shoulders, pulling her nearer. He lowered his lips to hers, a sheen of mockery in the green-brown eyes for him

143

and for her. His mouth tasted of wine and desire, arms enfolded her against the lean hardness of his body where the coarse linen of his shirt prickled her bare breasts and the leather of his britches stroked her naked thighs. The sensation sapped her will completely as his mouth brushed her cheek, scorched along the curve of her jaw, moved aside the cascade of chestnut hair to nibble the soft vulnerability of her bent neck. Ginny stood still, for once quiescent in his hold, allowing her mind to encompass only sensation as his hands moved upon her body, tantalizing, feather-light with their stroking caresses, mounting a delicate assault on all her senses so that, when he turned with her to the narrow tumbled bed, thoughts of treachery and rebellion were vanquished, and she was conscious of nothing but the perfection of the moment.

Ginny awoke to the peal of church bells interspersed with the call of the bugle. She was lying on top of the sheets, quite naked, her skin stroked by the cool morning air drifting in through the open casement. For a moment she lay, luxuriating in her body's relaxation and her mind's re-creation of the night. It was not possible to have enmity for one who at such times seemed indivisible from herself. But if she loved him as she knew she did, how could she plot against him as she was doing every waking moment? This morning, by hook or by crook, she was going to work against everything Alex believed in and worked for. She was going to evade his guard, deceive him absolutely, and if she was discovered, their love would be in the gravest jeopardy. It would be so much simpler just to yield, to accept that the king's cause was lost, as, in her heart of hearts, she knew that it was. But there were men — men like Edmund Verney and Peter Ashley — all over this land who refused to accept defeat, who were still prepared to give their lives, if necessary, as her father had done. She could not do less.

Downstairs, she found the unhurried atmosphere of a

144

Sunday morning. Breakfast was a leisurely affair, and everyone delicately refrained from any reference to her abrupt departure of the previous evening. Then Major Bonham dropped the bombshell.

"We have church parade at eleven, Mistress Courtney, and the padre will conduct the service at eleven-fifteen on the village green. The men put on a brave show; it will be something pleasant for you to see after yesterday."

Ginny gulped. "Your padre will conduct the service according to the new prayerbook, will he not, Major?"

"But of course," Major Bonham said. "The New Model Army does not subscribe to the superstitions of the old service."

"No," Ginny said. She had not thought of this complication. Parliament's forces would not worship in the old manner in the old churches. The traditional rituals were castigated as papist in origin and therefore dangerous. Most of the old churches had already been destroyed in the fervor of fanaticism, the silver melted down for arms, the paintings and altar cloths destroyed. The new priests were dour men, the new services plain to a fault, and there would be no taking of communion. Alex Marshall's brigade would not be worshiping with the townsfolk this Sunday morning, and where would that leave Parliament's ward? Would she be allowed to attend the service of her choice?

"Where is the colonel this morning?" she asked casually.

"Here," came Alex's cheerful voice from the door. "I give you good day, Ginny."

"Good day, Colonel." She offered him a distracted smile. "I must speak with you in private." She twisted her hands in a gesture of distress, keeping her eyes lowered. This game she must play to the hilt if she was to achieve her object.

"But of course." Alex looked concerned. "Something has happened to trouble you?" He held the door for her and followed her out into the passage.

"It is a matter of church," she said directly. "You will allow me the freedom to worship in the way of my father?" Alex was silent, and she went on swiftly. "It is a matter of conscience, Alex. You would not force me to participate in a service I find abhorrent."

"You will have to get used to it," he said carefully. "In a short while, the Puritan way of worship will be the only one allowed. All pageantry and superstition will be forbidden."

"That is not yet certain," she responded stubbornly. "And even if it were, is that not even greater cause to permit me to attend the service of my choice while there is still a choice. I wish to take communion as I have done every Sunday since my confirmation."

Alex punched a clenched fist into the palm of his hand, frowning deeply. "You make it devilishly difficult for me, Ginny. Personally, I have no objections to the old services, but in my position I cannot condone it. In fact, I would be within my rights and duties to prevent the conduction of such a service in the town; however, I had already decided that I would turn a blind eye. But if I permit you to attend, I must send someone with you, and I cannot command one of Parliament's soldiers to do such a thing."

"So you are saying I may not?"

"I am sorry," he said with genuine regret. "But you see my position."

"Then let me go alone." She looked at him directly. "At least, let me enter the church alone. The escort could remain outside, and I will give you my word that I will make no attempt to evade his guard." Technically, that would be true, she told herself in a vain attempt to quiet a clamoring conscience.

Alex gave vent to a series of soldier's oaths that accurately expressed his dilemma. Ginny, aware that they were not specifically directed at her, remained silent, admiring his fluency, hardly breathing lest she betray herself in some way.

"Very well." Alex made up his mind with his usual decision. "You may go, since I suspect it will be the last opportunity you will have. Next Sunday, we shall be in London where none would dare practice the traditional rituals. I have your word that you will go into the church and come out of it promptly at the end of the service by the same door?"

"You have my word." Her heart skipped with relief, even as she felt as if she had just emerged from the midden, soiled by deceit. How would she have answered him if he had asked for her word that she would engage in no subversion during the service?

Jed accompanied her to the church door. The soldier was monosyllabic, even more laconic than usual, giving Ginny the unmistakable impression that he disapproved mightily of this expedition. He took up his stance on the porch, legs parted, pike planted in front of him, eyes staring rigidly ahead, and ignored the townsfolk who hurried past him with lowered eyes at this powerful reminder of Parliament's strength and the knowledge that they were worshiping today on sufferance.

Ginny walked boldly into the church, nothing in her demeanor indicating the turmoil of excitement and trepidation roiling within. She received sidelong, curious glances as she walked up the aisle, looking for a vacant pew.

"Mistress, this way." The sidesman appeared in sober cloth, gesturing to a front pew immediately beneath the pulpit. Across the aisle sat Goodwife Brown and her family, all of whom acknowledged Ginny with the briefest inclination of the head. Although the church filled rapidly, no one joined Ginny in her pew, and she wondered whether this was by accident or design. The latter, probably, she decided. Anyone traveling with Parliament's army, regardless of status, would be a dangerous person to know.

The church had been stripped bare of ornaments, paintings, and silver, but the font had been left standing, as had the altar and the deep, dark-oak communion rail. The stained glass in the windows was still intact, and the priest, when he appeared, wore cassock and surplice as if the war had wrought no changes. Who or what was the red fox, Ginny wondered again as the service, comforting in its familiarity, began.

The great oak door creaked on its hinges, and she looked behind, down the aisle to see Jed closing the door behind him. He marched up the aisle and took a position at the end of Ginny's pew. Had the colonel ordered him to keep Parliament's ward under surveillance at all times? Or was Jed taking it upon himself to exceed instructions? Either way, it was a damnable happenstance. Supposing he insisted on accompanying her to the altar? Ginny forced herself to concentrate on the service, to keep her eyes on her prayer book although she knew the responses by heart. She must not give any indication that Jed's presence disturbed her in the least, must keep her eyes from sliding around the church, looking fearfully for some involuntary reaction that would betray them all.

Sweat trickled down from her armpits, beaded her upper lip, made her fingers slippery and awkward on the thin, precious paper of her prayer book. She could always take the coward's way out: attend the service and give no message. But she had promised the king to seize any opportunity, to do all within her power, and if the red fox was still prepared to risk his life by hearing the message, then would she deliver it.

The sidesman appeared beside Jed at the end of her pew, inviting her to approach the communion rail where the priest stood, a humble wooden cup replacing the customary silver chalice clasped in both hands. She stepped out of the pew, brushing past Jed, wondering if he could smell the sweat of fear, feel the tremors setting her limbs a-quiver to such a degree that she wondered if she would be able to walk steadily. Would he follow her? She trod up the shallow steps of the railing; Jed remained where he was, staring ahead. Other communicants followed, and as they knelt, the worshipers in the body of the church lifted their voices in the Psalm of David. The magnificent words of strength and comfort swelled, and as Ginny took the cup, tasting the wine, she heard the priest murmuring the traditional words,

148

then some others, his voice low and swift.

"If you would speak with the red fox, do so."

Under cover of the chanting voices, she gave King Charles's message, laying emphasis on his statement that he would not abandon his people, that he was not contemplating flight to France, that the cause was just and the fighting must continue. As she lifted her head, opening her mouth to take the bread the priest laid upon her tongue, she saw his eyes shining with joy, his expression uplifted with confirmation, and she knew that the message was a vital one and she must continue to pass it on at whatever personal risk.

As if reading her thoughts, the priest whispered, "You will find the red fox wherever you go about this land, if you have the courage to seek him out." Then he passed to the next communicant, and Ginny rose from her knees and returned to her pew, head bowed in an attitude of reverence as she slipped past Jed, filled with an overwhelming relief. Until their next halt, she was freed of the need for plotting, for deception, for fear.

Chapter Nine

After the noon meal, Ginny found herself at something of a loose end. Alex and his officers had excused themselves politely and were now ensconced in the parlor, presumably discussing matters not considered suitable for the ears of a ward of Parliament. A sleepy air hung over the inn, where even the servants were taking an afternoon nap. The kitchen was deserted, although the fire glowed bright, and various kettles were hung in its heat. Collecting a shallow wicker basket from one of the pantries, Ginny wandered into the stableyard, coming across those soldiers who cared for the horses and were billeted with their animals. They were lounging around in idle chat, tossing spillikins onto the cobbles, smoking clay pipes, or snoring sonorously in the mid-afternoon sun. Reluctant to disturb the peace of their indolent afternoon, Ginny crossed the yard and went out into the lane. No one made any attempt to stop her, but then she had permission to go where she pleased within the immediate vicinity of the inn.

On the way to the church that morning, she had seen wild strawberries growing in profusion along the hedgerow. Distilled strawberry juice had many excellent properties, particularly when applied to the skin, and had even been known to rid one of warts. The opportunity to pick a basketful was not to be passed up. The sun was hot, and Ginny tied her kerchief over her head, pushed her sleeves above her elbows, and hitched her skirt into her belt, leaving her ankles bare to the breeze. Voices coming from the fields beyond the hedge reached her lazily in the still air, but she hardly heard them, absorbed as she was in the pleasantly automatic task that allowed her mind to meander down whatever paths it happened upon.

The lane twisted and turned, and she simply followed it, oblivious of distance or direction until she heard the crunch of gravel behind her, startling her out of her self-absorption. Spinning round, she came up against a leather jerkin encasing a broad chest.

"What little wench 'ave we 'ere?" a voice boomed, as an arm encircled her waist. "Look'ee 'ere, Bart."

Ginny pushed against the chest with the hand that was not holding the basket, pulled backward against the arm where veins stood out like whipcord. A coarse laugh greeted her struggles, and another man appeared, grinning as he caught her chin. She smelled the beer on his breath, the rankness of his mouth where only the stumps of teeth held tenure, the instant before his lips seemed to swallow hers.

At this point, more angry and disgusted than frightened, she swore at them, kicking viciously at the calves of the man holding her. Her struggles seemed merely to amuse and excite them, and, catching sight of the insignia on the shoulder of one of them, she realized with horror mixed with relief that they were soldiers, members of Alex's brigade.

"You don't know what you are doing," she gasped through bruised and swollen lips as the lace at her bodice ripped. "If your colonel finds out —"

"And who's to tell 'im?" one mocked. "Come on, now, village wenches 're always glad of a tumble. Don't get enough of it these days, with only old men and little boys left at home." They both roared with laughter as they pushed her backward into the ditch, large hands groping hurtfully for her breasts beneath the ripped bodice. "Like it rough, do you?"

Panic swelled in her chest, suffocating almost in its intensity. They did not know who she was, and they were going to hurt her. With a monumental heave, she brought the basket of strawberries, upturned, down hard on the head of her captor. It could do him no real damage, but the basket stuck across his forehead, and strawberry juice ran down into his eyes, stinging and temporarily blinding him. With a bellow, he released her; the other one, his hands occupied with the fastening of his britches, grabbed at her a minute too late. Ginny kicked out, aiming with deadly accuracy for that part of his anatomy he had been in the process of revealing. He collapsed with an anguished roar over the injured member, and Ginny flew down the lane, headlong into Jed's arms.

"Easy now," Jed soothed, clicking his tongue in the manner he used to gentle a frightened horse. "I was wonderin' where you'd got to. It's all right now. Sit on the bank and wait for me." His voice was calm, but when Ginny, biting back her sobs, looked into his face, she saw that his expression was grimly intense, and he was looking at her momentarily disabled attackers.

She did as she was told, sitting on the bank as her legs began to shake convulsively, now the adrenaline had stopped pumping. Jed, burly though he was, would be no match for the other two, but curiously she had no fear for him as he walked steadily toward them, just as she knew that she was now safe. It was not hard to find the reason. With Jed's arrival on the scene, she was once again under the protective umbrella of Colonel Marshall.

Ginny could not hear what was said amongst the three of them, but she could sense their fear as the two soliders slunk away through a gap in the hedge. Jed came back and stood looking at her for a moment. "Ye're unharmed?"

"Aye." Ginny stood up, stiffening her wobbly knees. "A bit shaken, but no worse." Biting her lip, she said awkwardly, "I was lucky you came along."

"Seems to me, you were doin' all right for yourself," Jed responded. "Ye're a bonny fighter for a lass. But the colonel'll not be best pleased. Ye're a good ways from the inn, mistress. This lane runs right through the encampment."

"Does he have to know?" Ginny despised herself even as she made the appeal. "No, don't answer that. Forget that I asked."

A wintry smile touched the old soldier's thin lips. "I'd not tell him, but it's a matter of discipline. They can't get away with it, now they know who you are. They'll think the colonel's gone soft on 'em. Besides," he fixed her with a gimlet eye. "You wouldn't want it happenin' again, I reckon."

Ginny flushed, shaking her head. "Of course not. But I'll not venture so far afield another time, either."

"That'll be as well," Jed agreed. "Though I doubt you'll be gettin' the chance again."

It was a statement that seemed to require no response, and Ginny untied her kerchief, arranging it at her neck to cover the torn lace before trudging back along the lane beside the now-silent Jed. When they reached the inn, she told her companion that she would be in her chamber should anyone want her and, before Jed could argue, had fled upstairs to the quiet and privacy of her little room under the eaves.

The thought of being in the same room when Jed recounted the incident to his commander was too awful to contemplate, particularly in her torn gown, with bruised lips and streaks of dirt on her face and arms. She had time to change her gown, tidy her hair, and wash before the sound of boots was heard on the stairs.

"Mistress Courtney — uh — Ginny?" It was Diccon, sounding even more hesitant than usual. Ginny opened the door. "The colonel wants you," the lieutenant said uneasily.

"Mad as fire, is he?" Ginny said with an attempt at bravado.

Diccon sighed and relaxed somewhat. "I haven't seen him this angry in weeks," he confided.

"You are a comfort, Diccon," Ginny said with a rueful little smile. "I am already shaking like a blancmanger."

"Oh, I am certain he is not angry with you," Diccon said earnestly, standing aside on the cramped landing so that she could precede him down the stairs. Ginny just laughed, a hollow laugh of disbelief.

Alex was alone in the parlor, standing by the empty hearth. He gestured a curt dismissal to his aide-de-camp, and the door closed with soft finality behind Diccon. Ginny did not think she had ever seen anyone look quite so implacably furious as Alex at this moment. The green-brown eyes were metallic, the full, well-sculpted mouth set in a thin line, the lean, hard body taut as wire.

"What did they do to you?" His voice rasped harshly, like skin on a grater.

"I got away before they could do anything," Ginny said, then coughed to clear her throat where the words seemed to be stuck in sand.

"I want to know exactly what happened, what was said, and what they did."

Ginny recounted the tale as best she could remember, keeping her voice expressionless, her eyes anywhere but on the colonel. "They did not know who I was," she said at the last. "They thought I was a village girl."

"A reasonable assumption," Alex said curtly. "Parliament's ward was under strict instructions to stay close to the inn, and above all to keep clear of the camp. A wench, with a kerchief tied around her hair, sleeves rolled, and her skirt hitched up, wandering in the middle of the camp would be considered fair game."

Jed had presumably provided that uncomfortably accurate description, Ginny reflected. "I was picking strawberries," she said, deciding it was time to defend herself. "It was hot, and I was so absorbed I did not realize how far I had gone."

"If that is your only excuse, I consider it woefully inadequate," the colonel snapped. "Because of your careless disregard for my express orders, I am now obliged to discipline two of my men. Morale is low enough after yesterday as it is, without further blows."

"Supposing it had been a village girl they were intent on raping," Ginny fired back, "you would not consider that a punishable offense?"

"With luck, it would not have come to my attention," Alex

returned, with what Ginny considered appalling pragmatism. "Anyway, any woman foolish enough to hang around two-hundred deprived and lusting soldiers is asking for trouble?"

"That is so unjust!" Ginny stared at him, enraged now and no longer defensive. "We invite assault and worse, do we? Is that what you are saying?"

"On occasion," he said bluntly. "By ignoring the baser facts of life. Lust is one of those facts. I told you I could not guarantee your safety if you went near the encampment, and you chose to ignore that warning. Do you think I say these things just because I enjoy the sound of my own voice?"

He had adroitly managed to return matters to the point for which she had no defense. Facts were facts; they had been explained to her, and she had not taken them seriously enough. It was undeniably true. Had she taken them seriously, she would have watched where she was going. Now, an innocent afternoon of strawberry picking was about to have unpleasant repercussions for men whom no one would really blame. According to the lights of their fellows, and even their commander, they had behaved in a perfectly normal, understandable fashion, and she had brought those moments of panic-stricken horror, the foulness of that bodily contact, upon herself.

Wearily, she said, "If it was my fault, why do you not forget the matter? I will take the blame upon myself, and no harm was done after all, unless you consider the loss of a basket of wild strawberries, or a few seconds of panic."

"You were frightened?" he spoke almost as if it was the first time such a thing had occurred to him.

"Why should I have been frightened, when I invited the attack?" Ginny retorted bitterly.

"I am sorry, I did not mean that. My first thought was for your physical well-being. When I knew that you had not been hurt . . ."

Ginny shrugged. "May I go?" She turned toward the door.

"Not just yet." Alex sighed. "You must identify the men. Jed is bringing them here under guard. The business has been started and must be concluded in the only way possible. You will bear your part."

Ginny felt a chill at these words. There was a cold, resigned finality about them that she knew she would not be able to gainsay.

Nothing more was said during the long moments of waiting. Then the door was opened, and Jed marched in, wearing full armor as were the four corporals surrounding Ginny's erstwhile attackers. Ginny turned away from them, unwilling to see either pleading or accusation in their eyes.

"Mistress Courtney?" Alex spoke impersonally. "Are these the soldiers who attacked you in the lane?"

What would happen if she said "no?" Denied that she could make a positive identification? Would they escape without retribution, or would Jed's identification be sufficient? But Jed must have turned the corner of the lane too late to see anything but Ginny running toward him. Slowly, she turned to look at them and felt revulsion creep like a sticky slug's tail over her skin. She had invited nothing! "Yes," she said and walked to the door without a second glance at anyone in the room.

Alex made no attempt to stop her. He had intuited every nuance of her thoughts during that moment of silence when she had stood with her back to them, and he knew that, as always, she had made the courageous decision, but it was not over for her yet, as she would discover soon enough.

Ginny went up to her room, sick at heart, but unable to think what she could have done to alter this afternoon's inexorable path. The only thing she did know was that she could not face anyone at this moment. For a while, she busied herself mending the ripped lace of her gown, then, that task completed, she went to the window. The stableyard was deserted except for Jed who was grooming Bucephalus with a wisp of straw, burnishing the black coat. Jed would answer the question that she didn't want to ask, yet knew that she would get no peace until she did.

Running lightly down the stairs and into the yard, meeting no one on the way, she walked over to Bucephalus. Jed, whistling tunelessly through his teeth, acknowledged her with a nod that despite its brevity was not unfriendly.

Ginny ran her hand down the warm, sinewy indentation of the charger's neck. "What will happen to them, Jed?"

"A floggin'," he said impassively. "Twenty lashes at sundown."

Ginny made a strange, incoherent little sound, turning away. "It's a light sentence," Jed said. "They've got to be fit to march tomorrow."

"How can you be so callous?" But even as she accused the soldier, she knew that it was Alex who had pronounced sentence, Alex who had had practical thoughts of the morrow in mind.

Jed did not deign to reply, merely sucked on another wisp of straw, wetting it thoroughly before moving it down the horse's flanks.

Ginny went back upstairs, knowing that she should not be surprised, should certainly not be horrified. Flogging and death were facts of life, as freely applied to the civilian population as to the army. It had always been so. The whipping posts and stocks in the market squares were a familiar-enough sight, and she rarely thought twice about them. It had certainly never occurred to her to question the appropriateness of such retributive methods, and she was sure, although she had never heard him do so, that her father, the gentle John Redfern, in his capacity as magistrate, must have passed similar sentences in his time. The difference here was that she was in some way responsible. Even while common sense and an innate sense of justice told her that that was not so, she could not help feeling it. And if even Alex believed it, so would everyone else. Her position in the brigade would be totally untenable unless she could do something to repair the situation.

She remained in the stuffy little chamber for the rest of the afternoon, waiting in curious dread for sundown; yet still the piercing call of the bugle and the beat of the drums, sharp and alert in the gathering twilight, took her by surprise. Her heart began to thump as she went to close the casement, to shut out the sound. There was a swift tread on the stairs outside. Then the door opened, and Alex stood on the threshold, sword and sling buckled at his waist.

"Come," he said quietly, "it is time."

Ginny just looked at him, for the moment dumbfounded. He could only mean one thing. Dumbly, she shook her head, holding onto the back of the low, armless chair.

"Come," he repeated, extending his hand imperatively.

"No . . . no, I will not." She shook her head again violently. What kind of man was he, to expect this of her?

"You must," he said implacably. "It is justice, and it must be seen to be done."

"Not by me," she affirmed, her voice sounding stronger.

"Yes, by you. You will attend, and then you will fully understand that my interdictions are not made simply for the pleasure of power."

Ginny gripped the chair back tighter. "You would punish me in this way, then? By forcing the victim to witness the punishment of her attackers?"

Alex did not answer, instead reached for her hand. "Come along, Ginny."

Grimly, she hung onto the anchoring chair as he pulled her forward. "You cannot force me to do this, Alex. I will not come." The chair dragged across the wooden floor, as he pulled her, willy-nilly, toward the door. Ginny let go of the ineffectual anchor and with quiet desperation adopted the tactic of passive resistance by sitting down abruptly on the floor.

"Get up!" Alex looked down at her, jerking on her hand.

Ginny shook her head. "You will have to drag me or carry me every step of the way," she said with icy determination. "And I shall scream and keep on screaming."

Looking into those gray eyes, glowing with purpose, recognizing the stubborn set of that wide, generous mouth, Alex knew he was defeated. Like all good campaigners, he wasted no time in accepting the need for an orderly retreat. Releasing her hand, he gave her a mocking little bow as she still sat upon the floor, turned on his heel, and strode from the room.

Ginny waited until the sound of his step on the stair had faded before she stood up. She now knew exactly what she

158

was going to do and knew she had little time to waste. The camp would be deserted, and there would be no guards around the inn for as long as this punishment parade lasted. She collected what she needed from her baggage roll, the salves and strips of boiled cloth, the thick, herbal paste that would form a poultice if the cuts of the lash went deep. Swiftly, she ran down the stairs and out into the deserted stableyard. The drum was still beating, but it was the only sound, and there was no one in sight. Perhaps all the inhabitants of the inn had gone to witness the spectacle. No doubt, it would afford some of them considerable pleasure.

Once in the lane, she slipped through the hedge and found herself in the campground. Here there were guards, and when she was challenged, Ginny informed them in tones of complete confidence that she was here to tend the wounds of the prisoners. They would be expected to march on the morrow and would do so better if their pain was eased.

It was clear that the men knew who she was, just as they knew what had happened that afternoon. But her tone was so decisive and authoritative, the implication that she had the colonel's permission for her errand of mercy so clear, the sense of her statements so obvious, that she was shown without further question to the tent where her attackers would be brought.

As she waited, Ginny noted, with a degree of abstract interest, that she was not at all afraid. At any minute, the place would be filled with angry, disconsolate men, but they would not harm her now, whatever they might think of her. Whether she could get them to accept her presence and the very genuine help she could offer was the central question. If they did so, she would in some way be making amends, while at the same time indicating that she bore no grudge for the violence done her, that in her mind the matter was at an end. Curiously, she did not once think of what Alex's reaction might be if he were to discover her errand.

The drum, at long last, stopped beating, and the sound of marching feet came closer. Ginny sat quietly in the tent at the rear of the camp. There were voices outside; then the flap opened, and the two men were helped in by the four

159

corporals she had seen this afternoon. Ginny gave them no time to say anything but took charge with brisk authority, directing them to lay the men upon the pallets as she dropped to her knees beside them, rolling up her sleeves. She worked in silence, watched with amazement by a gathering, gawking crowd, and when the cuts were clean, she spread the herbal paste thickly before laying strips of cloth over the wounds.

"There, you will sleep easier now," she said, getting to her feet, rolling down her sleeves. "You," she gestured to one of the corporals who came over immediately, a look of wonder in his eyes. "In the morning, you will use this salve, and also in the evening until the cuts close. If you need me again, you may pass a message through Jed." Why she was so certain that Jed would conspire with her in this, Ginny had no idea, but she was quite certain. Picking up her basket, she left the tent, and the ranks of men opened to let her through. Ginny could feel no hostility, only puzzlement.

"Mistress?" A voice spoke suddenly, hesitantly. Ginny stopped and turned. "Can you do anything for this?" A soldier pushed through to the front, holding out his arm. Ginny examined the ugly, suppurating sore with a frown.

"This should have been seen to days ago," she said quietly. "I will do what I can." She again used the herbal poultice, bandaging the arm tightly. "Keep it dry and clean, if you wish to avoid malignancy. If there is no improvement in two days, send a message through Jed."

Suddenly conscious of the time, she began to hurry through the camp, although sensing that there were others who wished to speak with her. She did not know whether Alex would understand what she had done and why, and after this evening's confrontation, Ginny knew that another one so soon afterward would spell disaster.

Reaching the stableyard, she saw Jed talking with a group of his fellow soldiers, who looked at her askance and stopped their talk. Ginny went over to them boldly. "May I speak with you, Jed?"

Without a word, he moved away from the group in his customary economical fashion. Ginny told him in a few words what she had done, and what she was prepared to continue doing with his help. "It would be best if the colonel were not to know of this for the moment," she finished, meeting his eye.

"Aye," Jed agreed, stroking his chin, and that thin smile appeared again. " 'Twould at that, mistress. I'll not be tellin' him, but ye're a courageous lass, I reckon." He gave a snort of laughter as he turned away and went back to his companions.

Ginny hurried into the kitchen, suddenly conscious of the fact that she was ravenous. A leg of lamb was turning on the spit over the fire, Goodwife Brown was rolling pastry on the wooden table, a kitchen maid was mashing floury potatoes in a pot, another chopping fresh mint. The goodwife smiled at Ginny, the smile of conspirators, and Parliament's ward wondered with a sudden wash of weariness how many other conspiracies she would hatch under the nose of her lover and her enemy.

"Can I be of any help, goodwife?" she asked, placing her basket discreetly in a corner. She didn't particularly want to be seen with it; it might call for awkward explanations.

"That's kind of you," the goodwife said. "If ye'll fetch the soup into the parlor, I daresay the colonel and his men are good and ready for it." She cast Ginny a shrewd glance. "You too, I reckon. It's a bit peaky you are, this evening."

Ginny smiled, lifting the heavy kettle off its hook over the fire. "I'll not deny it's been a long day. Is the ladle on the table?"

"Aye, and the bowls."

Ginny carried the kettle with its fragrantly steaming contents into the parlor, glad to have this task to perform that would make her entrance seem natural and would mask her awkwardness at the prospect of having to face them all, and Alex in particular.

"Let me have that." Diccon sprang toward her as she pushed through the door, took the kettle out of her hands, and hefted it onto the table.

"My thanks, Diccon." She smiled and looked around the room. "May I serve you, gentlemen?" To her relief, she

161

could feel that her smile was natural, her voice easy, her hand steady as she picked up the ladle.

"Colonel?" She looked at him for the first time, eyebrows raised. "Do you care for soup?"

"Thank you," he said coldly. She forced herself to keep smiling, to ignore the ice in his eyes, the waves of anger radiating almost palpably from the rigidly held body. The atmosphere in the room was distinctly strained, hardly surprising with the colonel in this mood, Ginny reflected dourly, and after the grim business of this evening. She wondered if anyone but herself and Alex knew of her earlier victory and were thus able to attribute the colonel's wrath to the correct cause. It would be unlikely, she decided. Alex was not a man to broadcast his defeats.

Having served the men, she filled the last bowl for herself and was about to sit down in her usual place when Alex said in an expressionless tone, "I have matters to discuss with my officers, Mistress Courtney. You will not object, I trust, to dining in your chamber."

"On the contrary, sir," Ginny said, hiding her mortified hurt at this snub behind an expression of cold dignity. "I find that I prefer my own company." Picking up her bowl and spoon, she marched out of the room, leaving the door open. It was closed behind her with a firm, excluding bang. Under her breath, Ginny consigned Colonel Alexander Marshall to the fiery depths of Lucifer's kingdom. Her abrupt dismissal had been deliberately designed to humiliate her, she was under no illusions on that score. Not for one minute did she believe that he had business to discuss; he had been talking with his officers all afternoon. It had simply been Alex's way of reminding her that he could make life very uncomfortable for her if he chose to do so. Well, she was not going to eat in lonely isolation upstairs. Ginny went into the kitchen.

"My presence is not required in the parlor this evening," she informed the goodwife. "May I sup with you?"

"By all means." Goodwife Brown gestured to one of the girls to move up and make room for Ginny on the bench. "But I formed the impression that the colonel didn't want you in here."

162

"His wishes are a matter of supreme indifference to me," Ginny responded airily, taking a deep draft of October ale as the communal cup passed to her. Goodwife Brown smiled slightly but made no further comment.

The meal passed in cheerful talk and laughter, and Ginny began to feel much restored. It was certainly less of a strain eating in this company than in the presence of her captors, however flattering the attention paid her. And she had been dreading this evening's meal, dreading the knowing looks, the silent accusations, the awkwardness as they tried to avoid the one topic uppermost in all their minds.

She did not offer to help as the lamb and potatoes were taken into the parlor, feeling prudently that discretion in this instance was probably the better part of valor and she would do better not to draw attention to herself. There was no knowing what further embarrassment Alex, in his present mood, would decide to inflict upon her, should he conclude that she was disobeying some order. Soon the food and the ale produced an inevitable lassitude as the strains of the day took their toll. One of the stablehands began to sing, a riotous folk song that they all joined in and Ginny's head nodded as her eyelids drooped, and she smiled in sleepy contentment. War seemed far away at this moment in the warm kitchen amongst these friendly souls. She could almost have been back in her father's house, taking part in kitchen life as she had so often done . . .

It was thus that Alex found her, still sitting on the bench, her head pillowed on her arms, a dreamy smile curving her lips in sleep. He had wanted to hold onto his anger, the bitter anger at the defeat he had suffered at the hands of this ridiculously young, outrageously insolent creature who did not seem to understand the power he held over her very life, or who, if she did understand it, simply ignored it. Now, that anger faded, replaced with a much milder exasperation. Why had she not had the sense to got to bed? They would need to make a dawn start in the morning, their rest the previous night had been disturbed, wonderfully so, but fatiguing nonetheless, and her experience of the afternoon would have decimated a lesser woman.

He touched her shoulder. "Ginny, you silly girl, wake up."

"You'll be lucky," the goodwife said. "Beggin' your pardon, Colonel, but she's dead to the world, poor child. It's been a long and exhausting day."

"I am aware of that, goodwife," Alex replied stiffly. "She should have gone to bed long since." Slipping an arm beneath her shoulders, he lifted her to her feet. Her eyelids flickered, but apart from that there was no response from the inert figure sagging against him. With a resigned sigh, Alex picked her up in his arms. Almost deliberately, it seemed to him, a contented little whisper came from her lips, and she cuddled against his chest. Goodwife Brown smiled knowingly. She had thought there was rather more to the colonel and his prisoner than met the eye. But the girl was a genuine enough Cavalier for all that. Just another tangle brought about by this war. With an accepting shrug, she went to open the door for the colonel and his burden.

Alex carried Ginny upstairs and laid her down upon her bed, before beginning to undress her. Something penetrated Ginny's deep sleep, the feel of his hands on her, and she wriggled, seductive even in her semiconscious state.

"Stop it!" Alex directed shakily. He was having enough difficulty being objective about this task without blatant invitations, particularly when she didn't really know what she was doing.

Ginny smiled, a smile of pure mischief, although her eyes remained shut and he could have sworn she was at least two-thirds asleep. "Don't you ever again argue with me when I tell you to go to bed," he said vigorously, holding her against his shoulder as he dropped her nightgown over her head. "You have just demonstrated that you are totally incapable of making such simple decisions for yourself. Where are your arms, for heaven's sake?"

Obligingly, Ginny waved her limbs around under the folds of linen, and, with a muttered oath, her unusual and reluctant maid thrust them into the sleeves. "October ale," Ginny mumbled, in apologetic explanation. "Very good, but very strong."

"Dear God! Don't you know better than to drink that stuff

when you're tired?"

"Nothing else to drink," she said, dropping her head onto his chest. "Wine was in the parlor."

"I see," he said grimly. "So this condition you're in is my fault. I assume you misheard me. I didn't tell you to eat in the kitchen; I told you to eat up here."

"Don't do as I'm told," she mumbled, falling back on the bed. "Not unless it makes sense."

"I have noticed," he responded drily. "I can see that in future I am going to have to try very hard to ensure that we see eye to eye in matters that require your cooperation. What are you doing now?"

"Hair," Ginny muttered, struggling to sit up. "Have to brush it."

"Keep still and let me do it." Sitting on the bed behind her, he drew her backward against his chest, before unpinning the chestnut braids and brushing her hair with long, smooth strokes. Ginny sighed with pleasure, and her eyes closed again under the soporific rhythm. But when he laid her down again upon the bed, she reached her arms around his neck, and there was nothing sleepy about her voice this time.

"Stay with me, Alex."

He shook his head. "Not tonight, sweeting. We both need to sleep."

"A man of such iron self-control," she said with faint mockery. "So disciplined, so—"

"It would be as well for all of us if you had a little of that quality yourself," Alex interrupted smartly, getting to his feet.

"Are we friends again?" Ginny asked, still sounding wide-awake with no sign of October ale befuddlement.

Alex pursed his lips thoughtfully, considering the question as he stood looking down at her, hands planted firmly on his hips. Only when he saw a hint of anxiety creep into the gray eyes did he break his silence. "Until the next confrontation we are, my lover and my enemy. But if you value our friendship, you will not, however absentmindedly, venture near the men's quarters again."

165

"I would not be harmed a second time," she stated flatly, wondering if this was the moment to tell him of what she had done.

"That is no longer the point." His face had closed again. "Two men suffered this afternoon because of you, and as a result, the entire brigade suffered. You will keep well away from them at all times, is that clear?"

No, obviously this was not the moment to tell him what she had done and what she intended doing. "It is quite clear," Ginny said truthfully, closing her eyes to hide a betraying spark. She yawned. "You are right, it is late, Colonel, and I am very weary."

"I do not wish to quarrel with you." Alex bent over her, brushing her lips with his, stroking her hair away from her forehead. "Can we try to be a little easier on each other?"

"We can try," she said softly, "but the situation does not lend itself to peace. Except when we make love, we are at war, you and I."

Alex frowned, straightening slowly. "Then so be it. I give you good-night, my little rebel."

"Good-night, my captor." The door closed behind him. Ginny curled on her side. "Then so be it," she whispered into her pillow.

Chapter Ten

It was still dark when Ginny awoke, but sounds of bustle came from all around her. Voices in the stableyard drifted in through the open window, feet clattered along the stone corridors of the inn. She got up, dressed swiftly, and went downstairs.

"Good morrow, Ginny." Alex came out of a first-floor chamber, impressive in full armor. A quick glance around reassuring him that there was no one in sight, he took her chin between gloved fingers and kissed her hard. "I am going to drill the brigade on the green," he said. "I want you there."

"Is that an order or a request?" Ginny inquired in dulcet accents.

"Neither," Alex responded. "It is simply a statement. It is too early in the morning for your bee-sting tongue, mistress. I should be much obliged if you would dip it in honey; you will find honeycomb on the breakfast table." Laughing, he strode off, and Ginny made her way to the parlor in search of the promised sweetener. The colonel was obviously in a good mood this morning, a fact that would communicate itself to all and sundry, she reflected wryly. It seemed more than a little inequitable that one man's moods had the power to set the tenor of an entire brigade. Such power, she decided through a mouthful of honeycomb, was not at all good for the character, either. It was amazing that the

167

colonel was even tolerable much of the time.

"Ginny, are you ready?" Diccon appeared, also very smart in full regalia. "I'm to escort you to the green."

Ginny drained her cup of milk and wiped her mouth on the back of her hand before hastily buttering a slice of bread. "Would it be considered disrespectful to this martial ritual, if I were to bring my breakfast?"

Diccon looked nonplussed. "I don't know," he said. "It's not usual."

"No, I do not suppose it is." Ginny laughed and went to the door, bread and butter in hand. "But since I have not yet finished my breakfast, and we cannot afford to be late and earn the colonel's mighty frown, there seems little option."

"I do not know how you dare to say such things," Diccon confided, hurrying along beside her.

"Oh, pah!" Ginny waved her bread and butter in careless dismissal of this statement. "He is only a man—a powerful one, I grant you, but he's no divinity, Diccon." The aide-de-camp did not look totally convinced of this, and Ginny smiled to herself. Diccon's doglike devotion to his commander had not escaped her notice.

The drums sounded as soldiers came running from all directions to form lines on the greensward. Townsfolk leaned from their casements, children gathered, wide-eyed, at the edge of the green. Alex raised his eyebrows as Ginny and Diccon hurried over to him. "Have you no respect for ceremony?" he demanded of Ginny, indicating her traveling breakfast.

She shook her head, and her eyes twinkled mischievously. "Surely you would not expect me to forgo my breakfast, Colonel? I might become faint on the march."

"That would never do," he concurred with a chuckle. "It is bad enough having to stop every few yards so that you may pick flowers."

Major Bonham snorted with laughter, hastily suppressed, and Ginny grinned at him. "It would seem, Major, that an army on the march is no place for the untrained."

"It is certainly no place for the undisciplined," Alex said, but his eyes were smiling. "Could you at least refrain from

168

munching until the drill is completed? I do not wish to be distracted."

"I would not disturb your concentration for the world, Colonel." Ginny stepped back to stand beside the major, such an expression of alert expectancy on her face that they were all hard pressed to hide their smiles. Then the drums fell silent, and Alex's voice rang loud and clear across the green in the cool of early morning, and Ginny felt ashamed of her mockery at the magnificent spectacle, which she guessed had been put on as much for the benefit of the people of Newbury as in the interests of morale and discipline among the troops.

The day's journey was long and arduous, the sun beating down strongly, and Ginny thought of the two men, their backs lacerated by the lash, marching in armor in this heat where the sweat flowed freely, sticky and itching even for herself, on horseback, with unbroken skin and dressed relatively lightly. She had always been blessed, or cursed, with an overly vivid imagination and was soon suffering acutely in vicarious sympathy. Alex, noticing her suddenly abstracted silence, asked her what was the matter.

Ginny debated with herself for a moment. He had been going out of his way to be pleasant, to modify the habitual commanding tone of voice and choice of words. When she had teased him, even in front of his officers, he had taken it in good part. But would she be stirring up a hornets' nest again by referring to yesterday's debacle? It was a risk she decided to take.

"I was thinking about the men you had flogged yesterday," she said quietly. "Marching in this heat cannot be doing them any good."

Alex shrugged. "The punishment was not particularly severe."

"They will be feeling it now," she persisted in the same low tone.

Now what was she up to, Alex wondered warily. This was no casual conversation, of that he was convinced. He kept his tone neutral. "That is only to be expected."

So casual! Ginny looked at him. His face was quite expressionless. Yet she knew, who better, how gentle and tender he could be. "I have some ointments," she said tentatively. "They will aid the healing and will ease any discomfort they may be feeling now. I could ride to the back . . ."

The woman was utterly incorrigible! "Do you never listen to anything I say?" He spoke with controlled force, his voice low enough to be heard by her ears alone. "I told you you were not to have anything to do with the men. Have you forgotten?"

"No—no, of course, I have not forgotten. It is just that I can be of help, not just to those two, but maybe there are others with ailments or injuries. I have some skill in these matters as I told you."

"I do not wish to discuss this, now or at any other time."

And that, Ginny said to herself, was most definitely that! Well, she had tried; now it was up to herself and Jed to manage things without their coming to the colonel's attention.

Their accommodations that night were humble in the extreme. There was no inn in the tiny hamlet, and Alex said he and his officers would camp out with the men. A bed was found for Ginny in the only cottage that could provide one. She stood on the threshold of the mud-floored main room, where cats and dogs seemed to proliferate, smiled absently at the wrinkled crone who, in exchange for Parliament's coin, had agreed to be her hostess, allowed herself to be shown the cot set up at the rear of the room, counted the fleas with pursed lips, thanked her would-be landlady, and marched out into the street.

Jed, who had accompanied her on her visit of inspection, couldn't help his grin when she demanded in carefully neutral tones where the colonel was to be found. "Billet not to your liking, mistress?"

Ginny shook out her skirts, examining the folds for any clinging parasites. "A degree of discomfort I do not mind, Jed. Filth and fleas are a different case. Let us find the colonel."

Alex was to be found with his officers, all of whom had shed shirts and boots and were sprawled in cheerful relaxation outside a group of tents set up on the outskirts of the main camp. It was quite clear to Ginny that the prospect of a night in the open air was viewed with relish by them all. It was also clear that the thought that she was safely out of their way for the night was at least partly responsible for this relaxed attitude.

"Pray do not let me disturb you, gentlemen," she said, stalking over to them. "I am quite accustomed to the sight of men without their shirts, so you need not feel in the least uncomfortable. No, do not get up, I beg you."

"You have a problem, Ginny?" Alex braced himself for the worst. Virginia bore a most determined air, and he could smell defeat in the wind even before he knew the cause of battle.

"No problem," she said calmly. "I shall sleep under those trees over there. You need not mind me at all."

"Why?" he asked, keeping his tone only mildly curious.

"I have no desire to contract typhus," she told him succinctly. "Dirt, parasites, and disease make inevitable bedfellows. I prefer to take my chance out of doors. You may all pretend that I am not here."

"That would be difficult," Alex commented with a dry little smile. "If not impossible. You had better take the tent on the end, and it is to be hoped that your first taste of campfire cooking will not prove too unpalatable."

"I am not excessively nice in my requirements," Ginny retorted. "But I do not care for fleas and bedbugs."

"Understandable, Mistress Courtney," Major Bonham agreed with bland courtesy. "Will you not take a seat in our sylvan parlor?"

"Thank you." Ginny sat on the grass and pulled off her boots with a sigh of relief. "I think you should all call me Ginny, Major. Diccon and the colonel do, and it seems silly, in the circumstances, to stand on ceremony."

Alex felt their eyes on him. It could do no harm, he decided. With an easy laugh, he sat down beside her, giving his tacit permission for her suggestion. "Ceremony, my dear

Ginny, is something quite unknown to you, as we have already remarked."

Jed reappeared at this point with a flagon of wine. "Fire's a bit slow," he grunted, handing the flagon to Alex. "Supper'll be along in a bit."

"Perhaps I can help," Ginny said, getting to her feet, following Jed out of earshot, to where a brazier showed a sullen gleam. "How are the men?" she whispered. "Should I go to them?"

"They'll do," Jed replied in an undertone. "You'll not be able to go among 'em tonight without the colonel noticin'. In the mornin', you'll have a need to go into the bushes, I reckon. No one will inquire if you're away for a while in all the business of breakin' camp. There's one or two others who could do with some attention. Just follow me, when I give you the nod."

"It would be so much more sensible if the colonel would just see how unreasonable he's being." Ginny sighed.

"It's hard to change his mind when it's set," Jed informed her, shaking the contents of a skillet over the fire. "Always has been, even as a lad. That's not to say it can't be done though," he added. "By the right person."

"You think *I* could?"

"Mebbe," was the short reply. Silence followed, and Ginny, deciding that her cooking help was not needed and that Jed had clearly said as much as he was prepared to on that fascinating subject, returned to her companions.

She had always found food in the open air much more appetizing than its indoor equivalent, and Jed's efforts certainly did not go unappreciated. The flagon of wine was passed around, conversation was pleasantly desultory, with none of the formality attendant upon dinner in an inn parlor. It was not long before Ginny found herself resting against Alex's drawn-up knees, and if anyone noticed the intimacy, they gave no sign. It was also, Ginny realized, the first evening since this strange journey began that, for her, came to a natural close. There was no squabble leading to her banishment, and the stars were high in the sky when Major Bonham announced with a yawn that it was time to turn in.

"Whose tent have I appropriated?" Ginny asked, giving her hands to Alex.

"Mine," he told her, pulling her upright. "I shall sleep under the stars. I prefer it, anyway."

"Perhaps I would, also," she said with a wicked gleam.

Alex's eyes narrowed, but he said simply, "You may use my bedroll. Jed will find me another."

"Thank you, sir," she murmured, dropping him a curtsy. "But maybe we do not need a second one."

It was impossible not to laugh with her, Alex reflected, not to be entranced by those candid gray eyes where imps of mischief danced, by that wonderfully warm, generous mouth, by her deep-bosomed grace. She was utterly outrageous, utterly carefree, did not know the meaning of the word discretion, or if she did, seemed not to acknowledge any need for it. And when she was not driving him to the brink of fury, she was bringing him to the edge of distraction with the heady, invincible combination of love and lust that he knew she shared.

It was the latter combination that brought him stealthily into the tent, once the heavy silence of sleep had fallen over the camp. Ginny was waiting for him, sitting cross-legged on the bedroll, quite naked.

"I think you are a changeling," Alex whispered, dropping to his knees beside her. "There is a magical quality about you, definitely something of the fairy. But not a good fairy," he added, cradling one breast in his large palm, a long calloused finger tracing the enlarged aureola, tipping the erect peak that hardened and tightened in responsive longing. "A very wicked fairy, and you are going to be my undoing, I fear."

"Tonight, I am," she promised softly, running her hands down his bare chest, palming his nipples, slipping inside the waist of his britches, one finger playing in his navel. The fastening of his britches came apart under her urgent fingers, and she pushed them down over his hips, that seductive tongue peeking between her lips as she drank in the sight of those narrow hips, the concave belly, the slender trail of curly black hair leading the eye down to the hard, joyous promise of his arousal. "You are so beautiful," she whispered, enclosing him in her hand, reveling in the strong pulsing of his blood against her fingers, his involuntary stirrings of pleasure. "There can be no shame in this." Her head bent, and she took him between her lips, hearing his low moan of delight as her tongue stroked and turned, muscular and knowing as she lost herself in the giving.

The night air was a cool whisper on her skin, sensuous and arousing beneath the flimsy canvas shelter as their bodies twisted and slid, over and across, changing position with the ease and familiarity of long-established lovers. They laughed and whispered, and in the moment of fulfillment, Ginny cried out, unable to bite back the acknowledgment of ecstasy. She fell asleep in his arms almost immediately, and Alex lay in the darkness, listening to the night noises outside the tent, breathing in the mingled scents of her hair and skin. There would be little point in concealment after tonight, when any with ears to hear would know the truth, he thought ruefully, the instant before he, too, fell asleep.

Ginny woke when the bugle called reveille and for a moment, in the gray light of dawn, wondered where she was. Her bed was unusually hard, and the air unusually chilly on her bare skin. It was chilly, she decided, because there was rather more of it than she was accustomed to, but she felt marvelously invigorated, much more so than after a night's rest in a stuffy inn. There was no sign of Alex, but somehow her body knew that he had not long left her. She stretched in luxurious languor, knowing that she should get up, yet unwilling to lose too soon these precious moments of contemplation.

"Rise and shine, slug-a-bed!" Alex stuck his head around the tent flap. "I do not know what you can have done to deserve such consideration, but Jed is heating water for you, and the rest of us are obliged to wait for our breakfast until the fire is free."

Abruptly the sense of peace was shattered as she remembered the task she had set herself for this morning. Jed

174

would be waiting for her and for the right moment to take her into the camp. "Jed is one of nature's gentlemen," she said with a yawn, sitting up and reaching for her shift. "I have certain needs I must attend to, before I do anything else, though." Standing up, she smoothed the garment over her hips, then shook her head at Alex in mock reproof. "You play the voyeur, sir. Shame on you."

"It is irresistible, I fear." He watched as she climbed into her gown, then stood aside as Jed appeared swinging a kettle of steaming water.

"My thanks, Jed." Ginny smiled warmly at the soldier. "I will be back in a little while."

Jed nodded his comprehension, placing the hot water inside the tent. "If you bear to the right, mistress, behind the tent, you'll be certain of privacy," he said.

"It is to be hoped he is right," Ginny murmured to Alex, who laughed.

"You may be sure of it. You'll not be disturbed by any of us, at any rate. We've been up and about long enough to need only our breakfast.

"Then perhaps you would grant me a little privacy now, Colonel." She raised her eyebrows, and Alex instantly left her. Ginny swiftly gathered up her medicine basket, walking boldly out of the tent as if she had but one purpose in mind. Following Jed's instructions, she found herself in a small copse that skirted the camp. The rustle of her footsteps seemed the only sound until she heard a low and definitely human whistle. She stopped, whistled back softly.

"Mistress." A young soldier, scarcely more than a lad, popped up from behind a bush. "I'm to take you to the camp, Jed said."

Jed, of course, would be cooking the officers' breakfast, safely away from this act of disobedience. This boy could hardly be blamed for aiding and abetting Parliament's ward; only Ginny was in direct contravention of orders, and that was exactly how it should be. She followed the soldier without a word and soon found herself at the rear of the camp. A small group awaited her, amongst them her two attackers.

It was injury, not disease, she had to deal with, and Ginny guessed that the soldiers had their commander to thank for their generally fine state of health. They probably lived better and certainly with greater circumspection under his auspices than in the days before war had wrenched them from their cottages and allotments where they would have kept one step ahead of extreme poverty. She dispensed medicine and advice with a brisk objectivity, receiving in exchange only blunt courtesy. All the while, her ears were strained for the sound of an officer's voice. They presumably ventured into the ranks on occasion, and there were quite enough people involved in this tangle as it was. But then Jed was with them, she comforted herself. He would surely do something to avert her discovery.

Half an hour later, she was back in the woods behind the tent, wondering if Alex would remark on such an inordi-nately long time spent on answering nature's call. To her relief, there was no sign of any of them as she emerged into the clearing. The water in her tent was now tepid, but nonetheless welcome for that, particularly since she had become somewhat overheated in her haste to get back.

Feeling clean, cool, and inordinately calm, Ginny eventu-ally stepped out into the sunshine and looked around for Jed and signs of breakfast. There was no immediate evidence of either, only the usual orderly bustle that characterized Colonel Marshall's brigade. The minute she emerged from the tent, two soldiers fell upon it, dismantling it, hoisting her baggage and bedroll onto broad shoulders, and marching off to the supply lines. She tripped over a guy rope, was nearly knocked off her feet by a soldier moving backward with one half of some unidentifiable burden, and felt a very familiar pair of arms steadying her.

"You're in the way, sweetheart." In spite of the endear-ment, Alex's voice was crisp. "Be a good girl, and go and sit over by those trees until we're finished."

"But I'm hungry," Ginny wailed disconsolately but with utter truth. It must have something to do with open-air living, but the prospect of going breakfastless made her feel utterly desperate.

Alex roared with laughter. "Poor little thing, we can't have that. Jed has your breakfast somewhere."

"Well, somewhere isn't good enough," she stated definitely. "Where will I find him?"

"Go and sit over there." Alex gave her a little push in the required direction. "He will find you."

Jed did indeed find her within minutes, handing her bread and bacon, and a mug of ale. "All well?" he asked tersely.

Ginny nodded, her mouth too full of bacon to reply verbally. She chewed, swallowed, then asked, "No one remarked on the length of my absence?"

"Nah—too busy, like I said," Jed answered.

"You'll tell me if I'm needed again?"

"Aye, mistress, I will that." He walked off, leaving Ginny to consume her breakfast and watch the activity in a degree of contentment. She would have to start looking for the red fox again when they halted for the night, and maybe, if she could make contact herself, she could discover some news of Edmund and Peter. They would have had to come this way, if they had made landfall safely. But until this evening, she could have an utterly clear conscience and deal with Alex in perfect harmony.

It was amazing how wrong one could be.

The morning's march took them through quiet country lanes and sleepy villages, but there was something about the quiet that set the hairs on Ginny's neck prickling. They saw no one, although occasionally there was a rustle from a ditch or behind a hedge. Ginny felt unseen eyes on them, and when she looked at Alex riding tensely beside her, she knew that he felt them also. At one point, he fell back and engaged in a low-voiced conversation with Major Bonham.

"What is it, Diccon?" Ginny turned to the aide-de-camp riding on her other side. "Something is wrong."

"We're passing through a Royalist stronghold," Diccon said. "The colonel thinks they might try an ambush. It would be foolish; we must outnumber them in strength and weapons, but a surprise attack could do some damage."

"Diccon," Alex came alongside with the major. "Major

177

Bonham and I are going to ride ahead to the top of the Hog's Back. We'll have a good view of the countryside from there. Have a care for Ginny; she is your responsibility."

"May we not ride with you?" Ginny asked boldly. "I am a fearsome responsibility for poor Diccon alone. With Cavaliers behind every hedge, I might well be tempted to make a dash for it into the fields."

"It is an impulse you would bitterly regret," Alex said evenly, with little indication that he appreciated her levity. "However, if you wish it, you may both ride with us."

Ginny winked mischievously at Diccon and received a shy smile. "You would much prefer to ride with the colonel, would you not?" she whispered.

"Infinitely," he agreed, "but I could not have asked."

"Naturally not. That is why I did," she said cheerfully.

The four of them cantered up the steep face of the Hog's Back, a long, high ridge cutting through the Surrey countryside and commanding extensive views on either side.

"What are we looking for?" Ginny asked when they reached the summit.

"I don't know until I see it," Alex replied. "They'll not be fool enough to show themselves obviously."

Ginny could see nothing but flat green fields stretching to the horizon on either side. There were a few dots of cows, an occasional spiral of smoke from farmhouse or cottage, crops were sparse, there being few men left at home to plant and tend them, but apart from that, everything looked quite normal.

"Where the devil are they?" Alex muttered.

"Why are you so sure they are there?" Ginny asked curiously. This was a new side of Alex, tense but with a controlled excitement about him, as if he was preparing himself to do something that he knew he did well, and that he loved to do. Was it the prospect of fighting, Ginny wondered with a mixture of awe and dread.

"Can you not sense them?" Alex replied. "I do not wish for a skirmish. I cannot afford to lose any men or have to slow down because of wounded."

That calculating pragmatism again. When he spoke like

that, Ginny wondered what it was about the man that she liked, let alone loved. She turned Jen aside and rode to the edge of the ridge, shading her eyes against the sun as she looked toward the horizon. The town of Guildford lay some ten miles ahead, the cathedral spire visible through the sun's haze. Guildford was garrisoned with Roundhead forces, so they had but a short march to accomplish across enemy territory.

"If you are afraid of an ambush, why do you not continue to Guildford along the Hog's Back? No one could take you unawares up here."

"True enough." Alex smiled at her. "Quite a tactician, aren't you? But it is a very long way round, and I prefer to go as the crow flies. I have to decide whether the risk outweighs the advantage. Let us go back now. I think it is safe enough to halt the march for a short rest period."

The brigade halted in a large field, hedged on all sides. A small stream, bordered with golden marigolds, flowed along one side, and Ginny took Jen to water her. Looking over the hedge into the neighboring field, she thought she saw something on the far side that gladdened her apothecary's heart. Unless she was much mistaken, there was a large clump of pennyroyal growing against the far hedge. She slipped from the mare's back, knotting the reins so Jen could graze without fear of catching a hoof, and looked around for someone to tell where she was going. There was no sign of Alex anywhere, but somebody had presumably been designated to keep an eye on her. Let them earn their keep, she decided, prompted by that fatal imp of mischief. Since she had only the most innocent purpose in mind, she could wander off with a clear conscience and see if anyone noticed.

There was a gap in the hedge, the other side of the stream. Ginny discarded her shoes and paddled through the deliciously cool water. She was halfway across the far field, quite exposed, when the first shots rang out behind her. She obeyed her first instinct, which was to fling herself down on the grass and bury her head in her arms, waiting for the worst. Nothing happened, and slowly she realized that the noise of shouting, interspersed with shots, was coming from the field where the brigade was taking its ease. Alex had miscalculated, and the ambush he had feared had taken place.

Lying in the middle of this field was not going to do anyone any good, she thought rapidly. She needed to take shelter, and clearly that was to be found by going forward, not back into the scene of battle. Crouching low, she ran to the side of the field where the hedge afforded some cover. Then she crept around, putting as much distance as she could between herself and the sound of fighting. Why was she not afraid? The thought came and went as she gained the far side and the patch of pennyroyal. Now was obviously not a good time for herb collecting, she decided with an amazing degree of wry humor; she would go through into the next field and wait in the shelter of the hedge until there was some indication that it was safe to go back. Not for one minute did it occur to her to doubt that Alex would make short work of this inconvenient attack.

Alex's initial thought was for Ginny when the first shot rang out. "Get Virginia to safety," he bellowed at Diccon, flinging himself onto Bucephalus. After that, he forgot about her in the business of sorting out what had happened and what was now happening. The black charger hurtled down the field, and at the sight the men of Colonel Marshall's brigade stopped the disorderly, confused milling about that made the snipers' job so easy and formed tight squares, two deep, under the shouted commands of their officers. A musket ball whined over the colonel's head, but apart from a muttered oath, he ignored it. His men were now returning the fire, although they could not see their attackers, who had crept up on them in the ditches behind the hedgerows.

They were being fired on from two sides, but the squares held steady. When the front line discharged their muskets, they changed places with the line behind, who fired while their fellows reloaded. Then the maneuver was repeated. It would take more than a handful of snipers to withstand this orderly attrition and the limitless supply of ammunition.

Eventually, there were no returning shots. "Casualties?"

Alex demanded harshly of Major Bonham.

"Two dead, sir. Three injured," the major said. "We were lucky. Do we go after them?"

Alex shook his head. "We can't take prisoners on this journey, Major." They both knew what the alternative was if they engaged with the enemy, and the major knew that Colonel Marshall generally avoided gratuitous killing. "We'll carry the dead with us. Have the wounded tended to, litters if necessary; then draw the men up in formation. The sooner we get out of here, the better."

Alex rode over to Lieutenant Maulfrey. "Where did you put Ginny, Diccon?"

Diccon looked stricken. "I thought you had found her . . ."

"Found her?" Alex exclaimed. "What the devil do you mean, 'found her'? I told you to get her to safety."

"But she wasn't here, sir. I couldn't see her anywhere — I thought . . . I thought that . . ."

Alex had gone the color of chalk. "You do not think, Lieutenant. You obey orders. I told you to ensure her safety. Are you telling me that when you could not find her immediately, you decided to forget that order and follow your own pursuits?" His voice was as soft and deadly as the hiss of a cobra, and Diccon Maulfrey began to wish he had never been born.

"Beggin' yer pardon, Colonel." Jed brought temporary salvation. "Her mare is still here, and I think as 'ow she went into the next field before the shooting started."

"You saw her?"

Jed nodded. "I was about to go after her. Then all the commotion started—"

Alex set Bucephalus at the stream and the hedge, the magnificent black sailing effortlessly over the obstacles. There was no knowing what trouble she was in. The fields were crawling with Royalists. Of course, it was always possible that that fact suited her very well. And while he was out looking for her, the brigade was losing precious minutes in idleness. Anger and fear waged a battle for supremacy, and when he saw her, crouched over a patch of flowers at the far end of the field, anger won without further contest. Then he caught the flicker of movement beyond the hedge in front of her, a glimmer of white, and his heart leaped into his throat. It might well suit Virginia Courtney to fall into the hands of the rebels, but it most definitely did not suit him that she should.

Ginny heard the pounding of hooves behind her, turned, her hands full of pennyroyal. The charger was bearing down upon her, those huge hooves seeming about to run her down. She heard the unmistakable sound of a sword being unsheathed at her back, as a figure pushed through the hedge. Then Bucephalus was upon her. Alex let go the reins momentarily, leaned far down, clinging with his knees as he caught Virginia under the arms and swung her up, turning his horse with the pressure of his knees the instant the man with the drawn sword struck. The blade whistled harmlessly an inch from the charger's flank, and Ginny, who had no idea what had happened, felt the breath leave her body as she landed face down across the saddle in front of Alex, and Bucephalus galloped unchecked across the field.

"Let me up!" she gasped, outraged, still ignorant of their narrow escape, and, unfortunately, totally unaware of the extent of Alex's fear-induced fury. She struggled to right herself, at considerable danger to life and limb.

"Keep still!" Alex hissed, increasing the pressure of his hand on the small of her back as he pushed her down again with lamentable lack of delicacy.

Ginny, unthinking in her rage at his rough treatment, sank her teeth into his calf. Alex bellowed and brought his riding crop down on her upturned rear in a forceful reflex. Ginny's mouth opened on a shocked yelp. "I'll never forgive you, never!"

"When it comes to forgiveness, Virginia Courtney, you are on very thin ice," Alex gritted. "How dare you go off like that? Every minute my men stand in that field, they are in danger, but you did not think of that, did you? Any more than you thought of your own."

"That is not true! What was I supposed to do when all the shooting—" Ginny gave up, the jolting hurt her ribs and her

182

hip bones, and she felt sick in her upside-down position. And none of this was as bad as the gradually increasing fear that Alex, in his present mood, was quite capable of riding up to the brigade with her slung across his saddle like a sack of potatoes.

Mercifully, the charger's headlong gallop slowed to a canter, then a walk as Alex drew back on the reins. "You can walk from here," he said, pulling Bucephalus to a halt. With his hands under her arms, he steadied her as she slid down, holding her for the moment before her feet touched ground. Then he let her go and nudged his mount forward. After a few paces, he looked over his shoulder to where she still stood, unmoving. "In the name of the good God, what does it take to get through to you? Will you come along!"

Shaken and jolted as she was, as if every bone in her body had been dislodged, Ginny did not know how she had the strength or the courage to resist him. But it came from somewhere, from the deep-seated conviction that no one had the right to treat her as Alex had just done. "I'll not walk at your stirrup, Colonel." Her voice was quiet and steady.

The gray eyes were huge, smoky in their intensity, her face very pale, but she held herself as proudly as ever as she stared him down. Alex exhaled slowly, rubbing his eyes with finger and thumb of his right hand. "Very well. Put your foot on mine." He stretched a hand down to her.

Ginny took the hand, placed her bare foot on the booted one in the stirrup and sprang upward, turning with an agile twist to land on the saddle in front of him.

"Where are your shoes?" Alex said, noticing for the first time that she was without them.

"I had to wade through the stream to get through the hedge. I left them by Jen."

"I suppose it's too much to ask what you were doing?"

"I was going to pick pennyroyal; then I heard the shooting. I hid in the ditch until it stopped; then—then, I thought it would be silly not to collect what I had gone for in the first place. You made me drop them," she added.

"One of us was about to be run through by a gentleman with a sword, in case you hadn't noticed," Alex pointed out

183

with more than a hint of sarcasm. "The entire area is infested with rebels."

"Not to *my* way of thinking," Ginny retorted imprudently. "It is rebels I am riding with."

"Do you want me to turn you over again?" Alex demanded, quite at the end of his patience.

"You do, and so help me I will kill you," Ginny declared fiercely.

Fortunately for them both, at this point they broke through the hedge into the field where the brigade was drawn up in marching formation, and the pointless exchange of threats could be dropped without further loss of face on either side.

Alex rode over to the line of officers, all of whom were looking anxious, but none more so than Diccon, who was standing at the heads of his own mount and Ginny's mare. Without dismounting, Alex lifted Ginny to the ground, saying curtly, "You had better find your shoes." In the same tone, he said to Diccon, "Report to me after tattoo, Lieutenant Maulfrey."

Ginny found her shoes where she had left them and allowed the crestfallen Diccon to assist her to mount. The brigade moved out in somber silence, pikes and halberds catching the rays of the mid-afternoon sun. Ginny edged closer to the aide-de-camp. "What has happened, Diccon?" she asked in a discreet undertone. "Why is the colonel vexed with you?"

"I could not find you," Diccon muttered disconsolately. "And now, I expect, I shall lose rank at the very least."

"But that is absurd," Ginny maintained. "It was not your fault I was in the other field. I will talk to him."

"No — no, please, you must not, Ginny. I beg you will do no such thing." Diccon stammered in his urgency, his face scarlet with embarrassment at the thought of her intercession. "I did not look for you because I assumed, when I could not find you immediately, that someone else had charge of you. Or at least," he added miserably, "that is what I wanted to think, because I wanted to join the battle."

"Yes, I can quite see that having charge of some troublesome female prisoner cannot hold a candle to the prospect of being shot at," Ginny said sardonically. Diccon reminded her vividly at this point of Edmund trying to give her the slip so he could go and hunt hare without a mere girl tagging along. However, it did not seem entirely just that Diccon should be penalized because she had been more than capable of looking after herself. Mind you, as an advocate, Ginny reflected wryly, she might do his cause with the colonel more harm than good in the present frigid climate.

They reached Guildford without further engagement, and as they neared the town, the atmosphere lightened. They would be housed tonight in the barracks, Diccon told Ginny, and everyone looked forward to the prospect of being with their own kind for a few hours. They would be able to bury the dead with appropriate ceremony, and there would be field surgeons to tend to the wounded. The officers would dine in headquarters, and there would be the opportunity to gather news and information, which was in short supply on the road.

And there would be precious little opportunity for Parliament's ward to go in search of the red fox, not from the confines of a Roundhead barracks. Ginny kept her own counsel as they rode through the narrow streets, past the sentries at the gates to the barracks and into the square.

"Alex! Good God, man, but you're a sight for sore eyes." This hearty greeting came from a rotund but very smart colonel, much more elaborately dressed than Alex, who hurried across the yard toward them. "Ye're on the way to London, I'll be bound."

"Aye, Jack. Cromwell's orders," Alex said, swinging down and clapping the other on the shoulder affectionately. "I'm hoping we're to join the march to Scotland. And you?"

The other shook his head with a grimace. "We're to stay put and mop up this damn Surrey uprising. Rebels are all over the countryside. Did you have any trouble?"

Alex told him in a few words. "We've need of a surgeon and a burial parade, Jack."

"Those you shall have," Jack boomed. "And a haunch of venison, a pint of fine brandy and — " he winked salaciously, "for entertainment, my friend, your choice amongst the daintiest, most willing little wenches you've ever come across!" He rubbed his hands together, his laughter rich with anticipation and the pleasure of providing such unimpeachable hospitality.

Ginny coughed pointedly. It wasn't that she objected to the tone of the conversation; she had not been bred a Puritan, but it seemed necessary to remind Alex of her presence since she could not imagine where she was to fit into his host's plans.

"I do beg your pardon." Alex turned back to her, and there was a glint of humor in the green-brown eyes that Ginny hoped boded well for a speedy reconciliation. "Mistress Courtney, allow me to present Colonel Redincoate. Jack, this is Mistress Virginia Courtney, daughter of John Redfern."

Colonel Redincoate bowed politely, but his look was both speculative and admiring when he turned back to Alex, who had little difficulty in reading his friend's mind. "Are there any women in the barracks, Jack? Not of the kind you have just mentioned," he added dryly, lifting Ginny down.

Jack shook his head. "None that'd be company for a lady, I fear. Ye're taking her to London?"

Alex nodded. "As ward of Parliament. It's a long story, Jack. What the devil are we to do with her here?"

Ginny began to twiddle her thumbs, staring into the middle distance, whistling aimlessly. The two men stopped their discussion and regarded the subject with a degree of chagrin. "I shall be perfectly content with my own company," she said, once she was sure she had their attention. "I would not wish to interfere with your — uh — entertainment. I quite understand how I might be a hindrance in the pursuance of such a licentious program. But I do realize, of course, that soldiers must have certain — "

"That'll do!" Alex broke in swiftly before those dulcet tones could continue on their present devastating path. "For the moment, you'll stay with me, where I can see you." He gave a series of orders to Major Bonham about the dispersal of the troops and the arrangements for the burial service to take place at evening parade. The officers were told to see to the men under their direct command, then make their own arrangements for accommodation with the help of Colonel Redincoate's officers.

"Now, Jack, you may lead me to that brandy," he said, clapping his hands together with brisk finality. "And we must see where we are to put Mistress Courtney for the night." He motioned to Ginny to go ahead of him into the low, gray stone building and with a shrug, she complied.

They were shown into a long, gloomy, sparsely furnished chamber where the stone walls seemed to retain the chill of winter. The promised brandy appeared opportunely. Several men were engaged in serious conversation around a long table in the middle of the room, and at Ginny's entrance their eyes widened. Colonel Redincoate performed introductions, although it was clear that Ginny's anomalous position was giving him some trouble. As a prisoner, she hardly came into the category of guest, but her birth and breeding dictated that she be treated with all the respect due to a lady. But then an all-male barracks was no place for a lady.

Ginny accepted brandy, deciding that the events of the afternoon, together with this present awkwardness, which she was not enjoying in the least, warranted the spirits. Then she settled herself in a corner of the room, as far away from everyone as possible, and hoped that Alex would do something about the situation quickly.

"We've not a spare chamber in the place, Alex," Jack was saying. "Can you not billet her in the town? There's not a bad inn just down the road. She can sup there quite decently and leave us to our own devices."

Alex shook his head. "She's a committed rebel, Jack, for all that she doesn't look as if butter would melt in her mouth. There's no knowing what she'd get up to."

Colonel Redincoate regarded Virginia with renewed interest. "What d'ye intend doing with her, if she's a traitor?"

"I'll let Cromwell decide," Alex prevaricated.

"Too pretty for the hangman," Jack stated. "Fine skin, too.

187

It'd be a pity to see—"

"Quite," Alex interrupted.

Jack looked at him in some surprise. "Ye're not usually so nice in your notions, Alex."

Alex shrugged. "She has courage. I've never enjoyed breaking the truly courageous. You know that, Jack."

"Aye." Redincoate drank deep. "So, what's to be done with her tonight?" He grinned. "I'll happily share my bed with her."

Alex winced, resisting the urge to wipe the lascivious grin off the other man's face. "You can share yours with me, old friend. We'll put the lady behind lock and key in my bed, safely away from any wandering hands."

"Yours as well, I take it?" Jack gave him a conspiratorial grin. The icy stare he received in return brought a dull flush to his already ruddy complexion. "No offense, Alex," he apologized hastily. "I forgot what a Puritan you are."

Thus it was that Ginny found herself ensconced in a small chamber with a narrow barred window, furnished with a cot, stool, lantern, and chamber pot. "When you go to bed," Alex said quietly, "I shall lock you in and keep the key—for your own safety, you understand."

"Why can I not lock myself in?" she asked, reasonably enough.

"Because you might decide to go in search of pennyroyal or camomile in the middle of the night," he informed her. "And, while I do not think you could get out of the barracks undetected, I cannot vouch for your safety if you go a-wandering."

"Are you going to be quite horrid to Diccon?" Ginny asked, taking the bull by the horns.

"That is nothing to do with you," Alex said sharply.

"I think it is," she responded sturdily. "Since it was my disappearance that caused the trouble in the first place."

"It is *nothing* to do with you," he reiterated. "It is a military matter, pure and simple. For reasons of his own, Diccon chose to interpret his orders in a manner that suited him. That, my dear Virginia, is a serious, chargeable offense. As Lieutenant Maulfrey is well aware."

"Pah, such nonsense," Ginny said dismissively. "Sometimes, I think you are all little boys, playing at soldiers." Alex's jaw dropped ludicrously, but she continued, "Diccon wanted to join the fighting, and when he couldn't find me, decided quite correctly that I must be quite safe, so he went off to wage war. Do not say you blame him for that. I am sure, in his position, you would have felt the same."

"I might have felt it, but I would not have *done* the same," Alex said.

Ginny regarded him through narrowed eyes. "Be honest," she said. "When you were twenty, desperate for your first taste of action — would you not have done the same? He did not disobey orders, after all, just — reinterpreted them."

"You've a fondness for that young man, have you not?"

Ginny smiled. "As have you. And Diccon worships you."

"He knows what to expect," Alex said, frowning.

"Then surprise him. If you express yourself with your customary — uh — eloquence, I am certain you will achieve your object every bit as successfully as if you reduce his rank."

Dropping the subject, Alex offered her his arm. "Come, it is time for the burial service. As a member of this brigade, you will wish to attend."

It was very strange, Ginny thought, accompanying him outside, but she did feel part of this company, and she did wish to attend a ceremony of such sorrowful importance. She would have liked to have tended the wounded herself, but there was only so much one could accomplish in one day.

At the end of the service, the atmosphere of relief was palpable as they all turned to go inside, to drown the tensions of the day, to put death back where it belonged, a barely hidden, accepted fact of life. Only Diccon continued to look strained, and as he followed his commanding officer into the barracks, after the bugle sounded dismissal, Ginny decided he resembled nothing so much as a man ascending the scaffold.

She positioned herself in the corridor, round the corner and out of earshot of the room that Alex had been allotted

189

for the transaction of brigade business. It seemed a very long time before Diccon came out of the room and closed the door gently behind him.

"What happened?" Ginny whispered, beckoning from around her corner.

Diccon looked startled for a moment, then came over to her. "I never want to go through anything like that again," he groaned, leaning against the wall and mopping his brow with a heartfelt sigh.

"But are you still a lieutenant?" Ginny demanded impatiently.

"Yes." He grinned faintly. "I don't know why, but I still have my rank—although I feel as if I've been flayed."

There was, indeed, only so much one could accomplish in one day, Ginny thought again, lying on her narrow cot that night. But she was not dissatisfied with the day's accomplishments. It would have been better, of course, if she had not lost her pennyroyal.

Chapter Eleven

"Whatever is happening?" Ginny, at the sound of raised voices, looked toward the gateway of the barrack square the following morning.

"It's the night patrol returning," Diccon informed her. "Looks like they had some success, too. Caught a few rebels for the hangman." As if in confirmation of this statement, a cheer went up in the yard where Colonel Marshall's brigade was assembling in preparation for departure.

The night patrol consisted of some twenty troopers. With them they had a half-dozen prisoners, bleeding, broken men with bound hands, who stumbled ahead of prodding pikes.

Ginny, in distress, turned her head away from the sight, wondering if one could ever become inured to such horrors. Then something caught at the corner of her vision. Slowly, her hand over her mouth, she looked at the group again. "Peter." She spoke his name in a whisper, then shouted it. "Peter!" Under the astonished eyes of the men in the yard, before Diccon could react, she hurtled across the cobbles and flung her arms around a bowed, tattered, almost unrecognizable Peter Ashley.

"Oh, what have they done to you?" she murmured, in an agonized whisper, brushing the long, disheveled Cavalier locks away from a deep gash in his forehead.

"What are you doing here, Ginny?" Peter spoke through swollen lips. "Go away; you cannot be seen with me."

191

"Eh, mistress!" A burly trooper with a brutal mouth, caught her roughly by the shoulder. "No talking with the prisoners."

"Take your hands off me!" Ginny whirled on him in icy fury, slapping at the offending hand as if it were a gnat. "Lout. I'll talk to whomever I please."

The trooper gave Peter a kick behind the knee, and he fell forward onto the cobbles, unable to protect himself with his bound wrists.

Ginny flung herself at the soldier, curses and epithets flowing from her mouth with all the fluency of a mariner. She had punched him in the stomach, landed a solid kick on his calf before two other troopers pulled her off him. She fought all three of them with the desperate energy of a tigress protecting her young, heedless of her own hurts as they struggled to hold her.

Diccon, at last freed of his shocked daze, started running toward the fracas just as Alex and Jack Redincoate, deep in conversation, appeared in the doorway of the building across the yard.

"What in heaven's name?" Alex exclaimed. Ginny was visible only as a blur of blue serge as the skirts of her riding habit whirled around her in the struggle, but her eloquence could be heard clear across the square. Alex, who could not begin to imagine what was happening, ran as if all the devils in hell were at his heels, easily overtaking his lieutenant. "Release her!" At the bellowed command, the three soldiers came automatically to attention, and Ginny taking instant advantage of her sudden freedom, kicked out at them viciously, before dropping to her knees beside the winded Peter, who was struggling to stand up without the use of his hands.

Alex recognized him immediately and at last saw the light. "Get up, Ginny. This is no place for you." Bending, he took her arm.

Ginny shook him off. "You're as bad as they are," she accused him disdainfully. "He is hurt, but you would leave him lying here, to be kicked like a cur in the gutter."

"For God's sake, Ginny," Peter mumbled. "Alex is right.

192

Leave me be."

"I will not." Putting her arm around his waist, she hauled him upright, staggering under his weight. "Oh, what have they done to you?" she said again, wiping at the blood on his face with her kerchief.

Alex stood for a moment irresolute. Ginny didn't seem to understand that Peter Ashley was a rebel prisoner, and there was nothing either of them could do to help him now. Gently, he took her arm and spoke calmly and quietly. "You must come away now, Ginny." As he spoke, two of the soldiers, recovered from the furious onslaught that had temporarily disabled them, pushed forward and seized the prisoner roughly, one on each side.

"Leave him alone!" Ginny yelled, flinging herself on them again. Alex grabbed her, and she turned on him, kicking and scratching. It was like having one of the Furies in his arms. In desperation, he lifted her off the ground, holding her at arm's length with difficulty because Virginia Courtney was no diminutive sprite, but the lack of alternatives lent extra strength.

Ginny saw Peter being dragged off, partly lifted by his captors so his toes brushed the ground, and her wild gyrations ceased abruptly. "They will hurt him," she moaned and, when Alex set her down, began to weep helplessly. Alex took her in his arms, cradling her head against his chest as she sobbed brokenly. Jack Redincoate scratched his head in puzzlement, Diccon moved awkwardly back to his horse, Major Bonham looked inscrutable, and everyone else in the crowded yard stared at the sight of Colonel Alexander Marshall of the New Model Army comforting a Royalist prisoner who had just launched a violent attack on three of Cromwell's troopers and then on himself.

"I must go to him," Ginny sobbed. "He is wounded, and they are going to kill him, aren't they?" She raised her head from his chest on this last question, her eyes, although wet with tears, full of condemnation.

Alex could not deny it because he would not lie to her. "You must let it go, sweeting," he said gently. "It is war; Peter Ashley knows that. There is nothing you can do for him now."

"No . . . no." She shook her head in vigorous denial as if to shake his words out of her mind. "*You* can do something for him. You can stop them killing him."

"I cannot," he said with flat finality. "Two of my men were killed yesterday, three others sore wounded, by Peter and his like. It is the fortunes of war, Ginny."

She just stood still, looking at him, the tears running unchecked down her cheeks. Alex prayed that she would never again look at him like that, accusing, condemning, then accepting with a dull, lifeless resignation. Her nose ran, and she sniffed ineffectually. Her kerchief was stained with Peter's blood, and when she brought it to her wet face, it left pink smears. "At least let me see him," she said.

"It will do no good." Unable to bear it any longer, he pulled out his own handkerchief and mopped her face clean of blood and tears.

"He is going to die," she said fiercely. "What harm can it do, if I talk with him? And how can you know it will do no good for him to see a friend for one last time? Once you and he were friends, does that stand for nothing now?"

"It will distress you," he said inadequately. "You can do nothing for him, and that will distress you."

"And am I not to decide what suffering I am prepared to bear for my friends? If you are afraid I plan some treachery, then you may come too." This last was thrown in scornful challenge, and Alex sighed wearily.

"That is not what I am afraid of."

"Well, then?" Her tears had dried, and she stood no longer in need of comfort. Once again the courageous rebel prepared to battle the conquerors in a just cause.

Colonel Redincoate, from his vantage point discreetly to one side, nodded thoughtfully. Seldom had he witnessed such an interesting scene. His old friend, it would seem, had waded into rather deep waters. Couldn't really blame him. The Cavalier was every bit as courageous as he had said, and quite magnificent with it. She would take some taming, though; and what the devil would Cromwell have to say about it? Redincoate tore himself from the contemplation of this fascinating question and went to his friend's aid.

He coughed to alert Alex of his presence. "I see no harm in it, Alex, if the lady wants a few minutes' speech with the prisoner. It had best be soon, though," he added delicately, hoping he wouldn't have to expand on that. The rebel prisoners would need to be drained of all information before they met their maker, and soon Peter Ashley would be incapable of coherent speech with a friend.

Alex's grim expression showed that he understood. All his instincts told him to take Ginny away from here, as fast as possible, so that the healing could begin and she could forget what she had seen and what she knew was to happen, but he knew he could not make that decision for her. She was too strong, with a fine-honed inner strength that would carry her through whatever she set her mind to. "Five minutes," he said. "Then we leave. We have delayed enough already." He made his voice deliberately brisk and businesslike. "Jack, will you take her?" Then he turned without looking at her and strode back to his brigade.

"This way, Mistress Courtney." Ginny followed Colonel Redincoate into the square building into which the prisoners and their escorts had disappeared. An eerie scream, more animal than human, came from somewhere, and Ginny came to a shuddering halt. The colonel swore vividly before muttering, "This is no place for a woman."

"I'm sure you've made them welcome in here before, Colonel," Ginny snapped pointedly, once more in control of herself. "I have difficulty believing you show more consideration for female prisoners than you do for their male counterparts."

Colonel Redincoate found himself feeling some degree of compassion for Alex Marshall. He showed her into a small, windowless, stone-walled chamber containing only a stool. "If you will wait her, mistress, I will have the prisoner brought to you."

In a few minutes, the sound of shuffling feet came from outside; then the heavy door creaked open, and Peter Ashley came painfully inside and collapsed against the wall as the door slammed shut behind him. Ginny took the two paces necessary to reach him and helped him onto the stool. The tears were in her eyes again, but for his sake she must hold them back.

"This is madness, Ginny. Whatever can you be thinking of?" Peter protested, but he held her hands in a painful grip.

"I only have five minutes," she said, returning the grip. "Is there anything I can do for you? Any messages?"

"There is so much to regret," Peter said, as if in answer to her question. "So much to regret when you know you no longer have the possibility of changing things. I did not propose to Sally Turnham because I thought the war would be soon over, and I wanted to be able to fight it without thoughts of a wife at home. Tell her, will you, Ginny, that I died thinking of her, and regretting? My family, too, tell them . . . Oh," he sighed, "tell them whatever you think it will please them to hear."

"What of Edmund?" Ginny asked in a whisper the question that had been uppermost in her mind since she had first seen Peter. It seemed callous to ask him of someone else, when he was facing the ultimate loneliness, but she could not help herself.

"Please God, he is safe." Peter coughed and clutched his ribs with a grimace. "Whoresons!" he said bitterly. "They know where to put their boots. This war has made beasts of us all, Ginny. If it is not over soon, there will be no hope left for civilization." Ginny put her arms around him and held him, unable to say anything, since there was no comfort to offer. "Edmund went to aid the forces in Kent," Peter resumed with a visible effort that brought a sheen of sweat to his already ghastly complexion. "His wound healed well."

Ginny told him swiftly and in a whisper of her audience with the king, of his message that she carried, and Peter smiled weakly. "It is good to know that we do not die in vain," he said, then spoke with sudden urgency. "Do you continue to try to deliver your message?"

"I will continue to try," she said. "There is something you wish of me?"

Peter breathed shallowly for a moment, then said, "If you speak with the red fox — it is the code name, you under-

196

stand, for all who act as liaison between the people and our forces." Ginny nodded, she had already deduced that. "If you speak with him, tell him of the capture of the blue band, warn him that it is likely that by nightfall the positions of the others will be known." His face twisted in an ugly grin. "We can swear to hold out, but no one is fool enough to believe it."

Ginny shuddered but said nothing, merely gripped his hand, promising steadily, "I will pass the message without fail, Peter. Tonight, if it is humanly possible."

"Good." He managed a wan smile. "You should have been born a boy, Ginny. Edmund always said so." Then the smile faded. "But have a care. Those whom we once called traitors have no mercy for those whom *they* call traitors."

The door banged back on its hinges, and two troopers stood there. "Don't touch him!" Ginny said as they moved toward Peter. "Let him get up on his own. He's not going to run from you; you've made quite sure he can barely walk with your cowardly—"

"Hush, Ginny," Peter remonstrated, pulling himself up against the wall. She went to kiss him, holding him with all the power of loving friendship. "Pray that I make a good death, Ginny," he said, finally putting her from him. "It is all that is left for me now." Then, with the last dregs of strength, he walked unaided from the room.

Ginny stood in the cold, death-ridden room, blinded by tears, her soul a deep well of grief and horror. Jack Redincoate murmured something and motioned to the door. She marched past him, out into the yard, and over to the brigade where Alex and his officers stood at their mounts, waiting for her. "May God damn you all!" she said in ringing tones that included every man in the yard. "There is no cause on earth that can justify such carnage." Springing unaided onto Jen's back, she wheeled the mare and galloped toward the gate.

"Let her pass," Alex called to the sentries who had moved to bar her passage. "Follow her, Diccon, but just keep her in sight." The aide-de-camp mounted and went after her. Alex looked around the circle of silent men. "May God forgive us all," he said quietly, then mounted Bucephalus, and gave the order to move out.

Ginny galloped through the narrow streets of Guildford ford, having no idea of her direction and heedless of the passers-by who cowered against the walls of buildings at her impetuous passage. Diccon followed, rather more sedately, but fast enough to keep her in sight, wondering what he was supposed to do when she decided to stop—if she decided to stop. Would she come back with him willingly? Or should he just stay with her until the colonel came to his rescue?'

Ginny gradually became aware that she was being followed, as the wild grief and anger that had prompted her flight dissipated, as it had to, and she became aware of the world again. She reined in Jen, noticing with a surge of guilt the mare's wet neck, the flecks of foam around the bit, her heaving flanks. "Oh, Jen, I'm sorry," she whispered, leaning over to stroke her neck. The horse following slowed to a walk, and Ginny looked over her shoulder to where Diccon rode, at a careful thirty paces behind, his face anxious and solemn. "I am poor company, Diccon," she called. "But if you wish to come up with me, I'll not bite your head off."

Diccon trotted up, a look of transparent relief on his open countenance. "I think we should go back to the brigade—when you're ready to, that is."

"You're the colonel's watchdog, are you?" Ginny observed in a tone that seemed to indicate it didn't much matter one way or the other. "Well, I do not wish to get you into trouble again, so if you have been told to bring me back, then we had better go."

Diccon looked hurt. "The colonel did not say I was to bring you back. I was just to keep you in sight. If you do not wish to turn round, we will not do so."

"And where think you this road will lead us?" Ginny gave a short laugh. "To the end of the rainbow, mayhap. There was a time when one believed in such things—nursery comfort! But this is the world of grown men, isn't it, Diccon? A world where evil in the name of justice stalks the land; where men are beaten and broken and murdered because they hold a different opinion."

Diccon was silent, wishing fervently that he had not been given this task. He knew not how to answer her, how to comfort her. That was something for the colonel to do, and it was clear, after this morning, that it was something the colonel knew how to do. He had been puzzled by several obscure remarks made in the last day or so by Major Bonham and several of the other, higher ranking officers. Those remarks now made sense. The relationship between his colonel and Mistress Courtney was not as straightforward as Diccon had thought.

"Come, Diccon. It is time to return to the world." Ginny took pity on her companion. "I will pose you no more unanswerable questions. You know where your duty lies, do you not? If you do not ask the questions of yourself, then you cannot possibly be expected to be able to answer them for others." She turned Jen in the hedge-bordered lane, where the peaceful everyday scents of honeysuckle and roses mingled in the warm morning air, belying the presence of man's ugliness. Diccon, feeling as if he had in some way been reproved for some fault he did not know he had, followed her lead, and they rode in somber silence back into the town, where they picked up the London road and soon came up with the brigade. They rode past the ranks of marching men until they reached the front lines. Ginny was instantly conscious of the way the officers avoided her eye, and she remembered how she had cursed them in the barrack square, just as the whole, bitterly violent, degrading scene with the troopers returned in devastating clarity.

But she would not cringe or be ashamed of an outburst that had been so thoroughly justified. What she did not realize was that every one of them was fighting his own embarrassment, his own, suddenly awakened unease at his previously unquestioned participation in the events, brutal though they were, of this war.

Only Alex correctly interpreted both sides of this mute confrontation. They would be angry with Ginny for what she had made them see, and she would use her own anger, still a vibrant force, although thankfully controlled now, to defend herself. He himself felt only sorrow, for Peter and for

199

Ginny, and a vague practical irritation at the unfortunate quirk of fate that had brought Peter Ashley into the Guildford barracks this morning. Ginny had come face to face with the personal consequences of this war often enough already; she had not needed to touch it so closely for the horror to be brought home to her. War was his business, and Alex had long ago accepted the dark side of the coin. But he would have done anything to have protected Ginny from the knowledge so brutally forced upon her by the events of the morning; only there had been nothing to be done.

Throughout the day, Ginny rode slightly apart, and no one attempted to intrude on her self-imposed isolation. When they halted for the noon break, she refused all offers of food and drink with a mute headshake and went to sit on a grassy bank, where she picked daisies, idly threading them into the floral necklaces, crowns, and bracelets of childhood. It was a peaceful, almost restorative activity, occupying her hands and allowing her mind free reign. Renewed determination and icy purpose had replaced the grief and the rage. It was now imperative that she prevent others from falling into the hands of the enemy as a result of the capture of Peter and his fellows. If she continued to behave shocked and grief-stricken, it was possible that Alex's guard would be a little less rigorous. She certainly had an excuse for being left alone when they stopped for the night, and since no one appeared in the least inclined to disturb her solitude at the moment, it seemed hopeful that such consideration would continue for as long as she chose. She was aware of Alex's eyes on her much of the time, but the look was one of compassionate understanding, not the watchful scrutiny of captor for prisoner.

She felt no guilt at the prospect of this elaborate deceit, at allowing Alex to worry over her, at taking advantage of the lover's concern when it came to defeating the enemy in the person of that lover. A coldness had entered her soul when she had seen and heard Alex's refusal to save Peter. His reason had been, "It is war." Very well, then. So be it. She would manipulate every string she had to her bow without even the slightest pang that had afflicted her in the past.

Events conspired in Ginny's favor, and with the same cool detachment, she accepted the advantage fate had dealt her as if it were her due.

They stopped earlier than usual for the night in the village of Wimbledon, which boasted a substantial inn. Alex had debated whether to continue marching the last fifteen miles into London, but they would arrive late, and there was no knowing what accommodations could be found at that hour. Ginny was looking so pale and wan and dispirited, so much in need of featherbed comfort, hot baths, and good food, that he decided the delay was necessary. They would reach the city by noon tomorrow.

Ginny showed no reaction at all when they halted, merely dismounted and stood idly by Jen, staring into space while Alex talked with the innkeeper. In fact, her mind was racing. In a village of this size, she was bound to find those whom she sought.

"Ginny." Alex came over to her, his voice gentle. "You need to rest before dinner. I have managed to arrange a room of your own for tonight."

"My thanks," she said dully, "but I am not hungry."

"You have not eaten since early this morning," he reminded her. "If you wish for a tray in your chamber, we shall all respect your need to be alone."

She acquiesced with a tiny shrug and allowed herself to be escorted to a ground-floor chamber at the back of the inn, with a low window overlooking the garden. "My daughter's chamber, mistress," the innkeeper told her. "She'll bed with the maids tonight."

"Pray thank her for the sacrifice," Ginny said, smiling with an effort. "I would not normally ask it—"

"It is nothing at all. Pray do not mention it," the landlord said hastily. The poor young woman looked more dead than alive, as he told his wife in the kitchen a few minutes later. There was no knowing how those soldiers had been treating her, although the colonel was showing some concern for her well-being and had insisted that she was to be attended upon most scrupulously.

Ginny lay down on the bed to think how best she was to

201

accomplish her self-imposed task. A tentative knock at the door brought a young girl bearing a posset that, she informed Ginny, her mother had made up for the mistress, hoping it would give her strength. "I wish to talk with the red fox," Ginny said directly. "Do you know how I may do so?"

The girl almost dropped the cup, her eyes widening as she looked nervously at the half-open door behind her. "I don't know, I'm sure," she stammered. "We keep our noses out of trouble, mistress — so close as we are to London."

"Yes, I understand," Ginny said instantly. "I will not cause you trouble. If you cannot answer me, then I must find someone who can."

The girl bobbed a curtsy and left. Ginny sipped the posset thoughtfully. The red fox was obviously known in these parts; the girl had shown no puzzlement at what, to an innocent, would have been an odd statement. It was possible, of course, that the inn was owned by fervent supporters of Parliament, in which case Alex would know of her compromising question forthwith. But it would take rack and thumbscrew to pry anything else out of her, Ginny was quietly resolved. If the inn's inhabitants were simply neutral and genuinely afraid of trouble, then she had neither lost nor gained. If they were Royalists, she had made the first approach. For the moment, she could only wait.

A sudden commotion outside her door brought her off the bed. Voices and booted feet, spurs jangling under hasty strides, sounded. She heard an order to "saddle up," then Alex saying, "Diccon, if you wish for action, you may have it. We leave in five minutes." There was a loud rap on her door, and Ginny leaped back on the bed, bidding entrance in a plaintive voice.

"It is the very devil," Alex said without preamble. "I have to leave you here until morning."

"Why? Where do you go?" Ginny forgot to sound weak for a minute at the thought of what this could mean.

"Urgent business for Parliament," he said, uninformatively. "A patrol that I must lead. You will be quite safe here. Major Bonham will be in command in my absence,

202

and I shall leave three other officers with him. You would prefer to remain in your chamber anyway, I daresay?"

"Have I not said so?" Ginny returned, falling back on the pillows. "I do not wish to be entertained, so you may leave me to my own devices with a good conscience."

Alex frowned and came over to the bed. "I do not like to leave you when you are unhappy, chicken. And I do not like to feel that you hate me."

Ginny turned her head away, and he caught her chin, bringing her face round toward him again. "Do you hate me, sweetheart?"

"I hate what you do," she said in the low voice of truth. "And at the moment I am unable to separate what you do from what you are."

He sighed and straightened, releasing her chin. "It is to be expected, of course, but somehow it does not make it any easier. We will talk about it at length when we reach London, where we will have to come to some decisions, you and I." He left her then, making no attempt to kiss her in farewell, and Ginny felt a stab of desolation, then fear. What was his mission this night? Would he be in danger? Would he return whole in the morning?

They were not questions to be dwelt upon. What was important, was that she was alone with only the inscrutable Major Bonham to contend with. He would have orders to guard her, of course, but if even Alex had not seen through her act, she had little to fear from others. She would not be disturbed, maybe a check at bedtime, but that was all, and her chamber window opened directly onto the garden.

She remained where she was, listening to the bustle of departure, then the sudden silence. Major Bonham and Ensign Bryant were talking in the garden, outside her window — something about the disposition of sentries at the camp. Nothing was said about guards at the inn. Presumably they thought their own presence obviated such a necessity. The innkeeper called them in for dinner, and Ginny waited to see whether anything of interest would arrive with her own meal.

It was brought to her by an anxious-looking woman with

wispy brown hair escaping from her cap, faded blue eyes, and a thin, stooped frame. The resemblance to the innkeeper's daughter was unmistakable, however.

"Hetty said you wish to meet with someone," she whispered, placing a tray on the gate-legged table by the hearth. "We don't know anything, but if you go to the Black Cock at the end of the village, there may be someone who can help you."

"What time?" Ginny asked as her reluctant informant scuttled for the door.

"Any time after dark and before dawn," she was told. Then the door opened and closed.

Ginny remembered that they had passed the tavern on the way into the village. An uninviting-looking place, with flaking plaster, disheveled thatch, and glassless windows. A haven for rogues and vagabonds most like — and rebels, too. These days, there was little to choose between any of the groups who lived outside Parliament's law.

With excitement and a plan came hunger. The tray contained broth, a rather scrawny chicken leg, and boiled potatoes. Not exactly a feast, but beggers were hardly in a position to be choosers, and Ginny ate purposefully, if not with enthusiasm. The ale at least was tolerable and fortunately not as strong as the October ale in Newbury.

Having completed her meal, Ginny decided to show herself to the major and anyone else who might be interested in knowing that their charge was as monosyllabic and enfeebled as she had been all day, and that she was on her way to an early bed. A last visit to the privy would provide an unimpeachable reason for her appearance.

The major and his companions were smoking an after-dinner pipe in the garden when Parliament's ward passed them on her way to the outhouse. She acknowledged their distinctly awkward greeting with a small curtsy and a mumble that they could interpret how they pleased. On her return, she bade them a low-voiced good-night, which was politely given back to her. On regaining her chamber, she wasted no time in extinguishing her candle, knowing that they would see the sudden darkness in the window and draw the conclusion that their charge was innocently abed, nursing her spiritual wounds.

For two hours, Ginny lay in darkness, her ears straining for the slightest sound, her mind reaching to interpret every creak and squeak. At last, she was convinced that all she could hear were the night noises of the settling house. Remembering a trick she and Edmund had employed as children when they had wanted to go and watch badgers in the moonlight, Ginny pushed the bolster down the middle of the bed, bundling up her shift into a headlike shape on the pillow, drawing the sheet over it. It had satisfied the cursory checks of their nurse, so maybe it would work with soldiers, who, if they did check, would hopefully feel so awkward about intruding on her in the first place that they would not examine too closely. She slipped a dark, hooded cloak over her habit. She would swelter in the warm night, but it hid the white collar that might show up in the dark, and the hood covered the chestnut hair that could gleam inconveniently in the moonlight. The window had a broad sill, inside and out, and it was an easy matter to swing herself through and land soundlessly on the soft earth of the flowerbed beneath.

On her trip to the privy, she had noticed a gate leading out of the garden into the lane behind the inn. Would it be guarded? Ginny was almost positive that there would be a sentry posted at the front of the inn, as much for general security reasons as to keep her within doors. She slipped down the path between the fragrant ranks of wallflowers, came to the low gate, and paused. For as long as she remained in the garden, she could be accused of nothing. The minute she put her hand on the latch of the gate, she was engaged in subversion. The only sound, apart from her own breathing, was the persistent, willful, trilling song of a blackbird denying that it was night. No sentry stood with pike and halberd in the lane outside the garden gate. Closing her mind to the possibility of discovery, Ginny raised the latch and stepped outside her loosely guarded prison.

Clinging to the shadows of the ivy-clad stone wall, she ran

in the direction of the main village street. If there was a guard outside the inn, he would be facing that main street, but in order to discover a route to the Black Cock that would circumvent the street, she had to be able to pinpoint the tavern. There had been little rain in recent weeks, and the lane was fortunately dry, the muddy tracks of horses and oxen caked in hard, ridged peaks. The only light came from the quarter moon as the village of Wimbledon slept.

At the end of the lane, Ginny peered around the corner into the wider thoroughfare. The inn was on her right and, as she had suspected, a sentry stood at ease in front of the door. The Black Cock was to her left, at the far end of the village. She would not have to go past the sentry, but any unusual movement in this sleeping village would attract his attention. It would be safer to make her way through the back gardens of the cottages fronting the main street. Of course, her chances of setting every village dog in full cry were then dangerously high.

Chapter Twelve

The cottage gardens were separated by low stone walls, which presented little difficulty, although moving with stealth and in silence was not easy as Ginny's skirts became snagged on bushes and the sharp thorns of climbing roses. Once or twice, a dog began barking furiously, and she crouched in a shadow, hardly daring to breathe. A voice bellowed, something crashed, the dog yelped, and then there was silence again.

It took her about ten minutes to reach the garden at the back of the Black Cock, and once there, Ginny stood still in the darkness; having attained her initial goal, she was now not at all sure how to proceed. The tavern was a dark shape, crouching like some malevolent beast in the middle of an overgrown garden where the dank smells of damp earth, cess pit, and fermenting hops mingled noisomely. No light showed from any of the glassless windows, but the innkeeper's wife had said Ginny would find whom she sought between dusk and dawn, so presumably someone was awake to respond to a knock.

Suppose it was a trap, suppose this was nothing more than the den of thieves it appeared to be? Suppose those at the inn had good reason to deliver an unwary, innocent-seeming young woman into the hands of rapists . . . murderers . . . kidnappers? She was being utterly foolish. She had absolutely nothing to offer anyone with evil intent — except her body, a hollow voice reminded her. Ginny screwed her courage to the sticking post and boldly approached the low building where a heavy door was set into the stone wall. Her knock seemed to resound in the still night, and she shrank instinctively against the wall. Nothing happened. There was no sound from within. She stepped back and looked up at the windows. They were all tiny and set well above ground level, presumably to permit some light while providing only minimum access to inclement weather. She knocked again, more loudly this time, and rattled the latch. The door latch moved under her hand, and the door swung inward onto a pitch-dark passageway.

Her heart seemed to lodge in her throat, her hands to quiver with apprehension as she contemplated the unyielding blackness. Then the image of Peter sprang before her eyes, Peter and those others who would now be dead in Guildford barracks. Ginny stepped into the passage, but she could not bring herself to close the door behind her, shutting her into the unknown dark.

"Sykes, is that you?" A quavery voice cut the silence; a door cracked open at the end of the corridor, showing the faint gleam of candlelight.

"No . . . no, it is me," Ginny whispered ridiculously through her dry throat and parched lips.

"Who the devil?" Someone pushed past the owner of the quavery voice and came into the passage, holding a candle high. "A maid!" He gave a short laugh. "Close the door behind you, missy. We don't want any more uninvited visitors."

"I am come to speak with the red fox," Ginny said, the words coming out in a panicky rush. "They told me at the Hand and Shears that I might find him here between dusk and dawn."

"Come here, and let's get a good look at you," another voice, more cultured than the last, ordered from behind the candle bearer.

Ginny closed the door behind her, then stepped forward, some of her fear dissipated by the knowledge that the red fox was certainly familiar to these folk. She found herself in a small room that would be warm and snug in winter, but in the heat of summer and lit by tallow candles was oppressive. There were four men, an ancient presumably of the quavery voice, the large barrel-chested candle bearer, and a slim figure simply dressed but with the bearing and manners of a nobleman, and the fourth sat by the hearth, twisting the stem of a pewter goblet between his fingers, and whose long hair denoted the Cavalier.

"Who seeks the red fox?" The man with the cultured voice asked, beckoning her into the candlelight.

"I am Virginia Courtney, sir," she said, deciding simplicity was the best approach. "Daughter of John Redfern of the Isle of Wight, who died at Naseby."

"Have some wine, John Redfern's daughter," the man by the hearth spoke for the first time, stretching over to a table, filling another goblet from the flagon. "I drank with your father before his death. Let us drink to King Charles."

The speaker had already had more than enough, Ginny decided, judging by the slurred voice and the rather glazed eyes, but she accepted the goblet with a small automatic curtsy. "Can you direct me to the red fox, sirs? I have two messages of vital importance."

"How do you come to Wimbledon?" the burly one demanded, his eyes suspicious in spite of her introduction.

"With Parliament's army," she replied, hearing the sharp intake of breath. "There is a brigade quartered in the village, as you must know. I travel with them."

"Pray continue," the third speaker requested, his voice dry in the sudden silence. "I am certain there is more to be explained."

Ginny told them briefly of her history and position as ward of Parliament. "Traveling under Parliament's protection has enabled me to pass on the king's message in several places," she finished. "But I have a message of life and death to impart now. It is imperative that I speak with the red fox without delay. Every moment wasted could bring death."

"How can we be sure that you do not play a double game?" the drinker asked. The question was greeted with a rumble of agreement from the burly one.

"I bear the king's seal," she said simply, drawing the parchment from her pocket.

A reverent hush fell in the room, and it was the quality of the quiet that finally reassured Ginny that she was amongst friends. Only the king's most loyal subjects would react to his hand in such a manner. But there was one last question for her. "How have you managed to evade Parliament's guard to come here this night?"

"The colonel left on a patrol with most of his officers. Those who remain at the inn do not know me very well." She smiled. "They think that I am abed, and, indeed, I hope to be so before my absence is discovered."

"You will not then make your escape, having come this far?"

"Where would I go?" Ginny asked with absolute truth. "Besides, the colonel would leave no stone unturned to find me, and who knows what else he might turn up in the search? I'll not be responsible for reprisals, sirs."

They all nodded in matter-of-fact agreement. "So, this message of life and death, mistress? You may give it safely to all in this room and be assured it will reach the right ears."

Ginny told them of the events at Guildford, of her talk with Peter, of his message that the blue band had been captured, and that by nightfall it was likely that all the information they had had would be possessed by their interrogators. The news was received in somber silence.

"I will send runners." The slim, cultured man spoke at last. "If they leave immediately, they may be able to reach the others before the Roundheads get to them." He turned to Ginny. "We owe you a debt, mistress."

Ginny shook her head. "No, sir, no debt. I did my duty as

210

you will do yours, as . . ." Her voice faltered. "As Peter Ashley has done his." The man by the hearth crossed himself, murmured a prayer. "Do you have news of one Edmund Verney?" Ginny asked. "He is my cousin. Peter said he thought he had gone into Kent, but he did not know if he was safe."

"He passed through here two days ago," the ancient spoke, his voice firmer. "He was in good health and spirits, and we have not heard of his capture."

"Then the news is as good as I could have expected," said Ginny, putting her goblet on the table. "I must try to make my way back to the inn undetected, for your sakes as much as for mine. Is there anything further you would have me do?"

"You go to London?" the drinker asked.

"Yes," agreed Ginny. "After that, I do not know. Colonel Marshall is hoping to march with Cromwell to Scotland, but I do not know what plans will be made for me."

"There is nothing you can do in London; the city is all for Parliament. Your task is done, I think."

Ginny shrugged. "I will keep my eyes and ears open, nevertheless, and see what opportunities arise. Should you, perchance, come up with Edmund Verney, tell him that he is in my thoughts, and I pray for his safety."

She left then, retracing her steps through the back gardens, aided this time by a degree of familiarity and by the faintest lightening in the sky, the lightening of the false dawn. She had been gone perhaps three hours in all, and there were no indications of any disturbance in the village, of any changes in the situation that she had left, as she slipped thankfully through the garden gate of the Hand and Shears. The inn was still in darkness, the window of her ground-floor chamber still open, just as she had left it.

Ginny hitched herself up onto the broad window sill, swung her legs through into the dark room, jumped down just as a flint scraped on tinder and the darkness lifted.

She spun round like a top toward the door. Alex sat in the only chair in the room, leaning back negligently, his riding

211

crop across his knees, sword still at his waist, regarding her quizzically.

"Where have you been, my little rebel?"

Ginny thought faster than she had ever thought before. The lie must approximate the truth if it was to convince him. There was no innocent explanation she could come up with, like an urgent need for the outhouse in the middle of the night, since she had no idea how long he had been back. But he knew nothing of her role as messenger, and there was no reason why he should guess it. He would not, therefore, be able to ask the right questions, and thus, he could not force the truth from her as he had done that last time.

"I did not expect you back until morning," she said, unfastening her cloak as if this meeting were the most ordinary circumstance in the world.

Alex smiled. "That is rather obvious, my dear Ginny. We came across those we sought rather more quickly than I had dared to expect. I returned here in the hopes of snatching a couple of hours' sleep. A false hope as it turned out. Where have you been?"

"In the village," replied Ginny with an assumption of nonchalance.

Alex frowned and began to play with the thong of his riding whip with a curious sort of deliberation. "Please go on," he requested politely.

Ginny found her eyes riveting on the play of those long fingers as they stroked the plaited leather on his knee. Unease crept up the back of her neck, dispelling the moment of bravado. Did she really think he could not — would not force the truth from her?

"I went in search of news of Edmund," she told him. Alex nodded and waited, looking at her while his hands continued their purposeful fiddling. Ginny swallowed. "Peter told me . . ." She stopped, hoping to convince Alex by her hesitation and obvious reluctance that Peter's information about Edmund had been his most important communication.

"What did Peter tell you?" he prompted gently, tapping the crop in the palm of his hand.

"That . . . that Edmund . . . Oh, what good will it do to tell you?" she exclaimed with convincing desperation. "There is nothing you can do with the information."

"I will be the judge of that," he replied. "Now, hurry up. I would like to get some sleep this night." The leather made a soft, rhythmic slapping noise against his hand.

Ginny bit her lip. "Are you intending to use that?" she asked somewhat shakily, unable to bear the suspense a moment longer.

"This?" Alex said with almost credible astonishment, staring at the whip on his lap. "On you? Good God, no. Whatever could have given you that idea?"

"I cannot imagine," Ginny said, turning away from him now that the deadly spell of that menacing little game had been broken.

"You should know by now that my methods are a little more subtle," he said softly. "Not that it isn't a favorite instrument of torture," he added, as if imparting some fascinating piece of information. "In the right hands, it can be most effective. If one does not break the skin, one can prolong the agony indefinitely—"

"Stop it!" she exploded, knowing that he was reminding her of her own vulnerability, of her need for his protection from those who would use her with whatever cruelty took their fancies. His methods were indeed subtle, she reflected with bitter self-knowledge. Just with that little game, without even getting out his chair, he had weakened her.

"Peter said that Edmund had gone . . ." She stopped again, struggling visibly with herself, hoping he would be convinced of her overpowering reluctance to tell him. "Why must I betray him again?" Alex didn't answer her, and she said in a low, defeated whisper. "Edmund has gone into Kent to aid the forces there. Peter did not know if he was safe, but he said he would have passed this way. I thought that maybe there would be someone in the village who might give me

213

news of him."

"Where did you go to find this news?"

Some blessed instinct told her to tell the truth. "The Black Cock," she whispered.

There was a short silence; then Alex said, "I congratulate you, Virginia. Had you lied to me then, you would be in much deeper waters than you are now."

"How did you know that was where I would go?" She stared at him in a fearful kind of wonder. He seemed always to be a step ahead.

Alex smiled. "The Black Cock's reputation is well known in these parts. It harbored fugitives from the law long before this damned war. If a fleeing Royalist passed through Wimbledon, they would know of it in the Black Cock. Who told you to go there?"

"Peter," Ginny lied. "He said if we were to pass through Wimbledon, then . . ." Again she stopped, but this time out of the knowledge that expanding a lie tended to increase the risk of exposure.

"What news did you hear?"

"Why must I tell you?" she asked again. "It is old news. What good can it do you to hear it?"

"You know why you must tell me, little rebel. Just as you know you must pay the penalty for this night's work. In this, we are enemies, and while I acknowledge you have won a victory, I must minimize the consequences of that victory."

It was true, and she could not deny it. While Alex did not know the extent of her victory, she would come out of this triumphant, whatever penalty he decided to exact.

"Edmund did pass through several days ago. He was well and in good spirits. They have not heard tell of his capture since." She employed almost exactly the words used by the old man in the tavern, knowing that Alex would recognize the verisimilitude. Would he be satisfied?

She felt nauseated by the tension of the next seconds, while he sat still, examining her through narrowed eyes. Then, very slowly, he nodded. "You played a clever game

214

today, Ginny. I believed in your pain."

"And do you not think I felt it?" she demanded, suddenly enraged at the implication that Peter's agony had not really touched her.

"Oh, yes, I know you felt it. I did not realize, though, that you were capable of using it," he said briskly. "I will know better another time. I had thought I knew not to underestimate you, but we all pay for our vanities." Alex stood up. "It is time you were in bed."

"What are you going to do?" she asked, attempting to mask her apprehension.

"Had this just been between the two of us, I would have done nothing except watch you in future like a hawk," he told her. "Unfortunately, the entire brigade is aware by now of your little escapade, and you cannot be seen to go scot-free. Major Bonham, as your might imagine, is more than a little chagrinned. He was with me, you see, when I decided to check on you. The bolster is an old trick, Ginny, but I grant that in the dark it might have fooled someone who did not know the shape of you." A glint of laughter showed momentarily in the green-brown eyes. "The major insisted on sending a search party into the fields, which I allowed him to do to salve his conscience, although I knew you would be back when you had completed your business."

"How could you be so sure?"

"Because you could no more leave me than I could allow you to do so," he said simply. "We are tied by a Gordian knot, you and I. Get into bed now. Reveille is in two hours. I wish to reach London by noon."

Alex showed no inclination to leave the room, and Ginny realized that he was going to see her into bed quite literally. She felt strangely peculiar undressing in front of him as he watched with neutral, objective eyes that were a far cry from the sensuous eyes of the lover. Not that she had the energy for even the smallest spark herself, but it was a little galling to climb into bed and receive an almost fraternal kiss on the forehead. As he left the room, he said, "There is now a

215

sentry posted outside your window, should you make the mistake of trying another unorthodox departure."

Ginny muttered something childishly rude in response, and Alex chuckled, closing the door softly. The instant before she fell into a deep dreamless sleep, Ginny realized that she still did not know what penalty she would have to pay in the morning, but she did know that whatever it was she would bear it willingly, because she had won, hands down. A hapless prisoner, she had duped Parliament's forces, had acted as King Charles's messenger, had been instrumental in ensuring that any confession forced from Peter would have no ill effects, so that he could die without shame. And, last but far from least, as far as she knew, Edmund was still safe.

Two hours later, in the cold gray light of dawn, those last uplifting thoughts had no power to overcome the combined dead weights of fatigue, anticlimax, and apprehension. Hetty, the innkeeper's daughter, brought her white bread, with curds in a bowl, and a jug of cold water for washing. The cold water was cheerless, but salutary. The breakfast was equally cheerless, and the knot of tension in her belly made it impossible to swallow. Something unpleasant was going to happen to her today, and, since the object was to demonstrate to everyone that Parliament's ward had not escaped with impunity, whatever it was, was going to happen publicly.

It was almost with relief that she responded to Diccon's subdued knock on her door, his voice hesitantly saying that it was time to leave. At least now she would find out the worst. The lieutenant seemed to avoid her eye, and his response to her good morning was a mere mumble, all of which Ginny found far from reassuring. With Diccon, at least, she had always felt easy, however uncomfortable the situation.

She preceded him out into the street. The sky was heavy

216

and overcast in the gray light of early morning. The brigade was drawn up, the officers mounted at the head. Except for Alex, who stood between Bucephalus and Jen, holding the mare's bridle, his expression impassive. Ginny wondered if she was imagining the brooding, waiting quality of the silence that seemed unnaturally absolute for such a large group.

"I give you good day, colonel," she said, managing to sound as if it were the most ordinary morning.

"Good morrow, Virginia," he returned. "Come round here so that I may help you mount."

His voice was calm and even, but her pulse speeded and fluttered as she moved round to the far side of her horse. Alex put her into the saddle, then said quietly, "Place your hands on the pommel, please, one on top of the other."

It seemed to Ginny as if two-hundred pairs of eyes were upon her. She was too proud to ask why he wanted this and did as he said without a word. He placed a hand against her hip. "Move up a little; I want to be certain you can reach the pommel without strain on your arms." She inched forward, feeling the warmth of his palm through the material of her skirt. When he was satisfied with her position, Alex took his hand away and reached into the pocket of his jerkin, drawing out a broad strip of cloth. As she stared at her hands in mesmeric shock, he bound her wrists together.

"You may hold the pommel for safety," he told her in the same level tones, running a finger between the material and her skin. "The binding will not chafe if you do not pull against it. If you do fight it, the knot will simply tighten." Without another word, he fastened a thin, leather rein to Jen's bridle just above the bit, then swung onto Bucephalus, holding the leading rein loosely with his own. He raised his free hand toward Major Bonham, an order was shouted, the drums began to roll, and the brigade moved forward down the road to London.

Ginny wished, as she had so often done as a child, that she could make herself invisible at will. In those last desperate moments when discovery and retribution were inevitable, it had always seemed the only salvation. But it had not worked then, and it did not work now. She did not even have on her cloak, with the hood that she could pull down low over her face to hide her deep, mortified flush and the tears of embarrassment pricking her eyes. She could not allow them to flow, she thought with dreadful resolve. She could not possibly wipe them away discreetly with her hands tied, and it would merely draw attention to her predicament.

Damn Alex for hitting upon such an appallingly appropriate punishment for her offense. There was no cruelty, no pain, the cloth was soft as silk, the knot loose enough to permit movement of her wrists. But she was rendered completely helpless, obliged to hang onto the pommel to keep her balance, her horse obeying the dictates of someone other than her rider. Ginny's prisoner status was made manifest, and her captor was declaring to all and sundry that she would not have the opportunity to evade captivity again.

She found that while she was definitely angry, she could not help a certain begrudging admiration for his ingenuity, or the knowledge that some punitive action on Alex's part was justified. The consequences of their enmity had been understood between the lovers from the first. Alex had always said that he would protect the one whilst circumventing the other. Her best course now lay in graceful acceptance of this indignity that she had, with open eyes, brought upon herself. She had still won, after all.

That thought brought a tiny smile to her lips, and there was no longer any question of tears. She held her head high, straightened her shoulders, and began to take an interest in her surroundings. How soon would it be before they caught the first glimpse of London? She had never been to the metropolis, though Edmund had told her much of its glories, whetting her appetite unmercifully. The atmosphere would be rather different now, she imagined, when the riotous luxury of the king's court had given way to the sober decorum of a Puritan Parliament. They were approaching the city from the south, so they would have to cross the River Thames if they were to enter the center of the city. Would they do so by London Bridge, Ginny wondered, or take the horse ferry at Lambeth Palace? She knew from Edmund that there were no other routes across.

Now so absorbed in this fascinating question as to forget her annoyance at him, if not the cause of it, she was about to ask Alex, when he said suddenly, "Diccon, take Jen's rein, will you? I wish to ride ahead with Major Bonham."

Diccon obliged instantly, and Ginny cast the young man a sideways glance. "There is no need to be embarrassed at my predicament, Diccon," she said. "I brought it upon myself."

"Maybe so," the lieutenant muttered, blushing. "But it is no way to treat a lady."

"It is appropriate enough treatment for a rebel, though," she responded, sounding amazingly cheerful.

"If the binding is too tight, I could contrive to loosen it," Diccon blurted abruptly, his flush deepening.

Ginny looked at him in wondering surprise. "Oh, Diccon," she said, moved. "You would really be willing to invite the rough end of the colonel's tongue again, just for me?"

"I do not think it is right," he said steadfastly.

Ginny smiled and shook her head. "I am truly grateful, Diccon, but I am in no discomfort. See, the cloth is quite loose." She twisted her wrists in demonstration.

Alex came cantering back at this moment. "My thanks, Diccon." He took the rein, then looked at his aide-de-camp closely. A flash of amusement crossed his face, but he said only, "You may return to your place, Lieutenant." Diccon went off at once, and Alex observed to Ginny, "I have the distinct impression my star is falling in that particular firmament."

"He does not approve of the way you treat your prisoners," she responded. "I find his concern most touching."

"It is to be hoped that this calf love does not prove tedious," Alex said with a chuckle.

"Calf love? Whatever do you mean?" Ginny demanded in genuine surprise.

"Oh, come now, chicken, do not be naive. Poor Diccon is head over heels in love with you."

"Nonsense!" Ginny scoffed, then wondered uneasily if perhaps it were true. Why else would Diccon be willing to earn the displeasure of the commander he seemed to hero-worship?

"You may believe it or not as your please, but pray do not encourage him," said Alex with a small shrug.

"If my hands were free, I would hit you for that!" Ginny declared furiously. "How dare you imply I would do such a thing."

"I did not intend to insult you, Ginny," Alex said placatingly. "It's just that I do not think I am going to have the time to worry about Diccon's emotional stability. I would simply put you on your guard, that is all."

"Do we cross the Thames by London Bridge?" Ginny asked, avoiding a subject that seemed destined to lead to further acrimony.

"No, we remain on the south bank," Alex told her. "The main body of the army is quartered at Southwark, and we will find lodging there until I may meet with Cromwell."

"Oh." Ginny sounded as disappointed as she felt.

"If it is possible, Ginny, I will take you across the river, and you may see all there is to see," he promised with smiling comprehension.

"I will not enjoy being paraded through the streets of the metropolis in bonds," she said tartly.

"Well, if you behave yourself, perhaps, in a day or so, it will not be necessary," he returned smoothly.

A day or so! Ginny grimaced at the prospect. Clearly, she was going to have to come up with some invincible reasons for a rapid end to this disgrace.

Alex, well pleased with the speed of their progress, called a halt at Walworth under an overcast mid-morning sky. They would reach Southwark comfortably in a couple of hours, and a break for food, drink, and easement would not come amiss.

He lifted Ginny from her horse, cupped her elbow, and escorted her over to where a copper beech tree offered a broad trunk as a backrest, and moss-covered roots as a seat. "Give me your hands." She held them up as he unfastened the cloth and pocketed it.

"My thanks, sir," she murmured in dulcet tones, dropping him a mock curtsy, before sitting down and arranging her skirts around her.

Alex pursed his lips. "Have a care, chicken, lest I regret the inclination to be merciful. You will find it difficult to eat with your hands tied."

"I do not think that you wish me to starve, Colonel," she riposted, the gray eyes fearless in their challenge, amused in their knowledge that she was right.

Alex chuckled involuntarily, turning to take bread and cheese from Jed. "No, that would not suit me at all," he agreed, sitting down beside her. "I would not wish there to be one inch less of you."

Ginny could not imagine how Jed could have failed to hear the comment, but the soldier's wrinkled face remained graven as he put a basket of apples down between them. "There's water in the stream," he said, "if you've a thirst."

Ginny was hungry after her neglected, unappetizing breakfast. The bread was thick and crusty, the cheese ripe and strong, the apples crisp and juicy. Alex lay stretched out beside her on the moss under the copper beech, and in spite of last night and his retributive action of this morning, they were in perfect harmony. It didn't seem that it could be possible, yet it was so. They also seemed to be sitting in a fairy ring that no one else dared cross. No one approached them, the other officers taking their meal at a fair distance from the tree, on the bank of the stream.

Alex threw his apple core into the bushes and rose leisurely to his feet. "Won't be long," he said, strolling off toward a small copse. It was so much easier for men, Ginny thought resentfully. Women were not intended to spend their days marching in the open. She watched him return in an enviably short time, pause to exchange a few words with the group by the stream before coming back to the tree.

"Ready, Ginny? It's time we were on the road again."

"Would it be all right if I were to follow in your footsteps before we leave?" she asked pointedly. "Unguarded, if possible."

Alex regarded her with deliberate speculation, as if weighing up the situation. "Well, now," he pronounced thoughtfully, "I do not think you can get up to too much trouble in that copse. But beware of the nettles; I would not like to think of your delicate —"

"Oh, do stop!" Laughing in spite of herself, Ginny marched off toward the trees. On the way back, on impulse, she stopped beside Major Bonham. "I must apologize, Major, for the trouble I caused you last night."

A ghost of a smile touched the major's lips. "The fault was mine," he said. "I underestimated you, Ginny. My only comfort is that the colonel did too." She laughed, and it was returned, making her feel immeasurably better. It was one thing to be at odds with Alex, quite another to be so with these others whose life she shared.

Alex tied her wrists again, once she was back on Jen, but it didn't seem to matter quite so much this time, just some formality that had to be endured. Shortly after noon, they passed through the earthwork defenses of outer London. The sentries welcomed them, and a shouted exchange of comradely badinage took place as the brigade marched through. No attempt was made to halt this undisciplined jollity, Ginny observed, but then the brigade was returning home into Parliament-held London. They were amongst friends, and rigid rules of conduct could be somewhat relaxed.

In growing excitement, Ginny stared into the distance hoping to catch a glimpse of St. Paul's on its hill above the river, or one of the massive towers of the great Tower itself.

222

But the day remained gloomy, and visibility was low.

With her excitement came a return of apprehension. Here she would find no kindred spirit in kitchen or stableyard. She was a prisoner in the enemy camp with only Alex to intercede for her. And Alex seemed almost to have forgotten her presence, although he still held the rein that led her horse. His own excitement and tension was an almost palpable force, as it had been that day on the Hog's Back when he had contemplated the prospect of battle. Again, she shivered at the thought of the strange, alien quality of this man who knew her body so intimately, whose body *she* knew so intimately. What an extraordinary force was love and lust combined, strong enough to overpower differences of principle and temperament that should be utterly divisive.

Southwark was no more than an enormous army camp surrounding a cluster of buildings that had once housed the hamlet's inhabitants. The Globe Theatre, no longer needed to offer the best of theater for London's populace, stood on the banks of the river, neglected. Ginny looked at the building longingly, remembering Edmund tell of the wonderful plays he had seen there by Ben Jonson and Shakespeare. Would such entertainment ever be offered again?

The brigade halted before what had once been an inn, but was now clearly employed as army headquarters. Ginny was obliged to remain on her horse, which was held by a hastily summoned soldier, while Alex went into the building, and his officers, clearly knowing exactly what was expected of them, dispersed. The brigade seemed to vanish as she watched. They went in an orderly fashion, it was true, but at one minute there were two-hundred men drawn up in orderly ranks; the next, on a shouted command, they had gone.

Ginny became again acutely conscious of her captive state when there were no friendly faces in sight. She could not dismount with her hands bound, the soldier holding Jen seemed totally indifferent, and she wondered anew how Alex could be so callous as to abandon her in this fashion.

It seemed an eternity before he appeared in the doorway, in the company of two others wearing colonel's insignia. "Damnation," he muttered, seeing her. "I am sorry, I forgot all about you." He lifted her off Jen, and Ginny resisted the urge to kick him only with the greatest difficulty. "Go where you please, except into the men's camp," he said, "but return here in an hour. I will know then what we are to do next."

"My hands?" Ginny said.

"They stay as they are for the moment. I cannot put a guard on you, and I do not wish to lock you up, so this restriction must do instead."

Ginny watched him stride off down the street in the company of the others and felt forlorn, even as she wanted to stick a knife in his throat. How could he not care, not even imagine how lonely was her position? He was too busy, too absorbed in his own business. It would have been better if he had left her with Lady Hammond at Carisbrooke Castle.

Chapter Thirteen

There was no point repining, Ginny decided. She was here in Southwark, a mere hour's journey from London Bridge, and there was no knowing what the future held, but it was unlikely to be dull, that was for sure. With renewed spirits, she set off to explore her surroundings, giving her wrists an experimental twist, scrunching one hand up small to see if she could slip it free. All that happened was that the knot became small, hard, and much tighter, and the skin on her wrist bone reddened. She should have heeded Alex's warning, she thought crossly, giving up the struggle.

The first thing she noticed was that there were women, plenty of them, about the village. They stood gossiping in doorways, were to be found scrubbing clothes in wooden tubs, feeding chickens, hanging out laundry, kneading dough on wooden trays. But they did not seem to Ginny to be ordinary servants, in spite of the domestic nature of their activities. Something about their dress was not quite appropriate, a skirt was too short, a blouse falling off a shoulder revealing more than the mere swell of an ample breast, and they moved in such a way as to accentuate their womanly attributes. There was much laughter amongst them, and whenever a group of soldiers went past, there were cat calls and ribaldry.

The stared openly at Ginny, and one tall, buxom woman with flaming red hair and the white skin to match called out to her, beckoning her over to where she stood, leaning against the well with three others. "What you doin' 'ere, deerie?" she asked, not unkindly. "Not the place for the likes o' you." She fingered the good serge of Ginny's riding habit, the crisp white collar, then pointed at her hands. "You a prisoner, then?"

Ginny agreed that she was; it seemed simpler than complicated explanations about wards of Parliament. "I came in with Colonel Marshall's brigade," she offered.

"Eh, did you now?" One of the other women winked. "There's a fine gennleman, but hoity-toity." She sniffed, wrinkling her nose as if at a bad smell. "Always got 'is nose in the air, that one." By which, Ginny concluded that Alex did not amuse himself with whores and camp followers, since that was clearly what these women were.

She shrugged. "Do you live in the camp then?"

The red-haired woman laughed. "Wherever there's soldiers, deerie, that's where we live. And now that Cromwell's payin' 'em, it's a good living, ain't it, girls?" There was raucous agreement; then one of them said to Ginny, with more than a touch of scorn, "You thinkin' of tryin' it, then, duckie? There's worse ways to get by in wartime."

Ginny, remembering her two attackers of the foul breath and sweaty bodies, had difficulty believing this, but she muttered something neutral, having no desire to cause offense. "I don't suppose," she said tentatively, "that one of you would untie this knot for me?" She held out her wrists and, to her astonishment, saw them all jump backward as if she were holding a viper.

"Wat d'ye think we are?" the red-haired woman said. "Fools, or summat? Aidin' and abettin' a prisoner is a hangin' matter."

"I crave pardon," Ginny made haste to apologize. "I didn't mean to cause you any trouble. Perhaps you shouldn't be seen talking to me, either."

There were indeed some doubtful mutterings as to the

wisdom of conversing with a prisoner who seemed intent on escape, and Ginny left them, continuing in the direction of the Globe Theatre. The sound of a shrill scream from a nearby alley gave her pause. No one else seemed to be taking the slightest notice. She went swiftly toward the sound, then stared in disgust. Two women were rolling around in the soil of the kennel, screaming abuse at each other as they scratched, clawed, and yanked at their opponent's hair. A group of soldiers stood watching, yelling encouragement in the coarsest language. There was an awful fascination about the scene, and Ginny could not tear her eyes away even as she felt as degraded by the spectacle as if she were one of the participants.

"Come away, mistress!" Jed's hand seized her arm, pulling her away from the mouth of the alley. "What are you a-thinkin' of? You shouldn't be 'ere."

"The colonel said I might go where I pleased in the village," Ginny protested in what she realized was less than adequate defense for her obvious fascination.

"Somethin' must've addled his wits," Jed said unequivocally. "Unless he's forgotten the place is full of harlots. Most likely, he has," he added with an exasperated headshake. "It's the excitement, always drives the sense from him."

Ginny found this insight absolutely intriguing. Jed was talking about Alex as a grown man might talk of an irritating small boy for whom he had, nevertheless, considerable affection.

Jed clearly had no intention of permitting her to continue her walk and escorted her firmly back to headquarters, showing her into an empty, large, and rather dusty room that, judging by the faint, lingering smell of liquor, had presumably once been the inn's taproom. "You'll be quite all right here," he told her. "If 'n anyone wants to know who you are, just you tell 'em ye're waitin' on the colonel." With that, he left her, closing the door firmly in his wake. Ginny sat on a smooth window seat that had clearly been polished by generations of backsides and looked out onto the street where the scene was as lively as ever.

Alex, in the same company as before, appeared in about ten minutes, and Ginny watched as Jed went over to him. The batman spoke at some length, and Alex, to Ginny's eyes, began to look rather discomfited, pulling at his chin, as he glanced over at the inn. Then he nodded, said something briefly to Jed who saluted, rather pointedly to Ginny's way of thinking, and went off. Alex and the other two colonels came toward the inn.

When Alex walked into the room, Ginny was sitting demurely on the window seat, her bound hands resting in her lap, an expression of hurt innocence on her face.

"I gather you had some unpleasantness," Alex said. "I am sorry, I was not thinking clearly."

"It was quite horrid," Ginny murmured in a low voice, twisting her fingers, dropping her eyes to her lap. "Alex — they are . . . they are whores, I think!" This last was said in tones of such shocked modesty and innocence that all three men shuffled uncomfortably. "Could it possibly be so?" she asked, wondering how long she could continue the play before laugher gave her away. "Could they indeed be fallen women?"

Alex regarded her with growing suspicion. She had never before given him the slightest reason to suspect her of prudery, quite the opposite. It was certainly true that witnessing a cat fight of the kind Jed had so vividly described could have been a shock to one of maidenly sensibilities, but Ginny? No, she was made of sterner stuff than that.

"Mistress Courtney," he said, "will you take your eyes off your lap for one minute and look at me?" She raised her head slowly, and Alex gave an involuntary shout of laughter. The gray eyes were brimming with mischievous glee. "Wretch!" he exclaimed. "For a minute, you almost had me fooled. You were not even as shocked as Jed, were you?"

"It had a certain horrible fascination, to be quite truthful," she replied. "But I do not wish to see such a thing again. The whores themselves do not worry me, but — well, it was disgusting."

"I do not know what I can have been thinking of," Alex said with a rueful grimace. "It will be best if I keep you by me, in future."

"Yes, I think it will," Ginny agreed matter-of-factly. "Will you not introduce me to your colleagues?" She raised her eyebrows quizzically at the two men with him, both of whom were looking more than a little bewildered by the tone of the preceding conversation.

"Oh, I am sorry. Gentlemen, this is the lady I was telling you about, Mistress Virginia Courtney. Ginny, may I present Colonels Richards and Chambers."

Ginny rose from her perch, smiled, and attempted a polite curtsy. "You must excuse me, sirs," she said sweetly, "but I am unable to curtsy properly with my hands restricted in this manner."

"Give them to me," Alex said, then frowned over the knot. "Did I not tell you that you would merely tighten this by pulling against it? I cannot possibly undo it."

"Well, it is a great nuisance," Ginny retorted. "If I could have undone it myself, I would have done so."

"I do not doubt it," he said, pulling a knife from the sheath at his belt. "Mistress Courtney, gentlemen, is a most redoubtable rebel. Do not ever underestimate her." The cloth parted beneath the blade. "That should not have happened," he said softly, stroking with his thumb the reddened skin of her wrist bone.

The touch, so innocent seeming, sent a shock wave coursing through her down to the soles of her feet. The caress in his voice turned her bones to putty, and for a breathless second her fingers twined around his. What must Colonels Richards and Chambers be thinking, Ginny wondered distractedly, feeling that betraying flush warm her cheeks.

Alex gave her a knowing smile, well aware of the effect he was having and content to have it so. "Come," he said, "I will show you to your quarters. They will be a little primitive, I fear, but tomorrow we go to Whitehall, and you will be lodged in a palace."

Ginny clapped her hands in delight, her face radiant. "Truly?"

"Truly," he laughed. "I always keep my promises, even to intransigent rebels."

He showed her to a mere slip of a room, more of a cupboard than a chamber. "There are no other women sleeping in headquarters," Alex told her, "but you will not be disturbed by anyone."

"How can you be so sure?" Ginny asked, surprised at this sudden change of attitude. In Guildford, in the interests of her safety, he had locked her in at night and taken away the key.

"Because, chicken," he said slowly and deliberately, "I have the prior claim, and everyone knows it."

"Ah," she said, sucking in her lower lip. "We are to be done with secrecy then?" That would explain the openness of his manner with her in front of the colonels earlier.

"If you would have it so," he replied, taking her hand, lifting it to his lips. "After tomorrow, I can have no reason to keep you prisoner myself. I must either hand you over to Cromwell with the recommendation that he put you in the charge of a good Parliamentarian family until the fighting is done, or you throw in your lot with mine, sweetheart. Will you follow the drum?" The green-brown eyes were pinpricks of intensity as he asked the question that mattered so much to him. He had no other alternatives to offer. One day they might be able to talk of marriage, but not now when nothing was certain, not even life itself.

"Like those others out there?" Ginny gestured with her head toward the window.

"No!" Alex said, dropping her hand and transferring his hold to her shoulders. "That is not what I am offering, and you know it! Mistress, yes; whore, no!" The vigorous statement was punctuated with a hard shake, and Ginny, who had intended the remark to be a joke, realized that in some things they did not share the same sense of humor.

"It was said in jest," she protested. "Of course I do not think that."

"Sometimes I think I will never understand you," Alex grumbled. "You seem to hold nothing sacred. You have no respect for rank, you do not believe in obeying orders or treating ceremonies with the slightest reverence, or—"

"Then I am going to make a very poor soldier, aren't I?" Ginny interrupted this woeful catalogue with a grin. "Are you sure it will be a good idea?"

"No," he said savagely, jerking her into his arms. "I am convinced it will be the biggest mistake of my life, and we shall be always at loggerheads because you will never be where you are supposed to be and will be forever making mock of me in public and refusing to do as you are told." His hand pushed up her chin. "God's death, but I love you, Virginia Courtney." His mouth covered hers with bruising force, and she met the plundering tongue, thrust for thrust, matching his statement with her own passionate assertion. What was between them could not be denied. It would take its own course, and they would flow with it like logs down the rapids.

Alex drew back from her slowly and reluctantly. "I have to go for the moment, sweeting. There are division matters I must discuss with the others. You will dine with us, though, in one hour."

"If you promise not to treat me like a recalcitrant prisoner," said Ginny. "I will not tolerate being sent to bed in that irritating manner you have. Not if I now travel with you of my own free will."

Alex touched the tip of her nose with a long forefinger. "You will preside over the dinner table, Mistress Courtney, as if it were your own." At the door, he turned back to her. "I do not wish you to stay up late, though." The green-brown eyes danced merrily. "So make sure you take yourself off before I feel the need to remind you." Chuckling, he left her, and Ginny shook her head in mild exasperation, under no illusions that there would be true equality between them for as long as she rode as a member, honorary or otherwise, of Alexander Marshall's brigade.

A thought occurred to her. If Alex was safely occupied

231

and she had been given no orders to remain immured in this cupboard, she could go in search of Jed and see if anyone had need of physicking.

Jed was to be found sitting on a stone bench outside the inn, smoking a pipe and taking his ease in the early evening air. He greeted Ginny and her medicine basket with a grunt. "If ye're game, mistress, there's some who'd be glad to see you," he said, getting to his feet. "I'll show you where the brigade's quartered. Best you don't go wanderin' among the other regiments, though. Our own men'll have a care for you, but I wouldn't bet on the others."

Ginny spent the next forty-five minutes lancing boils, digging out a long splinter that had set up an infection in a corporal's thumb, and prescribing treatment for foot rot. They were far from serious ailments, but she knew the discomfort they could cause, and also how little ills, left untreated, could lead to the major horrors of septicemia and gangrene. It was a connection not generally understood, even by the educated, and she did her best to explain this as she worked, but with little hope that her audience would pay more than lip service to the lecture.

She regained the inn with just time to dispose of her incriminating basket and tidy her hair before Diccon, in his customary role as messenger, summoned her to the supper table. It was a pleasant-enough meal at which she did, indeed, preside, but when the table was cleared and packs of cards and dice appeared, together with the brandy, Ginny excused herself promptly. An officers' mess after a good dinner was no place for a woman, colonel's mistress or no. She lay in bed, listening to the riotous noise from the parlor below, wondering if Alex would come to her. After a while, in among the male voices, rose unmistakably lighter, female tones. Roars of laughter shook the rafters, there was an occasional crash as of a chair being upturned, slurred voices from the garden below her window as the revelers emerged for a few minutes of necessary relief.

She was just about to drop off to sleep, having given Alex up as lost for the night, when the voices from below rose to new heights, a roaring chant shook the flaking plaster on the wall of her cupboard, and booted feet began a rhythmic stamping. Curious beyond caution now, Ginny slipped from her narrow cot, caught up her cloak, and crept out onto the landing. The steep, narrow wooden staircase led down to the stone-flagged hall below. Halfway down, she stopped. The door to the parlor was open, and she had a clear view. The long refectory table had been completely cleared, and on it stood a woman, swaying her hips in time to the chanting and stamping feet as she fumbled drunkenly with the buttons on her chemise. Shouts of encouragement accompanied a disrobing that Ginny could not help but feel was somewhat inelegant. Diccon, his face flushed with brandy and excitement, could not take his eyes off the woman, and when her petticoat rustled around her ankles, his mouth fell open on an "ah" of wonderment. Had he never seen a naked woman before, Ginny wondered. Poor baby, he must be all of twenty. Surely he could not still be a virgin? Her eyes sought and found Alex among the slavering throng. He was sitting slightly apart, one leg crossed negligently over the other, a pewter tankard in his hand, watching the proceedings with an air of sleepy amusement.

Crossly, Ginny turned and went back upstairs. It was positively insulting that he should prefer such a spectacle to the prospect of a night of love-making in her arms, and so she would tell him in no uncertain terms as soon as she had the chance. The noise continued unabated, becoming wilder, if anything. Muted female giggles came from below her window; she heard Diccon's voice, sounding half-pleading, half-assertive, then the unmistakable sounds of someone retching miserably.

"Come on, lad, get your head down now." Alex spoke suddenly, his voice clear and commanding in the general cacophony, but with a note both amused and understanding. "You've had enough for one night, and I can promise you that you are not going to enjoy the morning." Diccon groaned, there was another giggle, then Alex's voice again, no longer amused, sending the giggler about her business.

Ginny smiled to herself in the darkness, listening to the sounds of firm steps and stumbling ones outside her door. She crept to the door, opening it a crack. Alex, with Diccon draped across his shoulders, was kicking open the door to the room opposite Ginny's cupboard. He tumbled the inert figure onto a bed on which reposed another soldierly figure snoring stertorously, then bent and pulled off Diccon's boots, before tossing a coverlet over him and leaving the room, shaking his head in a gesture expressing the resigned acceptance of a sophisticate for the youthful excesses of the naive.

Ginny almost whispered to him; then a better idea came to her, and she stayed still, peering through the crack in her door to see where he went. Alex disappeared behind a door at the end of the corridor, and Ginny chewed her nails for a minute wondering if he had a bedfellow. If he had, it would be one of the other colonels, since presumably rank counted even in such domestic instances. Over the next half an hour, Colonels Richards and Chambers came up the stairs separately, and both continued up to the second floor. Silence fell at last, and no one had entered Colonel Marshall's chamber.

Ginny left her cupboard, closing the door behind her with the utmost care. There was not a sound as she crept toward Alex's door and lifted the latch noiselessly. Wraithlike, she flitted across the dark room to the bed where a motionless hump could just be discerned in the gloom. The next instant, the world seemed to turn upside down, and she fought desperately against suffocating pressure filling her nose and mouth, an iron band clamped against her throat, hard, hurtful hands pinning her like a butterfly in a display case.

"Sweet Jesus!" Alex exclaimed, as his hands suddenly registered the familiarity of the body they were subduing. "You little fool, I nearly killed you! *Never, ever* try to take me by surprise."

It could have been no more than two or three seconds since she had approached the bed, but they were seconds Ginny would never want to relive. The smothering pillow

234

left her face, and, stunned, she stared up at him as he hung naked over her, and her eyes became fixed on the wickedly thin knife blade poised over her throat. "Why don't you wait to see who it is before you attack?" she croaked.

Alex shook his head in wordless exasperation and resheathed the blade, pushing it under the bolster. "Chicken, I would not give a groat for my chances of survival if I waited for an introduction to whoever is creeping around my bed in the middle of the night. Anyone on innocent business would know to announce himself loudly."

"I'll never make a good soldier," Ginny sighed. "It didn't even occur to me, and, besides, I thought you were asleep."

"I was, until you put your hand on the latch," he told her, swinging onto the bed beside her. "Don't ever do that again. My reactions are automatic and *very* fast. You were very close to having your throat cut."

"On the principle of act first and ask questions later," Ginny said with a shiver. "I do not care for soldiering, I have to tell you."

"But then you did not creep in here to be a soldier, did you, my sweet?" Alex asked softly, turning on his side, propping himself on one elbow. The green-brown eyes held a pensive look as he examined the face on the pillow beside him. A residue of that fearful panic still lingered in her eyes, in the tension of her skin over the high cheekbones, the set of the full mouth. With concentrated purpose, he took her lips, tasting, exploring, softly at first, then with increased pressure as he felt her melt beneath the gentle, insidious invasion, felt her fear and tension yield to the wondrous langour of slow-building desire.

His hand slid down to cup the firm mound of her breast, his thumb brushing over the soft linen covering the taut, straining peak. Ginny moved involuntarily, pressing herself against the long, lean nakedness, and he pulled her even closer so that she was made powerfully aware of the urgency of his need, the heat and throb of him through her thin night rail. She was boneless, pliant, and formless, an encompassing softness that he knew would receive and nurture

235

him.

Alex drew the hem of her nightgown upward, smoothing his hand along the fine, supple line of her leg to her hip. His hand slid round to her belly, palming the sharp points of her hip bones as his thumb played in her navel before he lowered his head and flicked the soft cup with his tongue. The slight stubble of his late-night beard grazed her tender skin, setting the muscles of her abdomen fluttering, and her hands raked through the auburn hair glowing bright against the whiteness of her belly as her hips lifted in wanton invitation. With one hand, he freed the sash constricting her waist, then pushed the gown upward, his lips following, nuzzling the gradually bared flesh, tasting deeply of a rose-crested breast as it was uncovered.

Casting the nightgown aside, he gathered her to him, rolling so that she came to rest above him, every curve and hollow of her body molded to his length. Ginny smiled down at him a little uncertainly as she adapted to this novel position. Understanding amusement flickered in the green-brown eyes, and the sculpted firmness of his mouth curved as he ran his fingers though the mass of chestnut hair, drawing it over her shoulders to enclose them both in a silky, fragrant tent. The calloused, swordsman's hand cupped her face, drawing her mouth down to his, and Ginny discovered the delight of initiation as her tongue penetrated deeply, tasting the brandy sweetness, before venturing forth on a voyage of exploration that left not a millimeter of his mouth and face untouched.

Her tongue darted into the tight shell of his ear, flicking in the whorls and contours, stroking as her teeth nibbled the sensitive lobe. She could feel his heart beating faster against her breast where the hair on his chest rubbed, faintly abrasive. The ridged muscles of his thighs pressed upward, powerful against her own softness, and the slight roundness of her belly fitted into the concavity of the one below.

His hands smoothed down her back, lingering over the tapering waist before caressing the flare of her hips moving into the slender length of thigh. The languid, seductive

236

stroking brought Ginny a seething excitement, a fluid fullness within as she pressed her body against him, encouraging the tightness of his hold. Then he parted her thighs and with a slow twist of his hips thrust into her welcoming body.

Ginny gasped with delight, moving with him as he thrust deeper, and she wanted to take him into the very core of herself, to encompass and hold him, indivisible in the ageless fusion. And as her body found its own rhythms, found where pleasure was centered, she moved ever faster, finding infinite delight as she strove to become a part of the man, to make him a part of her. There was no thought now, no sense of self, only the white-hot excitement of pure sensation rippling through her as he gripped her hips and drove upward with a great cry of joy, and for one miraculous moment she hovered on her own precipice, holding the throbbing power of his completion within her. Then she fell herself, in a wild shattering of golden sparks that ravaged her senses and left her in the quiet pool of surfeited joy.

She lay, stranded, beached upon him until the wild beating of her heart had stilled and she returned to the world, to awareness of the salt taste of his skin on her lips pressed against the hollow of his throat, to the sweaty slipperiness of their joined bodies as the fire that had consumed them retreated.

His hands flattened against her back, and he gently rolled her onto the bed beside him, moving with her so the moment of disengagement was prolonged and easy. "You are miraculous," he whispered, kissing her eyelids before collapsing with a groan of exhaustion onto the pillow.

"More entertaining than harlots stripping on the table?" Ginny inquired, even through her own exhaustion unable to resist the mischievous question.

"Did you see that?" Alex sat up abruptly.

"Mmmm," Ginny murmured, closing her eyes as if on the verge of sleep. "I could have done it better myself."

There was a moment of silence, and she risked a quick peep through her eyelashes. He was looking down at her speculatively. "I won't argue with you on that score," he said.

"Then why did you stay and watch?" Ginny demanded. "You looked monstrously amused."

"I was not amused," Alex protested, lying down again beside her. "I had thought to keep an eye on young Diccon. He is somewhat inexperienced, and, while I am all in favor of his losing his innocence, I would prefer that he not lose his shirt in addition."

"I saw you put him to bed," Ginny said softly. "It pleases me that the stern, implacable commander should concern himself with the health and well-being of those under his command." Her eyelids closed on this, a faint smile curved her lips, and with a little wriggle she snuggled against him and slept.

When she awoke, it was full day, and she was alone in the colonel's bed. Ginny stretched luxuriously and wondered why she had been allowed to sleep this long. Not even the call of the bugle and the summoning of the drum had penetrated her sleep. Blinking, she sat up and looked around the room she had only seen in the dark. It was sparsely furnished, but a jug and basin stood on a low table by the window, and her clothes were laid out for her on the end of the bed. At least she would not have to leave the colonel's chamber clad only in her nightgown.

Somewhat to her surprise, Ginny found that she felt remarkably well, not a whit fatigued after such a disturbed night, but she had not far to look for the reason behind this sense of physical well-being, and, at the memory, a slight flush stained her cheeks. Such shameless wantonness from the gently bred daughter of John Redfern! But it did not appear to disturb Alex, in the least — quite the opposite. With a little chuckle, she slid to the floor, raised her arms to embrace the new day, reveling in the soft air on her bare skin before pouring water into the basin and sponging herself down thoroughly. The bath in Newbury seemed a long time ago, she reflected, and another one should be contrived soon. It would be nice, also, to be able to wear something other than her riding habit. Maybe, if they were to stay for a few days in London, she could do so.

In spite of her bravado on the subject with Alex, Ginny felt slightly self-conscious as she left his chamber and was greatly relieved to find the corridor empty. Gathering up her skirts, she ran lightly down the stairs, making her way to the rear of the erstwhile inn where she presumed the kitchen would be found. Kitchens meant breakfast, and Ginny was ravenous.

She found the low-ceiling room with its blackened beams with little difficulty and, pausing on the threshold, was hard pressed to hide a smug smile. The men grouped around the long, scrubbed deal table were in various degrees of distress; haggard and drawn, they flopped in heavy-eyed silence. They were, without exception, the younger officers though. No one above the rank of lieutenant seemed to be suffering.

"Good morrow, gentlemen," Ginny said brightly. "You all look to me as if you have lost a shilling and found a groat. I expect you did not have enough sleep last night." Her eye fell on Diccon who looked as if he were about to expire. "Does your head pain you, Diccon?" she inquired, and when he attempted to nod, then groaned, wincing at the renewed thumps of agony, she went upstairs to fetch her medicine basket.

When she reentered the kitchen, she found Alex, Major Bonham, three captains, and Colonels Richards and Chambers. None of them appeared the worse for wear; presumably they had better heads than the younger ones or had behaved with more circumspection.

Ginny greeted them politely, trying to keep her gaze from lingering on Alex, as she shook drops from a tiny vial into a tin cup, mixed a little fine white powder to a paste with water, added the paste to the cup, stirred and placed it in front of Diccon.

"What is it?" he groaned, wrinkling his nose at the far from pleasant aroma.

"Kill or cure," Ginny said cheerfully. "If you can keep it down, you will feel better in no time. You may think yourself fortunate it is only a bad head you have, and not a case of the pox after last night's whoring."

239

Alex roared with laughter, and after a startled instant, those not in pain joined in. "I suppose you have a cure for that, also?"

"If it is not too far advanced," Ginny replied seriously. "An infusion of aloes and—You are laughing at me," she accused. "It is no laughing matter, as you would know if you have ever—"

"This is a most indelicate subject," Alex interrupted hastily before he was obliged to reveal any intimate details before the assembled company. "When you have finished ministering to these sore-headed profligates, we will set off for Whitehall. Diccon, I am sorry, but you ride with us." On that note of reasserted authority, he left the kitchen.

"Poor Diccon," Ginny said sympathetically. "Why do you not ask him if you can stay behind?"

A look of horror crossed the lieutenant's wan face. "And not go to Whitehall?" With desperate resolve, he took the tin cup and tipped the contents down his throat, watched with beleaguered interest by his fellow sufferers. Ginny surveyed him anxiously as the green tinge of his complexion deepened and his red eyes seemed to glaze. "Poison!" he choked, putting a hand to his mouth.

"Wait!" Ginny said imperatively. "You must keep it down."

An intent silence fell over the room as they all watched with gruesome fascination Diccon's struggles. After two or three minutes, his face cleared miraculously. "I do not think I shall puke after all," he announced.

"Good," Ginny declared with satisfaction. "Then you will be almost better directly. Not that you deserve to be," she added severely.

"Do not scold him, further, Mistress Courtney," Colonel Richards requested with a tiny smile. "I think he has suffered enough, do you not?"

"I daresay." Ginny returned the smile easily and turned to the imperative business of finding her own breakfast.

Half an hour later, they were on the road, Colonel Marshall, Lieutenant Maulfrey, Captain Baldwin of the colonel's brigade, Jed, and Parliament's ward.

Ginny could not control her excitement even as she told herself that a Royalist should not rejoice in the prospect of entering rebel-held London when its monarch rested a captive in Carisbrooke Castle. She gazed ahead, her eyes straining for the first sight of London Bridge, and told herself that for the first time since her odyssey began she could truly relax. She and Alex were at peace, each with the other, and, for the moment, there was no bone of contention waiting to rise up between them. There was nothing a Cavalier could do to aid the king's cause in this, the center of Parliament's power. For now, she was not in contravention of any direct order and had no intention of being so. There was no reason under the summer sun why there should not be perfect harmony between the lovers, their inherent enmity vanquished in the eye of the hurricane.

Chapter Fourteen

London Bridge, with its rows of houses and jutting cutwaters, was a wondrous sight for the girl who had never left the south coast of England. How could a bridge be so long, so strong that it could span the wide river, yet carry upon it an entire village? There were stores and street vendors, and her eyes grew ever wider at the variety of goods on display. As the travelers passed, mercers stood in doorways calling, "What do you lack?" and rolling out bolts of material for inspection. War had brought shortages and near starvation to the rest of the country, but London town seemed to have suffered no diminution in the supply of luxuries, let alone of necessities. It did not lack dirt, either, and Ginny wrinkled her nose at the stench produced by horse dung, rotting vegetables, and rags suppurating in the gutters under the heat of the summer sun. The city seemed shrouded under a choking, greasy canopy of smoke, and she covered her mouth and nostrils with her kerchief, looking at Alex for explanation.

"Sea-coal," he told her. "There is not enough wood in the city to burn, so they use coal instead. You will become accustomed to it." Ginny seriously doubted that but decided she had best ignore the villainous smell as well as she could if it were not to affect her pleasure in her first visit to the capital.

The Tower loomed gray and menacing on the far bank, and Ginny searched with unabashed curiosity for the iron portcullis at water level that marked Traitors' Gate. She shivered at the thought of all those who had made the final journey by barge along the river, disembarked at the green-slime-caked step where the river water slopped unceasingly, to be received by the governor of the Tower and escorted through the gate from which no one left.

On leaving London Bridge, they turned left and traveled along the north bank of the Thames. Alex regarded Ginny's wide-eyed wonder with a little smile and made no attempt to hurry their progress. When they came to a crowd, cheering and shouting in Temple Gardens and she looked at him for permission to go and see what was amusing them, he readily agreed but stayed where he was as Ginny and an equally delighted Diccon pushed through the crowd. They were back very quickly, however, Diccon clearly under protest to judge by his martyred air, Ginny looking dismayed.

"I have never before seen a bearbaiting," she said in reply to Alex's question. "It is quite appallingly cruel."

Alex frowned. "Parliament has forbidden such sport in the city," he said. "Together with most of the other public spectacles. That bearbaiting will not continue for much longer once the militia hear of it."

Ginny took small comfort from this. The sight of the wounded animal, tied to a stake, struggling to keep at bay the half-dozen hounds who snapped and tore at him, even as his great paws smashed their spines and ripped their flesh, had sickened her, and it was quite some time before her interest in the novelty of her surroundings revived.

They arrived at the Palace of Whitehall by mid afternoon, passing through the guarded gate into an inner courtyard where all was military bustle. Such surroundings were becoming very familiar, Ginny reflected, watching the orderly drilling of a squad of troopers, the swift, decisive stride of an officer on important business, listening to the hail of a sentry, the crisply bellowed orders that the recipients seemed

243

to understand although, to Ginny, the words bore little resemblance to the language as she knew it.

Alex identified himself to the guards at the massive iron and steel doors giving entrance to the palace, and after a few minutes a captain came out, saluted smartly, and told Alex that the commander-in-chief was in session with his staff and Colonel Marshall, together with his officers, was bidden to join them immediately.

Where did that leave Parliament's ward, Ginny wondered. Again a familiar situation, cooling her heels while the colonel went about his business. Alex's lips twitched as he read her expression correctly. "Come too," he said, lifting her off Jen. "You may wait in the antechamber until I have met with Cromwell. Jed will keep you company."

Whitehall resembled an army headquarters more than a palace, Ginny reflected, as they hurried behind the captain down long corridors stripped of their hangings and resounding with the tread of booted feet. She and Jed were left in a small, unfurnished antechamber while the others disappeared behind a heavy oak door, and Ginny paced restlessly, tapping her crop against her boots as she wandered between the small, diamond-paned window and the door, where she stood, pressing her ear against it. Unfortunately, it was too thick to afford much satisfaction for the eavesdropper, and Jed eventually told her in the tones of a privileged retainer to come away and learn a little patience.

At long last, the door opened and Alex emerged, beaming, looking for all the world as if he had just been told he had come into a fortune. His two companions were not much less delighted.

"Well?" Ginny demanded. "What has caused you to resemble the cat with the cream?"

"Later," he said. "Jed, will you escort Mistress Courtney to the Blue Boar on Market Street? Bespeak a decent privy chamber; I've a mind to be comfortable tonight. Ensure that Mistress Courtney has all she needs for her comfort and remain in the inn until I come." Taking Ginny by the arm, he drew her to one side, saying quietly, "I will come to you shortly, chicken. There are one or two matters I must attend to. Later we dine here with Cromwell."

"We?" She frowned, bemused by these sudden plans.

"Yes," he replied. "Cromwell wishes to see you."

"Why? I do not think I wish to meet him," Ginny said with sad lack of respect for the most powerful man in England. "And are you not to be lodged in the barracks?" This was all most confusing.

"No, I have decided to play the civilian tonight," he replied, answering her last question first. "Do not look so put out, sweeting. If you do as you are bid, you will have nothing to worry about." His lips curved in a teasing smile as the gray eyes flashed at this. "Go with Jed, now. I will undertake to answer all your questions anon." So saying, he gave her a little push toward the stolidly waiting batman.

The Blue Boar was a plaster-fronted, half-timbered building on a street so narrow that the top stories of the houses met with their opposite neighbors, forming an arch over the cobbled lane. Inside, it was solidly comfortable, with the gleaming pewter and brass and highly polished wood of the well-maintained establishment. Ginny and Jed were shown to a large, sunny chamber at the back of the inn, away from the noise of the street and overlooking a pretty garden.

"This do you, mistress?" Jed asked, looking around critically. Ginny said that it would do very well. The bed was large, piled high with feather mattresses and hung with clean chintz curtains. It was quite the most comfortable resting place she had been offered since leaving Alum Bay, and there seemed no question of her having any but one particular bedfellow.

The goodwife who had shown them to the chamber looked pleased with Ginny's approbation and begged to inquire if there was anything she could bring the mistress, besides warming pans for the sheets and a hot brick against the night chills.

"A bath," Ginny said with decision. "If you please, goodwife."

The matter was easily accomplished. A porcelain hip bath was placed before the hearth where, instead of hot coals, glowed a jug of brilliant poppies. Steaming water filled the tub, and a bunch of fragrant herbs was strewn on the surface, filling the room with the scent of lavender. There was even a cake of soap, that luxurious commodity that required so much effort to produce from the rendering down of waste fats and lye.

Jed didn't leave her until he was sure everything was as it should be; then he told her that he would be at the ale bench in the yard should she have need of him before the colonel arrived.

At last alone, Ginny savored a solitude that had not been hers for a week. She was guest, not prisoner, in this inn; there were no soldiers pounding the beat outside her door, no drums and bugles as constant reminders of war. When Alex came to her this time, it would be only as lover on neutral territory. Thankfully, she stripped off her habit and tossed it carelessly into the corner of the room. The gesture was satisfying, although common sense told her she would only have to pick it up again in a minute. After her bath, she would see if one of the inn servants could be persuaded to sponge and press it for her. With a sigh of pleasure, she slipped into the water, resting her neck against the curved rim of the bath, allowing her feet to hang over the far end.

When the door opened, she started almost guiltily. "What mischief are you up to?" Alex closed the door with a definitive click, laying a large parcel carefully on a chair in the corner of the room before crossing to the tub, his eyes hooded as they traversed her shape beneath the water.

"No mischief," she returned, feeling strangely vulnerable all of a sudden. "The bath is such luxury, I had fallen into a trance and was dreaming of heaven."

"There are many heavenly planes," Alex remarked, not taking his eyes off her as he shrugged out of his coat and pulled off his shirt. "But I think the bath is definitely a good idea."

"You must order your own," Ginny said, wriggling her toes.

"I would rather share yours," he replied, tugging off his boots and stockings.

"There is no room," she said unarguably.

246

"Then I must hurry you up. I will wash your back."

"Pray do not trouble, sir. I can manage myself." Throughout the by-play, the delicious tension built, wreathing and coiling between them, and Ginny continued to wriggle her toes absently until Alex dropped to his knees by the bath and seized her feet in both hands. Ginny squealed and squirmed helplessly as his fingers danced over the ticklish soles; then he bent his head, taking her toes in his mouth, sucking with a rhythmic fervor that seemed to transfer itself to every nerve center of her body. Half moaning, half laughing, she begged him to stop although she did not know whether that was what she really wanted and, when he did stop, knew that it wasn't.

Alex chuckled and felt around in the water for the soap, his hands deliberately straying into nooks and crannies where no soap cake could possibly have hidden. "Here!" Ginny said in mock irritation. "Is this what you are looking for?" Taking his hand, she slapped the soap into his palm.

"Among other things," Alex murmured, soaping the wash cloth. "Sit up and lean forward."

When she showed no signs of compliance, he moved behind her, encircling her waist with an iron-firm arm, lifting her up out of the water, bending her forward over his hand as he soaped her back with gentle, circular movements that nevertheless contrived to be very thorough. "Stop wriggling," he commanded when she struggled, more playfully than in earnest, and slipped his hand round her body, clasping one soap-slick breast.

"Bully!" Ginny accused him as his hold grew firmer under her struggles. "I did not realize quite how imperative was your need for a bath, sir. If you will unhand me, I will leave you in sole possession."

Alex dropped her abruptly, and she fell back into the tub with a splash that slurped water over the rim onto the wooden boards. He grinned at her indignant expression and picked up the towel from the stool where it lay. "Out." An imperative finger crooked, and Ginny rose, pink and dripping, from the fragrant water.

For long minutes, he looked at her until, with a shy smile,

she said, "Please do not look at me like that."

"But you are beautiful," he said softly. "I cannot help looking at you. Lift your arms behind your head."

Tremulously, she did so, feeling her skin stretch taut across her rib cage, her breasts rise with the movement. Alex exhaled on a long, slow breath. "I want you *now*," he breathed, "but I am rank with sweat and horseflesh and would not sully such sweet-scented skin." He tossed her the towel. "You must dry yourself, I fear, for if I touch you I shall be lost."

Ginny blotted the water from her skin, watching in her turn as he pushed off his britches and dipped into the soap-clouded water. "Allow me to wash *your* back, sir," she said, discarding the towel and coming to kneel beside the tub. Alex lay back under her ministering hands, his eyes closed in blissful peace as she soaped him from top to toe, running her fingers delicately down the sword scars on his ribs and thigh. How many more of those would he acquire before the fighting was done? The thought rose, unbidden and terrifying, and with it the dreadful memory of her dream that had haunted her as she sat, what now seemed an eon ago, on the dining room window seat while Parliament's colonel waited patiently for her breaking. She stopped, stood up, and reached again for the towel.

"What is it?" Alex asked, instantly aware of the change of mood.

"Why, nothing, Alex." Shrugging, she offered him a smile that should have been inviting, but was instead painful.

"You must not lie to me," he said quietly, stepping from the bath. "Not when we are lovers, sweet Ginny."

"I was suddenly afraid for you," she said in a low voice. "I do not think I could bear your death."

Alex came to her in one long stride, wrapping her in his arms, cradling and soothing her with soft murmurs as he eased them both onto the bed and simply held her until her shudders ceased and the peace of acceptance again entered her soul.

When he made love to her, it was with the utmost gentleness, taking her with slow, sure strokes into the green depths of oblivion, and then, when he felt her renewal, he possessed her again, but this time with a fierce, exorcising power that drained her of all but exquisite sensation and cleansed her thoughts of all fear.

"Sweetheart?" He brushed aside the heavy locks of chestnut hair obscuring her face. "We must get dressed. We are summoned to dine at Whitehall, if you remember?"

"Yes, I do." Ginny sat up. "Why am I to meet Cromwell? He can have no interest in a Cavalier prisoner, the daughter of a Malignant."

"On the contrary," Alex said dryly. "It is just those factors that do interest him. He also, I suspect, wishes to see for himself what creature it is that could so cause me to take leave of my senses."

"That does not sound altogether complimentary," Ginny said, swinging her legs over the edge of the bed where they dangled a good six inches from the floor. "In what manner have you taken leave of your senses?"

A sharp fingernail scribbled a path down her spine. "I have told my lord and master that I wish to assume responsibility for you personally. That means, my little rebel, that any crimes against Parliament that you commit will fall to my hand. It means I undertake to protect you and to make the necessary provisions for your keep, be it at my side or in the charge of someone I designate in my stead."

"You dare!" Ginny turned on him fiercely. "We agreed that I would follow the drum."

Alex laughed and pulled her back on the bed. "I have no intention of foisting you on any poor, unsuspecting soul," he declared. "We march to Scotland in three days, and I swear that I shall make a good soldier of you before the journey's done."

And afterward? But Ginny kept the question to herself. The trick of existence in these days of schism seemed to be to look no further than the next morning.

Alex suddenly leaped from the bed with a surge of energy and went to pick up the parcel that he had deposited on the chair when he had first entered the chamber. "I have a gift for you, Ginny, my love. It is to be hoped my eye is as good as I think it."

He dropped the parcel onto her bare thighs, and she looked up at him, startled. "What is it?"

"Open it."

She unfastened the twine and drew from its wrapping a heap of soft turquoise linen. Her eyes shot toward him as he stood, gloriously, unconsciously naked, watching her face intently. "It's lovely," she whispered, shaking out the folds to reveal a gown with a deep, scalloped lace collar, sleeves puffed full from the shoulder, narrowing below the elbow with a row of tiny buttons to the wrist. She had not had a new gown since her wedding. "I cannot accept it, Alex."

"And why not, pray?" His face darkened.

"But I cannot reciprocate," she said hesitantly. "I have nothing of my own . . ." She looked at him, helplessly, hoping he would understand.

"No," he agreed calmly. "You have nothing of your own but what is contained in that baggage roll." He indicated the only possessions she had been able to bring with her from her home. "You have no inheritance, no dowry, no guardian. The first two, I wrested from you as the fortunes of war; the latter role, I have in some measure undertaken myself." He let the statement lie for a minute, then said softly, "Will you argue with me, my raggle-taggle gypsy? Will you argue with my obligation to provide for you? Will you argue with the lover's right to give pleasure as he is able?"

"I will not argue with the latter," she said quietly, "and will accept the lover's gift. As to the first, no." She shook her head, the straight chestnut mane swirling vigorously. "I come with you of my own free will, and you are under no obligations, any more than I am obliged to accept your authority."

"And the authority of a husband? Would you accept that?" The question with all its implications hung in the room where the dust motes danced in the last rays of the evening sun.

"I would have no choice but to do so," she said eventually. "But we are not husband and wife."

"No," he agreed. "We are not. But I am responsible for

250

you, nevertheless. However, let us not discuss this further; it can only lead to acrimony. Put on the gown. I wish to see if I judged the size correctly."

Ginny, accepting the need to leave a discussion for which there could be no mutually agreeable conclusion, willingly obliged and received her own pleasure in Alex's clear delight in the accuracy of length, fit, and color that deepened and darkened her gray eyes, and drew attention to the burnished luster of her chestnut hair.

"You have a good eye, sir," she said, preening herself in front of her patchy reflection in the mullioned window. "Too good for one inexperienced in these matters." Her eyes twinkled roguishly.

"Not your concern, mistress," he said, adjusting the collar and turning her round to retie the sash. "There, that is better." His flat palm lingered for a moment on her bottom, then he sighed regretfully. "We must go, mistress mine. Cromwell does not forgive unpunctuality even from his generals."

"What?" Ginny whirled on him and took in his gleeful expression. "Truly? You are promoted?"

"It seems so," he said, trying to sound indifferent and failing miserably. "Lieutenant-General Marshall at your service, Mistress Courtney."

"Well, I may have little sympathy for the military mind," Ginny said, standing on tiptoe to kiss him, "and even less for the side you support, but I can still find it in my heart to be pleased for you."

Arm in arm, they descended the stairs, receiving the bobbed curtsies of the goodwife and her wenches, the bow of mine host. Ginny realized with a small shock that her wedding ring would not have escaped notice, and there would only be one respectable conclusion to be drawn. Well, let it be so. It could do no harm.

It was but a short distance to the Palace of Whitehall, and they walked, for once unaccompanied by soldierly escort, almost as if they were a prewar strolling couple. "It is to be hoped I do not say anything to offend your Mr. Cromwell," Ginny commented as they turned into the courtyard.

"That is certainly to be hoped," Alex concurred, pausing, his hand on her arm drawing her to a stop. "Cromwell has an exceedingly fiery temper, although it is generally controlled. He is also a most compassionate man and capable of much tenderness. But he will not tolerate lack of respect to himself. You would do well to accord him a degree of reverence."

"I reserve reverence for my king," Ginny said simply, "but I will try not to be impolite."

Alex was little reassured by this, knowing as he did Ginny's capacity for fearless, and generally unthinking, challenges. He had not sought this meeting between his Royalist mistress and his commander-in-chief, but Oliver Cromwell's invitations were in the nature of commands and not lightly rejected.

They passed into the great hall, thronged with officers, dressed like Alex in full uniform, soberly clad civilians, and ordinary soldiers strategically placed at the doors and windows. There were also women, Ginny noted with interest, and not of the Southwark barracks type either. These were the wives of the men who made up Parliament's court at Whitehall, men and women who, for the most part, had had little experience of power until they had taken the right side in civil war. Few of them would have frequented the court of King Charles, and Ginny felt her hackles rising as she examined the fine linens and lace of their gowns, the silk slippers, the glitter of jewelry. Out in the country, the king's loyal subjects were deprived of their lands, of their manors, of the basic necessities of life in many cases. They were hunted like vermin and when they were caught were tortured and strung up for the crows to pick. While these parasites bought for a song the estates of the nobility, proudly displayed the looted jewels, and behaved for all the world as if they were born landed gentry with an impeccable family tree behind them.

"I cannot stay here," she said abruptly and turned back to the door.

"You must!" Alex hissed desperately, seeing Cromwell beckon to him from across the room. "Take a hold of

252

yourself, for God's sake. If you antagonize anyone here, I cannot vouch for the consequences."

"Then you had better let me go," she replied tightly. "I am not afraid of confronting my enemies, but if you are afraid of such a thing—"

"You are going *nowhere*!" he rasped, hanging onto her arm with a frantic strength. "*You* chose to follow the drum, to stay by my side, and so you must do things you do not wish to do. You are going to make your curtsy to Cromwell and keep your indiscreet tongue still."

Slowly the sense of what he was saying penetrated the fog of fury clouding her brain. She was in the midst of her enemies, and only a fool would deliberately court trouble in such a situation. She could keep her integrity in a disdainful silence. With a haughty toss of her head, she allowed Alex to lead her over to the group of officers where Oliver Cromwell held sway.

Her first thought was that this supremely powerful man cut a poor figure. He was not much taller than she, plainly dressed in an ill-cut tunic with wrinkled sash, and his linen was not clean. There was a speck of blood on the narrow collar, and he had no hatband. Then she became aware of a strength emanating from the compact figure, his hand resting on his sword hilt as if it rarely left it, an intelligence to the florid complexion.

"Mistress Virginia Courtney, sir," Alex was saying, and the pressure of his fingers on her arm increased.

Ginny curtsied with care, according Oliver Cromwell just the depth she would consider suitable for a country squire. And she did not lower her eyes. The significance was not lost on Alex, or, indeed, on anyone familiar with the finer points of court etiquette.

Oliver Cromwell frowned. "I understand from General Marshall that you are considered a ward of Parliament, mistress. Is that a position you are content with?" His voice was sharp and unmelodious.

"I would prefer still to be my father's daughter, sir," Ginny replied in a tone devoid of expression. She did not add, "or my husband's wife," for that would be a lie, although it

253

would add even greater weight to her statement.

Cromwell glanced thoughtfully up at his newest general, who was staring stonily into the middle distance. "It is not Parliament's custom to cast the orphans of this war penniless upon the world," he said, "even when those victims be our enemies, Mistress Courtney. General Marshall acted correctly and compassionately."

"I am certain it must be as you say, sir," she responded in a flat voice. "I am hardly in a position to argue."

"What d'ye intend doing with her, Alex?" Cromwell, abandoning the attempt to persuade the prisoner of Parliament's point of view, addressed her protector instead.

"Do you mean at this moment, sir? Or in the long term?" Alex gritted, making no attempt to conceal his angry discomfiture at Ginny's insolence.

A glint of humor softened the commander-in-chief's stern countenance. "I leave the details to you, General. I am sure you are more than equal to the task. Now, what were you saying, Mr. Maidstone?" He turned away, after according Ginny a brief nod, and resumed his interrupted conversation with his steward and member of Parliament, John Maidstone.

"I did warn you," Ginny declared in an impassioned whisper to the frozen-faced Alex. "My father died fighting against that man; you could not expect me to accord him—"

"I expected you to accord him ordinary civility," Alex interrupted.

"So I did," she maintained stoutly. "I spoke only the truth. If Oliver Cromwell does not care to hear it, then more fool him."

"Well, fortunately it did no harm," he said with a sigh. "I cannot really blame you, but your sense of self-preservation is sadly unformed, my dear Virginia. Had he so pleased, Cromwell could have ordered you lodged with some loyal family in Spital Fields, or somewhere, and there would you remain."

"I do not think you believe that," Ginny said, hiding her relief at the cessation of his annoyance. "I do not believe I would remain there at all."

Alex chuckled involuntarily. "No, I do not believe you would either, my resourceful rebel. Let us follow the company into dinner." Guests were already seating themselves at long tables in the banqueting house, and servants were bearing in dishes as Alex and Ginny entered the noisy room where the air was heavy with the rich scents of perfume and spicy food.

"I am not going to the high table," Ginny said, hanging back, when she saw where he was leading her. "That is too much, Alex, to be stared at and prodded like the fat lady at the fair."

"Well, I am damned if I'll dine anywhere else," declared General Marshall, the youngest son of the earl of Grantham. "*You* may sit below the salt if you please."

Ginny did not please, so was obliged to grit her teeth and endure as he seated her at the table on the dais where dined Cromwell's intimates and the most powerful members of his retinue, feasting well above the common herd. She drew a fair degree of attention, but Alex, to her relief, made no attempt to draw her into any of the conversations he was having, introducing her only when it was unavoidable. Thus neglected, and content to be so, she was able to observe the company with as much dispassionate disdain as she pleased. Her platter was piled high with roast boar, her goblet constantly refilled with rich burgundy, and having little else to do, Ginny consumed the food absently. When Alex assisted her to her feet at the end of the meal, her legs seemed to have taken on the consistency of jelly.

"Take me back to the inn," she whispered with some urgency.

"What is it?" Alex looked at her in concern.

"Roast boar," she gasped. "It does not agree with me."

"It is not so much the boar as the burgundy," he chided. "I had thought you more inclined to circumspection."

"Oh, do not gloat," Ginny begged, hanging onto his arm. "I was so bored, I did not notice."

Alex clicked his tongue against his teeth reprovingly but, when he saw that she was in genuine distress, stopped teasing her and bore her out of the palace into the fresh air.

"That is better." Ginny breathed deeply. "But my head is spinning so."

"You must learn to hold your wine, child. It is fortunate Diccon is not here to take his revenge for the way you scolded him this morning. I seem destined to spend my evenings putting to bed intoxicated innocents." Alex was laughing, even as his arm supported her with strong comfort, half carrying her down the street.

"It is only because such rich living has not come my way for the last four years." Ginny attempted to recover her lost dignity. "It is Parliament who lives high on the hog, these days, not Royalists; and my head and my belly are no longer accustomed.

"That would indeed explain it," he agreed gravely, and Ginny giggled, a delightfully girlish sound that he had not heard before. It would be a great pity if it were only to be heard under the influence of burgundy, Alex thought, but then she had had little reason for indulging in girlish giggles since her girlhood had come to such an abrupt close.

The wine, however, did nothing to inhibit her when they attained the seclusion of their chamber. With mischief in her eyes, she proved how very much more adept she was than harlots in Southwark at the art of stripping, teasing, and tantalizing him, dancing just out of his reach until, driven beyond bearing, he seized her and threw her on the bed where she writhed, wonderfully soft and sinuous, until he drew her legs onto his shoulders, and plunged into the very center of her, and her body stilled in wonder, her eyes locked with his through the engulfing tidal wave of eternal pleasure.

Ginny fell asleep almost instantly as the wine finally took its toll, and Alex lay in the darkness wondering when next they would have such an interlude, when again they would be able to carve out a secluded oasis from the overpopulated military desert that he inhabited. He would not be able to act the civilian again in the foreseeable future; from tomorrow, he would have an entire division under his command, men who had probably been used to a lax order and would need much work to prepare them for the task they faced, if

256

they were to become efficient and, therefore, as safe as impending battle could make them. There would be little enough time for lovers' play in the days ahead, but they would take what they could, when they could.

Chapter Fifteen

The transitory nature of their interlude in the Blue Boar was brought home to Ginny forcefully over the next week. She hardly saw Alex, although she seemed to hear his voice constantly, crisp, impatient, and once or twice with that flaying edge that sent everyone in the vicinity scuttling. He had explained to her on the ride back to Southwark how it would be until they began the march to Scotland, and she had shrugged acceptingly. Now, she settled into a pattern similar to that adopted by the other women in the camp, busying herself with domestic matters about the headquarters building, and foraging in the surrounding fields for herbs and simples, replenishing her supplies and preparing medicines in the inn kitchen, filling the air with the distillation of spearmint and tilla, hawthorn berries and blackberry leaves.

If Alex was aware of these activities, he gave no sign, merely acknowledging her absently when they happened to meet around the inn or in the village. At the dinner table, the conversation was always of military matters, a simple continuation of the day's business with his officers, and the talk continued long after she had retired. Ginny lay on her narrow bed in her little cupboard, listening to the rumble of voices below — there were no more riotous evenings of debauchery with the camp whores — trying to stay awake until she heard Alex's step on the stairs, but somehow she never could, and he never came to wake her. The lover had given way to the soldier more thoroughly than ever before, and Ginny wondered a little desolately if, perhaps, the novelty had worn off, and she could no longer distract the man of war with the softer excitements of love and lust.

Unfortunately, when she did inadvertently intrude on his concentration, it was in a somewhat explosive manner that did not lend itself to softnesses of any kind.

Ginny had become rather careless in her physicking visits among the men. She now felt perfectly safe with them, was received warmly and gratefully, knew that what she was doing was important and necessary, knew also that she was more skilled and more knowledgeable than the army surgeons who amputated without consideration, took little care for basic cleanliness, and had little time for ailments that did not require the knife. She visited the camp morning and evening and was soon offering her help to men in other brigades. Since they were all now under the command of General Marshall, that seemed to Ginny perfectly right and proper.

Alex had originally intended to begin the march to Scotland within three days of his visit to Whitehall but soon realized that, in such a short time, he could not possibly lick the division into anything approximating the shape he considered necessary to accomplish the journey in good order. The delay made him irritable, his insistence on perfection made everyone else on edge, and tempers rose like the thunderclouds that suddenly appeared, promising a tempestuous end to the long, dry spell.

"Ah, mistress, you be needed in the camp." Jed appeared in the kitchen, looking for once slightly breathless.

"Is it urgent?" Ginny took a flat iron off the range and spat on the bottom to ascertain its temperature. There was a satisfying sizzle. "It has taken me half an hour to heat the irons, Jed; if I leave them now, they will go cold again." She shook out the folds of one of Alex's tunics and spread the garment on the table. "Not that the general would notice these days if his garments were wrinkled," she added. "Only it seems silly, if I am ironing my own clothes, not to iron his."

"Looked pretty urgent to me," Jed remarked, disregarding the matter of irons. "Man's bleedin' badly. It could be a matter for the surgeons, but—" He shrugged. "It come of a fight, and the general's become uncommon difficult about such things. If the surgeons get to hear of it, sure as life *he* will, and they'd as soon bleed to death."

Ginny pulled a face, well aware of the truth of this. "I'll fetch my basket." Abandoning the irons and the pile of clothes, she went upstairs, returning within minutes to where Jed was still waiting. "Where is the general, this morning, Jed? Do you know?"

"Conductin' a drill on the far parade ground," the batman informed her. "He'll not be back for an hour or so."

Her patient was bleeding profusely from a deep knife wound in the shoulder, but he and his companions seemed mostly concerned that the injury and its cause be kept secret from their superiors. Ginny cleansed and bandaged the gash, heedless of the blood dripping onto her apron. "You'll not be able to use that arm for some days, soldier, not even to carry your pike," she said. "How're you going to explain it?"

" 'Is mates'll cover for him," Jed said calmly. "You'd best be gettin' back, mistress; 'tis almost noon."

Ginny left the camp but found herself reluctant to return to the hot kitchen and the pile of ironing. The day was heavy, and thick clouds of gnats hung in the air as if waiting for the storm that would dispel the muggy tension. She made her way down to the river, hoping for a little breeze coming off the broad green and brown expanse of water that flowed between high banks. It was a peaceful spot, shielded from the camp and the village of Southwark by a screen of trees and shrubs. On the far bank, cows grazed serenely. Ginny glanced up at the salmon sky, remembering the old wives' tale that said cows grazing before thunder would produce curdled milk. Kicking off her sandals, she lay back on the grassy bank, curling her bare toes in the cool green grass that seemed to retain a little river moisture.

Alex came out of the trees a few yards away, smoothing with one pressing finger the irritable frown lines creasing his brow. He was in need of solitude and a quiet unsullied by repetitive, shouted orders and the tramp of boots. The forced inactivity that was yet endlessly busy was driving him to a near-intolerable pitch of frustration. The Scots had crossed the border, and every day Parliament's forces delayed in the south brought the enemy closer. That Parliament's army would defeat them when they eventually came up with the enemy, Alex had not a shadow of doubt, so the delay was not threatening, but for as long as the Scots remained on English soil, the war would drag on and the process of reconstruction could not begin. And he could not begin to think of his own future and how that future could or would be bound up with that of a proud rebel with a beesting tongue and an indomitable spirit.

So absorbed was he in these dismal reflections that he almost fell over the supine figure in his path. The irritation left him miraculously as he looked down at her, and she smiled, squinting her eyes against the bright spot in the clouds where hid the sun. Her hair was in one long braid hanging over her shoulder, and because of the oppressive warmth, she wore only a simple summer kirtle over a thin shift, no chemise and petticoats to trap the heat or obscure the lines of her body.

"Good morrow, General Marshall," said Ginny, sitting up and smoothing down her apron, lifting her face imperatively for a kiss.

Alex, chuckling, squatted on his heels and obliged. "Strawberries," he said thoughtfully, before tasting her lips again. "And honey." He sat down beside her with a sigh of relief. "If ever a man needed a brief respite, chicken . . ."

"Then let us stay here for the afternoon," suggested Ginny, taking his hand and tracing the fingernails intently. "I will return to the inn and bring a picnic."

"I wish it were possible." He sighed again, then frowned.

"What have you done to yourself, Ginny? You are hurt." He touched the bloodstains on her apron.

"Oh, no, 'tis not *my* blood," she said incautiously.

"Then whose is it?" The smile had left his face, the tenderness gone from the green-brown eyes. His eyes fell on the basket of bandages, salves, and medicines on the grass beside her. "What have you been doing, Virginia?"

Ginny decided that she had had enough of scuttling around on her errands of mercy like a spider escaping the broom. "A man from Colonel Chambers' brigade sustained a severe cut. I tended it for him."

"You what! How many times have I told you not to go anywhere near the camp?" he demanded furiously.

"You are being ridiculous, Alex," Ginny said, trying to sound patient and reasonable. "If you will just listen to me for a minute—"

"I asked you a question! How many times?" he interrupted.

Ginny gave up and allowed her own exasperation full rein. "I have lost count; at least half a dozen I should think."

Alex took a deep breath and hung onto his temper by a thread. "I will not tell you again," he said, with what he considered meritorious moderation.

Not so Ginny. "Good," she snapped. "The repetition grows tedious."

Alex paled, and that telltale muscle twitched in his drawn cheek. "The next time you go within a hundred yards of the camp, you will spend forty-eight hours in solitary confinement on bread and water."

Ginny lost her temper. "Yes, just like the baker who supposedly mixed chaff with his wheat, and the sentry who was three minutes late for duty, and the private whose jerkin was stained from campfire smoke and—"

"Yes," Alex roared, even more incensed at this further evidence of her intimacy with the camp. "Just like that." He sprang to his feet, standing over her, hands firmly planted on his hips. "For as long as you march with this division, Virginia Courtney, you will be subject to the same discipline as the rest of us, and don't you ever forget it."

Swinging on his heel, he strode off. Ginny leaped up. "Pigheaded dictator!" she yelled, picking up a rock-hard lump of river mud and hurling it at his departing back. Even as the missile left her hand, she prayed that it would miss its mark, but her aim was true and the distance short. The lump struck Alex squarely between the shoulder blades, and Ginny stood frozen to the spot, her hand clapped to her mouth, waiting in a sort of fearful anticipation.

Alex turned around very slowly, bent, and picked up the missile. He examined it thoughtfully, then tossed it into the bushes. "If I am a pigheaded dictator, you are a virago," he stated matter-of-factly and took a purposeful step toward her. Ginny took an equally purposeful one backward. This curious method of progression continued in silence for several more paces until Ginny suddenly stepped into air, straight off the bank to land with a squelch on her knees on the muddy bottom of the River Thames.

She struggled to her feet with a gasp, her hands coated with the mud that clung to her soaked skirt and encased her toes. Alex stood on the bank regarding her with some satisfaction. "That is quite the best place for you," he said. "It will cool your temper, and you may remain there until I receive the apology you owe me."

In other circumstances, Ginny would have agreed cheerfully that throwing rocks at people did indeed warrant an apology. But not under duress. She looked along the bank. It was steep for as far as she could see, and deeply cut away below the top so that scrambling out, while quite possible, would be an awkward maneuver and one quite easily hampered by someone above who had that intent. Alexander Marshall clearly had that intent.

Very deliberately, she flattened her hand, making a sharp wedge of it, then brought it down on the surface of the water in a vicious chopping movement that sent an arc of water straight at the bank to slap against Alex's chest. It was a trick she had learned in the sea when water fighting with Edmund, and she now employed it with most satisfactory results, driving Alex backward, away from the edge.

Just out of range, he stopped. "So you want to play, do you?" There was a rather alarming glint in his eyes, and Ginny was about to say that that was the last thing she wanted to do when he pulled off his boots and stockings. Open-mouthed, she watched in disbelief as he shrugged out of his tunic, then stood for a minute with his hands on his belt buckle, that same glint in his eye. She stared, wondering if he was really going to do what she thought he was. He was. The belt came undone and dropped to the grass; in one smooth, economical movement, his britches joined it, and Alex stood, lean, hard, and gloriously naked on the bank. And something about this entire, ridiculous business had aroused him mightily.

Ginny stood transfixed, thigh deep in the water, her gown drenched from the shoulders down. Alex jumped off the bank, landing beside her with a splash. "Take off your gown," he demanded, catching the rope of her hair and twisting it around his wrist.

"You are crazed!" She found her voice at last, although it was somewhat faint.

"Possibly," he said, taking another turn of the braid. "Having rocks thrown at one tends to have that effect. Take off your kirtle, unless you wish it torn."

A bubble of laughter grew in her chest, mingling with the undeniable excitement at his naked, aroused proximity. Her fingers fumbled with the hooks at her bodice, but at last they came undone, and she pushed the gown off her shoulders, down her body, over her hips, catching it on her foot, which she lifted clear of the water, grabbing at the soaked heap of material.

Alex released her braid to take the gown, which he wrung out carefully, then tossed onto the bank. "Get out now," he directed.

Ginny, who for one glorious moment had thought he was going to make love to her there in the river, was totally nonplussed. "I do not understand."

"You are not required to understand," he said calmly. "But

it is a perfectly simple thing I asked you to do, so do it. Get out of the water."

"Like this?" She indicated her shift that clung wetly and immodestly to every curve and hollow.

A glow appeared in his eyes. "That, little gypsy, is exactly why I want you to get out."

The deep sensuous glow was as exciting as it was reassuring. Alex was playing a game, and he wasn't sharing the rules, but experience had taught Ginny that Alex's games were never less than immensely rewarding.

She waded to the bank while he stood with hands on his hips watching through narrowed eyes. Scrambling up onto dry land was both awkward and inelegant, and she had little difficulty imagining the picture she must present, covered, yet not covered by the transparent, clinging shift.

"You've a delicious curve to your backside," Alex laughed as she finally reached the top. "Seldom have I been treated to such an alluring spectacle."

"Shame on you!" Ginny got to her feet and marched to the edge of the bank. "You are nothing but a satyr."

"A wild, lustful creature of the woods and streams," Alex agreed, striding out of the water, revealing the wildness of his lust. He sprang with enviable agility onto the bank beside her, then drew her wet length against him, tipping her chin. "I do not know how it is that you always manage to turn away my wrath. You yell insults at me and throw great rocks at my back, and desire takes me totally unawares. It's a magic you have, Virginia." His lips came down on hers with hard possession, and his hands moved to her back, pressing her into his body as if he would imprint her with his shape, before he pushed her down onto the grass, his mouth still locked with hers.

There was nothing gentle about this loving, no time spent on preparing her to receive him, but none was needed. Her own hands helped him eagerly as he pushed the sodden shift up to her waist with rough haste. An impatient knee nudged her thighs apart, and her hips lifted of their own accord as he cupped her buttocks, raising her as he penetrated with a

265

deep thrust that wrenched a gasp of pleasure from her. It was a different kind of loving, one where, although joined, they strove for themselves, clawing their separate ways up separate mountains, until, the instant before the fall, he spoke her name and his mouth seared hers, branding her as his own, and her nails raked the hard-muscled back, staking her own claim.

A clap of thunder and the heavens opened on them as they lay spent and breathless on the grass. Ginny began to laugh weakly, opening her mouth to catch the hard drops. "At least, now, my soaked condition will cause no comment." Spread-eagled, arms stretched wide, she reveled in the sensation as the rain beat down upon her filled and satisfied body.

Alex groaned as he looked at her and felt lust stirring again. "Such a glorious wanton, you are, my Ginny. Never could I have imagined being so in thrall. If I do not leave you now, we will remain forever in the rain on the banks of this river."

"Why not?" Ginny asked softly. "Put duty behind you for one short afternoon."

"I cannot. Do not tempt me." He began to dress swiftly in his rain-soaked clothes while she continued to lie on the grass taking her rain bath. When he was dressed, he bent over her, pulling her firmly to her feet. "You must not catch cold, chicken. Hurry back and change; the temperature will drop rapidly when the storm abates." He kissed the corner of her mouth, then said with quiet gravity, "I meant it, Ginny, about your going into the camp again. We may have made peace, but it alters nothing of what I have said."

It was pointless to reopen the argument, and she shrugged in mute resignation, bending to pick up her kirtle. Alex left, running through the rain, and Ginny dressed and made her way back to headquarters, laughing good-naturedly at the gibes her soaked condition invited from Diccon and the young officers taking shelter in the kitchen.

Something was going to have to be done, Ginny resolved, emerging pink-cheeked from the towel she had been using to

266

rub the water from her hair. How to convince that most infuriatingly stubborn man that in this instance he was quite wrong? Initially, he had had good reason for his edict, but those reasons no longer applied. If he wouldn't listen to her, though, how could she convince him of that? The problem lay entirely in the way he perceived military authority. The issue now was simply one of an order that had to be obeyed without question and for the sake of it. While that form of self-discipline was all very well for soldiers, whose lives and those of others might well depend on implicit obedience, it had no relevance for Ginny. She was needed in the camp, and not even General Marshall was going to deprive those who needed it of her expertise.

The storm passed by late afternoon, leaving the air cool and fresh, the sky a clean-washed, brilliant blue. Ginny went in search of Jed, having the firm conviction that the old soldier's wisdom in this matter would prove illuminating.

She found him in the stableyard, sitting on an upturned rainwater butt, cleaning tack. "Afternoon, Jed," she greeted him casually, fetching a three-legged milking stool from the barn and sitting down beside him. "That was a powerful storm."

"Aye," he grunted, spitting on the saddle resting across his knees and rubbing the saliva into the leather energetically. " 'Bout time, I'd say. Tempers was gettin' short."

"Yes," Ginny agreed, picking up a bit and dipping it in the bucket of water, rubbing with her fingers at the green-flecked stains made by Bucephalus' mouth. "And, on that subject, the general and I had a . . . disagreement."

"Ah?" Jed's faded brown eyes shot her a shrewd look. "Found out about visitin' the camp, did he?"

Ginny took the bit from the water and reached for a cloth, beginning to shine the metal with the intent concentration she brought to most activities. "He says that if I go there again, he'll put me in solitary confinement on bread and water for two days."

"Humph," murmured Jed in his customary laconic fashion.

"Do you think he would?" Ginny asked almost nonchalantly.

"Like as not," replied Jed. "If 'n he said so."

"Yes, that was rather what I thought," Ginny agreed dolefully. "Well, what's to be done, Jed? I cannot take the risk of defying him anymore, but the men need me." She placed the now-shining bit with the rest of the clean tack and picked up a stirrup and leather, methodically rubbing at the dull leather with a damp cloth.

Jed was silent for a while, and Ginny, content to let him mull over the problem, continued with her task. "General says you can't go to the men," he pronounced eventually. "Nothin' that says they can't come to you."

"What?" Ginny stopped working and looked at him, understanding dawning slowly. "You mean they could come to headquarters?"

"Don't see why not," Jed shrugged. "Give 'em a time posted in the camp when you'm available."

"It just might work." Ginny nodded thoughtfully. "And then, perhaps, that obstinate idiot will come to his senses." She looked guiltily at Jed. "I beg your pardon, I should not talk to you in that manner of the general."

Jed grinned. "Bit hard o' hearin' these days, mistress, particularly when it's summat I already know."

Ginny kissed him soundly on a leathery cheek, just as General Marshall on Bucephalus came clattering into the stableyard. "What did you do to deserve that, you old rogue?" he demanded cheerfully of Jed, swinging to the cobbles.

"Jed has more sense in his little finger than some I could mention in their entire bodies," Ginny told him with a teasing smile. "There is a haunch of venison for dinner, so I hope you are all hungry." The smile embraced the rest of the company who had ridden in with the general and was returned with the same natural warmth. Ginny went back to the kitchen to supervise the dinner preparations and put the final touches to the red-currant sauce, well satisfied with the outcome of her discussion with Jed.

The following morning, after breakfast, a trooper, barely a boy with no more than the lightest down on his chin, appeared at the kitchen door, bent double with griping stomach pains that a few questions elicited had begun after he had feasted on green plums from a neglected orchard in the village. He was a town lad from the north, and Ginny kept her caustic comments to herself as she mixed a herbal potion that would ease the gripes and keep him out of the latrines. No country-born boy would touch green fruit, but so many of these children had been flung into manhood and war before they had experienced anything beyond the four walls of home.

"Who was that?" Diccon inquired curiously, coming in from the yard.

Ginny told him, and then, because she could think of no good reason not to, explained the situation in its entirety. Diccon listened in some trepidation, wondering if simple knowledge would make him an accomplice. Ginny, guessing at his thoughts, laughed at him and told him he was a milksop to be concerned, but if he was afraid, he could keep out of the way when the men came in search of her.

Diccon bristled at this implicit accusation of cowardice and would have stomped off in a huff if Ginny hadn't apologized, much as she would have done to Edmund in similar circumstances, and Diccon, placated, became quite pink-cheeked with pleasure—until Alex's arrival in the kitchen sent him scurrying off with a muttered excuse.

"What the devil's going on, Ginny?" Alex asked. "First, I find you kissing Jed, and now Diccon looks as if he's just been given a glimpse of nirvana."

"Well, it's a little difficult to hold oneself aloof, when one is living in such close quarters," Ginny replied, reasonably enough.

Alex looked at her closely. "You are up to no good," he pronounced.

She smiled. "I cannot imagine what I could get up to here, surrounded by Parliament's army. I dare swear I am the only Royalist for miles around."

269

"That is what makes me uneasy," he said. "I know that you cannot possibly find an outlet for your subversive inclinations, but there is something about you at the moment that sounds the alarm—"

"Beg your pardon, sir, but the patrol is ready." Captain Baldwin provided the interruption, saluting smartly in the doorway.

"I am coming directly, Captain," Alex responded, still frowning quizzically at Ginny; then he shook his head in resignation. "I shall have to discover whatever it is later, I fear. We shall be back by sundown."

When the patrol returned an hour before sunset, Alex received the answer to his question in full measure. A line of troopers trailed from the kitchen door of the inn out into the yard. They were an orderly group, chatting quietly amongst themselves, and at the sight of the general sprang to attention.

"Find out what the hell's going on, will you?" Alex said in clipped words to Major Bonham before pushing past the troopers in the doorway and striding into the kitchen.

The youngster sitting on a stool at the table, his head bent as Ginny stood above him, a sharp object poised over his neck, leaped to his feet, stammering.

"Sit down!" Ginny said impatiently. "You should not make sudden moves when someone is about to stab you with a needle."

"At ease, trooper," Alex said, well aware that no blame for his presence in headquarters attached to the soldier. He said nothing to Ginny, merely sat down at the end of the table, one leg crossed over the other, and watched as she lanced the enormous boil on the soldier's neck, squeezing out the poisonous matter until the blood ran, while her patient endured in stoic silence.

Major Bonham came into the room, intent on giving his general the required explanation for this extraordinary occurrence. Since it was immediately apparent that the explanation was not necessary, he asked General Marshall in an expressionless voice if he had any further orders, for instance, the dispersal of the men outside.

Ginny, in the process of anointing the trooper's neck with a soothing salve, paused, her hands poised. Was Alex, the General Marshall of rigid principles and invincible purpose, beyond redemption? Would he see only the clever circumvention of his orders and not the need that justified the means? The man, Alex Marshall, would see the latter, but could that man be allowed to supersede the soldier?

"No, leave them be, Major," Alex said slowly. "It is to be assumed that they have good reasons for being here." He remained watching until the last man had gone and he had learned a good deal. While the general's presence caused some awkwardness, not one of the men seemed to feel any with Ginny in whom they confided symptoms, painful, embarrassing, or trivial, with remarkable ease. She was cheerfully matter-of-fact, did not blench at the most repellent sores and infections, and dispensed advice freely and with earthy bluntness.

As the lady of a great house, she would have been responsible for the health and doctoring of her household and, frequently, the tenants, but Ginny's skills and manner went far beyond such basic duty and ordinary training. The men treated her with the respect they would have afforded the wife of their liege lord, and the trust they would repose in someone who clearly had their interests at heart and knew beyond a shadow of doubt what she was doing.

When the kitchen was empty of all but themselves, Ginny began to put away her instruments and medicines, saying nothing to Alex who continued to sit at the table. He noticed how she washed everything with scrupulous care in boiling water, how she scrubbed her hands, and never had he seen anyone take this kind of care. He was no stranger to field hospitals, where one bloody body replaced another on the operating table, knives and probes were rarely even wiped between patients, blood-blackened bandages were replaced over suppurating wounds.

"Why do you concern yourself so much with cleanliness?" he asked eventually.

Ginny shrugged. "I do not know exactly why it should be so, but it seems that malignancy is less frequent if wounds are kept clean. A goodwife in Freshwater taught me much, and she was most insistent that cleanliness aided healing. But she did not know why, either." She laughed. "It is simple enough to do and takes but little time, so I do it." There was a short, but far from empty silence. Then she said, "Will the general permit me to continue doctoring his troops?"

"It seems the question should be, 'Will the general with a good grace permit you to continue?' " Alex replied. "Since it is clear that the general cannot prevent you."

"And will he?"

"Come here."

When she came over to him, he pulled her down onto his knee. "Alex, anyone could walk in," Ginny protested.

"Unlikely," Alex said dryly, "since I am certain everyone is aware that you and I have something to discuss that does not require an audience."

Ginny kissed his nose. "Is the general perhaps afraid that his consequence will suffer, if it is seen that I have defied him successfully?"

Alex smiled reluctantly. "If that were the case, I should be sorry for it. A short while ago, it probably was the case, but since an intractable gypsy entered my life, I have learned a few lessons. You may move freely among the men since you are clearly in no danger from them, and that was my only concern. However, you are not a free agent, chicken, not for as long as you follow the drum. There will be orders and restrictions, some of which you will not agree with, may not even understand, but you *must* agree to obey them, even if I do not have time to explain the reasons to your satisfaction."

Ginny sat upon his knee and thought this over. "I will agree on condition that you *do* explain them as soon as you have the opportunity, and that *you* agree to hearken to my opinions, however disagreeable they may seem." She punctuated the statement with a short, firm nod, pursing her lips.

Alex gave a shout of laughter. "You are a consummate negotiator, Mistress Courtney. There seems no end to your talents. We are agreed, then." He tipped her off his knee and stood up, the laughter fading from his expression. "We begin the march to Scotland on the morrow. It will be arduous and frequently uncomfortable, sweeting. It is to be hoped you do not regret your choice."

"I do not think there ever was a choice," she said with equal gravity. "Did you not once say that I could no more leave you than you could leave me? I will follow you to the gates of hell, my love, whatever the differences that lie between us."

Speechless, Alex took her in his arms, and they clung together in a moment of passionate confirmation that transcended all but the absolute commitment of a love that had come from nowhere, had not been sought, and could never be denied.

Part Two

That love would prove so hard a master

Chapter Sixteen

"God's death, but this northern clime is fit only for the divil!" Giles Courtney tossed the fiery contents of a metal pannikin down his throat with a disgusted snarl and limped to the door of the thatched hovel, which provided insubstantial shelter from the rain sheeting down across the Northumbrian hills outside. Insubstantial, maybe, but its inhabitants were a deal luckier than the massed army dripping under canvas beyond the door.

"Take it easy, Giles. Have some more brandy." Lord Peter Ottshore pushed the bottle across the table, exchanging a look with his companions. They could all sympathize with a man when an old wound, exacerbated by damp and cold, pained him anew. Giles Courtney had lain near death for nigh on two months, throughout the horrendous weeks of the retreat, and only a miracle had saved his leg. He was still far from strong, even after eighteen months holed up in the Scottish Highlands after the surrender of Oxford. But Courtney was a difficult man to sympathize with. He didn't suffer with grace or courtesy, and was overly ready to use the injury as excuse to avoid duty.

"This is a miserable billet we have found, by the Lord's name." James, Duke of Hamilton, commander of the Royalist forces, pushed through the ill-fitting door, slapping a sodden gauntlet against the palm of his hand. He tossed his hat with its bedraggled curling feather into a corner, on the hard-packed earth floor. "It's to be hoped we can get south of Durham before the rebels come up with us. That rabble out there," he gestured contemptuously to the camp outside, "haven't a soldier's bone between them. We need all the time we can get to knock 'em into shape."

"Raw recruits will be no match for the veterans of the New Model," a fair-haired colonel agreed. "But it's hard to drill them in this weather. Poor sods are soaked to the skin as it is, with small chance of getting dry."

"Won't do them any harm," Giles Courtney said sourly. "It's to be hoped they don't turn tail and run at the first sight of Cromwell."

"You've no cause to accuse them of cowardice, Courtney," the duke of Hamilton said with an edge to his voice. "They're untried, but no worse, and it's encouragement they need, not unfounded criticism. Aren't you officer of the watch?"

Giles Courtney flushed and muttered sullenly that he was, cramming his hat on his head before going out into the dismal evening. Eighteen months he had spent with this damned army, eighteen months of pain and discomfort with nothing to show for it but the prospect of a suicidal battle, throwing virgin recruits against the highly trained, disciplined veterans of Parliament's New Model Army. If he had had any sense, he would have kept out of it from the beginning, but his damned wife had thrown the death of her father in his face, and even his mother, weeping though she was, had pointed out that he was the only able-bodied man for miles around who had not declared himself for the king. And just what the devil were his wife and mother doing now? Someone would have got a message through to them after Oxford that he had been wounded near to death, but the retreat had been such a disorderly scuttle to the north, no further messages had been possible. Had he been conscious, instead of half out of his senses with pain, he would have insisted on being conveyed back to Dorset, but he had been bundled along with the baggage, tormented by surgeons. . . . And now, whenever it rained, which it did without cease, the pain in his hip blossomed exquisitely, and no one gave a damn. Virginia had some skill, as he remembered. Not of the tender, womanly kind with soft murmurs and cool hands and absolute attention to his every wish, even before it was articulated, but she produced potions and ointments that had the power to alleviate.

Virginia, his wife, bound to him with the indissoluble ties of duty. But, somehow, she was not dutiful. He could not put his finger on it, but he knew it was so. She did not contradict him, she was obedient, she lay beneath him without a murmur, she waited on him and accorded him all the respect due to her husband. But she was not truly submissive, truly dutiful. His mother had seen it from the beginning, had attempted to cow her daughter-in-law, had encouraged her son to assert his mastery in whatever ways were necessary. But there was something about those gray eyes that had prevented him from using physical means of subjugation, that had scared him even as it challenged him. It would not do so in the future, he thought. War and wounds had toughened him, and no weak female challenge would prevail again. The image of her body flashed across his mind's eye, and his loins stirred. He hadn't had a woman for eighteen months. God willing he would get back to the one who belonged to him, who could be spread and taken whenever her lord desired. . . .

Ginny looked down the hill, down at what once had been the peaceful, verdant orchards of Kent. Now, there was only devastation, the fruit trees cropped for fuel, and in vengeance, fields and gardens laid to waste. She looked at Alex, sitting like stone on the charger's back, gazing at what used to be the fertile lands of the Grantham estates. A gray stone manor house nestled at the foot of a small hill, but its park was no longer green, just the red brown of churned-up earth, scarring the countryside.

"Would it not be best to continue on your way?" she asked softly.

"I cannot. I have come this far and must go on. I must find out the worst, who is left alive . . ." His lips twisted in a grim smile. "There will be no welcome, of course. But if I may be of help, then I have to offer."

Ginny made no reply as the cavalcade moved off down the hill toward Alex's home. It was a small detour they made on the road to Scotland, and she had watched the agonizing process of decision as he had weighed up the knowledge that he would be regarded as an enemy at best, vilified as a traitor at worst by the kin whom he sought to help. She had offered no opinion, knowing that in this matter not even the lover had any rights, but a premonition of pain scudded over her soul as they approached the house, the pain that she would feel at his wounds.

The occupation of the Grantham estates had been thorough and vicious. The walls of the park land were tumbled, there were great bare patches on the grassland, where tents had been pitched and the blackened roots of tree stumps felled, presumably for firewood. Rich, brown plow land beyond the park was overgrown with thistles, with a few lean cattle scratching for subsistence. No smoke rose from the chimneys, and as they drew closer, they saw that the windows gaped, glassless, to the elements. The house looked shuttered and untenanted, except for a clothesline in what had once been the kitchen garden where hung a few garments flapping desolately in the breeze. Even the stone sundial had been smashed, the branches of the apricot tree wrenched from their tethers against the mellow stone wall so that they hung, broken, the fruit pulped on the ground beneath.

They rode beneath the gatehouse into the outer court, and there Alex gestured to his officers to remain, and he went forward alone into the inner court. Some instinct prodded Ginny into following. She looked up at the belfry and the weather vane, symbols of normality that alone seemed to have been untouched by destruction. Then a woman came out onto the steps, and Alex drew rein. Ginny followed suit, keeping behind him, not knowing whether he was aware of her presence or no; whether, if he was aware of it, he would bid her leave him to face the uncertainty of reunion alone.

"What more can you want with us?" The woman spoke slowly, weary with bitterness. "You left little enough standing on the last occasion, but I am sure you will find what little remains." She turned back to the door.

"Joan, do you not know me?" Alex spoke, his voice sounding strangely unlike his own.

The woman turned, brushed a straggling wisp of faded brown hair from her eyes. "Alex? It is you?" She shook her head in disbelief. "What have you come for? To gloat? To see what we have become? You will find here only the elderly and infirm, the women and the children. Your brothers are not here to stand against you; your victory will be easy enough."

Alex dismounted. "Joan, I am here to do what I can for you." He walked toward her, and she stepped back.

"You dare to offer Parliament's succor to those whom Parliament has destroyed?" The figure swayed, then crumpled on the step.

Ginny leaped from her horse, reaching the step as Alex knelt, lifted the inert figure against his shoulder. "She has but swooned," she said swiftly, feeling for the pulse, lifting the eyelids.

Joan Marshall opened her eyes, looking directly into the haunted ones of her brother-in-law. "Lie still," he said urgently as she struggled against him. "Ginny, what must we do for her?" He turned in appeal to Ginny who had stood up again, shocked at the women's scarecrow thinness, the face that had clearly once been pretty striated with deep lines.

"It is exhaustion, I think," she said quietly. "Lady, may I help you to your bed?"

"Not if you don't wish for typhus," Joan Marshall said, her voice stronger, acidulated now. "Take your army and leave us be, Alex. We've the sickness in the house, and you'll not be wanting to come too close, not even to destroy."

"Who has it?" Alex asked, ignoring his sister-in-law's tone, brushing aside her words.

"Little Joe," she gave him answer, and the tired blue eyes filled suddenly with the tears of utter desperation.

"Sweet Jesus," Alex whispered. "He cannot be above six

years old."

"How many days?" Ginny asked, her voice sounding a note of brisk matter-of-factness in the quiet court.

"This is the ninth," the sick child's mother responded. "So far no one else has succumbed."

"Has the fever broken at all?"

"No," Joan shook her head, "he is wild with it, and I can do nothing to ease him, although he will allow no one else near him." She stood up, allowing the support of Alex's arm as if there was no energy left for the old quarrels. "I must go back to him directly. I only came down because old Martha saw your troops and was like to fall into a convulsion. You know how she can be?"

Alex nodded. "I am here to help, not harm, and I will tell her so myself." He walked to the door, but Joan caught his arm.

"Alex, you cannot go to them. They would cut out their tongues rather than speak with you."

A ghost of a smile hovered over his lips. "Then I shall not expect a response, sister. I will do all the talking, but I must go inside in order to discover what needs to be done."

"Take me to the child, lady," Ginny said. "Perhaps I may be of help."

Joan Marshall looked at her curiously. "Who are you that rides with Parliament's army?"

"The general's mistress," Ginny said with brutal candor. "Virginia Courtney." She dropped a mock curtsy. "As good a Royalist as yourself, madam, for all that I love Parliament's general and trail Parliament's drum."

Joan looked at Alex in bewildered disbelief, and he smiled faintly. "Virginia is never one to beat about the bush, sister. She speaks only the truth. Virginia, this is the Lady Joan Marshall, my brother Joe's wife." Then he took Ginny's hand. "I do not wish you to enter the house, chicken."

"I am not afraid of the sickness," she said calmly. "I have nursed three people with it and have never fallen ill myself. It is a disease that passes me by. But you should not enter, or allow any of the men to do so, lest it sweep through the division."

282

Alex frowned, remembering how four years earlier the scourge of typhus had decimated the armies on both sides of the fighting, killing more than ever died by the sword. "I was afflicted as a child," he said, "so may enter with impunity. But you are right, no one else shall do so."

"Then will you fetch my basket?" Ginny asked, "and bring it to me. I will go with Lady Joan now."

Joan looked hesitant, and Alex said gently, "Ginny has some considerable skill, Joan, a gift aided with knowledge. Will you not trust her just because she rides with me?"

Joan passed a hand across her eyes. "I have no strength left for principles and causes. I will leave that to the men. Kit and Joe have enough hatred for you, Alex. You do not need mine, too."

"No." He shook his head, the green-brown eyes filled with a deep sorrow. "And my father, also, would prefer the son dead than traitorous." Turning, he went out to the far court where waited his officers.

Ginny looked after him for a moment, her heart filled with his pain; then she turned back to Joan. "We each make our choices, lady, and live with their fruits. The best we can hope is that the reasons for making those choices stand firm. Alex is a committed man; he would not and could not see any alternatives to the actions he has taken in this business."

"No," Joan said quietly, leading the way inside. "We all know that, but for his father and brothers, there are no extenuating circumstances."

"I do not think my father would find any, either," Ginny said. "But he died at Naseby, so is spared the grief of knowing that his only child has thrown in her lot with a traitor."

They passed through the great hall where the ripped paneling hung from the walls stripped bare of hangings. The stairs had been hacked loose, broken in places so that they had to tread carefully as they went up. "We live in the gallery," Joan explained. "We have found sufficient hangings and the bare necessities of furniture for the one room."

"And the child?" Ginny asked. "You do not keep him with the others?"

"No. We have taken up residence in a small chamber off the gallery." A tear rolled slowly down the thin, drawn cheek. "I fear that he will not last the night, and I am so afraid for the other children. For myself, I care not, but I fear to go near them, and the little ones do not understand." She opened a door at the end of a corridor, and Ginny found herself in the long gallery where a group of people looked up with eyes as hostile as they were fearful.

A string of tots hurled themselves at Joan Marshall, and she held them off. "Patience, I beg you take them."

A young woman rose swiftly from the window seat and came to her rescue, hushing the children who began to whimper.

"Are they come again?" An old voice croaked, and an elderly woman tottered forward, leaning heavily on a stick.

"It is Alex, Martha," Joan said. "He brings help."

"Help! We want nothing from the traitorous whelp," exploded a gray-haired man who looked able-bodied until Ginny noticed the club foot. "Who's this?" He waved at Ginny.

"Mistress Virginia Courtney," Joan said, somewhat helplessly. "I do not quite understand it, but she is no rebel, and she has some knowledge of the typhus."

"I am the daughter of John Redfern, of the Isle of Wight, widow of Giles Courtney, of the Dorsetshire Courtneys," Ginny said swiftly. "Will you not take me to the child, Lady Joan?"

Joan, with transparent relief, moved across the gallery and opened a door at the far end into a tiny antechamber furnished with a pallet and a stool. "They would not understand your relationship with Alex," she murmured.

"No, I am sure they would not. I do not quite understand it myself," Ginny said evenly, dropping to her knees beside the pallet where lay the almost inert figure of a small boy. She drew back the thin cover and raised his nightshirt, examining the red rash that covered his body. The child stirred, cried, and began to toss violently until he fell back, prostrated by the effort.

"We must break the fever," Ginny said, almost to herself,

feeling the weak, tremulous pulse. "It seems that the heart fails if the fever continues much beyond the eleventh day."

The child's mother moaned, a defeated little sound; then the door opened, and Alex appeared with Ginny's basket. He touched the child's burning forehead. "My godson," he said quietly. "My brother Joe's oldest child, after his father, the next earl of Grantham."

"I need a brazier," Ginny said, disregarding this information as totally irrelevant to the matter in hand. "With charcoal. Also, vinegar, and some hanging for the window." She indicated the window slit high up on the wall where, like the others in the manor, the glass had been broken. "Lady Joan, if you will bathe in vinegar and burn those clothes you have on, you will not carry infection to the other children. I will nurse the boy alone. Alex, I am sure you can do something about making the house more habitable. It is shameful that they must live in only one room. You must see what supplies they have, and augment them from those you carry. There is enough flour, corn, and meat traveling with the division to feed more than one army."

"I have already given the necessary orders," Alex said dryly. "You see to your business, Mistress Courtney, and leave me to mind mine, as you once told me to do."

"And monstrous enraged it made you," Ginny reminded him with a slight smile that she then directed toward Joan Marshall. "Do not despair, lady. I have seen worse cases, but it will be as well if you were to leave me with him. When he is on the mend, he will be fractious and demanding, and you will require all your strength. 'Twould be as well to take what rest you may, now."

"Come, Joan." Alex cupped his sister-in-law's elbow and propelled her back into the gallery. "Do as Ginny says and bathe and burn your clothes. I will procure the charcoal and brazier."

"You take your black, traitorous soul out of here, Alexander," the old woman hissed, waving her stick at him. "We've no need of the divil's aid."

"That is fortunate, Aunt Martha, since I am not sufficiently acquainted with the gentleman to beg him for favors," Alex retorted. "But you may vilify me as you please; I am not leaving here until I have done something to make the place habitable." He strode out of the gallery, down the stairs, and out into the sunshine. "Jed!"

"General?" Jed appeared instantly. " 'Tis criminal what they've done to the place."

"Aye," Alex agreed, hard-faced. "It bears the mark of Colney's troops. There'll be a reckoning between him and me." He was silent for a minute, as if forgetting what he had wanted Jed for. Then, with a soft oath he shook his head as if to dispel the train of thought. "Little Joe has typhus, Jed. Mistress Courtney wishes for a brazier, charcoal, and vinegar. Can you procure them?"

"Aye, sir." Jed saluted, but then couldn't help the question. "How bad is the little 'un, sir?"

"Bad enough," Alex replied shortly. "It's to be hoped the others remain well. Lady Joan has been tending him herself and has kept apart, so . . ." He shrugged. The progress of the disease was a mystery to them all. They knew only that once it caught hold, it spread like brushfire, cutting a swath of death through all who fell in its path.

"Colonel Bonham?" he called to the erstwhile major whose promotion had followed his superior's. "Quarter the men in the park; they can do little damage to it, now. Then I want working parties to shutter the windows, repair the doors, and clear the debris from the kitchen garden. I want firewood cut and stacked, and the pantries filled with supplies."

For two days, the Grantham manor resounded to the sounds of hammer and saw, to the cheery shouts of troopers who found themselves doing the tasks they had done all their lives until war had wrenched them from domestic toil and husbandry. And throughout, Ginny kept vigil by little Joe's pallet, the room darkened by a hanging over the window, the candle kept shielded to protect the child's aching eyes. The room was hot as the brazier burned, filling the air with the powerful aromatic scents of herbs that Ginny cooked in a skillet over the charcoal. Little Joe moaned and thrashed beneath the pile of heavy blankets that his nurse had requisitioned from the division. Whenever one scrawny little arm managed to push off the covering, she replaced it instantly, praying for the sweat that would bring the fever break. Every few hours, she raised the prostrated little body against her shoulder and forced a little of the herbal medicine between his lips in spite of the feeble resistance.

The food that Joan brought her remained mostly untouched; inactivity in the close atmosphere of the cramped space did little to promote appetite. On the evening of the third day, Alex and Joan both came into the little room, defying her interdiction.

Ginny waved them away impatiently. "You must not be in here. There is nothing you can do."

"You must take a walk in the fresh air," Alex said quietly. "I will watch Joe while you walk with Joan."

"That is not necessary," Ginny replied shortly. "And you do not know what to do for him."

"You will tell me," Alex answered. "It is necessary, or you will become ill yourself."

"Nonsense." Ginny brushed aside his hand as he moved to draw her off the stool. "I am perfectly strong, and this cannot continue for very much longer anyway. There must be a crisis soon, or . . ." Death was a fact of life they were all familiar with, and there was little point denying the truth.

"I will remain with you," Joan said, touching her son's wasted cheek with her little finger. "It is my place to be with him when the end comes." Her voice was strong; the last three days had restored her, had brought relief from the burdens of caring for the little group who looked to her for leadership, for all decisions. Alex had taken over that responsibility, sublimely indifferent to the castigations of the elderly until their comments had ceased. Yet his sister-in-law knew that he was not indifferent, that each barb lodged deep. It had been hardest for him with the children, who regarded their uncle from behind adult skirts, fearful as if an ogre had come amongst them. They had not seen him for four years, and most were too young to have any very clear memory of the young uncle who had laughed and joked with their parents, had played with the little ones and tossed them in the air. But they had heard much talk of the traitor, the man who had betrayed king and family, who had sent their grandmother into her grave, who was considered no longer of Grantham kin.

"In the morning," Alex said, "you will leave this room, Ginny, if I am obliged to carry you out." It was a small assertion, but he felt compelled to make it. He could not say to her, not now when his nephew's life hung in the balance, that he could not remain in Kent for more than one more day. He had done all he could to make the house habitable and had already delayed overlong in resuming the march to Scotland. If Ginny exhausted herself with nursing as she seemed inclined to do, she would have difficulty keeping up on a forced march, but he would not be able to slow the pace for her.

The door closed softly behind him, and the two women drew closer together beside the pallet in the hot, brooding silence, watching for the arrival of death. "Have you news of your husband?" Ginny asked, thinking of the child's father unaware of his son's agony.

"Not for some time," Joan replied. "He and Kit, Alex's second brother, were with the rising at Colchester. I received news that they still lived, but no more." She sighed. "Kit's wife has gone to be with her mother who is ailing, but she left the children here because the journey was too long and fraught. I cannot blame her, but I've much need of support." There was a short silence; then she went on with some difficulty. "I very much fear that they will all blame me for accepting rebel supplies. But what can I do? There is not enough food and fuel, and the children have been hungry. What are we to do in the winter with no glass to the windows, the doors hanging on their hinges, no fuel for the fires?"

"They cannot blame you in such a case," Ginny said, taking her hand.

"Oh, Ginny, you do not understand the extent of their hatred. Perhaps they would understand if the help had been offered by some rebel other than Alex. But they will not rest until they see their brother dead, and they would starve rather than accept food at his hands."

"And see their children starve?" Ginny demanded.

"I fear so. It is an unreasoning passion that holds them and their father. If they should come up with Alex, there will be bloody battle, and they will show no quarter."

Ginny shivered as she spoke what she knew to be the truth. "They should not expect any from Parliament's general, either, Joan, not if his cause is at stake."

The child suddenly moaned, his body convulsed beneath the covers, and Ginny reached for a cloth soaked in lavender water, laying it on his forehead, her face grim as she faced the knowledge that the convulsion could be the beginning of the end. The child's mother knew it, too, and held her son's burning clawlike hand, her face wiped clear of expression in the moment of despairing certainty. Little Joe was now so hot his skin seared Ginny's hands as she stripped away the covers and began to bathe the twisted, thrashing body with the lavender water. He cried suddenly and became still.

Joan laid the little hand back on the bed and stood up, turning away from Ginny as she yielded the fight and let grief have its way.

"It is over," Ginny said softly, straightening the covers. "Thank God for his mercy. I will make a syrup of rose hips directly, for he will be thirsty when he wakes."

"Wakes?" Joan swung round, her ravaged face bemused as hope waged war with disbelief. "Wakes?"

"Aye," Ginny smiled. "The crisis is past. He is sleeping peacefully." Joan fell to her knees beside the bed, and Ginny went out into the gallery, blinking painfully at the light. Her legs felt suddenly shaky, and she leaned against the wall, for the moment unaware of the circle of anxious eyes fixed on her.

"Mistress Courtney," Patience said hesitantly, "is there news?"

Ginny rubbed her eyes and shook her head with an impatient movement as if to dispel the cobwebs, then raised her head, her face tired but radiant. "Your pardon. The child will live."

Alex had been standing apart, looking down at the

devastation of his family's park through the now glazed window, when Ginny had come into the gallery. When she had leaned against the wall in a manner almost defeated, his first thought had been that little Joe had died of the typhus, and sorrow had welled, keeping him at the window for a moment, even as his mind reached out to her across the room. Then, when he heard her words, he strode over, taking her in his arms, heedless of the others who were too full of their own joy to pay much attention anyway.

"You are exhausted," he chided, his voice stern, belying the love and relief as he held her face between cupped hands and examined the drawn skin, the purple-smudged eyes, the gray cast of fatigue. "And you are grown thin."

That made her smile. "In but three days, Alex? It is not possible. I am as robust and round as ever."

"You are neither robust nor round," he asserted. "You must eat and sleep at once."

"First, I must make a syrup of rose hips for little Joe," Ginny said, pulling away from him.

"Patience and Aunt Martha will do that," Alex stated firmly. "Will you not?" He turned to the two women, the old and the young. "Mistress Courtney has done sufficient for the Granthams, I believe."

There was a harshness in his voice that made Ginny wince and protest softly, "I have done little enough, Alex. There is no call to speak in that fashion." But Alex had listened enough to the angry, ungrateful words, and while he was prepared to accept them for himself, he would not allow his family to ignore the obligation they stood under to a stranger who had given so much of herself without thought.

Ginny turned away from their embarrassment with a dismissive gesture and went to the door. Alex followed, catching her arm. "I am going to look after you," he said. "Come with me."

Too weary to protest, and, indeed, not loath to yield control in this moment of utter weakness, Ginny allowed him to take her hand and lead her through the corridors into the west wing of the house. Here, no attempt had been made to restore the rooms to habitability. Doors hung on their hinges, giving glimpses of ruined chambers where the wind whistled through smashed windows. Plaster dust and sawdust lay thick on the floors of the passage, and Ginny wondered why he was taking her on this desolate expedition, when all she wanted was to curl up in a corner of the gallery and sleep.

They came to a door at the end of the passage. Alex opened it, ushering her inside with an imperative hand in the small of her back. The room contained a feather mattress, the covering a little torn, but otherwise it was whole, a chair, table, and Alex's belongings.

"This was my boyhood room," he explained with a tiny smile. "I have taken refuge here with my memories. Sit down." He pushed her onto the stool, went over to his baggage, and drew out a leather flagon. "Take some of this, and I will be back in a moment."

There was brandy in the flask, and the first sip was almost enough to render Ginny unconscious in her fragile state. She sat on the stool and blinked bemusedly, feeling the warm lethargy seep through her. There was such utter silence in this deserted corner of the house she could almost imagine she was alone in the world. But the door opened again, and Alex came in carrying a round tin tub and a jug, both of which he placed on the floor. "I cannot find a proper bath," he said, "but this will do well enough. Stand up, now."

Ginny obeyed, taking another sip of brandy first. "Feels wonderful," she said.

"Yes, well, you may not have any more until you have eaten something," he told her, removing the flagon from her grasp before beginning to undress her with an efficient objectivity. "Stand in the tub." She stepped over the rim with unquestioning compliance and stood still, swaying slightly, as Alex sponged her body with cool water from the jug. "You are definitely thinner," he remarked, passing the cloth over her ribs, lifting her breasts in the palm of his free hand.

"I am capable of doing this for myself," Ginny murmured, although, in her state of satisfied exhaustion, the sensation of yielding control was quite wonderful.

"You are too tired to do it properly," Alex replied calmly,

sliding the cloth inside her thighs. "For three days you have been wearing the same clothes and have not moved from that room. You stand in sore need of a little soap and water."

Ginny chuckled weakly but did not disagree. Her eyes kept sliding to the feather mattress that seemed to become larger and fluffier at each glance. There was a knock at the door, and Alex draped a towel over her shoulders and went to open it. She heard Patience say something in a hesitant voice and Alex respond, sounding kinder than he had done before. Then he came back into the room bearing a steaming bowl and a hunk of rye brown bread.

"I am too tired, Alex," Ginny protested, knowing the food was for her.

"You will eat a little," he replied. "Tomorrow we must leave here and ride hard, sweetheart. You have to regain your strength quickly."

He crumbled the bread into the rich broth and patiently coaxed her to take enough to satisfy him, interspersed with sips of brandy. At last, she was allowed to curl onto the mattress, which proved to be every bit as soft and fluffy as Ginny had anticipated. It enclosed her in its softness, and she was asleep before Alex had drawn the coverlet over her.

He left the room quietly, although doubting that an earthquake would disturb the sleeper, and went back to the gallery where the others were having supper.

"Have you supped, Cousin Alex?" Patience asked in a tentative voice. It was the first time he had been afforded any signs of courtesy, let alone friendly acknowledgment, from anyone but Joan.

"Not yet, Patience," he replied with the warm smile that transformed the soldier's generally unyielding countenance. "I wish to talk with Joan first; then I will dine with my officers." The club-footed Jonathan Marshall humphed at this. "We shall be gone from here by tomorrow noon, Jonathan," Alex told him tonelessly. "I'll not come within your sight again, you may rest assured."

"And what of Mistress Courtney?" Aunt Martha demanded. "You'll leave her here to help Joan?"

"I'll do no such thing!" Alex exclaimed. "It is not her job to bear the burdens of the Granthams. It is for you to support Joan, something you will do a great deal more effectively if you spend a little less time complaining!" With that, he stalked into the little chamber where his nephew lay, attended by his mother.

"Oh, Alex," Joan said softly, "you should not have said that to Martha. It is hard for her with that inflammation of the joints, and she is in pain much of the time. Ginny said she would make up a poultice for her."

"Ginny is asleep, and if I have anything to do with it, she will remain so until just before we leave on the morrow," Alex stated with a degree of force. "She seems to think it her duty to aid the afflicted whenever they come to her notice, and I do not seem able to break her of the habit."

Joan smiled slightly. "Will you lift little Joe for me? I wish to give him some more of this physic. I am sure it is what has saved him. Ginny has been giving it to him every two hours."

Alex sat on the pallet, raising the scrawny little body against his shoulder, whispering soft reassurances as Joe whimpered. "Are you able to manage alone, Joan?" he asked bluntly.

"Now I am," his sister-in-law said steadily. "Had you not come when you did, I do not know what would have happened. Joe would have died, I am sure, and I . . ." She shrugged. "I was at the end of my strength, without hope or resource. Now, I am strong again and we can live, if not in great comfort, at least without too much hardship." She was silent for a moment, then bit her lip before saying, "I can but hope that when your brothers come to hear of your assistance, they will not castigate me too severely for accepting it."

"They were not always unreasonable," Alex said.

"No," Joan agreed, "but their enmity goes beyond rational thought. I pray that you do not come up against each other, else the blood spilled will be a dark blot on the Grantham escutcheon."

"There will be no brother's blood shed if I can avoid it," Alex said quietly, and Joan felt immeasurably comforted, although she could not say why, unless it lay in the sense that Alex was in command of so much more than his own destiny and could be safely entrusted with so much more.

"What of Ginny?" she asked, that thought following naturally from the previous one. "Does her future lie with yours?"

"I would have it so," he answered, getting to his feet. "But the future is a mere chimera, my dear Joan. When this war is finally over, if we still live and I am whole, not some wounded piece of war's flotsam, then we shall see."

Chapter Seventeen

"Ginny, we have to leave *now!*" Alex paced the gallery, his spurs jangling, his hand on his sword hilt, trying to keep a rein on his swelling impatience.

"In a minute," Ginny said over her shoulder. "Can you move your wrist just a little, madam? I know it hurts, but I wish to feel the movement of the joint." Aunt Martha, huffing and puffing, obliged, giving vent to a pitiful little moan.

"I will make a poultice to reduce the inflammation." Ginny straightened. "Patience, if you will come with me to the kitchen, I will show you how to do it, so that you may prepare fresh ones when I am gone."

Alex swore beneath his breath and strode out of the gallery, into the outer court where the division's officers waited under a lowering sky. "We are obliged to bide our time," he said in clipped tones through set lips, "until Mistress Courtney has manufactured a cure for Aunt Martha's arthritis!" His audience maintained a prudent silence, keeping their expressions neutral. Alex looked up at the sky. "There will be a deluge before this day is done," he muttered. Five minutes later, he snapped, "Diccon, fetch her!"

There was no mistaking the command, or the fact that the general had finally lost patience. Diccon went into the house at a run. "Ginny?" he called through the echoing hall. There was no reply, so he thundered up the broken staircase, paused, heard the murmur of voices, and burst without ceremony into the gallery. "I beg—beg pardon," he stammered, at the incredulous, indignant faces turned toward him. "But, Ginny, you must come at once. The general is about to explode."

"Oh, pshaw!" Ginny waved a dismissive hand. "Five more minutes will make no difference, and I must see little Joe before I leave. There, now, madam. Does that not feel better?" She turned back to Aunt Martha.

"Ginny, please," Diccon pleaded urgently. "You do not understand. The division is drawn up and ready to leave on the instant. The general will not stand to be kept waiting any longer."

Diccon appeared to be quite genuine in his urgency. "Very well, I will come directly," Ginny said. "Tell him that I am coming." She went over to the pallet in the corner where the little boy had been moved, now that the danger of infection was past, back amongst the company.

The aide-de-camp wrung his hands in pathetic indecision. He did not dare return to the general without Virginia since that would be tantamount to disobedience, but the longer he delayed the greater would be the commander's ire.

Joan read his expression correctly. "Ginny, I will accompany you downstairs," she said with a soft choke of laughter. "That poor young man looks as if he expects to be drawn and quartered on the instant."

"At times, your brother-in-law is a veritable bully," Ginny told her unequivocally. "But he does not make *me* quake in my boots." She examined the child's eyes carefully and felt his pulse. "I do not think there will be a relapse if you do not allow him to overtax his strength. Keep giving him the medicine. It is prepared from foxgloves and has some tonic effects on the heart. If there has been any strain, it will help to counteract it."

"Ginny," Diccon almost whimpered, and she got off her knees.

"Yes, Diccon, I am coming right away." But she did not join him until she had gone round the room making her farewells. Joan was hard pressed to keep a straight face, and even more so when they gained the courtyard and Ginny greeted Alex, whose face was black as thunder, with a cheerfully insouciant apology.

Alex clenched his fists tightly and waited in grim silence until the two women had completed an extended good-bye. Then he clasped the dilatory Ginny around the waist and lifted her onto Jen where she landed with a jarring thump. "You may have been a civilian for the last three days," he told her furiously, "but you will please remember that you are now back in the army, Virginia Courtney, and an entire division is not to be kept cooling its heels at the whim of a headstrong girl."

"I had matters to attend to," Ginny countered, aware of the interest this heated exchange was generating in the courtyard, but unable to accept the public rebuke without defending herself.

Alex chose to ignore that and went over to bid farewell to his sister-in-law. "I do not think you will ever have the last word," Joan whispered, chuckling. "Mistress Courtney is more than a match for a mere general."

At that, Alex smiled reluctantly. "I am afraid you are right, sister, but I shall persevere, nevertheless." They embraced, briefly and silently, each knowing that this might be the last occasion on which they would ever meet. Alex mounted Bucephalus, and the group rode through the gatehouse and into the park where the division waited in marching order.

The drums sounded, sharp and alert, and they moved out under the gray skies, down the driveway and out into the country lane. Alex did not once look back, although Ginny kept her head turned toward the house nestling in the lee of the hill until it was lost to sight. In Joan Marshall, she had felt something she had hitherto not experienced — a sense of sisterhood, of shared emotions and attitudes that sprang, not just from similar experiences, but from the universality of the female condition. She had had no true women friends; in her childhood there had been Edmund, and he had provided her with all the friendship she desired. Her husband's sisters had made no secret of their dislike of her, and, until the last three days, she would have said that the friendship of her own sex was an irrelevancy, something she neither wished for nor needed. Now, she felt a deep regret for what she was leaving behind, for the fact that she must lose so soon what she had so recently discovered.

She glanced sideways at Alex. His expression remained somewhat severe, but it was impossible to tell whether that had still to do with her keeping them waiting or was caused by his own thoughts on leaving his ancestral home for possibly the last time. No one seemed inclined to disturb his silence, and the atmosphere became as leaden as the skies.

"How far do we ride today?" Ginny ventured.

"The far side of London," she was informed without warmth. "It will be slow going when the rain begins, and we are already two hours later than I had intended."

"I did not keep you waiting two hours," Ginny protested.

"I had already delayed the start because I was loath to wake you," Alex snapped. "We must now march without a break until we make up lost time."

Ginny decided that further conversation was going to be fruitless and lapsed into silence. The rain began in half an hour and settled into a relentless, impenetrable, soaking stream that turned the ground beneath them to thick yellow mud churning under the horses' hooves and the marching boots, splattering britches and leggings. It dripped down the back of Ginny's neck in a cold, wet trickle fed by her drenched hair. The heavy serge of her riding habit became sodden, clinging to her thighs and chafing the underside unbearably as she was forced to move in the saddle with the rhythm of Jen's gait. No one talked, each locked in his own miserable discomfort, except for a brief exchange between Alex and Colonel Bonham as to whether they should stop for a half-hour's break.

Ginny did not know whether she wanted the decision to be for or against the breathing space. She did not think, if she once got off the mare and was able to pull the soaked material away from her raw skin for a blissful while, that she would be able to bear the agony of returning to the saddle again. She thought enviously of the men in their leather britches which the rain scarcely penetrated, running away as if off an oiled skin.

The decision fell against a halt, and the long, dark day wore on. After six hours, the benefits of her lengthy, unbroken night's sleep had dissipated, and Ginny was as bone tired as she had been yesterday after three sleepless nights. But she could not begin to imagine what she could do about it. It was unthinkable to ask Alex for special consideration, to demand that he stop the entire division for the night because this pursuivant of the drum needed to take her rest and anoint her raw flesh. He had warned her that the journey would be arduous, and she had accepted the conditions, but a cheerful imagination had not matched the wretchedness of the reality of unceasing rain, wet serge, and unutterable weariness.

She seemed eventually to fall into a sort of trance where physical miseries became inseparable from herself and from each other. She shivered with cold, flexing her numb fingers in her gloves, curling her deadened toes in her boots. Her back ached with the effort to keep it straight, shoulders set, to keep concealed the extent of her weakness. In spite of all her efforts, however, tears of misery rolled down her cheeks, mingling with the rain so she made no attempt to brush them away, aware that, as true darkness fell, no one would be able to see her face clearly.

For an hour, Alex watched Ginny anxiously. He had no way of knowing the full extent of her wretchedness, could only guess at her weariness, and for a while he was fooled. Then she sniffed suddenly, biting her lip fiercely, and he realized she was crying. Cursing himself for his stupidity, he reached over for Jen's bridle, drawing the mare alongside Bucephalus. "I am going to lift you up," he said. "Help me by putting your arms around my neck."

Ginny looked up at him bewildered as the words penetrated her daze. She saw the green-brown eyes filled with concern, the hard lines of his previous expression dissolved with the tenderness that she knew belonged to the lover.

"Ginny, did you hear me?" he asked urgently, twisting and

bending down from his saddle. "Put your arms around my neck."

As she raised her arms in almost hypnotized obedience, he caught her beneath them, lifting her bodily from the saddle and settling her in front of him. Diccon, who as usual had been riding on her other side, took Jen's reins so that he could lead the mare. An involuntary groan of relief escaped Ginny as she turned sideways on the saddle in front of Alex, taking the weight off her sore thighs, leaning into the supporting arm that held her against his chest. His buff leather coat provided minimal comfort, but Ginny was beyond caring, knowing only that she no longer needed to keep her body upright, that Alex provided all the support she needed.

"Brave girl," he said gently, "but foolish with it. I had no idea how you were suffering. You must tell me much sooner next time."

"It is only the chafing that became unbearable," she said. "The cold and wet I can endure as well as any."

"What chafing?" He frowned down at her.

Ginny explained the problem somewhat diffidently, wondering whether a man who was accustomed to leather britches could begin to understand. But it seemed that Alex did. "I think," he said matter-of-factly, "that we must contrive a pair of britches for you. Apart from this specific problem, you will find it more comfortable to ride astride on long journeys. Jed will look out a suitable saddle for your mare."

They were riding through countryside that showed little sign of habitation, only a scattering of cottages here and there offering no welcome or possibility of shelter for such large numbers. Alex again consulted with Colonel Bonham, who seemed to find nothing strange in a tactical discussion with his general, when the general was cradling a wet female form against his chest. A group of cavalry troopers, led by Jed, was sent on ahead to scout out some form of shelter, however inadequate, since the evening was drawing in and food and rest were now become imperative for more than Ginny.

They rode back within twenty minutes to report a large barn and outbuildings on the outskirts of a small farm. The farmhouse was ruined, destroyed by fire, but the farm buildings still stood, and there was straw in the barn, a little moldy, certainly, but relatively dry and better than no bedding at all.

Alex nodded. It would do because it had to. Orders were passed back, and the pace picked up as the thought of journey's end lent renewed vigor. Ginny, when she was set tentatively upon her feet, found to her relief that she could stand and was spared the mortification of having to be carried. "Let us see what hospitality this palace can offer us," Alex said cheerfully, striding into the barn, the rest following. It smelled of moldy hay, manure, and damp stone, but there were plenty of hay bales, and a rickety ladder led up to the hayloft. "Up with you," Alex said to Ginny, leading her to the ladder. "You will have your privacy up there and can get out of that soaked habit. I will have your baggage and medicines brought as soon as the men have been dispersed."

Ginny climbed up the ladder, holding her wet skirts to one side. Something scuttled across the floor as she stepped into the loft. Rats! She pulled a face, but was too relieved to find herself somewhere relatively dry and free of motion to care what fellow inhabitants there were. It felt a little peculiar, getting out of her clothes without a door between herself and the very male voices coming from below. It sounded rather as if everyone was doing the same as she was, stripping to their undergarments, using their shirts to dry their hair. She heard Alex cheerfully make some ribald joke and felt that flash of admiration for him again. He always knew exactly how to raise morale, how to show by example that one could and should rise above minor inconveniences be they rain, inadequate shelter, or Royalist ambushes.

She was soaked to the skin, but remained shivering in her shift until Alex's voice came again and the top rung of the ladder standing above the loft floor shook as he put his foot on the bottom. "Dry clothes," he announced. "You were fortunate that your baggage found shelter under some tarpaulin. Jed, I suspect, has your interests very much at heart. More so than mine, at least, since everything I possess is as wet as what I have on." He grinned at her, and she had the unmistakable impression that he was enjoying this, that hardship and discomfort were mere grist to the soldier's mill. "Turn around and let us see how much damage has been done."

Ginny submitted to being turned around so that he could lift up her shift and examine the backs of her thighs. His voice was very sober, however, as he said, "What do you have that I can put on?"

"Is it as bad as it feels?" she asked, trying for a light tone.

"If it feels as bad as it looks, sweetheart, you must be in agony," he said succinctly. "You'll ride with me again, tomorrow. Now, tell me what I may put on."

Ginny found the salve in her basket and handed it to him, gritting her teeth as he smoothed over the rawness. But imperceptibly the stinging gave way to a spreading warmth, and she heaved a sigh of relief. "That is better. My thanks. If you have any more of that brandy, I shall be quite restored." Her smile was strong as she turned back to him, and Alex tipped her chin to kiss the corner of her mouth.

"You have all the makings of a soldier," he teased. "It is only your lamentable tendency to insubordination that causes difficulty." When she opened her mouth in indignant protest, he kissed her again, laughing. "I will bring you brandy and food, chicken, but I fear you must stay up here, since below there is a scene of some considerable dishevelment."

"Must I sleep alone, with only the rats for company?" she asked in mock distress, rummaging through her baggage for her warm flannel robe that kept the winter drafts at bay and should prove equally useful in a chilly, damp barn in summertime.

"No," Alex said. "There seems little point in such pretense. I will protect you from the rats, and we will keep each other warm."

The next day, Ginny rode on Bucephalus, in front of Alex, able to wear a simple linen gown and sit in such a way as to spare her chafed skin. That evening, when they made

302

camp, Alex brought her a pair of leather britches.

"They fit," Ginny said in amazement, buttoning them up. "How could that be?"

Alex laughed, but would only say, "Jed has many skills." He regarded her through narrowed eyes as she preened delightedly, striding up and down the small chamber the general had requisitioned above the village forge. "I am no longer convinced that it was a good idea," he said thoughtfully. "They accentuate all those curves that are normally hidden by your skirts. You are a sight to enflame even the most jaded spirit. And since my spirit is far from jaded . . ."

He lunged for her, but, laughing, she drew back, saying with slightly pink cheeks, "You must control your ungovernable lust, General, for a few days. I find myself a little indisposed."

Alex frowned, then his expression cleared. "I cannot tell you what a relief that is, chicken. I have been much afraid that I would get you with child."

A shadow passed across her face, and she turned away, busying herself with the clothes she had discarded. "You need not be afraid of that. I am barren."

"How can you possibly know that?" Alex caught her by the shoulders, swinging her round to face him.

She shrugged. "You forget I was married for some considerable time. My inability to conceive was not through want of trying on my husband's part." She presented the brutal truth flatly, and Alex winced. He had found it easy to forget the fact that Giles Courtney had once possessed the body that he felt so passionately was his and his alone. It had been easy because he knew she had not been touched by the other man, not in the ways of love. She had been as innocent of loving as any virgin. Now the candid statement was like an open-handed slap, and he flinched from the images thus produced.

"I have a staff meting," he said abruptly, going to the door. "Do not wear those britches around the camp, if you please. They are for riding only."

Ginny looked at the closed door and shook her head with sad resignation. Alex's thoughts had not been hard to divine, but why should the reminder of a long-dead man concern him? Men were most definitely a puzzle. She lay down on the lumpy pallet that was all the bed this humble accommodation could provide, linking her arms behind her head, wondering how Alex would have reacted to the information that she was barren if they were contemplating marriage. It was one thing, and a very convenient one, for a mistress to be unable to conceive, but for a wife it was disastrous. Alex would want sons; cut off from his roots, disowned and disinherited, he would need to found his own branch of the family, his own dynasty in the land that he had fought for and would continue fighting for, if not with the sword, then with words in Parliament during the process of reconstruction. But she had told herself never to think of the future, never to speculate, never to permit even the slightest hint of future planning. To do so brought only desolation as she had just discovered.

During the ensuing days, there was little time for thought and even less for planning beyond the moment. The march took them through the Cotswold hills where signs of the battles of the first war that had been fought around Oxford, brought home to them all the futility of victory if it was to be so short-lived. Ginny could sense the anger rising among the men as well as the officers, angry and embittered that they had to endure this discomfort, face death and privation again in a renewed struggle that Parliament's previous victories should have taught the Royalist rebels would be without gain. With this bitterness came a desire for vengeance, a resolve to exact an eye for an eye. And it was a resolve that General Marshall appeared to support. While he would permit no plundering, he turned a blind eye when his troopers uncovered a nest of wounded Royalists with whom they had much sport before putting the wretched men to the sword. When the division was harassed by groups of rebels who came nibbling at the edges of his army like caterpillars at a leaf, he showed no quarter in revenge, pursuing them across the countryside, refusing to take prisoners, abandoning the wounded to the tender mercies of his men.

Ginny watched, sickened by the ruthless cruelty, the blind indifference to suffering. On one level, she understood the reasons for it, understood that Alex, by allowing his men to express their bitter rage in this way, was preventing the inevitable dispiritedness, weakening of morale, loss of discipline, grumbles that could lead to mutinous action that he would have to punish with relentless severity — all the ills that were inevitable concomitants of a forced march undertaken in conditions of hardship. But understanding could not excuse, and, while her love for the man remained undiminished, her despair at the soldier's barbarity drove a wedge between them until she could remain silent no longer.

One afternoon, they rode into a small village just outside Melton Mowbray, to be greeted with much enthusiasm and excitement by the villagers who came eagerly to the commander of this magnificent division, full of tales of the excesses committed in the countryside by rebel troops; who presented for inspection six captured Cavaliers who had been discovered red-handed stealing horses to take them north to join the duke of Hamilton's forces and the Scots, whom no right-minded Englishman would accept as master.

General Marshall listened to the charges, his expression almost indifferent as he sat upon his horse in the village square, his officers around him, the division drawn up upon the green. "Hang them," he said simply, when the peroration was done.

"No!" Ginny forgot her place, forgot that she must never in public challenge the general's authority on serious matters, and there was no more public arena than this. "Alex, you cannot do that; you cannot allow such a barbarism."

"Be silent!" he thundered, his eyes blazing like green fire in the deeply tanned face. "You dare to tell me my business!"

Ginny flinched beneath a fury, the extent of which she had not experienced before, but she stuck to her guns. "You remember what you said of General Colney, in Winchester? That he was a butcher who did not understand how to make punishment an effective deterrent. How excesses achieved nothing. Has there not been enough excess? What possible good can hanging these men do? Whom do you hope to deter by their deaths? There is no one here but Parliament's loyal supporters." Without waiting to see the effect of her words, she turned her horse and galloped out of the village, heedless of the stares of the men who, while they could not have heard the exchange, knew that some confrontation had taken place between the general and the division's physician.

A frozen silence held the group in the square, a silence broken only by the chomping on a bit, the pawing of a hoof on the cobbles. Alex allowed the stillness to seep into his bones as he absorbed Ginny's words. He knew why the estrangement had come between them in the last weeks, but he had accepted it as a consequence of duty. It was his duty to subjugate a rebellious land and maintain the morale of his troops who were entitled to their revenge. If it was harsh and cruel, then it was because war was harsh and cruel. Virginia did not seem to see this reality, and perhaps it was hardly surprising. One did not expect the weaker sex to be intimately acquainted with such realities as a matter of course, and somehow, in his need to have her beside him, he had neglected to anticipate this. However, maybe, on this occasion she had a point. What would be gained by executing the prisoners out of hand? They would reach Nottingham tomorrow, and he could afford to take prisoners that far. The authorities there could deal with them.

"Captain Baldwin, hold the prisoners under guard. They march with us to Nottingham in the morning. Colonel, dismiss the troops to their quarters; we will make an early halt this day, a few hours' rest will not come amiss. Lieutenant Maulfrey, will you go in search of that firebrand, please? I do not want her roaming the countryside alone."

Diccon saluted, unable to hide his grin, and went about a task that he infinitely preferred to ordinary duty. It took him an hour to find her, though, and when he did so, it was only because he saw a riderless Jen grazing tranquilly in front of a small, tumbledown cottage set in a neglected garden behind a broken fieldstone wall.

Dismounting, he tethered his own horse to a wavy sapling and rapped smartly on an ill-fitting door. There was no response at first, and he knocked again, calling her name. The door opened then, and Ginny stood blinking at him in the daylight that provided a sharp contrast to the gloom of the cottage at her back. "Is it you, Diccon?"

"I have been sent to bring you back to the village," he said, peering over her shoulder to where a toothless crone sat by the fire, stirring something in an iron cauldron. The hairs on the back of his neck prickled as a wall-eyed cat brushed against his leg, and he took an involuntary step backward, away from whatever witchcraft was contained in the dilapidated hovel.

"I am not coming back," Ginny stated flatly. "I have supped full of horrors these last days, and I will not lay my head in a place where the gibbets swing beneath my casement. You may come for me in the morning, when you are ready to leave. I will stay here with Dame Barton, who has much wisdom to impart."

"There are no gibbets," Diccon said uneasily, wishing he were miles away from the ancient dame and her cat and the aromatic contents of that cauldron in the spider-hung cottage. "The prisoners are to be taken to Nottingham, and the general doesn't wish you to roam the countryside alone."

The old woman cackled scornfully at this. "She'll be coming to no harm," she said, "too much sense and too much knowledge, that one, for all that she's got a babe's head on her shoulders."

"You flatter me, dame," Ginny laughed, before saying seriously to Diccon, "There are to be no hangings?"

Diccon shook his head. "We're to stop early for the day, give the men a chance to cook a decent supper and look to their clothes and armor. We'll all be glad of the respite."

"And the general?" she inquired, eyebrows raised. "What is his mood? Perhaps I would still be better advised to pass the night here with Dame Barton?"

"I could not say." Diccon shuffled his feet, embarrassed. "He did not appear greatly annoyed after you had left."

"Then I will return, but not yet. You may go back and tell

the general that I am quite safe, and that I am learning from Dame Barton, who has knowledge of some most effective simples."

Diccon had little doubt of that, although for preference would have substituted the word spells for simples. But he had no authority over Ginny and could see no alternative to his returning to the village empty-handed. "May I, at least, say what time you will come back?"

"Before supper," Ginny reassured him. "Dame Barton has little enough for herself, without sharing it."

"True enough," the old dame said with another cackle. "But there's nettles aplenty out back. They'll make a fine soup, if someone's prepared to pick 'em."

"Off you go, Diccon." Ginny gave him a little push. "You are not at all comfortable here, and I am wasting precious time. There is much I would ask Dame Barton." She closed the door on him firmly, and the lieutenant remounted and rode disconsolately back to the village.

"Could you not find her?" Alex demanded, anxiety rasping harsh in his voice.

"I found her, sir, with an old dame some two miles away. She said she would return for supper, but wished to talk with the crone." Diccon grimaced. "Unsavory place it was, sir—smelled of witchcraft."

"Oh, do not be absurd," Alex reproved briskly. "This fear of witches grows to epidemic proportions. I'll have no further talk of it."

"Sir." Diccon saluted stiffly, hurt apparent in every line of his rigid body.

Alex controlled his quivering lip. "You are dismissed, Lieutenant." When Diccon had gone, he turned back to the others, gathered in the kitchen of a substantial farmhouse that was to provide their quarters for the night. "I'll not encourage this rabid talk of witches. It grows worse the further north we march. It is getting to the point where every old woman with a cat and a little skill at physicking is suspect." Knowing that did little to ease his mind at Ginny's prolonged absence. If she was in suspect company, exchanging recipes and cures, picking herbs in the fields, she could

308

easily fall foul of superstitious countryfolk. He sighed in weary exasperation. He was no longer concerned about her rebel activities; the Royalists hereabouts were on the run, the uprisings quelled, and there was little harm she could do to Parliament's cause. Neither was he afraid that she would attempt to leave him. But now, it seemed, he had something else to fear from her lone wanderings, and attempting to forbid those wanderings would inevitably lead to a major confrontation.

When she eventually appeared, however, she brought him something much more pressing to worry about. She burst into the farm kitchen, drawing off her gloves, tossing her hat onto the table. "There is dysentery in the camp, Alex."

Alex groaned. "How do you know?"

"As I was coming back, a corporal waylaid me, wanting to know if I had anything to help him because he'd been stopping every mile or so along the march today, he and the rest of his troop."

There was silence as they all absorbed the implications of this. Dysentery would run like wildfire throughout the division, the march would have to be slowed to a snail's pace to accommodate the need for constant stops, and the men would grow weaker by the day. "As far as I could gather," Ginny went on calmly, "it is only the one troop so far. I told the sergeant to dig separate jakes for them and pitch their tents away from the others. They should cook and eat separately. It would be best not to march tomorrow, so that it can be determined if the outbreak has spread further, and those who have it can be immediately isolated."

"God's death! I cannot afford another day's delay," Alex exclaimed, pummeling his clenched fist into his palm.

"If you do not, you will be able to make little speed in a day or so when the entire division is afflicted," she pointed out unarguably. "At present, the symptoms do not appear to be severe, and we can hope to keep it contained. I can help a small number of men, but not the entire division. I do not have sufficient sulphur."

Sulphur, Alex thought. What the devil had sulphur to do with dysentery? Presumably yet another of Ginny's mysterious but potent healing formulas. He paced the quarry-stone floor until he could accept the inevitable, if not with a good grace, at least with resignation. "Very well, we will remain here tomorrow. It will provide the opportunity to drill the division and smarten things up. There has been some laxity on the march. I will leave the arrangements to you, gentlemen." He nodded at his colonels. "I will hold a review of the troops on the green at ten tomorrow. It will be a sight for the villagers and will inspire the men."

"Presumably not as well as a hanging," Ginny muttered, unable to help the sardonic comment. The room emptied as if by magic, leaving only the general and his troublesome lady. "I crave pardon," Ginny said swiftly. "That was unnecessary."

"Since you emerged victorious in the matter, I would have to agree that gloating over your victory is indeed unnecessary," Alex responded in a tone as dry as dust. He filled a cup with wine, took a slow sip, regarding her over the rim. "I cannot help what you do not like, Ginny. I would spare you if I could, but these things, while unpleasant, are necessary."

"Unpleasant!" she exclaimed. "Is that what you call the floggings and the pillory and the hangings? The torture of a helpless prisoner with no information of value is a mere unpleasantness?"

"The men need an outlet for their fury," he said. "You forget that they face battle and disease, that they have been forced to leave their families for the second time in seven years, and all because there are those too stubborn to acknowledge the truth of final defeat."

"I cannot accept that." She turned from him. "My energies go in saving lives, General, not in taking them. In relieving suffering, not in creating it. We can never reach agreement on this."

"Then can we agree to differ, sweetheart? I cannot bear to be so estranged." He spoke softly, surprising Ginny, who had expected a snap of impatience at her refusal to see his point of view. "I listened to you this afternoon and will do so again, although I cannot always promise to follow your

310

advice."

"That is concession, indeed," Ginny said with a shaky little smile. "I cannot bear to be estranged, either, my love, but I cannot bear the unnecessary shedding of blood. In battle . . ." She shrugged. "There, it is necessary, I suppose."

"Will you come upstairs?" he asked quietly. "I have great need of you."

In the chamber abovestairs, they resolved their differences in the only way they could, in the ephemeral joining of bodies that brought the joining of selves, and the reaffirmation of the magic that bound them through all divisiveness.

Chapter Eighteen

"Colonel Bonham, will you tell the general that I am gone to have further speech with Dame Barton?" Ginny came into the kitchen the following morning, drawing on her riding gloves.

"You will not watch the review?" the colonel asked. "It will be a rare sight."

Ginny shook her head. "I do not doubt it, sir, but I have not had the luck to find such a one as Dame Barton in many months. I will sit at her feet and learn this day. Perhaps she will have some new insights into the dysentery or will know where I may acquire more sulphur."

Colonel Bonham smiled. "I will inform the general, Ginny. May I tell him what time you expect to return?"

Ginny frowned. "I do not really know; it will depend on the dame and what plans she has. Perhaps you had better say not before supper; then he will not worry, and if I am back earlier, it will not matter."

The colonel bowed gravely at this very sensible proposition, but he was unprepared for the reaction when he passed the message on to the general.

"Damnation!" Alex swore. "I do not wish for her to roam the countryside, and particularly not in the company of witches and warlocks!" Colonel Bonham coughed. "Oh, I do not mean that exactly," Alex sighed. "But it is how such folk are designated by the ignorant in these parts, as well you know. I will go in search of her after the review, although how I am to bring her back without a scene, I cannot imagine. Mistress Virginia Courtney does not take too kindly to restrictions on her movements, as I am sure you are aware."

The colonel confessed that he had indeed noticed this on one or two occasions, and Alex chuckled ruefully, leading Colonel Bonham to reflect that the advent of Mistress Courtney in his life had wrought some changes for the better in General Marshall, had certainly had an agreeably softening effect on the rigidly principled commander.

When Ginny reached Dame Barton's cottage, she discovered she was not the only visitor. A distraught, middle-aged couple, holding a pallid, inert baby, huddled against the inside wall, watching in the gloom as the old woman mixed a paste in a mortar, grinding it with a pestle and muttering to herself.

"Good morrow, dame," Ginny greeted her cheerfully, pushing through the door. "What's to do?" She smiled inquiringly at the couple.

" 'Tis the babe," the dame said. "Has a sleepin' sickness." She grunted. "Folks don't come near the old woman most times, 'ceptin' when they're scared to death of death itself."

"May I see the child?" Ginny held out her arms, and the mother gave her the baby.

"It is our only child, mistress," she said in a low voice. "A miracle after all these years, and there'll not be another; I'm at the end of my time."

Ginny nodded and carried the infant out into the sunshine, laying it on the grass and beginning to unwrap the swaddling blankets from the little limbs. The father demanded with nervous anger to know what she was doing. "I wish to see him properly," she replied, examining the naked body carefully. "How long has he been like this?"

"A week," the mother answered. "He was quite well until a week ago. You know of these things, mistress? Like the dame?"

"Dame Barton has more knowledge than I," Ginny replied, "but I have some small skill, although I confess this puzzles me. There is nothing to indicate what it could be." Wrapping the child again, she handed him back to his mother and returned to the cottage. "What think you, dame?"

"Somethin' lackin' in the milk," the old woman said briefly. "Seen it several times." She put the paste on a broad, damp green leaf and rolled it tightly, then stood up, groaning as her stiff limbs creaked, hobbling outside to where the couple waited. "Give him this, goodwife, and find a healthy wet nurse as soon as may be. Your milk's not good."

With hastily garbled thanks and the exchange of the leaf for a coin, the couple made off with the baby across the fields. Ginny watched them go, her lip curled slightly. They could not wait to get away from the old dame and her dilapidated cottage and her potions, until the next time they found themselves in straits desperate enough to warrant the dangerous contact.

The morning passed rapidly and pleasantly in the fields and hedgerows where they gathered flowers, herbs, and berries, Ginny listening and noting all the while as Dame Barton imparted her wisdom in throwaway statements. It was early afternoon when they returned to the cottage, and at the sight that met them, Ginny went cold and sick with fear.

A crowd milled around the cottage, brandishing staves and rope. The wall-eyed cat hung head down from the branch of the sapling, and the dame's few sticks of furniture, her cooking pots and scraps of linen were flung higgledy-piggledy onto the grass. Dame Barton gave a great cry of sorrow and anger when she saw the murdered cat and tottered toward the group, who turned faces, twisted with the fear that breeds unreasoning hatred, toward the two women. An ugly murmur rose and swelled, and the group advanced on them.

"What is the matter?" Ginny tried to sound calm, to keep her voice from shaking. "What business have you with Dame Barton? You have no right to—"

"Rights!" someone exclaimed. "Witches have no rights. Seize 'em!"

"No! You are mad—let me go—" Ginny fought the hands that grabbed her; kicking, clawing, and spitting, she struggled against inevitable captivity, but they caught her wrists, bending her arms up against her back so she cried out in pain, yanking on her hair until she thought it would be pulled from her scalp. "I am no witch!" she yelled frantically, feeling the rough cord pulled tight around her wrists, seeing Dame Barton on her knees, sobbing as she was punched and kicked while they bound her hands also.

"The witch finder'll tell soon enough," the middle-aged woman of this morning hissed, bringing her face close to Ginny's. "My babe's going to die because of your witchcraft, yours and the dame's. I heard you whisper your spells over him when you laid him naked on the grass, poking at him, laying the devil's curse on him."

"You are talking nonsense." Ginny tried to turn her head away from the hot breath, fetid with rage, that blasted her face, but her head was held fast by whoever still hung on to her braid. "There were no spells, and I did not touch the child except to see if his limbs were whole."

The woman hit her in the face with her open hand, using the full force of her arm, and Ginny fell into a shocked silence, as her ears rang and she tasted the blood from her cut lip. There were no words to convince this mob of her innocence, but if they were to be taken to the witch finder, then at least she would hear the charges laid clearly, and perhaps they could be answered.

The mob dragged them through the fields, Ginny stumbling as she was poked and prodded, and her heart went out to Dame Barton who had neither youth nor strength to help her counteract the roughness of her handling. Where were they taking them? Not to the village where the division was quartered, but away from it, so there seemed little chance that someone who knew her might see her plight and come to her aid. It would have to be a substantial hamlet if it boasted a witch finder. . . . The reflections raced through her head as she thought of and as quickly discarded plans for escape. There were none, unless some miracle brought rescue, or with sweet reason she could convince a mob mad for vengeance and an implacable witch finder with his pins.

Alex had little time throughout the morning to give thought to his wandering mistress. After the review he went on an unannounced walk through the camp, stopping to talk with the troopers as they scrubbed clothes in wooden wash-tubs, bent over their cooking pots, cleaned armor. The general joked and laughed with them, listened to grievances and opinions as if they were of genuine importance to him in the business of commanding the division, and gave short shrift to an incensed surgeon complaining about the orders given to isolate the troopers with dysentery. Such a precaution seemed ridiculous to the chirurgeon, unheard of in all his days in the army. "Well, now you *have* heard of it," General Marshall said curtly, "and I'll hear no more from you, unless you've a wish to visit the guardhouse!"

He strode back to the farmhouse, his good mood somewhat dissipated, and gave orders to Jed to saddle Bucephalus. "Diccon?"

"General?" The aide-de-camp appeared instantly.

"Furnish me with directions to this dame's cottage," he demanded, cutting a slice from the loaf of barley bread on the table, taking a deep gulp of ale. He listened while consuming this hasty repast, then went back outside to where Jed was waiting with his horse.

"Like me to come too, General?" Jed asked.

"By which you mean that you've a mind for the outing," Alex responded with a chuckle. "Aye, by all means bear me company."

It was a peaceful ride on a sunny afternoon across the fields to the stone cottage, and the two men rode in the companionable silence that came from long intimacy. As the cottage came into sight, Alex let fly a string of oaths, spurring Bucephalus forward, Jed on his sturdy cob pounding behind. A small boy was picking through the pathetic heap of Dame Barton's possessions as Alex flung himself from his horse before the animal had come to a full stop.

"What the devil's been going on here?" He shook the lad vigorously, and the boy whimpered, his eyes wide with a fright that stoppered his tongue.

"Easy now, General," Jed said. "If he's got anythin' to say, you'll not hear it if you shake him like a terrier with a rat."

Alex's eyes fell on the dead cat swinging from the tree, and with another oath he pulled his knife from his belt and cut the animal down.

"Took 'em for witches," the boy babbled. "Both of 'em, the young 'un and the old."

"Where?" Alex snapped.

"To the witch finder—in Mowbray," his informant replied. "Swim 'em, like as not."

The color drained from the general's face, leaving it gray beneath the suntan. "How long ago, boy?"

The lad squinted up at the sun and frowned. "Sun was over yonder trees," he said, pointing.

"A good two hours, I'd say, General," Jed put in quietly. "We'd best get a move on."

Ginny closed her eyes against the sounds, the smells, the press of bodies jostling her in the market square of Melton Mowbray. A trestle table stood in the center of the square, beside it the witch finder in a suit of broadcloth worn shiny with age and none too clean. Dame Barton was laid upon the table, rough hands stripping the frail old body, exposing to the crowd the wrinkled skin and sagging breasts, the fleshless thighs and haunches. Ginny tried to blank out her mind, tried not to think of what they would do to her when they were finished with the dame.

The charges of witchcraft were jumbled, a mishmash of stories involving stricken crops and cows with the murrain, of mother's milk turned sour, and someone's aunt struck down with agonizing pains and a doll stuck with pins found in the barn. But the most damning evidence came from the parents of the child for whom the dame had provided medicine. Upon receiving just a touch of the white paste on the tip of his tongue, the babe had gone into violent convulsions and was now worse than before. In vain, did the old woman protest that that was an effect to be expected, that the child would not die, that they should continue with the potion, and with a healthy wet nurse he would regain his strength.

They pointed the finger at Ginny, who had muttered curses over the helpless babe, had stripped him and laid him down on the grass, prodding at his limbs with evil bewitchment, so that they would convulse and twist. There was nothing to be said in defense, Ginny thought, as the lethargy of desperation crept over her like a paralysis. They would examine her for the mark as they were doing with the dame. The witch finder would stick the long pin into her flesh to see if she would bleed, and then, because the evidence would not be conclusive, they would swim her, throw her bound into the river to see if she would sink or if the pure water would reject one who had dishonored her baptism by becoming a witch. Either way, death was inevitable.

They had finished with the dame now and cries of, "to the river to swim the witch," went up. The scrawny, naked old woman was carted off to the riverbank, and hands seized Ginny and flung her onto the table. Again she tried to close her mind, to take herself out of her body so that she would not feel the shame of exposure, but she could not blank out the hands on her skin, rough and calloused, as they pulled away her clothes, and she could not shut out the ribald comments as she felt the warmth of the sun on her body, laid bare upon the table. The witch finder would discover the mole that so delighted Alex, high up on the inside of her right thigh, and he would stick the long pin into its center to see if it would bleed, and if it did not, it would be proved the witch's mark. She did not know if it would bleed, knew only that she wished for death, *now*; that there was nothing in life that could compensate for this degradation, or for the appalling fear that set her limbs quivering and black spots dancing behind her eyelids. The witch finder raised the long, sharp pin, drove it into a small freckle on her abdomen, and the black spots coalesced and swallowed her in merciful oblivion.

The two horsemen pounded down the dusty lane that led into the village of Melton Mowbray. There was no sign of life, the cottages with their front doors standing open, their tenants gone to view the spectacle in the square.

Alex had feared for himself on many occasions; he had known the liquid weakening of his gut, the uncontrollable shaking of his legs and hands that preceded the moment of danger, then the cool, clear flow of adrenaline once he was in the midst of the worst. Now he was afraid for someone other than himself, and the symptoms were the same, but there was no relief because he was not facing the danger himself. Bucephalus, unused to the spur, thundered into the market square, rearing up on his hindquarters at the unkind prod. The crowd around the table fell back, gazing upward in fear-struck wonder as if the devil himself had come amongst them on his black charger. And, indeed, the man with the blazing green eyes, flourishing a broad sword, the sun glinting off the close-cropped auburn head could well have emerged from satanic depths, so wrathful was his mien.

Alex saw the still figure on the table, the silky smooth skin that he could feel just by looking at her, the tactile curves of bosom and hip, the soft dark triangle at the base of her belly that would yield to his curling fingers. . . . Then he saw the bright spot of blood on her belly, harsh against the whiteness of her skin; he saw the man in his worn, shiny suit holding the pin from which blood dripped; and with a bellow of rage, he flung himself from his horse, cutting a swath through the crowd with wide sweeps of his sword.

Jed stilled Bucephalus with a symphony of low, clicking noises, gathering up the reins, averting his eyes discreetly from the table and its inert offering. Then the sight was blocked out by the broad frame, and pandemonium broke loose as Parliament's general raged, heaping curses and threats of perdition on a now-terrified mob, who shrank away from a man who had the power to carry out those threats, who could hang every man jack of them for traitors if he so wished. The witch finder went down to the cobbles under a fist that brought instant unconsciousness, and Ginny came back to reality as she was pulled into a sitting position, an arm, familiar in its strength, behind her back, the comforting, familiar scent of Alex driving away the nightmare as her head was buried in his shirt. Her arms were pushed into long sleeves, and she was no longer naked under the sun and the burning eyes of strangers in the middle of a market square.

For a moment, almost overpowered by relief, Ginny thought she would swoon again as Alex picked her up in his arms and pushed his way through the stunned crowd to where Jed stood holding the two horses. Jed took the burden while Alex mounted, then reached down for her, and throughout Ginny was unable to say anything, shivering and shaking with the aftermath, her throat dry as the desert, her tongue seemingly swollen against the roof of her mouth. Then, as the certainty of safety finally became fact in her mind, that the arms around her, the broad, shirtless chest at her back were real and not figments of a fevered, petrified imagination, she remembered Dame Barton and what they would be doing to her, those who had taken off the one witch, more interested in the new sport of swimming the crone then staying to watch the witch finder prick the young one.

"Alex . . . Dame Barton . . ." She struggled to sit upright on the saddle. "You must save her. They have taken her to the river to swim her."

"Dear God, Ginny! Is it not enough that I have to pluck you naked from the filthy hands of those swine, without —"

"Please . . ." she whispered, the gray eyes haunted, bright with intensity. "She is old, and they have hurt her already. They will murder her if you do not do something."

He was defenseless against those eyes, against the pleading for his compassionate response to the suffering of an old woman who meant nothing to him, was just another victim of superstition and fear, her only difference from all those

320

others lying in the fact that she had attracted the friendship of Virginia Courtney. He turned his horse to the river.

Jed kept his own counsel as he followed on the cob. If the general chose to ride bare-chested around the countryside, with a seminaked woman on his saddle, rescuing witches from the river, it was not Jed's business. However, if asked, he would venture the opinion that Mistress Courtney had the devil's own ability for finding trouble, and if the general had a grain of common sense, he would keep a close eye on her in future.

A small stone bridge traversed the river, and as they reached the middle of the bridge, Ginny gave a cry of outrage and would have flung herself from Bucephalus if Alex had not grabbed a handful of his shirt at her waist. The old dame was a waterlogged bundle bobbing in the middle of the river. On the banks on either side stood a jeering crowd of men, women, and children throwing sticks and stones at the bundle, from which thin gray wisps of hair straggled on the brown surface of the water. What had once been Dame Barton went down beneath the water as a plank of wood struck her head, then bobbed up again.

Bucephalus pounded across the bridge and onto the far bank. Alex leaped to the ground and snatched a hooked pole from the hand of a laughing farmer, whose jeering mirth ceased abruptly at the palpable fury radiating from this man. Ginny had been left on Bucephalus and, while she would willingly have essayed the leap to the ground way below, was conscious of the fact that Alex's shirt barely reached her knees and she could not possibly leave her perch with any decency.

Alex fished at the inert bundle with the hook, catching at last on one of the ropes that bound it. He drew the old woman to the bank and waded into the shallows to lift the sodden, shapeless mass that now bore little resemblance to humanity.

Ginny pressed her hand to her mouth as she swallowed the bitter lump of nausea that rose in her throat. They had tied the dame, bent double, her wrists bound to her ankles, and the figure lay in this contorted position, water dripping

321

from the thin gray straggles of hair on her body where blood streaked from the missiles that had found their mark. One eye hung loose on the thin cheek, and Ginny, careless now of modesty, fell from Bucephalus and crawled into the bushes to vomit helplessly in disgust and shame at man's inhumanity to man.

Alex cut the bonds and straightened the pathetic, saturated, shrunken frame of what had once been a woman, that still bore all the marks of womanhood, but as a travesty. What would Ginny expect him to do now? Exact vengeance on this brutish, now-silent group? On one or two of the faces there stirred a flicker of conscience as the mob fury died and they saw what it had led to. It was hard to imagine there would have been anything evil or menacing about that ruined bundle lying in a puddle on the grass.

"Bury her!" Alex swung round slowly, his eyes hard as he stared at each member of the crowd. "Decently!" He turned to the soldier, standing rigid by his horse. "Jed, see that it is done. If it is not, bring word to the camp, and I'll have every man, woman, and child pilloried!" Without waiting to see the effect of his words, he went over to the bushes where Ginny still crouched, no longer retching but sobbing weakly, his shirt clinging damply to her back where the cold sweat filmed.

"It is done," he said gently, stroking her back. "You must begin to put this behind you now." Bending, he drew her to her feet, lifting her ravaged face as he wiped it dry with his kerchief. She made no protest, submitted in silence to being lifted again onto Bucephalus, averting her eyes from the scene at the riverbank.

"You!" Alex pointed suddenly at a woman in a long, fringed shawl. "I want your shawl." He tossed a coin on the grass in front of her and twitched the garment from her shoulders. "You may replace it with the clothes you ripped from your witches!" He handed the shawl up to Ginny. "Put this around you, you cannot possibly enter the camp in only that shirt."

Ginny recoiled from the garment as from something loathsome, but she knew he was right and grimly wrapped

322

herself in the voluminous folds of material that came well below her knees.

They rode back to the encampment in silence, Ginny still shivering periodically, Alex struggling with his anger now that he knew he had her safe. His earlier, dreadful fear for her was still vivid in his mind, and he did not think he would ever be able to banish the image of her inert body, lying exposed in the market square, or the image of what had once been Dame Barton and the thought that half an hour later, and it would have been Ginny he fished from the river.

There was no possible way their return could be accomplished without drawing attention — not when the general had no shirt and Mistress Courtney was bare-legged, bare-foot, and wrapped most strangely. Alex looked neither to right nor left as he rode into the village and up to the farmhouse. Ginny, who had suffered so much already this afternoon she had thought herself immune from ordinary mortification or embarrassment, found that she was wrong. Her cheeks flamed at the concerned faces of the officers gathered around the farmhouse door, and the minute her feet touched ground she fled upstairs, clutching the shawl around her.

"What the devil happened, sir?" Colonel Bonham followed Alex into the kitchen. "Is Ginny hurt?"

"No — by some miracle," Alex returned shortly. "At least, she is unharmed physically. There are other wounds that will take considerable healing." He poured ale from the pitcher and drank deeply before telling the colonel the full story.

"Should I send a detachment to Mowbray, sir, to aid Jed?"

"Aye, that you can, Nick. 'Tis a good thought, though Jed'll stand in no need of support. But a show of strength against those murdering louts will not come amiss." Alex drained his tankard and went upstairs to the chamber he shared with Ginny. The door was locked. "Virginia, open the door." He kept his voice low, without annoyance, but there was no response. He repeated the request calmly, listening for any sound beyond the oak. When, again, there

323

was nothing, fear began to nibble at the edges of his calm. What was she doing? Her experiences of the afternoon could have been enough to overset reason . . . No, that was ridiculous. Ginny was level-headed, always rational. He tried again.

"Ginny, if you wish to be alone, I understand, but I want you to unlock the door."

Ginny, curled on the bed like a small, wounded animal, heard the sounds of his words but not the sense. She remained still and silent. Alex felt the nibbling fear threaten to blossom into full-blown panic. "If you do not open this door by the time I have counted to five, Virginia, I will have it broken down!" It was no idle threat, half-a-dozen broad soldiers and a battering ram, and this solid, iron-hinged door would crack like a boiled egg. Three of his officers appeared at the head of the stairs, drawn by his voice that was no longer even. Alex swung his booted foot at the door with full force and bellowed, "One!"

The violent sound penetrated Ginny's daze, and her eyes snapped into focus. Another kick accompanied a shouted, "Two!" She leaped from the bed, suddenly totally aware of her surroundings again. Her fingers fumbled with the bolt, yanking it back as the door shivered beneath a third blow. The door flew open with such violent force that she was obliged to jump backward, catching a brief glimpse of the startled faces behind a livid Alex. "Don't you *ever* lock yourself in again, do you understand me?" He was in the chamber, and the door slammed behind him on the interested group.

Ginny just stood and looked at him, blinking, for the moment speechless. "Do you understand?" he repeated, glaring at her, hands firmly planted on his hips. Ginny nodded. "Quite apart from the fact that I was concerned for you, my possessions were behind that door, and I need a clean shirt," he said rather more quietly, somewhat mollified by her total lack of resistance.

"I beg your pardon," she said. "Somehow, I didn't seem to hear you properly."

"Mmmm." He scratched his head, his expression softening. "Well, perhaps you had better wash out your ears, because I will not tolerate a repetition."

"No," Ginny agreed meekly. "Shall I pass you a clean shirt?"

Alex looked at her suspiciously but could see not a flicker of her usual mischievous teasing in the gray eyes. She appeared subdued to the point of being cowed, but instead of gratifying him, this condition merely served to rouse his anger again, as yet further evidence of this afternoon's terrors. "I have something to say to you," he stated, "and you had better listen carefully because I only intend saying it once." He took the shirt she handed him with a muttered word of thanks, waiting for some reaction to his uncompromising statement. When there was none, he continued in the same tone. "Not only will you never again leave the camp unescorted, but you will go nowhere without my specific permission. If I am not available to give it on any occasion, you will wait until I am. Do I make myself clear?"

Ginny felt the first slight stirrings of annoyance piercing the numbness. She did not think, at this moment, that she would ever want to leave the camp again, with or without an escort, but that was something for her to decide. "There is no need to use that tone of voice," she said, turning to pick up the shirt that she had discarded earlier.

"There is every need!" Alex swung her round to face him. "I am not prepared to endure such an afternoon again. If you dare go off without my permission, so help me, I will—" He stopped, unwilling to articulate the threat that came easily to his lips but that he knew he would be unable to fulfil.

"You will what?" Ginny taunted, some of the old fire back in her eyes.

Suddenly he smiled. "A wise man, my dear Ginny, does not utter either threats or promises that he knows he cannot keep. Promise me you will do as I *ask*."

"I will promise not to leave the camp unescorted," she said slowly, "and I promise that I will tell you where I am going beforehand. Will that do?"

"Perfectly, since any escort you have must have my permission to accompany you, it all comes to the same thing, it seems to me." His eyebrows lifted, lightly mocking, waiting for the flare that would tell him she was almost back to herself again. But instead she crept into his arms, burrowing against his chest, and he carried her over to the bed, lying down with her, stroking her hair while she wept the pure tears of release and eventually fell asleep, drained but cleansed.

Chapter Nineteen

Nottingham Castle was a gray, forbidding mass of stone, Parliament's pennant flying from the keep. There were other, less attractive decorations adorning the castle walls, but Ginny now scarcely noticed the severed rebel heads. There was too much to do worrying about the living, without fruitless anguish over the long dead.

The division was to be quartered overnight within the castle, the general and his officers, because of overcrowding, in a requisitioned inn in the town. Alex reached this agreement in consultation with the castle's governor, then came over to Ginny who, in her usual retiring fashion in unfamiliar surroundings, had seated herself in a corner of the messroom while waiting for dispositions to be made.

"Chicken, I have many matters to discuss with the officers here. We shall be in conference until dinner and probably long into the night. Do you wish to stay in the castle until after dinner? Or would you rather go to the inn now, sup there on your own, and retire early?"

Ginny frowned. The idea of spending the rest of the day alone in a strange inn in a strange town was not appealing. "I do not wish to be in the way, but I would prefer to stay here. If I may go freely among the men, I too have matters to attend to, some physicking—one or two injuries that require attention . . ."

Alex nodded. "Go where you wish within the confines of

327

the castle, then, and I will send Diccon to find you when we dine."

Ginny went out into the inner courtyard. It was a dark, brooding cobbled square where the sun was a stranger, unable to strike down over the high stone walls that seemed perpetually damp, as were the mired cobbles beneath her feet. With a grimace, she crossed the square and went through the arch in the wall that gave onto the larger, sunnier outer court. Here there were soldiers, some of whom looked slightly askance at the extraordinary sight of a young woman in their midst. She approached the sentry at the main gate to ask where General Marshall's division was to be found.

"Far side of the keep, mistress," she was told. "On the west hill." The sentry saw her bewildered expression as she looked around the courtyard, trying to work out how to reach the far side of the donjon, and took pity. "Hey! You!" He beckoned at a passing corporal. "The mistress here has business with General Marshall's division, on the west hill. Show her the way, will you?"

"My thanks, trooper." Ginny smiled at the sentry, then at her escort, who simply nodded, striding ahead of her toward one of the circular towers standing at the corners of the court. She scurried after him since he seemed disinclined to slow down for her through a bewildering series of long passageways, whose gloom was but slightly alleviated by narrow slits high up in the walls. Heavy, iron-barred doors with shuttered peepholes were set into the walls. Cells, Ginny presumed, as she hurried after her guide, holding up her skirts to prevent soiling them on flagstones that looked as if they had not seen a mop and water in years. Alex had told her not to wear her britches on today's ride to Nottingham, on the grounds that they would be in strangers' company overnight, in the midst of an army that was unaccustomed to the sight of a respectable female in such guise.

After countless serpentine twists and turns, the corporal opened a door at the end of a narrow corridor, and Ginny found herself outside the castle, at the top of the grassy hill sloping down to the town. The slope was covered with tents, hardly a blade of grass visible, and the scene under the afternoon sun struck Ginny, after the dreariness of the castle, as immensely cheerful. The familiar call of the bugle summoned and dismissed in its regulatory, incessant fashion as she made her way, skipping over guy ropes, toward the formation of tents flying the pennant bearing Alex's shield. Her escort acknowledged her thanks with another curt nod, then turned, and made his way back to the castle.

She spent a pleasant hour among men whom she now thought of in much the same way as she had thought of the tenants and servants of the great house at Alum Bay. She heard many a story of the families left behind as she tended to the minor ailments and injuries and dispensed sulphur to the dysentery sufferers, who seemed to be getting no worse, at least, and the sickness appeared to be still contained. She left the camp when the position of the sun and the smells of cooking from the braziers indicated suppertime. No soldier, friendly or otherwise, appeared conveniently to offer guidance as she went back into the castle, and Ginny resigned herself to relying on her imperfect memory to lead her safely through the warren of passages.

She was halfway down one of these passages, not a soul in sight when she heard the eerily familiar sound for which not even familiarity could provide inurement. Ginny paused at the barred door in the wall, pressing her ear against it. The moaning came again, low but unmistakable. Standing on tiptoe, she pushed back the shutter over the jailer's peephole, but it was too high to afford her a view of anything but the wall opposite. The cell was in almost complete darkness anyway. She glanced up and down the passage. It remained deserted. The groaning came again, but this time there were words, indistinct but recognizable.

"God damn your eyes, you miserable bastard! Come in, or get your black soul away from that door, and let me die in peace!"

Obviously, the occupant of the cell had heard the opening of the peephole and assumed his jailer was casting a cursory eye over his prisoner. Ginny pulled back on the heavy bolts.

They were heavy and had not seen oil in many months. It took her nearly five anxious minutes of alternately pulling and twisting, while the bolts scraped in complaint, the noise sounding to her ears like the clamoring of church bells in the damp silence. At last, the door swung open with a protesting whine and Ginny stood in the doorway, accustoming herself to the gloom, wrinkling her nose at the fetid stench.

"Who the devil —?" A ragged figure, lying on a filthy straw pallet against the wall, struggled onto one elbow, every movement obviously causing him excruciating pain, but the blue eyes still flashed with the angry spirit that she had heard in the cursing tongue. "No devil," the man said, sinking back on the pallet. "I'm closer to death than I thought. 'Tis an angel come for me."

"No angel," Ginny said, coming into the cell, putting her basket on the floor by the pallet. "Flesh and blood, I assure you. Where are you hurt?"

"Don't tell me that after leaving me to rot in this sinkhole for five days, the bastards've decided to send me a nurse?" The man laughed, then coughed, a trickle of blood sliding from the corner of his mouth. "Get the Cavalier fit for the hangman, is that it? Fit enough to dance on the end of the rope . . ." He coughed again.

"Do not talk," Ginny instructed him, wiping the blood from his mouth. "Show me where you are hurt." She pulled off the thin, blood-caked blanket and then gagged at the stench of corruption. The jagged edge of his thigh bone pointed up through the swollen, livid flesh already turning bluish-green. Biting her lip, she sat back on her heels. "The leg must come off." It was a brutal truth, but one the wounded man must already know.

"Too late for that now," he said. "If they'd wanted me to live, they'd have done it before." There was a moment's silence, then he croaked, "Is there water, for the love of God? They left a pitcher, but God damn them, it is out of my reach."

Ginny filled the tin cup from the pitcher by the door and held it to his lips. It was true. He had not the strength to survive an amputation of the limb, even if his captors could be persuaded to provide the surgeon to perform the operation. That slow, fierce rage filled her again. They had thrown a desperately wounded man into a cell and left him to die as slowly or as quickly as his wounds would dictate, and she could do nothing, absolutely nothing to save him. But she could ease his condition a little, and she could create such a scene with Alex that he would be forced to intervene and at least have the man moved so that he could die like a man and not like a rat in a cess pit.

Fighting her nausea at the reek of putrefaction, she cleansed around the wound and bandaged it, then washed the thin feverish body with cool water that brought a moment's easement. "Were you wounded in battle?"

"Skirmish," he said with an effort, closing his eyes. "Not enough of us left for a battle, all we can do is harass the rebel bastards and try to get up with Hamilton's forces . . ."

A string of the foulest oaths Ginny had ever heard suddenly came from the corridor outside, and booted feet thundered, coming to a screeching halt in the doorway. A trooper, pike at the ready stood there, still cursing until he saw that his prisoner had not moved and the intruder was a mere woman in a serge riding habit, bare-headed, carrying a wicker basket. "Who the devil are you, wench?" He grabbed her arm with a painful wrench.

Ginny drew herself up to her full height, ignoring the pain of the soldier's grip. "Fetch General Marshall," she demanded without raising her voice.

He didn't drop her arm, but the grip loosened, and a flash of uncertainty appeared in the bloodshot eyes. "What's the general got to do with you?"

"That is no concern of yours, soldier. Do as I say, and fetch him immediately. Otherwise it will go hard with you, I promise." She was every inch John Redfern's daughter, and he released her arm.

"Come out of here, mistress. This is no place for the likes of you," he said, almost beseeching.

"It is no place for the likes of any but rats," she spat. "Maybe you are only following orders in your treatment of this man, if so you will not be held personally responsible. If

331

not . . ." She stared at him, then repeated. "Fetch General Marshall here, *at once*. I wish him to see this man."

"I can't do that, mistress." The soldier looked aghast. "Generals don't concern themselves with . . ." He gestured helplessly.

"Then summon your superior officer, and *he* may fetch the general." Having started on this course, Ginny didn't see how she could back down, but the thought of Alex being summoned from a high-level conference by some bewildered sergeant at the orders of his troublemaking mistress with her inconveniently humanitarian propensities was more than a little intimidating. He would probably be furious, but he would certainly come.

"You may lock me in with the prisoner if you are afraid I will spirit him away on some magic carpet while you are gone," she went on, seeing him waver. "For heaven's sake, man, get on with it!"

Impatiently, she gave him a push, and the arrogant gesture seemed to convince the trooper that he had best do as she said. The heavy door slammed, the bolts were shot, and Ginny's heart plummeted to her boots. That suggestion had been made out of bravado, and she had not been prepared for the reality of imprisonment in semidarkness with a dying man. The cell contained only a pail, the straw pallet, and the pitcher of water.

The sergeant in the guardhouse listened incredulously to the trooper's halting tale. "A woman with the prisoner in fifty-seven? You been drinking, man?"

"Come and see for yourself, Sergeant. And she's no wench, either. Proud as a queen, givin' me orders, tellin' me to fetch General Marshall for all the world as if the general hisself was her servant."

"But where'd she come from?" The sergeant looked around, bewildered. Enlightenment came from the sentry on the main gate who had just been relieved.

"Rode in with the general's division," he informed the sergeant. "Went looking for the men some time back.

Orders are she's to be let alone to go where she wants." He shrugged and grinned salaciously. "Keepin' the general's bed warm, I'll be bound. 'S all right for some."

A rumble of agreement went around the circular chamber, together with a few lewd remarks. The sergeant scratched his cropped head. "Well, I dunno what to do fer the best. Guvnor'll 'ave me 'ide if 'n I disturb 'im fer no reason."

The sentry grunted. "That General Marshall's a bad man to cross, I've 'eard tell. If his lady wants summat 'n you don't jump, could lose more than yer 'ide, to my way o' thinkin'."

There was a silence as the unhappy sergeant cogitated. "'Left 'er in the cell, did you?" he asked the trooper.

The trooper nodded. "Locked the door 'n all, so she's there all right an' tight."

"Shouldn't 've done that," the sentry pronounced judiciously. "Not locked 'er in."

"Got no right interferin' with the prisoners," the trooper said stoutly. "Guvnor'd say the same. 'Is prisoner, after all."

"Ye're right!" The sergeant sprang energetically to his feet. "We'd best lay it before the guvnor wiv no more ado. Com' on, lad."

When the knock came at the messroom door, one of the junior officers went immediately to answer it. He returned to the room looking nonplussed. The governor and General Marshall were deeply involved in a discussion about dispensing pay to the troops in the castle, and the ensign coughed apologetically.

"What is it, Ensign?" Alex looked at the young man impatiently. "If you wish for our attention, you do not need to cough, standing there like a goose waiting for Christmas."

The young man's ears reddened. Not being a member of the general's staff, he was unused to the acerbic tongue or to the emphasis placed on correct bearing. "Beg your pardon, sir." He saluted stiffly. "Sergeant Smith says that the young lady wishes to see you at once."

"Well, send her in," Alex replied.

"It seems she's with a prisoner, General, and wishes you to go to her."

"What prisoner?" the governor interrupted. "How'd she find the prisoners?"

"The prisoner in fifty-seven, sir," the ensign said. "I don't know how she found him, sir, but the guard says he was doing a routine check on the corridor and found the door to fifty-seven open. The young lady was inside and refused to leave until the general came."

"Is this prisoner by any chance wounded?" Alex inquired with a prickle of foreboding. There was an uncomfortable silence. "Well, Governor?"

"Near death," the governor replied. "By all the odds, he should've died two days ago, but he's a stubborn so-and-so, like all the Calverts."

Alex sighed, drawing his own conclusions. It was typical of Virginia to put him in this impossible situation. He was a guest in the castle, and what the governor did with his prisoners was no business of General Marshall's. He could not go around demanding changes just because something was happening that offended Ginny's sense of decency. It was also outrageous of her to cause this kind of scene, in front of total strangers, and in the middle of what was proving to be a very difficult session as it was.

"My apologies, but if you'll excuse me, Governor, I'll go and sort this out. It will not take me many minutes."

"I will accompany you." The governor pushed back his chair firmly. Alex could hardly blame him for wanting to see for himself what was going on on his territory, but he would have preferred his confrontation with Mistress Courtney to have had no witnesses. However, he was obliged to acknowledge the governor's presence with a gracious smile and grit his teeth as the rest of the room followed for all the world as if the circus was come to town.

"Who are you?" the prisoner asked as the door clanged shut behind the jailer. His face was twisted with the effort to speak lucidly, but the eyes were still clear.

"Virginia Courtney, daughter of John Redfern," she said, sitting on the floor beside him, ignoring the chill as the

334

damp stone struck through her skirt. "As good a Royalist as any."

"Aye, you must be cousin to Edmund Verney," her fellow prisoner said.

"You know Edmund?" Ginny asked eagerly. "Can you give me news of him? Have you seen him?"

"Two weeks ago," he replied. "But what do you do in Nottingham Castle demanding the attention of Parliament's most feared general?"

"Oh, it is a long story," Ginny said dismissively. "Tell me of Edmund quickly before they come back. I had news of him in Wimbledon, but none since."

"If you've a mind to find him, he's not more than ten miles distant," her companion said with a weak chuckle. "There's a few of us left, gathering up the stragglers for the march north."

"Where?" Ginny asked breathlessly, then saw the man's eyes sharpen suspiciously.

"Is this the latest trick they've come up with? Boots and screw haven't got a thing out of me, not even lying here without food or water, unable to reach the pail . . ." He coughed again. "Send a pretty woman, pretending to be a loyal Royalist who somehow has access to Parliament's generals, with hands as soft and skilled as . . ." His voice faded, and an expression of disgust crossed his face.

Ginny reached into the pocket of her skirt, drew out the king's parchment, faded and cracked now, but the seal was still clear. "I will not betray you," she said softly, holding it before his eyes. "The king himself trusted me to bear his message, and I have done what I could since we left the Isle of Wight. Will you not tell me where I may find my cousin? I would see him, perhaps for the last time."

Footsteps sounded outside, and she thrust the parchment back into her pocket. "Grantly Manor," the prisoner whispered. "Ten miles to the east as the crow flies. Outside Grantly village."

"Virginia, this time you have gone too far," Alex said in clipped tones, pushing into the cell, then stopping with a gasp, putting his hand over his mouth. Behind him stood the governor, Colonel Bonham, and several others whom Ginny did not recognize. They all reeled at the stench, stepping backward into the passage.

"It is not pleasant, is it, gentlemen?" Ginny said coldly, getting to her feet, deciding that attack was her best form of defense. "This man is dying, Alex. He is sore wounded, and the wound is mortified. He has been left to rot away. Will you not allow him the right to die with some decency?"

"He is not my prisoner, Ginny," Alex said with a weary sigh. "I have no authority in the matter."

"General Marshall has no authority?" She looked at him in scathing disbelief. "I have noticed that General Marshall has whatever authority he chooses!"

Alex flushed with anger, aware of the men behind him, the ordinary soldiers behind them, all listening to the cold contempt of this slip of a girl who had caused him nothing but trouble ever since he had first laid eyes upon her.

The frail figure on the filthy straw laughed. It was amazing such a sound could come from that broken form. Alex looked down at him, met the clear flash of blue eyes that somehow retained their dignity and humanity in spite of the appalling degradation of his position. With swift decision, he turned on his heel and instructed the governor in cold, clear tones. "Newton, get this man out of this hellhole immediately. I want a report on his condition after dinner."

"I will stay with him," Ginny said.

"You will not," Alex said with all the force of restrained exasperation. "He will be looked after. You have made your presence sufficiently felt for one day; now be satisfied with that. There is always tomorrow when you will find God-only-knows-what other matters to plague me with."

He was only exacting natural vengeance because of the way she had spoken to him so publicly, Ginny told herself, but it did nothing to ease her bitter anger at this deliberately humiliating speech. There was nothing she could do about it, however, any more than she could resist his hold on her wrist as he marched with her out of the cell, pushing through the interested spectators, hauling her along beside him back to the messroom.

"Sit over there," Alex instructed her curtly, pushing Ginny over to a wooden settle against the wall. "I'm sending someone to find Jed, and as soon as he gets here, he will take you to the inn."

Ginny said nothing but sat down, her lips set tight, her hands clasped in her lap, staring into the middle distance. The men resumed the earlier discussion, but the tension in the room was thick enough to cut with a knife. The governor looked as outraged as he felt at the general's public, unilateral usurping of his authority, but he was outranked by General Marshall and could do nothing but obey the order. His eyes kept sliding to the still figure of the woman on the settle. What the devil was Alexander Marshall doing, fighting a war with a woman in tow? A woman with a scold's tongue to boot, one she didn't scruple to use. It didn't fit with what he had heard tell of the general — a man who took nothing from anybody. Yet here he was, doing the bidding of some arrogant wench who needed a taste of the birch to bring her to a proper sense of her place.

Alex, well aware of the train of the governor's thoughts, found himself much in agreement with them. The governor had funds that Alex wanted to get his hands on for troops, who were in sore need of boots and stockings on this damnable march. He could requisition some proportion of those funds, but not enough. The rest he had to cozen out of the man, and his chances of doing that in this atmosphere of hostility were now remote.

"General?" The door burst open to admit an excited Diccon who came to a stammering halt as his commander raised an eyebrow at this unceremonious entrance. "A patrol has just returned, sir," he said more moderately. "They have a prisoner who said there's a sizable group of Royalists holed up in some manor house about ten miles from here."

Ginny went cold, but with a supreme effort of will she did not alter either her expression or her position.

"Where exactly and how many?" Alex inquired, unable to hide the glitter of excitement in his eyes at the prospect of action.

Diccon looked crestfallen. "The prisoner died, sir, before they could get any more out of him, but they think it's the last stronghold in the area from where the rebels have been launching attacks for the last few weeks."

"What think you, Newton?" Alex looked at the governor. "You know the area, and you know the nature of the rebels around here." The deliberate deference to the governor's superior knowledge in this matter was designed simply to placate.

Newton pondered with a weighty frown while Ginny sat like an effigy, her ears straining to catch every word. "There's quite a few of them, we think," he pronounced eventually. "They've caused us some considerable damage in losses of men, horses, equipment . . . That fellow Calvert was one of 'em, but we couldn't get a peep out of him." He glared at Alex who, with a bland expression, chose to ignore this reopening of an old sore.

"Any idea where this stronghold might be?" he asked instead. "We might as well scoop them up whilst we're here. It should not delay us overlong."

"You intend to go after them yourself?" Newton asked. "It is surely a task for my troops."

"I do not wish to offend you, Newton," Alex said with ominous quiet, "but it seems to me you have already had ample opportunity to dispose of this troublesome nest of rebels. Besides, my men will be glad to see some real action again. It will be a little foretaste of what is to come."

Ginny's scalp crawled at this cold-blooded discussion where fighting and killing were simply facts, where Alex issued the reminder of what they were all marching to with such blithe calm. So much had happened during the march that she had been spared the time for reflection when she would be unable to escape the acceptance of the battle that would end everything that was for the present familiar — end it one way or the other.

"Bring me a map of the area, Diccon," Alex was saying. "Let us see if we cannot rout out these rebels once and for all." His voice was rich with satisfaction, with the anticipation of pleasurable action, and Ginny thought of Edmund with a silent wail of despair. Alex would find him, and this time there would be no mercy. She had too often seen what happened when rebels were taken to have any illusions. The best they could hope for would be a clean death by the sword. She knew with absolute certainty that Alex would find them and defeat them, that to hope that he would not be able to discover their whereabouts, or to hope that they would succeed in vanquishing Parliament's general was living in a fool's paradise.

"You wanted me, General?" Jed appeared in the doorway.

"Oh, yes . . ." Alex looked up, slightly distracted. In the absorption of the last few minutes, he had forgotten all about Ginny. Now, he straightened from the map that Diccon was spreading out on the table and glanced over his shoulder at her. "Take Mistress Courtney to the inn, will you? See that they provide her with a decent supper in a privy chamber, and remain with her until she retires."

He was disposing of her in the same way he would have given orders for his charger's comfort and stabling. Ginny stood up, her fury for the moment superseding her dismay at the news she had just heard. "A word with you, General, if you please." Insolence dripped from her tongue, disdain in the tiny curtsy accompanying what had not been a request. She walked to the door and stood waiting for him.

The muscle in his cheek twitched, and he curled and flexed his hands as if at any moment they might take on a life of their own. Ginny, seeing the convulsive movement, knew that she had gone too far but was too angry to care. He would not lay hands on her here, although he would undoubtedly exact the penalty in some way at some other time; Alex always did. He left the table and came to the door. Jed stepped away discreetly.

"I wish to sleep alone this night," Ginny stated in a low voice, but the words were carefully articulated, her eyes never leaving the Arctic green of his.

"You need have no fear that you will be disturbed, madam," he replied. "I would not trust myself to be alone with you." Swinging on his heel, he returned to the table, the look on his face sending all who knew him into a prudent, attentive silence.

"What've you been up to now?" Jed asked with his usual familiarity as they left the castle. "Haven't seen the general so put out since the last time you crossed swords with him." The old soldier chuckled richly. "Yesterday, I reckon that was."

"It is not funny, Jed," Ginny said and would say nothing more. Jed shrugged and lapsed into the silence that he found so comfortable, quite unperturbed by this unusual reticence. When they reached the inn, she told him that she wanted no supper, that her head ached and she wished only to be alone behind a closed door. This blissful condition was rapidly achieved, although Jed insisted she take a tray behind the door with her.

Once alone, Ginny began to pace the floor in an agony of indecision, but it was not really indecision, since she knew what she had to do. It was just that her heart and soul shrank from the consequences of that action. She had hoped to slip away, to see Edmund for one last time, but then she would have come back, would cheerfully have told Alex what she had been doing, if not where she had been. And, while he would have been annoyed that she had broken their agreement not to leave the camp unescorted, he would have understood. As he had said, the Royalists were on the run; there was nothing she could do to harm Parliament's cause any longer. But that was before he had heard of this active group of rebels who, if she warned them of imminent attack, could escape to fight another day. By saving Edmund, by fighting for the king's cause this one last time, she would be directly betraying Alex, something she had not done before. She would be using her intimacy with him to spy on and foil his plan in a personal attack. Alex would be bound to see it differently from the holistic conflict of Cavalier against Roundhead. It *was* different, there were no two ways about it. And how, having betrayed him, could she return to him? A man of such invincible principles would not be able to forgive such treachery. Even if, by some miracle, she could keep her escape and her actions from him, she could not live with that deceit herself.

340

But she had no choice. Whatever loyalty she had toward her lover, she could not stand by while her dearest friend, closer to her than any brother, stood in danger of his life and she could save him. And if Edmund came to harm at Alex's hands, she would not be able to forgive Alex. The circle was vicious in its completion.

If only she and Alex had not parted in animosity. Tears pricked behind her eyes, and fiercely she swallowed the lump in her throat. There was no point in being maudlin about a mere detail in the greater tragedy of their separation. There would be time enough later when the task was completed. And if they had not quarreled, her absence would have been discovered as soon as Alex returned to the inn. As it was, he would not venture into her chamber this night, and Diccon would be sent to summon her in the morning, by which time the die would have been cast.

It was always possible, of course, that Alex would set off before morning on his expedition to mop up the rebels. Ginny stood frowning, one leg in her britches, the other paused in midair. On horseback, they could eat up the ten miles in less than an hour. On foot, she could not hope to do more than four miles an hour. Jen was well out of reach, stabled in the castle with the cavalry horses. How much of a start did she have? She finished dressing quickly, calculating all the while. They would have to decide where the rebels were first, and it was possible there would be several likely places that would have to be checked out. It would be a piece of appalling ill luck if they hit upon Grantly Manor at the first. And they had no idea that anyone might forestall them. Therein lay her major advantage. They would dine first, also. Alex was never careless of his men's well-being and would not throw them into a nonurgent engagement on empty bellies. The men who would make up the party would also have to be selected and prepared. This was not an expedition that would require an entire division. Presumably he would take only men of horse; foot soldiers would move too slowly.

No, they could not possibly leave for at least four hours, Ginny decided, going to the window. The boughs of an apple tree scraped against the second-floor casement. She hadn't climbed a tree in years, Ginny thought, swinging one leg over the sill, surveying the gnarled fruit tree, picking out her best route to the ground with a practiced eye. Britches made life a great deal easier, of course. She inched forward until she sat astride the branch, then gingerly brought one knee up, then the other, reaching up to grab the overhead branch as she pulled herself to her feet. The bough creaked ominously beneath her weight, and she progressed rapidly to the safety of the sturdier trunk.

A few seconds later she was on the ground in the darkened garden. Voices and laughter came from the tap-room, and the yellow glow of lamplight filled the open casements behind her. She melted into the garden shadows, shinned over the stone wall, and landed with a soft thud in the lane behind. A moment to fix her direction east against her memory of the setting sun, and Ginny set off on her mission of betrayal and rescue.

Chapter Twenty

"We've so little ammunition left, Edmund, we may as well strike camp here and make our way north." Joe Marshall paced the long gallery of Grantly Manor, his shadow, caught by the flickering flame of the tallow candles, climbing huge and insubstantial on the bare walls. He had his youngest brother's auburn hair, but Joe's temples were silver, and threads of the same weaved through the long locks curling on his shoulders. The set of the mouth and the jaw was similar, but the elder's face was lined and drawn.

Edmund Verney, thinner but tougher and wirier than he had been on leaving the Isle of Wight, looked up from the musket he was cleaning. "I was thinking, ever since we lost Jack Calvert on that last raid, that we've perhaps pushed our luck far enough. Newton may be an indecisive, bumbling idiot, but even he's going to decide he's taken enough at some point. I vote for the northern march. We'll come up with Hamilton's army near the border."

"Do we go separately or as a body?" a young man with flowing locks and a blue sash asked.

"Every man for himself," Kit Marshall pronounced. "An entire troop, even one as small as ours, would hardly escape detection in the countryside." He peered out of one of the long windows, staring down at the overgrown driveway below. The moon was full and something moved in the shadows of the box hedges beside the drive. Frowning, he looked more closely, signaling with his hand for silence in the room behind. All seemed still again in the garden below.

"What is it?" his brother asked softly, coming to stand beside him.

"Thought I saw something," Kit replied. "A figure over by those bushes. Who's on guard below?"

"Will Bright and Keith." Joe stared down, then stiffened. "Damnation, but ye're right, Kit. Someone's down there and up to no good, I'll be bound. How the devil did he get this close without alerting the guards?"

"Probably asleep," Edmund said with a scathing grin. "Let us go and invite our visitor inside. We must not show ourselves lacking in hospitality." He drew his sword and went swiftly to the door, the Marshall brothers following.

Ginny crouched in the shadows, looking up at the faint glow from the long windows that must be from the gallery. The house was of simple design, long and low with two wings set at right angles to the central portion. It was far from grand, probably once the dwelling of a local squire, and nestling as it did in a valley, separated from Nottingham by a low hill, was insignificant enough to escape notice. She had come upon it by traveling due east as the prisoner had said. There was a small hamlet about a mile down the road, and here was a house. She had been walking for what must be close on two and a half hours. This must be Grantly Manor. But how was she to declare her presence without running the risk of being shot, or run through more likely since it was a quieter method of disposing of unwelcome visitors?

The question was answered for her with shocking abruptness. A hand came from behind, clamping itself over her mouth and nose, and she felt the unmistakable prick of something very sharp against her spine. The sensation kept her still, and she hardly dared to breathe lest she provoke its penetration. The suffocating clamp over her mouth prevented speech and she resisted the urge to bite deep into the fleshy, salt-tasting palm.

"Sensible of you," a voice spoke gruffly. "Let's get you in the light and see what nocturnal visitor we have." The sword point pricked deeper, and Ginny obeyed the prod eagerly, almost tripping over herself in her anxious haste to keep ahead of it. The hand remained over her mouth, but as they emerged into the full moonlight, the voice said incredulously, "It is but a lad!" Then, more incredulously yet, "Well, I'll be damned! It's a maid." The hand left her mouth, although the sword remained at her back. "Just what in the name of the good God is a maid masquerading as a lad doing here in the middle of the night?"

Ginny twisted her head to look up at her captor and gasped. There was no mistaking the family likeness. It could be Alex, five years hence, who was returning her scrutiny. "Joe or Kit?" she heard herself ask before questioning the wisdom of such an inquiry at this juncture.

"Kit," the man said slowly. "It seems you have the advantage of me, girl, but not for much longer. In with you." The businesslike prod drove her through the suddenly opened door into a square hall. "Look what I've turned up in the bushes," Kit said to the others standing there. "A maid in very provocative clothing who knows Kit and Joe Marshall, it seems."

Ginny had eyes only for Edmund, leaning carelessly against the newel post, looking amused. Then the amusement died. "Ginny!"

"Yes, it is I, Edmund," she said. "It is so wonderful to see you. I have been so afraid for you, these last weeks, after Peter . . ."

"Peter? You have news of Peter?" Edmund bounded across the hall to her.

Before she could tell him, Kit Marshall expostulated, "Would one of you enlighten the rest of us?"

"I am as much in the dark as you," Edmund replied. "What the devil are you doing here, Ginny? I had thought you safely on the Isle of Wight . . ." Then a shadow crossed his face. "Colonel Marshall . . . ?"

"Lieutenant-General," Ginny interrupted, looking at Alex's brother, dreading to see what she knew from Joan that she would see—implacable enmity, murderous loathing at the very sound of his name. It was exactly as she had feared. But the bellow came not from Kit, but from another man who came in from the garden behind them.

"What have you to do with that traitorous, rebel blackguard?" Joe demanded, grabbing her arm so that she winced and Edmund stepped forward.

"Leave her be, Joe," he said with sudden menace. "Your damn brother took her prisoner when Peter Ashley and I escaped the Isle of Wight, and it's a score I'll settle with him if I get the chance."

"Oh, stop it!" Ginny exclaimed, unable to bear it any longer. "You are wasting precious time. I did not come here to listen to your—" She stopped. How could she possibly defend Alex in this company? How could she even hint at the true nature of her relationship with the most detested man in Parliament's army? She had come here to warn them against that man, after all. She was on their side, not Alex's. The bitter dregs of that truth hung sour on her tongue.

"What *did* you come here for?" Kit asked, belatedly sheathing his sword.

Ginny stepped away from him thankfully. Even in the minutes since Edmund's disclosure, she had been conscious of Kit as her captor, of the sword still at her back. "Alex is at Nottingham Castle," she told them. "A prisoner, before he died, told of your stronghold, but he died before he could be—be persuaded to tell them the exact location." She swallowed. "Alex is intending to come after you. He does not know, of course, that Edmund is here, or you." She gestured to the Marshall brothers.

"How did you know to find us? And what do you do in that traitor's company?" Joe fixed her with a piercing green eye.

Ginny decided on the lie that had once been the truth. "I am made ward of Parliament, tantamount to prisoner, because I have been working for the king. General Marshall has made himself personally responsible for me." She looked his brothers in the eye. "It was a kindness on his part, since otherwise I would have shared the fate of all rebel prisoners."

"How did you find us, Ginny, if the prisoner died before furnishing our hiding place?" Edmund asked in the silence that had followed her statement — a statement that made perfect sense to him since he remembered the scene on the beach at Alum Bay when Alex Marshall had taken her prisoner for himself.

"Another prisoner, I do not know his name. He was close to death, but I tended him a little, and when I said who I was, he mentioned Edmund. He told me how to find you just before they took him away."

"Jack Calvert," someone muttered. "Dark hair, blue eyes?"

"Aye," Ginny smiled with sad memory. "And unvanquished."

"Jack," stated Edmund quietly, and there was a moment's silence as they remembered the dead.

"I had thought to try to escape, to see Edmund again," Ginny resumed with difficulty because she was uncertain how to put her original plan, which had included returning to Alex. She decided it was not necessary to enter into detail; they would assume her motive was escape pure and simple, and it would do no harm to let the assumption lie. "Then I heard talk of the planned expedition, and I knew that I must come and warn you. You cannot defeat him," she said simply. "He has an entire division at his disposal, all the ammunition he needs. The only thing he does not have is time. If he does not find you, he will not take the time to pursue you because he cannot afford to. There have been too many delays already — dysentery and such like." She shrugged, loathing herself for the words of betrayal.

"How soon will he come?" Kit asked, turning to the stairs.

"It depends how long it takes him to fix upon this place," Ginny said, following the others upstairs to the gallery. "He does not know that I have come to warn you. He cannot know it, since he does not know of my conversation with Jack Calvert. It is to be hoped that he does not yet know of my absence either."

"But we can assume we have little time," Edmund said. "Do we stay and fight?" He looked around the intent circle.

"You cannot," exclaimed Ginny without thought that her utterance had no place in the decision these men must make for themselves and not at the bidding of a mere woman.

347

"You will not defeat him, I have told you."

"Hush, Ginny," Edmund admonished gently. "We have heard you and are, indeed, indebted to you more than we can ever repay, but this is not something in which you can have a say."

"I crave pardon, gentlemen." She went over to the window, depression and the deep sense of loss creeping into every cranny of her soul. If they stayed to fight Alex and lost, then she had thrown everything away. But she could not appeal thus to Edmund, not without telling him the untellable truth.

The discussion raged in the background, but the majority opinion seemed to be in favor of flight. Only the Marshall brothers remained silent, and Ginny watched them covertly. Their faces were closed and set, the eyes distanced as if they saw something other than the scene in the gallery. It was not hard for Ginny to imagine what they saw—their traitorous, rebel brother finally overcome at their hands, and the family honor avenged.

"So, we are agreed," Edmund, who seemed to be the group's spokesman, said eventually. "We part company, those who will to go on to the border, the others to make for the coast to take ship for Holland and join up with the prince of Wales." He came over to Ginny, taking her hands and smiling at her, the old Edmund of the reckless brown eyes. "We will try this venture together then, Ginny, as so many before. In Holland we will prepare to return in triumph and restore the king to his rightful throne. It is agreed."

Beneath this plan lay the absolute assumption of their marriage. Ginny murmured something that could have been consent as her inner turmoil roiled. Of course, Edmund assumed that she had escaped for that very reason; it was their original plan, after all, once they had left the Isle of Wight together. But how could she even contemplate such a thing? And then what choice did she have? Alex would see her desertion for the personal treachery it was; would see that she had chosen loyalty to Edmund over loyalty to him, would not see the pragmatism that lay behind her choice—

that she had come down on the side of saving life. Edmund would have died if she had chosen otherwise, but Alex, God willing, would have survived in either event.

"What say you, Ginny?" Edmund asked, puzzled at her hesitant reticence. "You seem unsure."

"No—no, I am not unsure, Edmund," Ginny lied, trying for a smile. "It is just that everything is so confusing—happening so quickly."

The explanation seemed to convince Edmund, who squeezed reassuringly the hands he still held and kissed her in a fraternal fashion that made her want to weep for a lifetime of lost passion—the secret of a passion that she knew she must now take to her grave.

"The rest of you must go," Joe spoke finally. "Kit and I will stay here. There is something we must attend to."

"What on earth do you mean?" Edmund demanded. "The two of you cannot stand alone against an entire brigade."

"The two of us can stand alone against our brother," Kit told him quietly. "We have long waited for this opportunity. We will be waiting for him, and when we have done what we must, then shall we take our chance. We will have the advantage of surprise."

Ginny felt the cold fear creep up her back. Alex would not be expecting to walk into an ambush fueled with the heat of personal vendetta. He would ride as always at the head of his troops, calm and relaxed, the reins held loosely in one hand. True, he would have breastplate and gorget as protection, sword at his hip, an armed troop at his back, but he would be expecting to fight fair, if he had to fight at all. He would not be on the lookout for snipers with but one target who knew he was coming although he knew nothing of them. In her anxiety to save Edmund's life, she had jeopardized Alex's.

"To remove Parliament's general once and for all would be a brave stroke for the king," Edmund said slowly. "More far reaching in its effect than disposing of an entire troop. And I too have a score to settle with General Marshall."

"No, Edmund," Ginny whispered, her hand at her throat. "You have no quarrel with the man who spared your life

349

once and did not then take advantage of information I gave him to pursue you." But the words were whispered to herself because, to articulate them clearly, she would have to reveal the truth to this company, and that truth would not alter the resolve of Joe and Kit Marshall to rid the world of the traitor, however it might affect Edmund. What would Edmund think of her — the willing mistress of such a man, no better than a camp follower except that she trailed the drum for love, not coin?

"Ginny, you will leave with the others," Edmund was saying, his eyes shining. "They will take you to a safe house near King's Lynn, and when I come, we will take a ship together across the North Sea."

Ginny shook her head. "How do you expect to escape from this house, Edmund, if you kill the general? Do you think his men will not come after you? They have undying loyalty for their commander and will tear you limb from limb."

"Leave that to us," Edmund said with a reassuring smile. "We will make our plans."

For all the world as if she was some stupid female who could not be expected to understand the complexities of the male mind. If matters had not been so desperate, Ginny would have found it amusing. Edmund had not always been so inclined to dismiss her thus; clearly his present company had corrupted him.

"I am not leaving," she said with a credible assumption of calm. "I am not prepared to wait at King's Lynn amongst total strangers, looking for your arrival when I know you will not be able to leave here alive."

"You must!" Kit Marshall spoke angrily. "This is no place for a woman, and our business with Alexander Marshall is no concern of yours."

If you did but know, Ginny thought as she shook her head. "I stay."

"But, Ginny." Edmund took her hands again, his voice pleading. "Do not be stubborn in this."

"Do not talk to me of 'stubborn,' Edmund Verney," Ginny cried. "I have played my part in this war also, as well you

350

know, and I have the right to decide my own fate."

Edmund could not gainsay her and looked helplessly at the Marshalls. Joe shrugged. "Nothing to do with us. She's your responsibility, Edmund."

"I am no one's responsibility," Ginny snapped, marching into the center of the room. "You are quite mad in this and will ensure all your deaths if you attempt this fratricide."

"It is no fratricide," Kit stated. "The man is no brother of ours, no son to our father. It is our task to rid the world of a traitor who was given life and nurtured by our family. If she will not go alone, Edmund, go with her. The Marshalls will deal with their own."

"I am staying," Ginny repeated. "Whether Edmund goes or stays, it matters not. I remain here." She did not care what they made of that, knew only that she could not run, leaving Alex to his fate, that if she could not stop this with words and sense, then she must find some other way.

"We are ready." One of the others came into the room, thrusting a pistol into his sash. "We have three hours until dawn." The farewells were brief but carried the intensity of friendship forged in battle and adversity, the sad acceptance of their lost cause. All in Grantly Manor knew that there was no longer any hope for His Majesty unless Hamilton's forces could pull off the miracle. The only sensible course of action now was to retreat, join up with the prince of Wales in exile, and gather men and arms for the return.

After their departure, a heavy silence hung over the gallery as the candles waned and the three men primed their muskets, waiting. Ginny sat alone in a shadowy corner of the room on a chair with a woven seat. There was no way of telling how long it would be. She wondered if he knew of her departure, if he had come to her chamber to make peace before he left and had found her gone. Would he have searched for her, or assumed she would return when she was ready, as she had done at Wimbledon—returned from her mission and found him waiting for her in the calm certainty of the indissoluble knot that tied them?

The first streaks of gray appeared in the sky, and the three men drew close to the windows, looking out over the drive.

Only Edmund was truly aware of Ginny's presence, and with that awareness came the first faint inklings of foreboding. He remembered the way she had leaped from the boat at Alum Bay, had said that it was right thus, that it was what she wanted. He had not questioned such curious statements then because, in that strange situation, they had not seemed overly strange. He had simply believed in the sacrifice she was making for Peter and for him. Now he wondered what lay between the Roundhead general and Virginia Courtney that kept her in this place in contradiction of her own statements of the futility of remaining.

Hunger took her at last out of the gallery and down to the kitchen, but she found little of substance there, those who had left had presumably taken what supplies there were against their own hunger on the journey. There was a little brawn, though, and some salted cod and a flagon of cider. She ate absently, wondering whether she should reverse her journey, run out now and alert Alex to the ambush awaiting him. There was a certain morbid humor in the picture of herself running desperately between the two camps reporting the actions and intentions of each to the other in a vain, stupid attempt to avoid the bloodshed of those she loved by those she loved. It was a situation that somehow seemed to encapsulate the whole damnable dilemma of this godforsaken war. Heartsick and weary, she went back to the gallery to offer Edmund some cod and a mug of cider, which he took, giving her a sharp glance with his muttered thanks.

Wandering to the window, she looked out as the sky lightened into full day. Perhaps Alex would not come after all. Perhaps, having drawn a blank at several places already, he had decided he could not afford to delay further. Perhaps, even now, the drums and bugle were rousing the division to muster on the parade ground of the castle in preparation for departure. The scene was now so familiar; she could see it in every detail, could hear the voices, the pawing of the hooves. . . . She could hear that now, through the opened window, the unmistakable sound of hooves, the jangle of a bridle. The three men heard it too. They moved soundlessly to the three central windows, shrinking against the narrow

352

strip of wall between.

"Get back, Ginny," Edmund hissed, seeing her standing there, heedless, in full view of anyone coming down the drive. She stepped to one side, shrinking into a corner by the last in the row of windows, peering round out of the window. He was riding as she had known he would be, no helmet, the early sun catching the auburn-glinting hair, striking off the silver breastplate and the hilt of his sword. He rode, as always when approaching some military destination, some ten paces ahead of the front line, quite alone. Behind him, Ginny could discern Diccon, Colonel Bonham, and several other familiar faces, mostly junior officers, included presumably so that they might increase their experience of action before the big battle.

She was conscious at this moment of only one thing, of how much she loved him, of how much she wanted him with every nerve and cell of a shamelessly lusting body. The click of a flintlock resounded like a bell clapper in the deathly hush of the gallery, hurling her out of the wondrous daze that seemed to have brought on a creeping paralysis, so her limbs moved as if through cotton wool as she saw the three men raise their muskets to their shoulders, all trained on the one man, riding, because of her, oblivious into the valley of death.

Ginny moved behind the three men, then, like a panther on his prey, sprang at Kit who stood in the middle. She cried Alex's name at the top of her lungs as the force of her body threw Kit against his brother, and Edmund spun round in astonishment. Kit's musket discharged into the air above, the shot burying itself in the ceiling with a hail of plaster dust.

Alex had been looking carefully at the house, looking for signs that it might be inhabited by those whom he sought. They had tried three places during the night's march and drawn no cover, but there was something about the brooding quality of the silence that hung over this neglected manor that made his nose twitch. The grass in the park might be high, the bushes tangled, the beds choked with weeds, but the place was not untenanted. He could smell it and feel it,

353

and so could Bucephalus who stepped higher, lifting his nose to the wind. In the last four years, they had ridden together up to too many houses where the inhabitants hid from them, hoping they would turn and ride away again, for either man or horse to be fooled.

He heard Ginny's shout the instant before the bellow of the musket. Bucephalus, too well trained to react with fear, quivered in readiness for the order that would send him forward into the attack. But Alex was frozen for a moment that seemed infinite, his eyes riveted on the struggle in the window. It was Ginny; he had heard her voice, he could see her framed in the window, unmistakable to the eyes that knew every curve and hollow of her body, every millimeter of skin, every gesture . . . but she was back at the inn in Nottingham, nursing her anger as he had been nursing his. Yet she was here, fighting with the equally unmistakable figure of his brother. Then two other figures appeared in the window, and she seemed to be locked with all three of them, calling her warning all the time. At last he moved, hurling himself from his horse to take cover in the box hedge as a musket roared again, and the ball whistled into the dust just behind Bucephalus. Had he been astride his horse, it would have taken his head with it. Pandemonium broke out in the ranks, a pistol was discharged, but erratically this time now that its target had disappeared, and Alex, from his position by the hedge, bellowed orders that brought the cavalcade wheeling through the hedge and out of the line of fire from the window.

Ginny ceased her frantic efforts to wrench the weapons from the Marshalls, who, cursing viciously, were struggling to reload although they knew now that the advantage of surprise was lost.

"Why?" Edmund asked quietly, his face white as whey, his own musket unfired, hanging loosely by the stock from his hand. "What is that man to you?"

"I could not allow you to kill him," Ginny said in a flat voice, without answering the question. "But I cannot allow him to kill you, either." She bit her lip. "I will go down and talk with him."

"What is he to you?" It was Kit this time who seized her by the shoulder, swinging her round to face him.

Ginny looked at the three faces where desperation and disbelief mingled. "All and everything," she said. "He is all and everything to me. I betrayed him for Edmund's sake, but I could not allow you to kill him, not even for Edmund's sake. I am sorry, my dear." She put a hand on her cousin's arm, but he drew back from her, and she let the hand fall.

"His mistress?" Edmund asked in the same quiet tone. "You are the mistress of a rebel general?"

"I would ask you to believe that, despite that, I remain loyal to the king," she said painfully. "Why else would I come here?"

Edmund muttered something incomprehensible and turned away, back to the window. "They are reforming," he told them. "But their muskets are trained on every corner of the house. Do we take the cellar route?"

"What route?" Ginny asked and then shriveled as she saw denial on every face. She was one with the traitor outside, not to be trusted although she had come to them in good faith, and if they had left with the others as she had begged them to do, they would all now be safe.

"Not I," Kit said. "I'll not skulk from a rat, creeping through passages to flee across the fields."

The morning quiet was suddenly shattered by a tremendous pounding from below. Someone was hammering on the oak front door, hammering with the vigor of an invader who would have entrance despite all opposition. Ginny moved to the door of the gallery. "Where are you going?" Edmund rasped.

Ginny shrugged as if nothing mattered any longer. "You will do what you feel you must. I will do the same." She went slowly down the shallow flight of stairs, her hand running over the smooth cherrywood of the banister, feeling its shape and texture as an irrelevancy, yet as if its solid reality were all the grounding she had in a world where friends became enemies, where lovers who had accepted a form of enmity as inescapable now faced the smirch of personal betrayal and desertion.

She drew back on the heavy bolts even as the hammering on the other side continued. When the sounds of her efforts penetrated, the noise outside ceased. She pulled the door wide, stepped into the morning light, and closed the door gently behind her.

Alex was back on Bucephalus, looking much as he had done the first time she had seen him when he had ridden to take possession of John Redfern's lands and property and John Redfern's daughter. Behind him ranged six lines of cavalry with small sword and musket. The man of horse who had been battening on the door with the hilt of his sword stepped back as Ginny came out, and there was a moment of utter silence.

Alex looked at her, and the gray eyes, unflinching, met his. She had betrayed him, he thought, asking the question with his eyes and reading the answer in hers. She would have left him if the choice had been hers. Again he read the truth. But he did not know why, knew only the sense of emptiness as faith and trust crumbled. Yet she had saved his life. But then one would save the life of a dog that one was fond of, after all. Deliberately, he dismounted and crossed the gravel toward her, his booted feet scrunching on the tiny stones.

When he reached her, Ginny said softly, "Your brothers and Edmund Verney are within. Only they remain."

"And you," he added.

She nodded. "And I, but my presence is for the moment unimportant. I would ask you, in the name of humanity, of pity, and of decency, for their lives." When he said nothing, she knelt before him on the gravel. "In the name of humanity, of pity, and of decency; in the name of the love that we shared, spare their lives. What will be gained by further bloodshed?"

"They would shed mine," he said.

"Must that rob you of nobility?"

"Stand up," he said. Ginny rose to her feet. "I owe you two lives, Virginia Courtney," Alex said. "My nephew's and now mine own. I will give you my brothers' lives for those two." He stopped, and the silence hung heavy between them. He knew now why she had come to Grantly Manor; she had come for Edmund Verney's sake. "You would have left with your cousin?" She made no reply, but as before her eyes told him the truth. Alex felt used and shriveled like a sere leaf. "I will have your life in exchange for your cousin's," he said, his eyes holding hers in the intense quiet as fifty men watched a play, the dialogue of which they could only guess at.

The bright head bowed in acknowledgment and acceptance. It was inevitable, a bargain decreed by fate. They were in some way possessed by each other, and she had always belonged to him and always would. But there was one thing more she had to have. "And safe passage also," she said. "Not to fight in this war again, but home to their wives and children for your brothers, to the coast for Edmund. Otherwise, their lives alone would be a valueless gift."

"Very well." Alex spoke with slow deliberation. "But it is the last time you will ever range yourself with those who stand against me. Whatever I decide to do with your life that I have bought this day, you will remember always the bargain you struck, and where your loyalty now lies."

"I will remember."

"Then find me parchment and a pen that I may write the orders for safe passage."

Leaving him standing before the door, Ginny went into the kitchen where she had earlier seen a bunch of goose pens, an inkpot, and a sand caster. She could find no parchment until opening a drawer of the dresser, she discovered a bundle of receipts written on but one side of the vellum. She took her findings into the hall, laid them on a square oak table, and sharpened the quill with a knife before going to the door again. "It is ready for you."

Alex stepped into the dim light of the hall, and for a few minutes the only sound was the scratching of the quill on parchment. He dusted the ink with the sand caster and handed her the documents, one eyebrow raised as he waited for her approval. When she had finished reading, he said, "You may tell them that they have twenty minutes to leave this place. They must go out through the back as I do not wish to see them, and I do not wish my men to. After twenty minutes, the house will be searched."

Ginny nodded and went upstairs. The three men still stood in the gallery, and it was clear from their bearing that they awaited capture. She handed them the documents. "He will have the house searched in twenty minutes; you must be gone through the back way by then."

"We are to accept the mercy of that—?"

"Yes," Ginny interrupted Joe fiercely. "You will accept it for Joan's sake and for little Joe who, three weeks ago, lay at death's door. Your wife is desperate for your strength. Has she not borne enough that you would throw your life away for some footling stiff-necked notions of pride?"

"You have seen my wife?" Joe stared at her.

"Aye, and nursed your son sick of the typhus." She glared at him. "Go, for God's sake. No one is asking for gratitude or apology, for anything except that you take what has been given you and make good use of it." She looked then at Edmund, who held his own paper between his hands. "I would ask for forgiveness, my friend, if I believed there was anything to forgive. But I have remained true to king and country. What is between Alex Marshall and myself has nothing to do with this war, although the war touches us at all points."

"What will you do now?" Edmund asked. "You have foiled the general's plans. Will he grant you safe passage also?"

Ginny shook her head. She would not tell Edmund of the bargain. "I remain with him, Edmund. I do not know what he intends, but it is my destiny, and I am content to have it so."

"That is not like you." Edmund frowned. "To yield control in that way."

It was not, but she found that she had meant it when she had said she was content to have it so. She had made enough agonizing decisions in the last weeks that the thought of having all such matters decided for her brought only relief. Maybe Alex would take her life in the literal sense, as a rebel spy in his camp. Maybe he would leave her behind, a prisoner in Nottingham Castle, maybe . . . But there was no point speculating. He would do what he would do.

"Then it is farewell." Edmund held out his hand. "We will not meet again."

"No, I do not suppose we shall." She took his hand, and her heart wept at this cold, estranged good-bye. "God go with you, Edmund."

"And with you, Cousin." He let go of her hand and walked to the door, then suddenly spun round with a cry of sorrow. "Damnation, Ginny! I do not care whose mistress you are. You have always been true, and I do not believe you could ever be otherwise." He held out his arms, and she ran into them. They clung together as Kit and Joe quietly left the gallery.

Then Ginny drew back with a little sob. "You must go, Edmund. The twenty minutes must be almost passed, and Alex will not delay longer." With a supreme effort, she managed a tiny smile as she stood on tiptoe and kissed the corner of his mouth. "This war *will* end, love. Who knows what twists and turns fate will deal us? While we have life and health, there is always hope that one day we will find each other again."

"Aye." He agreed with her because there was too much pain in denial, pressed her hands one last time, and left.

Ginny remained in the gallery for a few minutes until she was sure her tears were swallowed, then went downstairs, out into the sunshine where her arrival was the signal for the troopers to move into the house. At a signal from the general, she went to stand beside him. He said not a word to her, and Ginny could feel no warmth in him. His expression was stern, the eyes hard, and he held himself straight beside her so that not even his sleeve would brush her arm.

Chapter Twenty-one

This time, Alex bound her hands behind her back, and she walked, as she had once refused to do, at his stirrup, the troop of horse keeping to the pace that she set. This time, Ginny was not conscious of a sense of humiliation. She was a rebel spy, she knew it, they all knew it, and all, even her friends, avoided her eye, avoided even looking at the figure trudging steadily along beside Bucephalus. Of necessity, she kept her eyes on the ground, side-stepping ruts and stones that could trip her easily in the unbalanced state caused by her bound hands. No one spoke.

Diccon seethed with anger whenever he glanced at the general, so grim and implacable, staring rigidly ahead as if he did not even notice Ginny on the ground beside him. It did not matter to Diccon what she had done; he knew that there had to have been insuperable reasons for it, and that the general should treat her like any common prisoner filled the lieutenant's soul with rage. She had been walking now for two hours, and the sun was getting high; yet a quiet dignity radiated from the silent figure, and Diccon, although he had long ago accepted that she was unattainable, ached with the love that could only find expression in service.

Alex was not indifferent, although nothing showed on his face. He was in a torment of doubt and indecision. She had betrayed him, had deserted him, would have left him for

360

Edmund Verney. But *was* that the true picture? He had also always known how deep ran her affection — no, love — for her cousin. And now he knew that it ran so deep that it transcended the love or loyalty she had for *him*. But should that wound him as sharply as it did? He had always known that she could serve her own cause at the expense of his as and when she could. Had she not simply served both her cousin and her cause? Somehow, she had found out about Grantly Manor. Could he blame her for doing what she had always said she would when she had the chance? He would blame himself for relaxing his guard. Naïvely, he had thought that danger was now insignificant, that with her physicking and the love she bore him, she had other things to think of. She had played him for a fool, that was for sure. But it would never happen again. Not now that he had her life and exclusive loyalty, given to him in exchange for her cousin's safety. But God damn it! He would have that life and loyalty given to him freely, not as part of any bargain, when he did not know, could not tell, whether she considered her cousin's life dearly bought.

Ginny continued to put one foot in front of the other doggedly, refusing to remember that she had not slept the previous night because the thought brought a wash of fatigue with the knowledge that exhaustion was both justifiable and inevitable. But her boots seemed weighted with lead, and her pace slackened. As she fell back, Alex slowed his horse, and the rest were forced to do the same to avoid overtaking the general and his prisoner. Her foot caught against a mud-ridged cart track, and she stumbled, unable to use her hands for protection or balance, onto her knees.

Diccon, heedless of his commander, flung himself from his mount. "Ginny, are you hurt?" He helped her upright. "You must ride my horse. I will walk."

"You will do no such thing, Lieutenant," Alex pronounced coldly. Diccon swung round, mutiny on his lips and in his eyes, and met the cool gaze that held his until, against his will, his eyes dropped. Alex nodded slowly. "Now you may untie her wrists."

Diccon made no attempt to struggle with the knot but

pulled his knife from his belt and cut through it. Ginny murmured her thanks, shaking out her arms to relieve the knot between her shoulder blades. "Come." Alex stretched down his hand. "Diccon, help her up."

Ginny put her hand in Alex's, felt his fingers close tight and firm around hers, put her foot into Diccon's palm, and went up as he tossed her. She settled onto the saddle as she had done in the past, except that this time, because of her britches, she could ride astride and did not lean against Alex, and the arm that came around her to hold the reins was no cradle into which she could slip. Instead, she held herself upright, as if she rode alone.

No longer hampered by the need to keep to a walking pace, the cavalcade increased its speed, and they reached Nottingham within the hour. Ginny was set down at the inn; Diccon instructed to remain with her until further orders. Alex and his troop went on to the castle where he would presumably make some report of the night and morning's activities to Governor Newton. How much of the truth would he tell, Ginny wondered. Not enough to incriminate her, presumably, or else why was she left here and not taken in ignominy to the castle? She was too tired to ask questions of herself or of anyone and, with a word of excuse to Diccon, went to the chamber she had occupied the previous day. Her belongings were still there, the bed unslept in, nothing disturbed. It was as if she had never left it, and perhaps no one here knew that she had. Perhaps, if she went to bed and fell asleep, she would wake and the whole wretched business would vanish into the land of nightmares where it belonged. . . .

An hour later, Alex came into the chamber. He had had a thoroughly unpleasant session with Governor Newton when he had been obliged to admit failure of the enterprise of which he had had such high hopes. While admitting failure, he had also been forced to keep the real truth from the gloating governor, since disclosing Ginny's part in the fiasco would be tantamount to branding her a spy, and he would be hard pressed to find adequate reason for saving her from justice. His pride and his dignity had both been pricked raw by the encounter. His trusting love had received a staggering blow that left him confused and bewildered. He had wasted half a day on a futile exercise; he and the members of the troop had had a sleepless night; and now the cause of all this trouble and grief was sleeping like a baby, one bare round arm thrown over the coverlet, the lustrous chestnut hair spread thickly upon the pillow, the sable eyelashes forming half-moons on her pale cheeks.

"Wake up, Ginny!" He shook her naked shoulder roughly, and when she moaned and rolled over, burrowing into the pillow, he yanked the covers off her, shutting his mind to the sight of her curled body, so soft, tender, and inviting. Ginny clung stubbornly to the black depths of unconsciousness until something cold and wet scrubbed roughly across her face and she came to, shuddering at this brutal awakening, washed by the nausea that came from being torn so abruptly from the depths of her first sleep. Bemused, she looked up into the furious face hanging over her, and, caught off guard in her weakened state, tears of self-pity filled her eyes.

Hurt and frustration were the coals that fed the fiercely glowing brazier of his anger, and Alex did not want to see the tears. "How dare you go to sleep!" he blazed. "I have already wasted half a day because of you. Because of you, fifty men have gone without sleep to no purpose and can look forward to none until this night." He pulled her off the bed as he spoke. "We leave here in five minutes, and if you must ride like Lady Godiva, then so be it!" With that, he stormed out of the chamber, slamming the door in his wake.

Ginny, her hands trembling and heart beating fast with the shock of her rude awakening, struggled to put on her clothes again. She could not think clearly, was aware only of how wretchedly unwell she felt, how even her skin seemed to ache. She stumbled downstairs, still fastening the buttons on her shirt, petrified of what might happen if she did not appear by the decreed five minutes.

Jed passed her on the stairs in too much of a hurry to greet her. He entered the chamber she had just left, emerging in a few seconds with her baggage roll. Outside, Alex, astride Bucephalus, waited and fumed. Jen, saddled, stood

363

patiently. Ginny mounted without assistance, and Jed, having swung himself up onto his cob, stowed Ginny's baggage behind him, and the three of them rode back to the castle where the division stood ready to move out.

The next few days were sheer misery for everyone. The general was almost unapproachable, setting a furious pace that raised blisters on the feet and frayed tempers. They never made camp properly because they stopped too late at night for anyone to have the energy, and, besides, the general decided they could not afford the time involved in striking it the following morning. So they slept in barns and outhouses, or under the stars, eating without the comfort of fire so they all grew heartily sick of stale biscuit, cold bacon, pickled herrings, and whatever other supplies they carried that required no cooking.

Ginny felt filthier than she could ever remember. There seemed little point in putting fresh linen on a dirty body, and since the opportunity never arose for washing either clothes or herself, she gave up all attempts to keep herself respectably tidy and slept in the clothes she had ridden in all day, assuming that she smelled no worse than anyone else and probably was the only person to notice anyway.

Alex spoke to her only to give her an order or bellow because she was in the way. Since this was the only way he communicated with anyone these days, Ginny could not feel singled out, but her unhappiness increased hourly. She knew that she was responsible for Alex's mood and, therefore, responsible for everyone else's misery. Once or twice, she attempted to broach the subject, but he always cut her off with mortifying impatience and walked away. She began to wonder whether the bargain they had struck could possibly be affording Alex any satisfaction. He certainly did not appear to be any happier than anyone else, but perhaps he was deriving some twisted pleasure from punishing her with this icy indifference and the unusually careless disregard for the well-being of others that he must know upset her.

Ginny set her teeth and went about her usual business in grim silence. The march took its toll of the men, and her services were much in demand during the brief halts. She took to rising before dawn, going into the fields to collect the herbal ingredients for her medicines but always with Jed to accompany her. At first, he had no solution to offer on the general's evil temper, merely telling Ginny that he had seen it several times before, and while it was the devil's own business while it lasted, he would recover his usual equilibrium eventually.

"In the meantime, an entire division is to be made to suffer," Ginny retorted. "There is no justice in that, and the general prides himself on his sense of justice, does he not?" Jed grunted. "If he must punish *me* then I will accept it willingly. I caused him grievous hurt, I know that." She smiled sadly. "I would make it up to him, if he would allow me, but I cannot come within ten paces without having my head bitten off."

"Folks 'ave always been afeard of his black moods, even when he was a lad," Jed said thoughtfully, laying a bunch of spearmint in her basket. "His sainted mother, rest her soul, would do anythin' to stop 'em, wouldn't let his brothers upset 'im, or anyone else, for that matter. Might 've been better if 'n she had."

Ginny sat back on her heels and surveyed the weather-beaten, wrinkled face intently. "Are you suggesting that perhaps someone should *not* be afraid of this black mood, should perhaps show him that they are not?"

Jed shrugged. "Stands to reason you expect what you've always 'ad, seems to me. General expects folks to run scared when he's vexed like this, and then I don't think 'e knows what to do about it. Can't stop bein' vexed just like that, now, can 'e? Not with everyone shakin' in their shoes."

"You make him sound like a thoroughly spoiled little boy who's thrown a tremendous tantrum and is scared and bewildered by the effect it's had," Ginny said with a laugh.

"If the cap fits," Jed responded laconically. "Best be gettin' back, now, mistress. Don't want to upset the general by keepin' the division waitin' again, do you?" He winked, and Ginny chuckled, feeling better than she had done for days.

At six o'clock, after a grueling day in the early August heat, Ginny saw what she had been waiting for — a wide, clear river running between lush green meadows shaded by broad oaks and copper beeches. She nudged Jen forward, out of the front line to ride beside Bucephalus some ten paces ahead of the rest. "General, I think we should stop here for the night," she announced without preamble.

Alex looked at her in blank astonishment. "You what?"

"I think we should stop here for the night," she repeated calmly. "There is water for bathing and cooking, and if we stop now, the men can light their fires and have a hot supper for once."

"And since when have you been in command of this division?" he demanded icily, with a sardonic twist of his lips.

"Since its general seems to have forgotten to concern himself with the welfare of his men," she returned smartly. "They are suffering from blisters and foot rot because they have not had time to air their boots or wash their stockings. They are sore from marching in armor at this insane pace you have set. They all know that speed is of the essence, but one early halt is not going to make that much difference, and they will march all the better for it on the morrow. Besides," she went on swiftly, seeing him momentarily at a loss, "I stink, and if I do not bathe and change my clothes within the next half-hour, I shall be quite unable to stand my own company, let alone yours." Twisting over her shoulder, she called, "Colonel Bonham, the general has said we may halt the march for the day and make camp beside the river."

There was nothing Alex could do about it, short of engaging in an unseemly brawl on the public highway with this outrageous woman who had so surely cut the ground from beneath his feet. He gestured assent to the colonel, but the habitual black glower showed no sign of lifting, deepened if anything. At the sight of it, Ginny put her chin up. She was going to force a response from him before the morning at whatever cost. A blazing row, however ugly, had to be better than this frigid wasteland, and it was high time General Alexander Marshall realized that one person, at least, was not afraid of his temper.

366

The men of the division, once dismissed from their ranks, behaved like children released from the schoolroom, pulling off their boots and stockings and wading into the river with great shouts of glee, splashing water over dust-coated heads and clothes. Tents went up and fires were lit in double-quick time; soon the aromas of cooking drifted with the smoke across the meadow, and the sounds of singing and the strumming of a mandolin filled the evening air.

The officers' tents went up equally rapidly, the general's, at Jed's instruction, set a little apart. Ginny took possession immediately, without waiting for a signal from its rightful owner who, if the past nights were anything to go by, would sleep in lonely isolation under the trees. She found her precious sliver of soap, a towel, and clean undergarments and wrapped the whole in her kirtle of green chintz before leaving the tent, clutching her bundle and setting off toward the river.

"Virginia!" Alex's voice bellowed, arresting her before she had gone three paces.

She stopped but did not turn, saying into the air ahead of her. "Yes, General. What may I do for you?"

"Where do you think you're going?" He strode across the grass toward her, lowering his voice in deference to those others around them who made great show of ignoring the scene.

"I am going to bathe in the river," she replied succinctly. "As I told you I would."

"Well, I am telling you that you may not," he snapped.

"For what reason?" Ginny demanded indignantly, moving off without waiting for his response.

"Come back here!"

"No," she threw over her shoulder, "not until I have bathed."

Alex caught her, seized her hand, and pulled her into the trees out of sight of any fascinated spectators. "You will do as I tell you," he gritted. "You may not bathe in the river because, in order to ensure privacy from the camp, you will have to go quite some way away, and I will not permit you to go far afield without escort, as well you know. Jed will bring

367

you water to the tent, and you must make do with that."

"It is not good enough," she said furiously. "I must wash my hair, and I *will* bathe properly. If I must be escorted, then you will have to come." She tugged at her imprisoned wrist. "Let me go. I am sick to death of your ill temper and your unfairness. It is bad enough that you should have the power of inflicting misery on so many without your using that power to satisfy your own self-conceit. When I have bathed, I will prepare you some hiera picra which will purge the choler from your stomach!" Alex, so taken aback by this forceful speech, loosened his grip on her hand, and she twitched free, marching away from him, not deigning to run, knowing that if he was determined to stop her, he could do so simply by virtue of superior strength.

Alex watched her break through the trees again so that she was back in sight of the camp, contemplated forcing her to do as he bade her, then dismissed the idea as undignified. No one had spoken to him in that manner since he was a child, and in with his fury lurked something uncomfortable that he did not wish to examine closely. If she was determined to bathe, then would he have to accompany her. A week ago, the prospect would have brought only pleasure, he thought sourly, and he would most probably have shared the bath with her. But he was so damnably confused about the way he felt about her these days, the last thing he could afford was to lose what little perspective remained to him in the seductive glories of her body.

He strode briskly in pursuit, catching her up as she rounded a bend in the river. Ginny stopped and looked around, ignoring her companion as she tried to decide whether this particular spot would serve her purpose. "It is not far enough away," Alex told her firmly. "We will go around the next bend, if you please."

"If you are to stand watch for me, I fail to see what difference it makes how far away I go," Ginny said with deliberate impudence.

Alex's lips thinned, but he refused to rise to the provocation and maintained instead a lofty silence as they progressed around the next bend where they found a small, stony beach that Ginny decided would be perfect. Alex flung himself on his back on the bank, gazing deliberately upward into the early evening sky as she threw off her clothes with a sigh partly of relief and partly of disgust at their sweat-stiffened, dust-caked condition. Ginny cast a glance at the supine figure, then shrugged, telling herself that she felt far too bedraggled and filthy to wish to attract his attention anyhow. Squaring her shoulders, she marched to the water's edge and dipped her toe in experimentally. The water was cold, much colder than the southern rivers of her home county.

Alex turned his head, watching her through half-closed eyes. He hadn't meant to but somehow couldn't help himself. She had a magnificent back, long and narrow, the spine straight as a die. As he watched, she unpinned her hair and let it fall down her back, running her hands through it to free the kinks. His eyes roamed greedily down her length, lingering over the nipped-in waist before traversing the neat roundness of her buttocks that he could feel just by looking. His hands curled, cupping the muscular curves in memory, then flattened to stroke over her thighs, again so long and slender, down to play in the soft hollow behind her knee. It always made her squirm and wriggle when his tongue licked that sensitive spot. He smiled and, forgetting that he was not supposed to be observing the nymph at her ablutions, turned on his side, propping his head on his elbow, and watched with unabashed pleasure.

Ginny waded waist deep in the water, holding her arms out at her sides, the cold making her catch her breath as it crept up over her ribs. Unable to bear the slow torture of gradual immersion any longer, she plunged headfirst beneath the water and emerged with a gasp, shaking out her wet hair. Alex chuckled to himself.

Ginny still had her back to him, so was blissfully unaware of his far-from-covert observation as she soaped her hair and body with scouring vigor before plunging back beneath the water, finding it invigorating rather than cold now that she was used to it. Still clutching the precious sliver of soap, she swam across the river to the far bank, glorying in the

369

feel of the water on her clean limbs cleaving the water with all the power of the skilled swimmer. Alex watched the white shape beneath the water, still smiling appreciatively as the curve of her backside broke the surface. At the far side, she rolled onto her back, keeping herself afloat with a lazy paddling motion of her legs. The crowns of her breasts, hardened by the cold water, rose clear to be stroked by the soft air.

It was really rather more than flesh and blood could be expected to bear, Alex reflected with a degree of pleasurable discomfort. Then, with a jolt, he remembered why he had not intended to be seduced on this bathing party. Lusting after her was all well and good, but it simply added to his confusion. He flung himself onto his back again. Why would she have left him? What had he done to deserve that? Certainly, they had had an unpleasant squabble over the wounded prisoner. Ginny had behaved without due circumspection in the presence of that damned governor, and Alex had retaliated in his usual fashion by treating her publicly like a recalcitrant and exasperating responsibility. It was a familiar-enough pattern; on previous occasions they had made up with an exchange of apologies and another inch of compromise on either side. But not content with betraying his plans to the enemy, she had been fully intending to run away with the enemy. He could understand, just, why she had felt the need to run to Edmund's rescue, and he would have forgiven her easily enough once she had come back and they could have had it out. But he could neither understand nor forgive the fact that, having gone to Edmund's rescue, she had then been intending to throw in her lot with her cousin, just as she had been about to do that morning at Alum Bay. If his brothers had not been there, had not decided to lie in wait for him, if Edmund had not decided to do the same, she would have flown the coop with the rest of them, and he would not have discovered her absence until he returned empty-handed to Nottingham. He would not even have known where she had gone. Since he would not have discovered Edmund, he would not have been able to make the connection. It was hopeless. He could not begin to understand.

Ginny swam back to the beach and emerged from the water with a marked flash of chagrin that her watchman had not even stirred from his supine pose, gazing up into a most uninteresting sky. Picking up her towel, she trod deliberately over to him. Alex did not move until she tossed her soaking wet hair forward over her head and a rain of river water fell upon his chest.

"Damn you, Ginny!" Alex sat up, brushing at his shirt. "I am soaked. What are you thinking of?"

"Only that you could do with a bath, sir," she replied promptly. "If you will not take one for yourself, then I must encourage you." Laughing, she shook her hair over him again. "I will even lend you my soap."

"Stop it!" Alex roared, grabbing her ankle. "I am not in the mood to play games."

"No, you are only in the mood to sulk and look black and make everyone's life a misery," she retorted, kicking lightly at his ribs with her free foot.

"Don't you talk to me like that, Virginia Courtney." Alex released her foot and sprang upright. His arm brushed her bare breast, and he jumped back as if he had been scorched. "Put your clothes on at once."

Slowly, Ginny shook her head. "Not until you agree to talk about this that is making you so wretched, and everyone wretched with you." She planted her feet firmly, put her hands on her hips, shoulders back so that her breasts were thrust forward with a defiance to match her jutting chin.

Alex inhaled sharply. She was so damnably beautiful, and his aroused body throbbed with longing, even as his wounded spirit kept him from yielding to that desire. "Get dressed," he repeated with creditable calm. "There is nothing to talk about, and you cannot continue to stand stark-naked in this field."

"I most certainly can," Virginia said, not moving a muscle.

"Do you want me to take my hand to your backside?" His words were clipped, as he took a menacing step toward her.

Ginny stood her ground, narrowing her eyes, the tip of

her tongue running over her lips. "Whatever gives the general pleasure," she murmured in dulcet tones.

Laughter welled deep within him, taking him totally by surprise. He turned away hastily, lest she should see it in his eyes, and went rapidly down to the beach, throwing off his clothes. He was now in sore need of dousing with cold water — and not just for its cleansing properties.

Ginny watched him with a rueful little smile. She had not really achieved her object, but a little progress had been made. He had been forced to respond to her, at least, without taking refuge in that icy withdrawal. She dressed in her gloriously clean clothes and sat upon the bank to comb out her hair. Alex was in the river for an inordinately long time, and he did not scorn the soap when she tossed it to him. Neither, however, did he say anything further to her when he finally came out, merely helped himself to her towel before pulling on his britches.

"You do not want to put that sweaty shirt on again, now you are all clean," Ginny observed in domestic manner. "Or your stockings. I should go back to the camp as you are and find clean clothes."

"Thank you for the advice, Mistress Prim," he said sarcastically. "I did not need it, however. If you are quite finished, let us go."

That evening, Ginny went to considerable effort to lighten the mood around the campfire, deliberately including the general in her cheerful chat, although she was very careful not to tease him as she had done in the past. Her efforts were aided by the creature comforts of hot food and a sack posset that she made for them with warmed wine. The general, while he bore no part in the conversation, at least made no disparaging remarks and remained in the group, sitting with his back against a tree trunk. Ginny ached to go over to him, to lean against his knees while he stroked absently through her hair in the old way. She ached because of the hurt in his eyes that seemed to have lost their clarity of purpose, but how could she put it right if he would not talk about it? Would not allow her near him? She sighed. At least, though, she had made matters a little easier for everyone else by taking a stand this afternoon, and Alex, while pride would perhaps not allow him to acknowledge it openly, would recognize that she had been right and would act accordingly in future. The consequences of her actions now rested entirely between herself and Alex, where they belonged. But it was so lonely. Biting her lip hard to keep back the tears, Ginny got to her feet. "Gentlemen, I must bid you good night. The opportunity for an early and relatively comfortable night is not one to be ignored."

In the chorus of good nights, Alex's silence went unnoticed by all save Ginny. But then what could she expect? She lay in the tent, breathing in the scents of crushed grass and wood smoke, listening to the low murmur of voices from the campfire that eventually lulled her to sleep.

The sensation that woke her was so light, so exquisitely tantalizing that for a moment she did not know whether she slept or woke. Something was moving over her skin, something insubstantial, incorporeal. Her eyelashes fluttered, and she whispered a little murmur of dreamy pleasure. Then her eyes snapped open. "Alex?"

"Hush, not a word," he commanded softly. "Not a word, not a movement." The green-brown eyes burned their message as she lay looking up at him, baffled by this strange visitation. There was something different about his expression, not stern exactly, but not soft with love either. Something determined, purposeful, as if he had come to a decision after long agonizing. "I am come," he said quietly, "to take possession of my own."

Her breath seemed to catch in her throat as his meaning became clear. She opened her mouth to speak, but he placed two fingers over her lips, pressing firmly. "No, you will not speak, my own, and you will lie quite still."

A flicker of apprehension crept up her spine. What would he do with her? He had just reminded her that she was his, had given herself to him in exchange for Edmund's life; but this was not what she had meant. Yet, he had the right to interpret the bargain as he chose; it had been made with no conditions. Alex had pulled the covers from her while she slept, and for the first time in his presence, Ginny felt

373

overpoweringly conscious of the vulnerability of her naked-ness.

Alex removed his fingers, then very lightly brushed across her lips with the fine tip of a delicate sable brush. She knew then what she had felt in the half-trance between sleeping and waking. The brush flicked across the shell of her ear with a sweet and piercing pleasure that drew a gasp from between her parted lips, then moved to trace the curve of her cheek and down to her collarbone. His eyes remained locked with hers as the brush drifted down to the mound of her breast, touched and stroked until her nipples tightened and the slow languorous delight began to build deep in her belly. The delicate instrument of pleasure fluttered across her abdomen, painted in her navel, dipped lower over the rippling skin of her belly. His free hand parted her thighs with gentle, yet inexorable insistence, and her throat seemed to close in an anticipation so intense that it verged on pain.

The brush trailed upward over the tender satin of her inner thighs, and still he held her with his gaze, the fine mouth relaxed, yet unsmiling. He drew circles, smaller and smaller circles inside her thighs, moving ever upward. Hot tears of near-unbearable prescient delight scalded her cheeks as her body tensed, waiting as the brush hovered. The waiting seemed to stretch into infinity, and the deep secret recesses of her body filled and throbbed. In that moment, Ginny finally understood that this was for her, that this strange possession was to give her ultimate joy even as she was branded by the giver of that joy.

Then, when she had almost ceased to expect it, he touched her, a delicate, light caress of the brush that made her body thrum like the plucked string of a lute. He opened her with delicate fingers, parting her soft petaled center to paint with exquisite artistry until she slipped over the edge of reality, mindless and sensate, a body that existed only to be pleasured by the one man who knew how to give that pleasure — and so possessed her.

Only then did he smile in the old way, cover her mouth with his as he gathered her against him, sliding into the tender, opened body with the ease of temptation, with the pulsing throb of his need, and she held him tight within her as joy peaked again and again. He drew her knees up, pressing them against her body as he penetrated deeper into her very core, and the explosion ravaged them, tore them apart even as it renewed.

He did not leave her body once the tempest had expended itself, but instead slipped his hands beneath her buttocks, clasping her tightly so that she held him within. "Why would you leave me?" he asked. "I have not been able to understand what I had done that you would go with Edmund Verney."

The tears that had never been long absent in the last hour trickled down her cheeks. "I thought that I had betrayed you, and you would not want me back. But I had to save Edmund. If you had killed him, then you and I would have been destroyed whether I stayed or no. But I *did* betray you. Not just fought for my own cause, which I have done many times since we came together, but I hurt you directly. I had thought you would see only disloyalty."

He shook his head. "I was hurt that you would betray me to save another, but it was no mortal wound, little rebel. You did not think you could trust me enough to come back and face me afterward?"

"I am sorry," she whispered. "But you are a man of strong principles, my love. Strong enough to overcome all ties of kinship, to accept total severance from those you must always have held most dear. How could I know it would not be the same with me?"

"Nothing could ever keep me from loving you," he said with fierce insistence. "Not principle, not duty, not even the thought that you did not love me in the same way. It is that thought that has racked me these last days. But not for one minute have I loved you one iota less than before."

"I understand that now." She reached her hand to trace the chiseled mouth with her little finger. "I could not have borne to have left you either, love. I would sooner be with you, even though you loathed and despised me for my treachery, than live in passionless friendship with Edmund."

Slowly, he moved out of her, drawing her head into the

crook of his arm as he lay down beside her. "There will be no further mistrust between us, and, God willing, no further need for you to ply your trade against mine, my lady Cavalier. Only the one battle lies ahead now; then all will be over, and we will begin anew, you and I, as England begins anew."

"God willing," she said. "If your life is spared and Parliament's force victorious . . . if . . ." But there were too many "ifs." Only the advent of tomorrow's dawn was certain sure.

Chapter Twenty-two

"Courtney, you will range your troop of foot on the right wing, behind Peter's horse." The duke of Hamilton indicated the position with his knife point on the rough sketch map resting on a trestle table outside his tent.

Giles Courtney indicated understanding with a grunt and shifted his aching hip. "It's the devil's own luck that Cromwell decided to come round behind us," he said.

"Aye," Hamilton agreed, looking out across the countryside to where Parliament's army was camped. "Had he attempted to bar our march south, we would have met him with full force and in good order. As it is—" He shrugged. "As it is, the damn sections are scattered all over the place, and it'll be days before we can get a full muster and a coordinated plan of attack and defense."

There was a reflective silence in the group of Royalist officers. Those necessary days were ones Cromwell would not allow them. Faced with the choice of meeting the Royalist army head on and attempting to prevent their deeper intrusion into England, or going behind them and placing himself between them and Scotland, he had taken the latter option. It was a decision that had paid off, since the Scottish army, caught unawares, was divided into sections near the town of Preston, each section unprotected by its fellows and thus particularly vulnerable to attack.

"*They* look in good-enough order," Giles observed, articulating the gloomy thought in everyone's minds. The rows of tents belonging to Parliament's army seemed to stretch to the horizon, and there was something about the neat orderliness of their lines that struck at the struggling optimism of the Royalist force. By dawn tomorrow, they would be locked in final combat with the opposing army — an army of highly trained, highly disciplined veterans who had only memories of past victories to inform their courage.

The duke of Hamilton looked at Major Courtney with a degree of contempt. It was not necessary to speak aloud the knowledge that they all carried. "Our cause is just," he said curtly. "God fights on our side, and with His aid we will be triumphant."

Giles made no response although his spirit rose in resentment at the implied rebuke. What possible point was there in denying the truth? And if God was on their side, He had certainly taken His time about proving it. This army would go into pitched battle tomorrow with nothing but the memory of defeat to bolster their courage. He walked away from the group by the tent and climbed a low hill overlooking the next day's battleground, at present merely an enormous tract of land lying between the two opposing armies. Tomorrow, it would ring with the bellow of cannons and muskets, the clash of steel, the shriek of wounded horses, and the cries of the injured. The soft green meadow would be trampled, churned beneath hooves and boots, reddened with the blood of the unlucky.

Would he again be one of the unlucky? He smiled without humor. Of course, general opinion would say that he had been one of the lucky at Oxford — not dead, not crippled. But this time, if faced with the choice of death or a repetition of those months of agony, Giles Courtney would choose death. He no longer cared who won or lost this war; king or Parliament, what did it matter who governed the land? It was high time Englishmen went back to their houses and their farms, picked up the even tenor of their lives, bedded their wives, raised their children, managed their affairs as they had always done. In the soft, green, seaside county of Dorset was his home, the stately Elizabethan manor house in rich parkland, and in the manor house was his wife, waiting for him, and he would return to her whole or not at all.

"Diccon, if you do not keep still, I cannot possibly do this!" Ginny admonished the lieutenant impatiently when her needle came unthreaded for the sixth time as Diccon leaned forward eagerly to join in the conversation around the table in the farmhouse kitchen that formed the headquarters for General Marshall's division.

"I can manage without the button," Diccon said, shaking out his sleeve. "I will have chain mail on top of my shirt."

"And a loose sleeve will ride up beneath it and be most uncomfortable," she retorted. "Take the shirt off, if you cannot be still."

Alex grinned as the spat continued: Diccon was so excited at the prospect of tomorrow's battle, Ginny so thoroughly determined to prick the bubble with her maternal concerns. "Give her the shirt, Diccon. It will be easier in the long run," he advised. "Chicken, if you must ensure that we are all clean, pressed, and tidy for battle, could you do so quietly? What I have to say is important, and I do not wish anyone to be distracted." It was said with a smile, and she could not possibly take offense.

"I will leave you to it," she said, replacing her needle and thread in her workbasket. "I need a little air." Outside, in the dusk, she walked slowly down the narrow street of the village of Preston where Cromwell's officers were quartered. His own headquarters were in the tavern at the head of the street. With a rueful smile, Ginny acknowledged that her anxiety over Diccon's missing button, her fussing over all of them in the last days was a displacement of her real fears. She could not say how afraid she was for their lives, how frighteningly lunatic she thought their eager, excited anticipation of the morrow's bloodshed. Even the experienced campaigners evinced this excitement, although much more muted than that of the untried youngsters. Alex was as taut as the string of a fiddle, but Ginny knew that it was the controlled tension of the expert, the tension that would ensure maximum performance. If there was any of anxiety or fear in it, it was not visible, even to her who knew so well every twist and turn of his moods.

As she walked back to the farmhouse, acknowledging the saluted greeting of the sentries about the village, she saw Alex come out into the street, standing motionless for a moment as if he were sniffing the wind. Her heart lurched with love and the sense of loss as she recognized that the lover was now gone, the soldier paramount in that magnificent frame, so tall and broad and powerful. His hands were the hands of a swordsman, no longer of a lover, so gentle and tender as they drew the notes of perfection from her. The man was preparing himself for the killing time, and the time of loving was, for the moment, over.

She came up to him and stood beside him, saying nothing. He looked down at her and smiled. "I am going round the posts, would you like to accompany me?"

Ginny nodded. "I would bid farewell to those who will not return."

"It is war," he reminded her quietly, as he had done so often before.

"Do you think I do not know it?" she replied.

Nothing more was said as they walked out of the village and into the field where the main body of Cromwell's army was drawn up, Alex's division amongst them. An officer appeared, saluting with his sword at the sight of the general, but Alex told him softly that he wished to move around without ceremony and did not wish the troops to be alerted to his presence. They walked from company to company in the gathering dusk. Whenever the general was recognized, the men sprang to attention, standing tall and proud, bearing Alex's insignia on their shoulders, his pennant flying from their tents. He talked with them, not as general to foot soldier, but as soldier to soldier, and Ginny saw the way they responded, the way their eyes lit up, and they stood, if possible, even taller.

The men of horse were quartered separately from their comrades of foot, but they offered the same impressive stance. The horses were being tended for the night, magnificent beasts for the most part, although none was Bucephalus' rival. Ginny wondered, with that same desolate pang, how many of those majestic beasts would return to be watered and groomed tomorrow night.

Far away, across the expanse of land separating the two armies, she could discern the shadowy figures of the enemy sentries pacing in the dark, preparing themselves for the morrow, thinking much the same thoughts as the men on this side—thinking of their wives, their children, their homes, or of a time when Englishmen would again be at peace in a land unravaged by civil strife.

In the forward lines, the atmosphere was different, the nearness of the enemy palpable. Here, they were ready for battle, preparations already made, pikes sharpened to a fine edge. These were the men who would launch the first attack, and a grim silence hung over them. It was with relief that Ginny turned back when Alex was ready to leave, and they returned through the lines to the village.

"Will you come to bed?" she asked softly as they approached the farmhouse.

Alex shook his head. "Not tonight, sweetheart. I will take what rest I may with the others."

"Indeed," she said with a faint smile, "I would not be responsible for sapping your strength, General."

"You would renew it, rather," he replied. "But I cannot have comforts that are denied others, not on the eve of battle."

"No, of course you cannot." Ginny sighed. "May I then stay up with you? *I* do not have to fight tomorrow and may sleep all day if I so choose." Her tone was ironic, meant to amuse, but it did not succeed.

Alex shook his head. "I would like you to go to your chamber, sweeting. I know the waiting will be hard for you, but I must think of my men first, and your presence tonight will be a distraction and a constraint that they do not need."

Ginny accepted the rejection, accepted in silence the woman's place in the background where she would not be a distraction or a constraint as men went about the all-important business of death-dealing. Accepted it only be-cause she had no choice.

Throughout the night, she lay listening to the rumble of voices below, the occasional quick tones and step indicating a messenger from Cromwell's headquarters. In the dark hours of early morning, there was silence. Were they sleeping? Or just preparing themselves in the meditative quiet for what lay ahead? In the hour before dawn, her door opened, and Alex trod softly to the bed, his body encased in armor, his helmet in his hand. He stood looking down at her, and Ginny said, "I am not asleep." She sat up, lifting her arms to him.

"No, I did not think you would be." Bending, he clasped her hands behind his neck, placing his lips on hers in a kiss of searing sweetness. "Farewell, my own."

"You will not say, 'until tomorrow'?" Ginny whispered, trying not to cling to him.

"No," he replied gently, disengaging her arms. "I will not make promises I cannot be certain of keeping."

"As you said once before, in a different context." Ginny smiled, blinking back her tears. "A wise man does not issue threats or promises that he cannot keep." She touched her fingers to her lips, then to his. "Farewell, my love. God go with you."

The door closed softly behind him, sounds of movement came from downstairs, of voices whispering although there was no need for such quiet. Then came the silence of emptiness, and Ginny knew she was alone.

Within the hour, just as day broke, the sounds of cannon reached her and continued throughout the day. A heavy pall of smoke veiled the battlefield, and she could see little of the action, even from her position atop a hill at the back of the village. But as the day wore on, she saw the encampment below begin to seethe like an anthill, figures scurrying with burdens between the tents, carts moving between the camp and the pall of smoke. Slowly, Ginny went back down the hill. If they were bringing in the wounded, then there was work for her to do.

It was grim work, and she forced herself to stay where she

was most needed, with the men waiting outside the field hospital, waiting for the attention of the hard-pressed surgeons within. There were some whom she could deal with herself, if it was only a matter of removing a bullet, dressing a wound, splinting a fracture, but Ginny was no surgeon, and for those who required amputation there was little she could do to ameliorate the knife and the bitten bullet. Throughout that interminable day, amid the roar of cannons and the heat and haste surrounding the broken bodies, she longed to go up to the farmhouse, to discover if there was news, to go to Cromwell's headquarters and question the runners. Where was General Marshall in that inferno? Was he still astride Bucephalus, leading his men? He was not among the wounded, that much she knew, as she scrutinized every blood-soaked, twisted figure, her heart in her mouth as relief at not finding him warred with the dread of what could be happening to him out there amongst the guns and the swords.

At nightfall, the guns fell silent, and only the acrid stench of smoke remained, hanging heavy in the air. Ginny drew a blanket over the body she had been tending on the grass and straightened slowly. The man was dead, the hole in his gut the size of a man's fist, and death had been a mercy. She wiped her hands on her blood-stained apron and for the first time allowed herself to feel the bone-weariness.

"Mistress, the general says you're to come back to headquarters now."

"Jed!" Ginny swung round, then flung her arms around the sturdy figure as if he embodied a whole world of solidity and comfort. "The general . . . he is well?"

"Aye." Jed nodded, patting her back with steady rhythm. "He's well, but he needs you."

"How did you know where to find me?" Ginny stood upright again, smiling through her tears of relief.

"Not hard to guess," Jed responded with a faint chuckle. "General knew you'd be here, and if 'n you weren't brought back, you'd be here all night."

Stumbling a little now with utter fatigue, Ginny left the camp, following Jed back to the village. She found an exhausted group in the farmhouse kitchen, but one quick look and she knew they were all there, drawn and tired with faces blackened by smoke, but no one was missing. She fell into Alex's arms with a low cry, for once heedless of the audience but knowing, as he held her, stroked her face, and whispered to her, that it did not matter who witnessed this reunion.

"You are blacker and bloodier than the rest of us," Alex said, voicing his concern, drawing her over to the table where cold meat and wine stood. "You have been working with the wounded all day?"

"Most of it," Ginny agreed, taking the cup of wine he handed her. "Is it over?"

The look on their faces showed her how naive was the question. Alex shook his head. "We held the day, chicken, but it is far from done. We have crushed perhaps three sections of their forces, taken some two thousand prisoners, but it is not sufficient to cry victory as yet." He sat down on the long bench at the deal table, pulling her down beside him. "You must eat something." He sliced bacon from the flitch, bread from the round loaf.

"I am not hungry." Ginny looked at the offering with a grimace of distaste. "The wine I am glad of, though."

"You *must* eat something," Alex insisted.

Ginny swallowed a few mouthfuls to please him, then settled back in the circle of his arm, listening to their talk, sipping her wine until a pleasant haze settled over her and her eyelids drooped.

She was hardly aware of anything when Alex lifted her off the bench and carried her upstairs, laying her on the bed. "I have to discuss tomorrow's battle plan with Cromwell, sweetheart," he explained, pulling off her shoes. "Are you able to undress yourself?"

"Do not be foolish." Ginny sat up with a supreme effort. "I require no nursemaiding, General, any more than you do."

"What could a man not achieve with you beside him?" murmured Alex, bending to kiss her. "You have more courage in your little finger, my raggle-taggle gypsy, than has half a division put together."

When he had left her, Ginny washed off as much of the dirt and blood as she had energy for with the cold water in the ewer, then pulled off her clothes, and crawled onto the bed. She was only vaguely conscious of Alex, still fully dressed, falling much later onto the mattress beside her, asleep almost before his body hit the feathers. The knock at the door in the black hour before dawn awoke her, and she lay watching as he girded himself in chain mail and armor, buckling sword and sling about his waist. Again, they said farewell as if it would be the last time, and again she was left alone in the house, listening to the roar of cannons.

It was three o'clock that afternoon when she staggered out of the hospital tent, desperate for air that did not reek of blood, for quiet that was not rent by the groans and cries of the wounded and dying. When first she saw Bucephalus, pounding up the aisle between the tents, she thought her eyes were deceiving her. Then she knew that they were not; she could not imagine Alex as vividly as she now saw him, riding as if all the devils in hell were at his heels. He carried something in front of him over the saddle, and as horse and rider drew closer, Ginny saw that it was a body. Alive or dead, she had no way of telling, but she was running toward them as Bucephalus reared to a halt and Alex threw himself to the ground and lifted the figure from the saddle.

His eyes were haunted, his face gray. "It is Diccon," he said simply as Ginny reached him.

"Oh, God, no," she whispered, pressing her fingers to her lips. "Dead?"

"I do not know." Alex laid Diccon on the ground, looking helplessly at Ginny, the green-brown eyes pleading as if she would be able, if she chose, to make everything all right again.

She dropped to the ground beside the still figure, fumbling with the catch of his helmet. Alex, his fingers more experienced, helped her, pulling it away so she could reach for the pulse in Diccon's neck, raise his eyelids to examine his pupils. The pulse fluttered faintly, and when she saw the blood pumping from the main artery in his leg, Ginny was surprised it was there at all.

385

"I need a tourniquet," she said, pressing her hands below the hole where the musket ball had entered with such force that it had torn through bone, muscle, and sinew to leave an exit wound that bled as severely as the entrance. "Untie my apron, Alex." He did so swiftly, twisting it for her as she instructed, then tying it tightly where her hands had been. All the while, Ginny knew their efforts were futile; yet she could not bring herself to tell Alex as he worked so feverishly to save the life of his young aide-de-camp. Later, she would hear how he had seen Diccon go down and had charged alone into the melee of enemy troopers to pluck the boy from the ground where he had fallen. Then he had left the battlefield with him, bringing him to the only person he could think of who could be trusted to do the right thing. The woman whose fondness for Diccon Maulfrey ran as deep as his own.

"It is no good, love," Ginny said at last, moving her fingers from Diccon's throat. She looked at Alex and saw a glaze of tears in the green-brown eyes that carried a deep remorse mingled with the grief. "You are not to blame," she said softly, taking his hand.

"Such a pitiable waste!" he declared in a fierce whisper. "I could have kept him behind the front line, but he was so damnably eager—he reminded me . . ." Without finishing his sentence, Alex remounted Bucephalus and rode, grim-faced, back to the slaughter.

Reminded you of yourself, Ginny finished for him, as her own tears for Diccon flowed freely. The young man's death had broken through the soldier's emotional barricades erected to preserve him from the blows of personal loss and the questioning of purpose that would bring diminution of courage and a wavering from the straight and narrow paths of duty.

There were other casualties that day amongst the officers of General Marshall's division, but they were not major ones, and Ginny found her own skills more than sufficient to deal with the sword gash in Colonel Bonham's upper arm, the shell fragments embedded in an ensign's cheek. But she had not the skills to heal the grief that hung heavy upon them all, or to fill the gap in their number. She seemed to hear Diccon's voice, full of enthusiasm, his ready laugh, but every time she looked over to the place on the bench that he had made his own, it was empty.

On the general's orders, they buried Diccon that evening in a quiet, intensely personal ceremony attended only by his own troop of men, his fellow officers, and Ginny. It was again evidence that Alex knew what he was about when it came to dealing with the spiritual as well as the physical welfare of his men. The ceremony was cathartic, laying to rest grief as the body was laid to rest, and they returned to the farmhouse with renewed purpose, only Ginny knowing that it would be a long time before Alex lost his sense of guilt, the remorse lurking in his eyes.

The Battle of Preston went into its third day, but by that morning reports of the enemy position indicated that victory lay waiting for Parliament after one more concerted attack on the remaining sections of the Scottish army. When the men left at daybreak, they were talking, laughing even on occasion, the deadly serious atmosphere of the preceding two days dissipated by the thought that this day should see the end and bring success.

Ginny, standing at her casement, watched them ride out and wondered at how they could be so lighthearted. There was no less danger in today's fighting, the swords, the cannons, the muskets and pikes and halberds were the same weapons, capable of inflicting the same wounds. Her day's work amongst the casualties would be no lighter.

Giles Courtney surveyed the train of artillery with a jaundiced eye. It was well defended with firelocks and rear guard forces and to a practical mind inclined to pessimism presented an impossible target for his own small troop of foot and Lord Peter Ottshore's horse. But if they could not seize that artillery, then the battle and the war were as good as lost. Peter raised his sword and his voice in a rousing yell. The drums beat loud, and the assault began as the small group threw themselves against the enemy defenses. Rebuffed, they withdrew, reforming for a second attempt. Peter's horse went down with a scream as a musket ball lodged in the powerful chest. His rider rolled free and ran back to join with Giles and the foot soldiers bringing up the rear in support.

The troop of enemy horse bearing down on them from the right scattered the foot to the four winds. Giles saw an enormous black charger, lips drawn back against the bit in a fierce grimace, eyes red like some creature from the depths of hell, his rider, head and body encased in armor, only the eyes visible through the visor, cutting a swath through the Royalist troops with a sword that he wielded to devastating purpose. For a moment, the two men's eyes locked; then the sword flashed, aiming unerringly for the tiny chink between Giles Courtney's helmet and his gorget where the protective metal did not meet. As the rider struck, a Cavalier musket fired. Alex felt the intolerable pain in his chest when the ball crashed against his breastplate, driving the silver inward as it penetrated his flesh. Then he felt nothing more.

Bucephalus wandered, aimless and riderless, in the chaos as the final battle raged fiercely around the artillery train. By some miracle, the charger escaped injury, musket balls and pistol shots whistling harmlessly by as he roamed without direction until he found his way out of the inferno and cantered back to the camp.

Jed, who had returned to the camp with a wounded ensign, saw him first. His heart leaped to his throat. There was only one explanation for the horse's riderless state. But as Jed ran after him, he saw Ginny hurtling down from the field hospital toward Bucephalus, reaching him just before Jed.

"Where is he?" she demanded wildly of the horse, seizing the reins. Then she saw Jed and asked the question again, her eyes frantic in a face as white as death.

Jed shook his head. "I don't know, mistress. I was not with him. If he's wounded, they'll be bringin' him out."

"I must find him!" Ginny began to run toward the battlefield, Jed pounding after her. He caught her at last and hung onto her with every fiber of a strength that was hardly sufficient against the desperation-fueled strength that in-fused Ginny.

"Be still, now," he said. "Ye cannot go into that. General'd have my hide if I let you—and yours, too, for being so foolish."

Ginny moaned and thought she was going to be sick, but the sense of Jed's words finally infiltrated her fear-crazed, fog-ridden brain. "If he is in there, wounded . . ." she said slowly, articulating the words as if she had only just learned how to speak. "If he is in there, wounded, and they do not bring him out, he will be killed."

"Go on back to the hospital, and leave this to me." Jed turned her back to the camp and pushed her. "I'll find the general, don't you worry."

With dragging step, Ginny went back to the camp, looking over her shoulder at the smoke haze obscuring the scene in the field. For an hour, she sat on the trampled grass outside the hospital tent, unable to continue with her work, hardly hearing the sounds of pain around her, as her mind was filled with dreadful images. When men came running and shouting up the hill, she stared unseeing; then what they were saying finally penetrated her daze. The Scottish army was on the run, leaving the field to Parliament. Cromwell was pursuing them. The three-day battle was finished, Parliament's victory so unequivocal that the Royal-ist army would never recover to fight again. The war was over.

Slowly, painfully, Ginny got to her feet. There was no sign of Jed, no familiar face she could turn to for help. If the battle was done, then she would search for him herself, as she had known in the deepest recesses of her soul would happen since her waking dream on the window seat in the house at Alum Bay. She would search through the flotsam of Parliament's dead and dying.

Dusk was falling, adding to the lack of visibility in the smoke-hazed field as Ginny picked her way through the shapes of men and fallen horses. Why had no one seen what had happened? He could not have been alone when disaster struck. But then Ginny could not picture the chaos of that final charge, when hand-to-hand fighting had broken out and no one had had time to look to their comrades. Something grabbed her ankle, and she shook herself free impatiently, then, horrified at herself, looked down. The soldier muttered vague and incoherent words through swollen lips, and she pulled herself together, looking around, noticing for the first time that she was not alone in the grisly business of searching through the dead. There were parties of stretcher bearers, and she called one of them over.

"This man is alive, trooper."

The trooper looked amazed at the sight of a woman in the midst of hell but called to his comrades, and Ginny went on her way. When she saw Jed, kneeling beside a body, she knew he had found what they sought, and a great calm washed through her. "Is he dead?" she asked evenly when she reached him.

"All but," Jed said, his face twisted with pain.

"Let me see." Ginny knelt at his side. Jed had removed Alex's helmet, and his face seemed extraordinarily peaceful, eyes closed, mouth relaxed. She felt for his pulse, without much hope, but it was there. Not strong, but in the name of the good God, it was there! She looked at the mess of his chest. It did not appear to be bleeding much, which could be a good or a bad sign. "Get him up to the house, Jed," she said urgently. "I cannot look at his wound properly here, but tell them to be gentle. The bleeding must not start up again."

"Ginny?"

She heard the voice from the past. It was weak but unmistakable, although for a moment she thought it merely some part of this waking nightmare, a figment of her feverish imagination that had run riot in the last several hours. Distractedly, almost without interest, she glanced sideways at the body lying beside Alex. And found herself looking into the eyes of her husband. His helmet was beside him, and he was bleeding copiously from a sword wound in the neck. As she stared at him, his eyes closed, and he lapsed again into unconsciousness.

For a moment, she was frozen, encased in ice, unable to

think or to move. Then Alex moaned, and his eyelids fluttered. "I am here, love," she whispered, taking his hand. The stretcher bearers came running, and she looked again at Giles Courtney, still unconscious. She had not seen him, had she? She would walk away from this field of death and fight for the life of the man she loved, and forget that she had imagined seeing her husband. As one of the enemy wounded, he would be amongst the last to receive attention. He would surely die out here, as he was supposed to have done nearly two years ago.

Jed was looking at her strangely, and she realized that she was staring at Giles, and there was loathing and despair on her face. "Tell them to bring that man, too, Jed," she said quietly. "He is my husband, whom I thought dead since the surrender of Oxford." Then she walked off beside Alex's stretcher.

It was Jed's turn to stare, at first in utter incomprehension, then with pity and understanding. He said nothing, though, merely called over another pair of stretcher-bearers, giving them orders to bring the wounded Royalist up to the village.

In the farmhouse, Ginny barely acknowledged those who had escaped hurt and, knowing that their commander had not come off the field unscathed, waited in near-intolerable anxiety for news. Brushing aside their questions, she directed the stretcher-bearers to the chamber abovestairs, telling them to lay Alex carefully on the bed.

"Where shall we put the other one, mistress?" Jed asked hesitantly, not knowing how to refer to the unconscious man.

"Anywhere," Ginny replied. "I will look to his hurts later. For the moment, he must take his chance. You must help me with the general's armor, Jed. I cannot see what damage has been done."

"Ginny?" Alex opened his eyes, his voice weak but clear.

"Aye, love, I am here." She smiled at him, even as she cursed inwardly that he had regained consciousness before they had managed to cut away the mangled breastplate. She took his hand. "Hold tight now, my love."

He clung to her hand, gazing fixedly into her eyes, as Jed sawed through the metal, shards of which were buried in his flesh under the impact of the musket ball.

"I would give you brandy," Ginny said, "but if the lung is perforated, it will only make things worse." Her voice was cheerfully matter-of-fact, masking her anguish at his agony, her fear of what she would find. The fierce grip on her hand slackened abruptly, as Alex mercifully passed out again. "Hot water, Jed, quickly, and cloths so that I may clean this and see the worst before he comes to."

The musket ball was lodged between the third and fourth ribs, both of which were fractured. But his breastplate had slowed the impact so that heart and lungs had escaped, and the ball had not sufficient force to reach his spine. Ginny felt her heart lift. If she could remove the musket ball, the fragments of bone, and the silver from his breastplate without undue loss of blood, close up the wound, splint the ribs, and if mortification did not set in, there was no reason why he should not eventually be as good as new.

She told Jed in a few words what she had to do, and when Alex opened his eyes again, reaching for her hand, she explained to him, also. "It seems I'll live," he said with a painful grin. "Do your worst, gypsy."

"Knock him out, Jed," Ginny instructed levelly, dipping her knife in the hot water.

"You do, soldier, and I'll have you facing a drumhead court-martial," Alex threatened, some of the old fire in his voice.

"Take no notice of him, Jed," Ginny said.

Jed glanced at the determined young woman with her knife, then at the man whom he had served since boyhood. With an apologetic shrug, he drew back his fist, bringing it accurately and with carefully judged force against Alex's chin.

"My thanks." Ginny smiled at him. "My hand will be steadier if I know he cannot feel the pain I am inflicting."

She worked as swiftly as she could, using a twist of silk to hold open the wound as she probed for the fragments and the musket ball. When Alex's eyelids began to flutter, Jed tapped him sharply on the chin again, and he became still. "Never forgive me for this, 'e won't," muttered Jed, but he did not sound particularly worried about such an eventuality as he held the candle high to cast the greatest light as Ginny worked.

It was an hour later before she was satisfied that she had removed all that she could see. "It is to be hoped I have missed nothing," she said with a frown, wiping away the blood from the torn flesh. It was an ugly wound, but somehow, cleansed, it seemed less alarming. "I must close this. If he wakes again, Jed, we must leave him this time. It cannot be good for him in his weakened state to be rendered unconscious so violently."

Jed nodded and reached for Alex's leather belt lying over the stool. When Alex resurfaced with a groan, Jed pushed the belt between his teeth and took his hands, holding them still as Ginny stitched the wound, fighting her own nausea even as she knew that if she lost courage at this point, she would have done as well to have left him on the field or abandoned him to the butchers in the field hospital. But at last it was done, and she wrapped clean bandages in overlapping strips around his torso, tightly to restrict movement that would disturb the fractured ribs.

"I will prepare a potion that will help him sleep," she said quietly to Jed. "We must watch now for fever and inflammation. Will you stay with him? I must go to . . ." But the words "my husband" stuck in her throat, and she left the room without saying them.

She found Giles laid upon a bed in the chamber across the hall. He was barely conscious and rambled as she removed his armor and his clothes, noting with abstracted interest the twisted scar high on his hip. The wound that was supposed to have killed him, she assumed, turning her attention to the deep sword cut on his neck. Throughout the wandering of his fevered mind, however, emerged a thread that bore her name, and she had little hope that, when the delirium had passed and he regained his senses, he would have forgotten her presence on the battlefield. What possible explanation was there for it, except the truth? And how could she tell that truth to her husband? And how could she leave her lover, now that her husband was here to stake his rightful claim? But how could she stay with the lover, now that the husband was here to stake his rightful claim?

Chapter Twenty-three

For three days, Giles Courtney drifted in a fevered world peopled by hallucinatory figures who tended to him efficiently and attentively, if impersonally. But throughout, some memory constantly eluded him although he was troubled by a vague but definite feeling of unease accompanying it. On the fourth day, he opened his eyes on a small chamber, was physically conscious of the contours of the mattress beneath him, of the fact that he was thirsty and weak, but apart from that quite clear-headed.

"I'll not allow him to be bled, Jed; he is weak enough as it is. Those damn chirurgeons would be advised to leave my patient alone!"

The voice was raised in exasperation, coming from outside his half-open door, and finally the elusive memory fell into place. Giles Courtney stared up at the ceiling. It was his wife's voice, well remembered although that authoritative note of decision was not one he had heard often during their marriage. It was not one he would have wished to have heard. He remembered the moment on the battlefield, the moment when the sword had bitten into his neck; then he remembered hearing her voice through the mists of semi-consciousness as he lay, bleeding, on the ground. *But what the hell was his wife doing here in the middle of the war?* The question assumed monumental proportions as he lay there, and that feeling of unease became no longer vague, but took on definite shape.

"If you gather me snails, Jed, I will distill some snail water this afternoon. It is a certain remedy against hectic fevers and will do the general more good than all the cupping in the world." Ginny put her hand on the door of her husband's chamber and pushed it fully open, glancing at the figure on the bed. She saw immediately the change in his face, the lucidity of the eyes and, with sinking heart, stepped completely into the room, pulling the door to behind her. "You are better, I see." Coming over to the bed, she laid her hand on his brow. "The fever has broken. I will bring you a peppermint caudle directly. It will help you regain your strength."

Giles gripped her wrist as she turned to go. "Where am I? And what do you do here?"

"You are in a farmhouse in the village of Preston," she told him. "Parliament won the day, and you were wounded in the neck. I discovered you on the battlefield and had you brought here." She paused, then went on. "You are being cared for in the enemy camp. I do not know whether you are considered a prisoner or not. But I suspect not, since the main body of the army has gone back to London for dispersal, and only those unable to travel remain."

"And what does my wife do in the enemy camp?" he demanded, the light blue eyes narrowing.

"It is a long story, Giles," Ginny said. "We had heard that you were killed after Oxford. I left Courtney Manor and returned to the Isle of Wight to care for my mother who died some six months later. My father's house and estate were sequestered as the property of a Malignant. I was made ward of Parliament." She shrugged with a fair assumption of carelessness, as if there was no more to the tale. "Rest a little now; you are still very weak." She left him then, before he could find the words to stop her, but she knew that he would not be satisfied with what she had told him. No man of sense would be, and she still could not decide what lie would be plausible, or even if she cared enough to keep the truth from him.

All her thoughts and energies were for Alex, whose

recovery was alarmingly slow. Whether from shock or loss of blood, Ginny could not decide, but he remained in a high fever, rarely lucid, and the flesh around the wound was hot, red, and swollen. For the next few days and nights, she left his side only to prepare medicines and poultices, spelled by Jed when fatigue overcame her. In her anxious absorption, she almost forgot Giles Courtney, locked in the chamber across the hall, leaving his care to Jed.

One evening, when she sat on the window seat in Alex's chamber, watching him as he tossed restlessly, Jed came in, closing the door softly behind him. "Askin' a deal of awkward questions, 'e is," said the soldier, a backward jerk of his head toward the passage serving as identification of the awkward questioner. " 'Ard not to answer 'em, mistress."

"No." Ginny bit her lip. "I do not wish to put you in an awkward position, Jed, but I do not wish him to learn the general's name. Giles Courtney will guess most of the truth, if he has not already done so, and I must live with the consequences, but he must not know the identity of . . ." She sighed. "What a pickle it all is, Jed. I do not know which way to turn, and I can make no decisions until I feel sure Alex has turned the corner to recovery. Oh, how can I ever leave him?" She looked at Jed, her eyes filled with pain, but he had neither answers nor comfort to offer her, and Ginny went over to the bed to smooth back the hair from Alex's hectic brow. The green-brown eyes opened for a minute, and for a minute she thought there was recognition in them; then, with resignation in her soul, she left his side and went to her husband.

Giles was up, limping around the small chamber, his brow furrowed with impatience and frustration. "Where the devil have you been?" he exploded at Ginny. "I have seen no one but that sour-faced trooper who behaves like a jailer and won't even give me the time of day."

"Jed is not one for idle talk," Ginny said. "But you should be grateful for his care. He has tended you well."

"And why am I not to be tended by my wife?" demanded Giles. "Who is it that you are with day and night?"

"There are other sick men," Ginny attempted to reason

397

with him, "some with wounds graver than yours."

"But none with a superior claim to your attention than your husband," he pointed out, his face tight with suspicion. "Or am I mistaken?" His fingers closed over her shoulders, biting deep. Ginny winced, tried to turn away from the pale eyes that glared with angry mistrust. "Why would a ward of Parliament be dragged behind the drum across the length and breadth of England, madam? Will you tell me that?"

"I will tell you nothing, Giles," she said, making up her mind at last. "You may draw whatever conclusions you wish; you will hear nothing further from me on the subject. You were presumed dead, and in such a time of schism all the rules of custom have been shattered. Suffice it that I *am* here and was able to save your life. If you wish to return to Dorset, to consider your wife as one dead, then I will make no attempt to persuade you to do otherwise."

"Whose whore have you been?" he spat. "Or are you available to all comers — so long, of course, that they fight for the traitors' cause?" He raised his hand threateningly.

Ginny looked him in the eye, fearless because she felt only distaste and contempt. "No one's whore," she replied. "But if you're determined to believe it, then do so." She shrugged, twitching out of his hold. "You should be strong enough to leave here in a day or so. There is no one who will prevent you."

Giles felt the slow, corrosive burn of the cuckold simmer in his soul, and with it the overpowering need for vengeance on the woman who had betrayed him. He found that he did not care with whom she had betrayed him, or how many there had been. It was enough that she had been unfaithful to him, who rightfully owned her, and a traitor to the Royalist cause. He would not release her but would reclaim her for his own, reassert the husband's rights, and hold her for the rest of her life in the prison of a vengeful marriage.

"I will not leave here without my wife," he declared as she reached the door. "Whatever you have done, you are still my wife, madam, and we have a lifetime in which you will learn the true meaning of that position. There is not a court in the land that would deny my right to take you back to your

398

home."

Ginny shuddered as the words fell with a soft hiss on her ears. Giles was right; she was his chattel, and he had the legal right to force her acquiescence. He could take her back in shackles as a runaway wife, and people would wonder only at his forbearance, the depths of his forgiveness in taking her back under his roof, in not casting her from his door, penniless and unprotected. But he would not do that because she had let him know that that was what she wished for. The vindictive side of her husband was one she had always known, although previously it had not often been directed at her but at her servants, a horse that had fallen at a jump, a dog who failed to retrieve the bird — anyone or anything that failed to accord Giles Courtney the respect due to his consequence, or to augment that consequence created and bolstered by his doting mother and sisters. What greater blow to his self-esteem than the knowledge that his wife had been unfaithful? He would not tolerate that blow, and his pride would not tolerate the thought that she had left him. So, he would take her back and hold her fast in Dorset, and whatever unkindness he showed her would be repeated in full measure by his womenfolk.

Without a word, she left the room, turning the key again before going downstairs and out into the street. She had always known that if Giles insisted, she would have to go back with him. Her only hope had lain in the thought that, suspecting the truth, he would have cast her off, no longer worthy to be called his wife. She could have remained then with Alex for as long as it was possible, as his mistress only, since she had a husband already, and, besides, Alex must find a wife who could breed him sons. She had accepted that fact long since and would have been content with whatever arrangements they could make. Now, she did not know whether she wanted to scream or cry with her anger and her grief at this evil twist of fate. Supposing she left Giles, ran away from Preston? But she could not implicate Alex in such a crime by continuing to keep company with him. Stealing away another man's wife was a crime against the moral fabric of society that would bar him from holding any prominent position in the land, would ruin the career on which his heart was set. And if she ran from Giles but not to Alex, what future was there for her? Penniless, an outcast, with no kin, no home. She had no choice but to accept imprisonment.

The following dawn, she stood by Alex's bed, looking at that beloved face for the last time. "Jed, if you will continue with the snail water and the poultice, I believe he will make a good recovery. The fever is down some this morning, and I do not think there is danger of gangrene now."

"And what do I tell him when he asks for you?" Jed demanded. "When he knows ye're gone, it will set him back by weeks."

"Do not be angry with me, Jed." Ginny blinked back the tears. "You know I have no choice. If I stay here in defiance of my husband, he will discover the general's identity easily enough, and nothing will save Alex's career once the truth is shouted abroad."

"Per'aps the general'll call him out and kill 'im for you," Jed suggested pragmatically.

"That is foolish, Jed. I do not hold with killing, as well you know," she said sharply. "Had that ever been a solution, I would have left my husband to bleed to death on the battlefield."

"Can't think why ye didn't," the soldier muttered. "Easier all round, seems to me." Then, seeing her face, he relented. "You got to do what seems right to you, mistress, even if it makes no sense to me, and it won't to the general."

"It will, if you explain the whole to him," she whispered. "I would stay until I could explain it to him myself, but I dare not." She did not say whether it was her husband she was afraid of, or herself, but Jed guessed shrewdly that it was the latter. Once Alex was well enough to talk, he would not allow her to leave him, whatever reasons she might produce for doing so, and she would be unable to withstand him.

The door suddenly burst open, and Giles Courtney, dressed for travel, stood there. "Who is he?" he demanded, making to cross the room. Jed moved fast, and Giles found himself outside in the passage borne backward by the force of that stocky soldier's body.

"None of yer business, sir," Jed said, closing the door behind him. "You leave the mistress to make 'er farewells in peace."

"You insolent blackguard!" Giles raised his fist, but Jed was quicker and stronger, seizing his wrist and twisting it as he side-stepped expertly. Giles's face went gray with the pain as the twist tightened, and he finally bent double in submission. "You'll pay for that!" he gritted through clenched teeth, rubbing his wrist when Jed released him.

Jed's lips twisted in a sardonic grimace of disbelief. Ginny came out, her eyes sheened with tears, biting her trembling lip. She walked past them both as if she did not see them and went outside where an ill-sprung coach awaited them. It would be a wretched, jolting journey that lay ahead of them, but Giles was not strong enough to ride, and his hip was paining him more since the fever. They faced perhaps two weeks shut up in bitter enmity and discomfort, until they reached whatever awaited them in Dorset.

"Jed, damn your eyes, man! Where the devil've you got to?"

The irritable bellow reached the old soldier as he ascended the farmhouse stairs, a steaming jug of water in hand. "I'm comin'," he grumbled. "Only got one pair o' legs, General." He entered the chamber and sighed at the sight of the general sitting on the edge of the bed, struggling with his stockings. "Let me do that," he said, setting down the jug. "Though what you think ye're about, goin' out with the fever only gone two days, I dunno, to be sure."

"I cannot abide one more minute shut up in this damn prison!" Alex exclaimed, trying to hide his relief as he fell back against the bolster and allowed Jed to draw on his stockings. He was so damnably weak, no more strength than a kitten, but if he lay on that bed for one more minute, just thinking—well, he'd be inclined to cut his throat!

Leaning heavily on Jed, he went downstairs and out into the street. The village bore all the signs of its recent occupation by armed forces, and the battlefield below was a grassless, mud-churned mess for as far as the eye could see. There were few people around, the villagers occupied with trying to resume their old lives, the few members of the army left nursing their strength and wounds as Alex was doing. But there was no nursing for the deepest wound, he thought wretchedly, pacing slowly beside Jed. Why had she not stayed, not trusted him sufficiently to find some way out of what he had to admit was the most damnably tortuous dilemma? She had said little enough about her husband, sensing that he did not wish to hear of the man who had first known her. But Alex had heard in her silences that Giles Courtney had been no friend to his wife. What would such a man do with a faithless wife, one who, in the name of passion and love, had thrown in her lot with the enemy? Would he accept the excuse that she had thought him dead? Forgive and forget? From the brief description Jed had given him of Giles Courtney, Alex doubted it.

His sleeping and waking hours were tormented with worry for her, as much as he ached with loneliness. From time to time, he would feel a spurt of fury that she had *again* walked away from him, breaking the bargain made at Grantly Manor, and he would fantasize about laying hands on her — and then the anger would become muddled with the feel of her softness, the sound of her voice, her laughter, and he would want to weep with the desolation of loss.

He knew that practically she had done the only thing possible. If her husband asserted his legal right, the lover had no claim, and the woman no choice in the matter at all. But she had not even given him a chance to find a way around it, had not waited long enough for him to recover consciousness so that they could at least have discussed it, have made some plans for the future. Even if she had had to go with Courtney, they could still have planned something . . . but she had walked out of his life without a word, leaving him too feeble to do anything about it, too weak even to sit a horse!

Jed, feeling the general's weight grow heavier on his shoulder, glanced up anxiously at the tall figure beside him. The general seemed shrunken somehow, thin as a rail and stooped, his face haggard, his eyes sunken. It was not surprising after such a long illness following a near-mortal wound, but it was the blow to his spirit that would keep him enfeebled unless Jed could come up with something.

"Reckon you'll be needed in London, soon as ye're fit to travel, General," he said. "Plenty of work to be done there. There's talk of bringin' the king to trial."

"Aye," Alex agreed dully. " 'Tis not an action I'll support. There's no call for regicide."

"Sooner ye get there and make your views known, sir, the better," Jed said with a cheery note of enthusiasm. "Can't hang about up north forever, now."

"Hanging about up north was never my intention," Alex stated acidly. "But perhaps you'll tell me how I'm to leave, when I can't walk ten paces down the street without your support!"

Jed refrained from comment since there would be little point in it, but he determined to prod the general frequently about his views on the possible execution of the king. If he could be encouraged to take up a definite stance on the matter, nothing would stop him from hurrying back to London to put his principles into effect, and in all the ensuing bustle, maybe he could be induced to put thoughts of Mistress Courtney behind him.

Night after night, Ginny would edge gingerly to the far side of the bed, away from the sprawled, stertorously snoring figure of her husband. His outflung limbs left little space for her, and she was petrified of touching him lest he wake and attempt to renew the conjugal assault on her body that a drunken stupor had mercifully and as always brought to an incomplete close. Giles Courtney had never been anything but an inconsiderate lover, but now, faced with his impotence, humiliated and frustrated by the woman who had betrayed his bed, he was careless of hurting her, pinching

403

and prodding, breathing over her the fumes of the brandy that he took ostensibly to dull the pain of his hip. In fact, the brandy bottle appeared at the breakfast table and remained at his side until he retired.

Once and only once, Ginny had attempted to remonstrate with him, to point out the deleterious effects of this constant imbibing, had offered to prepare a soothing poultice for his hip. The tirade that had broken over her head in a white-hot, intoxicated fury had left her shaking and frightened for her physical safety for the first time. Since then, she had kept out of his way as far as it was possible.

They had found Courtney Manor intact, having escaped occupation by Parliament's forces, but crippling fines had been levied on the family for their part in the war, and they were forced to sell off vast tracts of woodland and borrow heavily. As a result, stringent household economies were instituted by Lady Courtney, something that did not concern Ginny in the least, but seriously affected the equanimity of her three sisters-in-law and her husband who felt, after his years of fighting and hardship, that he was entitled to the comforts and luxuries that had hitherto been his due.

Nothing had been said about the circumstances in which Giles had met up again with his wife, and his mother and sisters assumed that he had journeyed to the Isle of Wight to fetch her back. Her desertion on her husband's supposed death, however, rankled, and no opportunity was lost to increase the misery of her existence.

The winter of 1648 dragged interminably. The country was in a turmoil as the king was seized and taken from the Isle of Wight to Windsor. On January 30, 1649, he was executed on a scaffold specially erected outside the banqueting house at Whitehall. Ginny, sickened at the news, left the house on a raw February afternoon, and rode down to the sea. That time of her audience with the king at Carisbrooke, when she had taken his seal and pledged herself to further his cause in Parliament's despite seemed an eternity past. Just as did the time she had spent at Whitehall, dining in that banqueting house at the high table with Parliament's newly appointed general. Where was Alex now? Would he have supported the king's execution? Was he well? The image of the green-brown eyes softened in love or snapping with exasperation hung in her mind's eye, the feel of his hands touched her skin. There seemed little point in existence any more.

The sea crashed gray against the stony beach in the horseshoe-shaped cove, inviting her with its implacable rhythm that all the misery in the world could not alter. She could swim out to the farthermost edge of the headland where the current was strong. The water was cold enough to numb the limbs of the strongest swimmer, and it would not take long to slip down into the cradle of oblivion. . . .

Each day she cherished the thought that perhaps today Alex would come riding on Bucephalus, up the gravel sweep to hammer on the great door, to catch her up in front of him and ride away with her. Of course he would not; she had left him without a word, without the slightest hope that they could ever come together again, not in Giles Courtney's lifetime. But even knowing that it was impossible could not destroy the dream that kept her alive, shielded her from the pinpricks of unkindness from her in-laws and the nightly brutality of her husband, who, in angry failure, would blame her and call her whore, leaving her to lie awake throughout the long reaches of the night, crying inside for the loss of love and passion.

The cold, gray familiar sea beckoned again with its promise of surcease. Resolutely, Ginny turned away from the invitation. The bed she lay on was largely of her own making, and she had never before lacked courage. To give one's life as Peter Ashley and Jack Calvert and Diccon and so many others had done was a fine and splendid thing, but to take it because things were not as one would wish them to be was a cowardly act, and one that would negate the sacrifices of all those others.

Back at the house, she paused outside the small parlor, listening to the most unusual sounds of her mother-in-law's voice raised in altercation with her son.

"Eavesdropper, keyhole peeper," a voice hissed behind her, and she spun round guiltily to face the malicious glare of

Giles's youngest sister Margaret.

"I was just about to join my husband in the parlor, as it happens," Ginny lied, quite unable to bear such a mean-spirited accusation. Since Margaret showed no intention of leaving, she was obliged to follow through and open the door.

The two within stared at her, for the moment silenced by their surprise. Virginia never appeared among the family except at the dinner table and never took part in exchanges, be they acrimonious or harmonious. "Good morrow, husband, madam," she greeted them calmly, dropping a polite curtsy. "I trust I do not intrude."

"As it happens, the matter concerns you," Lady Courtney said stiffly. "Although your opinion is of little interest and even less importance."

Ginny dropped another curtsy in ironic acceptance of the truth and waited.

"We are to go to the Colonies, it seems, to repair the family fortunes," Giles stated, limping irritably over to the sideboard where the brandy bottle stood. "My mother seems to think it is the only way we shall be able to maintain Courtney Manor for our heirs—not that there's much sign of them," he added morosely, glaring at Ginny with red-rimmed eyes over the bottle.

"May I ask, madam, why the Colonies would achieve this miracle?" Ginny inquired, ignoring her husband's remark.

Lady Courtney, although she would die rather than admit it, had developed a certain reluctant respect for her daughter-in-law. There was a hint of steel beneath the appearance of obedience and dutiful respect that the other woman recognized, just as she saw the weakness of her son. Giles would never amount to anything left to himself, but with his wife behind him, it was just possible. Anyway, it would certainly be worth enlisting her support. So she answered the question with none of her customary sharpness. "My uncle's son and his wife went to the Colony of Virginia some fifteen years ago, receiving a land grant from the London Company," she explained. "They were planting tobacco. I received a letter two weeks ago, and it seems they are doing well. There is still much land available." She handed Ginny a pamphlet of the kind issued by the companies promoting emigration. "Our neighbors, the Hallidays, received this in London. Their son is sailing on the next vessel leaving Southampton under the auspices of the London Company."

Ginny examined the pamphlet critically. It was full of flowery promises of fabulous riches and untold amounts of land waiting to be seized by the bold and the farseeing. No mention of the hardships she had heard tell of, of the wilderness and the disease, of the painted savages who massacred whole settlements. She remembered listening to an old mariner given hospitality by John Redfern some ten years ago, telling of the massacre of 1622, of the land seething with wildlife that the settlers could neither tame nor catch for the pot, of the way they had to hew land for cultivation out of the wilderness and swamp. But it was also true, that since then matters had improved somewhat, and if this pamphlet was to be believed, some forty thousand souls had been conveyed to the Colony of Virginia in the last fifteen years, and the planting of tobacco was the road to fortune.

It was also the road away from the agony of memory and loss, she thought. A better road, surely, than the one offered by the sea this afternoon. It offered escape from this prison, where every day was the same, bound by malice and duty in hostile company. True, it would not take her away from Giles Courtney, but it would take *him* away from the women who kept him ineffectual and without purpose with their doting servitude. Who could know what he might become in a new land where he had to stand on his own feet, face challenges that might, at least, take his mind off tormenting his wife? It could be no worse, and the possibility that it might be better was sufficient. Alex was lost to her so completely already, that a separating ocean was of no moment.

"I find the idea appealing, madam," she said. "It is written here that the next ships will sail at the end of April. We have two months to make our preparations. It will be sufficient time, I think."

Lady Courtney smiled. "I see no reason why we cannot accomplish everything in that time, daughter. Giles, you must journey to London within the week and meet with the men of the London Company. You will receive a land grant from them and details of your passage."

And thus is was settled, Giles reflected in moody resignation. Settled between his mother and his wife, as it had been settled that he should declare himself for the king four years previously. That decision had brought only disaster; there was little reason to imagine that this one would be any different.

Chapter Twenty-four

On the last Saturday in April, Giles and Virginia Courtney stood with twenty other passengers on the deck of the *Elizabeth May* watching the port of Southampton recede as the vessel, under full sail, picked up speed with the fresh breeze and danced across the waters of the Solent, heading for the Needle Rocks and the English Channel.

Ginny stood riveted to the deck rail, watching the Isle of Wight come closer until she could see the house on the headland above Alum Bay. It looked just as it had when she had left it ten months ago, but it was not hard to imagine what ten months of neglect had wreaked in the gardens and fields of the estate, and the house would be dusty and mildewed. But perhaps it already had new owners, staunch Parliamentarians rewarded for their services. She swallowed her tears. It was over, all over. The past was gone and she had only the future to face. And the immediate future would require every vestige of strength and courage if it was to be embraced with even a modicum of dignity.

She went down to the between deck area where the passengers were to be quartered during the voyage. With a headroom of a mere four foot seven, only the children could stand up. It was an area designed for cargo, not people, and no attempt had been made to modify it for its new purpose. Voices were already raised in argument as the passengers laid claim to deck area, rolling out their pallets, arranging their chests, in which reposed all their worldly goods, as boundary fences around them.

Giles had established an area in one corner, and Ginny had to give him credit for picking a relatively choice spot and hanging on to it with all the grim determination of a spoiled child with a disputed sweetmeat. The cackle of chickens rose from the hold below where they hung in cages above the water barrels, sacks of flour, and grain, the flitches of bacon, sides of beef, hogsheads of pickled herring and salted cod, the casks of ale that would be all they would have to drink once the water was used and they were far from land. A child began to wail, an exasperated hand cracked, and the wailing doubled in volume.

Ginny went back on deck. Three months of that, if they were lucky, and once in the open sea the gratings would be battened down, and they would be herded into that space, lit only by oil lamps, cooking, washing, eating, sleeping, performing all the most intimate activities — privacy a lost word.

A seaman pushed past her, hauling on the topsail halyard, and one of the officers bellowed at her to get below. Ginny contemplated telling him that she was probably every bit as capable of sailing the wretched ship as he was, then decided against it. Three months was a long time, and it would be impolitic to set up backs before they had even left the Channel. A cursory glance had shown her that the sailors' and officers' quarters were palatial compared with those between decks. The bunks were long enough and wide enough to accommodate the human frame, but most important, they were fore and aft the main deck with access to light and air. In the forward cabin, also, was set up a brick fireplace with arms and hooks for cooking pots. Ginny wondered if and when the passengers would have access to those facilities, or would they be condemned to cooking below decks even in calm seas?

Alex rode through the verdant Dorsetshire countryside, his heart pounding uncomfortably, his hands sticky in his gauntlets although it was a chilly May morning. He did not know why he was doing this, except that he had to be sure that she was alive and well. He would not go up to the house, he would not even try to see her, but in Lulworth village he would make general inquiries, and Jed would ask around also. Between them, they would be able to glean a relatively accurate picture of life at Courtney Manor.

But the information he received at the ale bench of the Stag and Hounds rendered him dumbfounded for a full five minutes. Esquire Courtney and his lady wife had taken ship for the Colonies at the end of April. It was said they were bound for Virginia, a good destination for Mistress Courtney, the goodwife chuckled, setting a foaming tankard at his hand, being as how she was so named herself. Of course, the fines for Malignancy had been monstrous heavy on the Courtneys and it was said that only by planting in the Colonies could they hope to maintain the estate by sending monies home to Lady Courtney, who had a good head on her shoulders, better than her son's, the goodwife added with a lowered voice. The young mistress, also, kept a clear head for management and was much missed in and around the village, such skill she had with the simples. But such a sad lady, as she was, hardly ever smiled since she had come back after the war. Quite dreadful it was to see such unhappiness on such a pretty young face. Not long for this world, they had all been feeling, and there were some that said she spent an unnatural long time looking at the sea. The goodwife nodded significantly. Not that anyone was accusing the poor young thing of harboring wickedness — but . . .

Alex muttered something noncommittal, and the woman's chatter eventually ceased. Tossing a coin on the bench, he remounted Bucephalus and rode out of the village, his mind in a turmoil. Jed rode stolidly at his side. He had heard every word of the goodwife's discourse at the inn, and one

411

look at the general's face made it clear that he would not welcome interruption.

The New World! Alex shook his head in disbelief, yet wondered why he should find the news so surprising. It was a route taken by many Royalists in the aftermath of defeat. Having lost their lands here, for many it seemed the logical course, to go where land aplenty lay for the taking, where fortunes could be repaired. But had Virginia gone willingly? Or had she gone, the submissive wife at the insistence of her lord, staring back at the island of her birth, wondering where lay the man she had loved and left, whether he was thinking of her, whether he needed her? She had not been happy, that much he knew. Not even resigned, if the goodwife had been telling the truth. And *he* was wretched. Life had no savor any more. Not even ambition could compensate for the loss of that undisciplined rebel with the bee-sting tongue, and the glorious, passionate nature, and the river of compassion that flowed in her veins.

The familiar lethargy of grief slopped over him, and his shoulders sagged. Jed glanced sideways and sighed, recognizing the signs. "Seems to me ye'd do well to go after the mistress, sir," he said directly. "Not goin' to get anythin' done, mopin' and moanin' all the time."

"She is another man's wife, Jed," Alex snapped. "Do you think I have not thought of going after her? There is talk, these days, in Parliament of making adultery a capital offense! I cannot risk her life as well as her reputation. For mine own, I care not a jot."

"It was your life and career *she* was thinkin' of when she went off," Jed pointed out. "Don't think she cared too much about her own either. Besides," he added casually, "that husband of hers looked mighty sickly to my way o' thinkin'. Should be surprised if he survived the voyage. Short o' women they are in the New World, or so they says; a pretty young wider woman'd be snapped up before she ever set foot on land."

"In the name of the good God, what are you getting at, Jed?" Alex demanded, although his companion's meaning was perfectly clear.

"Things change, that's all," Jed replied tranquilly. "But if 'n ye're not around when they do, can't do much about it . . . stands to reason."

Alex looked around at the peaceful, tamed countryside that he loved, that he would have given his life to preserve, had nearly done so, in fact. There was soldier's work to be done in Ireland where Cromwell was fighting for reconquest, and there was politician's work to be done in London now that both the king's office and the House of Lords had been abolished by act of Parliament. The authority of Parliament rested solely with the army now, and a New Model general held power in the palm of his hand. But it was all empty; the once-sweet cup of power and ambition contained only the sour dregs of disappointment and loss. Without Virginia, he might as well as retire, a reclusive, miserable man in his thirtieth year, to a cottage in the countryside and breed goats.

The soft splash as the body hit the water was become a sadly familiar sound these days, Ginny reflected, turning away from the deck rail with those of her fellow passengers fit enough to attend the cursory burial service for the sixth of their number to succumb to the scurvy sickness in the last week. No one was well, not even the seamen, and they at least had light and air for much of the time. The passengers sweltered in the fetid atmosphere between decks, where the stench of vomit and the groans of the sick, the pathetic wailing of the children combined to create a little, dark, hot hell.

Ginny, even in the fiercest storms created by the cross winds, escaped the miseries of seasickness but was kept endlessly occupied with the sufferers. Giles was now so debilitated, he could barely crawl forward to the pail, and if his wife was long from his side, he heaped curses and execrations upon her head between pulls at the brandy bottle that he guarded jealously beneath his pallet. Ginny's

413

one fear was that the brandy would run out before they could touch land and replenish the supply. At least when he was drunk, he was insensible much of the time.

The ship rolled and pitched unmercifully, the storms sometimes so fierce and the seas so high that they were unable to carry any sail and were forced to hull on the wild gray ocean. At these times they made no progress except to plunge into the deep troughs that threatened to swallow the frail vessel as it heeled over until the masts were parallel with the ocean, and it seemed as if it would never right itself again. Throughout, Ginny felt only a curious sense of serenity, unaffected by the desperate cries and prayers of her companions. She was a child of the sea, and it had always been her second home. She had never had any illusions about its sudden treachery, but, curiously, the prospect of drowning did not alarm her. Her life was not in her hands any longer, and fate had dealt her enough twists and turns to resign her to destiny. And a destiny that did not include Alexander Marshall was one she viewed with supreme indifference. Let it bring what it would.

It was almost four months to the day that the *Elizabeth May* and her two sister ships sailed into the land-sheltered water of the Chesapeake Bay. They had stopped for a week in the Indies for repairs and supplies, and the renewal of fresh food and water had done much for the sick. Even Giles, pale and weak though he was, was able to stand at the rail beside his wife, gazing at the rich green shores of the New World.

Their destination was the settlement at Jamestown established forty-two years earlier and, as the *Elizabeth May* turned into the broad reaches of the James River, Ginny felt for the first time since the morning she had walked away from Alex in Preston a stirring of interest, the faintest flicker of excitement. So different it was from her own Isle of Wight, so lush, the shoreline studded with tall trees reaching to the water's edge. There were other craft on the river, small sailboats for the most part, but also canoes, their sailors waving at the convoy of tall ships, at the passengers crowding the rail now, life returning to their eyes and voices at the prospect of the journey's end.

Here and there along the shore, the trees had been cut back from a landing stage jutting into the river, and a cart track ran from the shore to a house standing in a cleared ground and facing the river. There were figures at work on the land, seemingly industrious despite the heat of a late August sun that was more powerful than any Ginny had ever experienced. August . . . she had not seen Alex for a year. Was he well? Was he alive? Married to the daughter of some staunch Paliamentarian, who would give him sons and manage his household with Puritan competence and advance his career with a substantial jointure and family influence . . . Dear God, when would the sense of loss finally recede? The grief leave her with some serenity? Everytime she thought it was over, the desolation and the wanting hit her with renewed force as if to punish her for the moments of forgetfulness.

"There'd best be someone to meet us." Giles, his voice its now-habitual whine, broke into her reverie. "They should have received the letter on the *Deliverance* last month. If not, I don't know how we're to manage."

"Easily enough," Ginny replied, thankful for the interruption that gave her something else to think about. "If the letter did not reach your cousins, then we send a message from Jamestown. There must be an inn in the settlement where we may lodge, and people willing to advise us."

"Willing to rob us, more likely," Giles muttered petulantly. "And how are we to manage to keep close the silks, the china, and the furniture if we're not to be met? Where are they to be stowed once the vessel lands and we stand around like ninnyhammers waiting for deliverance?"

"Maybe, if we do not stand around like ninnyhammers waiting for deliverance, husband, we shall be able to have a care for those things," Ginny retorted, exasperation sharpening the tongue that she usually kept blunted in her husband's presence. "I for one am quite capable of having a care for myself."

"When there are men around, ready and willing to lie with a traitor's whore, you may be," he hissed viciously, and Ginny blanched. She was by now accustomed to the accusation, but during the voyage and Gile's sickness he had been more circumspect in its utterance, presumably because he needed her attention and could not enforce it in the conditions prevailing on board. Turning away, she went down to their quarters to see to the final stowing of their possessions in preparation for landing.

A great cheer brought her back above deck, and she stood with the others as the *Elizabeth May*, sails lowered, dropped anchor in the deep waters off the peninsula where stood the fort and township of Jamestown. Small craft and canoes bobbed around them, sent out from the landing stage to transport the passengers and their goods to shore. The arrival of ships from England was obviously a great event, judging by the numbers of people on the shore. Of course, the vessels carried goods eagerly awaited by the colonists, luxuries that they could not manufacture for themselves but that they could buy with the profits from their now well-established tobacco plantations. They also carried letters from home, and there must be few of these transplanted folks who would not be glad of news, Ginny reflected. Then there was no time for reflection in the urgent bustle of landing. Giles seemed incapable of doing anything except giving orders to people who ignored them and bellowing ineffectually whenever he saw some article that belonged to the Courtneys being tossed into one of the waiting craft.

"Giles, they are not going anywhere but to shore," Ginny said as he lamented the disappearance of a pair of decorated andirons from Courtney Manor. "We shall follow them ourselves, if you will but climb into that canoe. I will remain on board and ensure that everything else follows safely, and you may receive the goods on shore. Is that not a good plan?"

Much as he would have liked to have found fault with the plan, Giles could not, and he scrambled down into the bobbing canoe, manned by a grinning lad of about eleven, to be paddled ashore where he made a great nuisance of himself, insisting on examining every chest and bundle as it landed on the dock to see if it contained Courtney belongings.

Ginny was one of the last to leave the *Elizabeth May*, helping her fellow passengers into the small boats that seemed suddenly insubstantial to bodies that had become accustomed to the heaving decks of a one-hundred-ton vessel. At last, however, she also stepped onto the soil of the New World and felt instantly giddy as her feet found solid ground after four months of movement.

"Virginia!" Giles called imperatively from the far end of the landing stage. "Everything is here, but I can find no one who is expecting us."

Ginny looked up the short track that led through cultivated plots to the stockade of the fort. Outside the stockade there were buildings, but from this angle it was difficult to judge the layout accurately, or to decide how much of the settlement existed outside the fort. "Why do you not hire one of those children to stand guard over our belongings, husband, and we will go up into the town? Your cousin Harrington must be well enough known in these parts for us to be able to gather some information as to how we might contact him."

It was another suggestion with which he could not argue, and Giles was in the process of negotiating a price with a would-be guard of his possessions when a red-haired, pink-cheeked man in fustian britches and calico shirt came hurrying down the path. "Esquire Courtney?" he called over the throng.

"Over here!" Ginny called back in ringing accents, waving her kerchief to attract his attention.

"Ah, mistress, right glad I am to have found you," the man puffed, reaching them. "Tom Brigham at your service, bondsman to Esquire Harrington."

"Bondsman?" Ginny inquired, eyebrows raised.

"Debtor's prison, mistress," Tom Brigham informed her succinctly. "Three more years, and I'll be a freedman, God

417

willing. 'Tis a grand land then. Got my eye on some three-hundred acres up Wolstenholme way."

"What's that to do with us, man?" Giles asked testily. "Let us remove our belongings from this public place before we all melt in this damned heat." He wiped the back of his hand over his brow, and Ginny noted with a pang of guilt her husband's waxen, sweat-beaded complexion. He was still far from recovered from the depredations of the voyage, and irascible arguments in the heat were not going to improve his health or his temper.

"Indeed, Master Brigham," she said swiftly, "if you can direct us to some shade, we shall be right glad of it."

"I can do better than that, mistress," Tom Brigham said cheerfully, shouldering one of the bundles. "There's a chamber bespoke for you at the inn, and we go down the river at dawn to Harrington Hundred. No, leave those, sir," he gestured to Giles who was struggling with a chest. "There's lads aplenty glad of the work, and they're honest enough." He chuckled. "Place is too small for theft to pass unnoticed, and they'll not risk three days in the stocks — not in this heat."

Giles was obliged to be satisfied with this assurance, and they followed the bondsman up the track toward the stockade. The dark muzzles of cannon poked through embrasures in the bulwarks, but they were the only signs that one was treading a potentially hostile ground. Around the fort, a sizable community had sprung up of brick and frame houses and shops set on cleared ground among the trees that provided much-needed shade from the pitiless afternoon sun. Everywhere, there was tobacco; it grew beside the streets, in the market square, and in every cottage garden.

"Here we are, then." Tom Brigham stopped outside a fairly substantial brick building. "The King James will see you comfortable for the night."

Accommodations, however, were cramped and far from comfortable by London standards. Ginny found herself allotted bed space in a crowded chamber above the wash house, while her husband shared equally cramped quarters above the stables. The arrival of the ships, the need to accommodate those passengers who were not immediately transported to their final destinations, and also those colonists who had come to town to collect goods and mail from the vessels left the inn bursting at the seams.

Tom Brigham having undertaken to retrieve all their possessions and have them loaded onto the boats that were to convey them to Harrington Hundred the following morning, Giles eventually succumbed to his wife's gentle persuasion and took to his bed until dinnertime. Ginny, fastening a kerchief about her head against the sun, set out to explore the town.

It was a bustling, thriving place where the sound of hammer on anvil rang out from the forge, horses tethered outside, patiently awaiting the blacksmith's attention. Dogs roamed the streets freely, apparently sufficiently domesticated to leave alone the chickens and ducks pecking in the gardens of row houses and cottages, and to ignore the pigs and goats that wandered around with them. By far the largest building was the church, and, as Ginny discovered when she entered into conversation with a young woman tending her garden, it was also the most important one. Services were held twice daily, and only the bedridden and dying were excused an attendance enforced by the stocks and whipping post in the marketplace.

When the bell chimed, summoning the townsfolk to evening service, Ginny, as a result of her conversation, was prepared. Giles, on the other hand, ranted against canting Puritans all the way down the street. "Hush," Ginny said, looking uneasily at the closed faces of those around them. "You must not talk thus of their customs. We are newcomers and have no say as yet."

"I do not need *you*, woman, to tell me what I may and may not do," Giles declared. "Sundays, high days, and holidays are sufficient for church going, without this trekking back and forth to the pulpit every morning and evening."

"Perhaps it is a little less strict out of town," Ginny offered, hoping to placate him sufficiently to ensure his silence on the subject. As his wife, she would be tarred with the same brush, whatever her own views on the matter, or however circumspectly she behaved, and she had no desire to fall foul of the Church elders this early on. The thought of Giles in the stocks was one that could, on occasion, afford her a certain grim pleasure, but it was not an experience she wished to bring upon herself.

Fortunately, her husband lapsed into silence and endured the lengthy service, in the company of every man, woman, and child residing in Jamestown, with little more than an irritable grunt and some fidgets.

Hare pie in a rich claret sauce with quartered onions and thick lardons of bacon provided some compensation at suppertime, and Giles was introduced to a fiery spirit known as whiskey that the innkeeper said with well-deserved pride was now more highly favored in these parts than English ale.

"Excellent!" Giles agreed heartily, settling into the ingle-nook, accepting a clay pipe from a fellow drinker. "As good as brandy, I declare."

"Cheaper, too," someone chuckled. "Made right here, some ten miles up river out of Indian corn."

Ginny's eyebrows lifted. Her husband had found para-dise, she thought sardonically, gathering up dishes and taking them into the kitchen. Cheap, readily available spirit to keep the miseries at bay! It boded ill for a life where only energy and vigor could overcome the forces of wilderness, could succeed in establishing the farm and plantation that was supposed to repair the Courtney fortunes.

She went up to the chamber above the wash house, early enough to stake claim to one of the coveted outside edges of the bed, leaving her three bedfellows to argue over the other. But it was a long time before she fell asleep as the mattress seemed to move beneath her with the rhythm of the sea, and strange noises came from outside, noises of an alien land where the wildlife was unfamiliar and strange flying things buzzed and whined. Much later, she heard her husband's voice from the yard below, thick and slurred as he staggered to his own bed above the stables. She had that to be thankful for, at least. Since they had left Southampton, she had been spared his angry, frustrated fumblings. Only the desperate or shameless would have ventured intimacy in the crowded conditions between decks on the *Elizabeth May*, even if he had not become sick soon after sailing into the Channel. But she could not expect circumstances to continue in her favor once they were settled. They would hope to stay with the Harringtons until they could build their own house on the five-hundred acres granted to them. Perhaps, the Harringtons contained a large family in a small house, and a privy chamber would not be available for their guests. On that semioptimistic thought, Ginny fell asleep.

Dawn brought a renewal of bustle, raised voices from the yard, the sound of horses' hooves, the chink of bridle and bit. Ginny sprang from bed with a resurgence of her old energy. She was here, safely landed in the New World, and a new life awaited her. Throwing on her clothes with more than her usual speed, she hastened down the stairs, crossed the yard, and entered the kitchen where Tom Brigham was to be found, eating a veal collop at the table.

"Good morrow, mistress," he greeted her cheerfully. "As soon as you've broken your fast, we'll be on our way."

"By all means," Ginny agreed, spreading a crust of bread generously with slip-coat cheese. "But someone should wake my husband. He was late in his bed last night and will be heavy-headed this morning, I'll be bound."

The innkeeper's wife shot her a shrewd glance. "Depends on how good a head he has for the whiskey." She poured Ginny some red-currant cordial.

Ginny took it with a word of thanks but said no more on the subject of her husband's head. It ill-befitted a wife to appear critical of her husband in any company, but particularly not with servants and strangers.

Tom Brigham went to call Giles, who eventually appeared, sullen and morose and disinclined for talk, which suited Ginny admirably. At the landing stage, they found canoes being loaded with supplies and the Courtney possessions. A burly negro supervising these activities was introduced by Tom Brigham as Jonas, a freed slave who had originally come from Africa as an indentured servant but had been taken into perpetual bondage until Robert Harrington had freed him last year.

Ginny had found herself somewhat puzzled by the system of labor operating in Virginia, and her questions in the inn of the preceding evening had seemed lamentably naive, eliciting a degree of patient humoring and mockery with the information. There were convicts and bondsmen like Tom, either sent out by the government or bought by planters for their artisan skills, and indentured servants willing to sell their craft and labor in exchange for passage and the prospect of owning their own land once their indentures were worked out. And then there were the negroes brought from Africa by Dutch and English traders to be held in perpetual bondage by those who bought them to work the land. Originally, they had come as indentured servants like their white counterparts, but for some reason a new system had evolved, and now they were owned.

It was very curious, Ginny thought, following Tom aboard the small sailboat that was to carry the passengers, and somewhat distasteful. But again she reminded herself that she was the stranger here, at the moment only a guest, and had no right to question the customs and organizations of her hosts, not until she had established a place for herself. The question of labor, however, was one she and Giles were going to have to face for themselves soon enough. It was to be hoped Cousin Harrington was willing to be free with advice and suggestions.

The journey up river took three hours, and Ginny enjoyed every minute of them. After half an hour, she persuaded Tom to yield up the tiller, which he did willingly enough when he realized how skilled she was, and he settled down with his pipe to enjoy the morning sun and the peace, as the river wound its way between the green shores where richly colored birds dipped and soared amongst the broad leaves of the majestic trees. Broad rippling circles on the surface of the water indicated the presence of large fish, and gigantic dragonflies and butterflies darted low over the bullrushes. Narrow creeks ran through the marsh land on either side of the river, and every now and again a canoe would appear, negotiating the creek to make its way out into the broad thoroughfare of the river. The paddler would hail Tom and his little fleet of canoes, and there would be an exchange of news or some pleasantry. Clearly, spread out though they were, the tidewater planters and farmers maintained close contact, Ginny thought. There was probably a good reason for it, too.

"Are there Indians close by, Master Brigham?" she inquired, following through on this thought.

"Name's Tom, mistress," he said, puffing contentedly on the copper-bowled clay pipe. "Aye, there'll be plenty of 'em, watching us from the forest. But you'll not see them, unless they want to be seen."

Ginny shivered at the thought of all those unseen eyes buried in the thick foliage lining the shore. "Do they ever come out — I mean, into the town or the settlements."

"Bless you, yes." Tom chuckled, and Ginny again felt naive as she had done with her questions about servants. "They come out to trade, and we go to them to trade. There's been no real trouble with the Powhatan for quite some time. Although," he added, "it's best to be ready for it. You'll find we keep our swords and muskets handy by the door."

Harrington Hundred stood on some eight-hundred acres of land, a square, substantial brick house, its glazed windows and pantiles indicating prosperity, at the summit of a broad slope facing the river. Another square building stood beside the landing stage. "Tobacco warehouse," Tom informed Ginny. "Shipyard's over to the left."

The Harringtons were obviously most prosperous, Ginny decided, looking at the hustle and bustle of the shipyard where the husks of boats rested on cradles, swarmed over by an army of carpenters. Shipbuilding would be a most useful business in this water-based community, almost as profitable as tobacco. As they tied up at the landing stage, ready hands helping them ashore, a loud whoop of glee came from above. Ginny looked up to see a veritable tribe of children come hurtling down the slope from the house. Behind them, at a more stately pace, came a woman whose gown of crisp starched muslin shining from application of the chintz glazer made Ginny feel wrinkled and travel-soiled, as indeed she was.

"Cousins, I bid you welcome," the woman said, a smile wreathing a plump and benevolent countenance.

Ginny took the outstretched hand, laughing as the horde of children swarmed around her skirts, babbling questions without giving her time to answer them. "Mistress Harrington, we stand in your debt," she said simply, looking around for Giles who seemed backward in making his own greeting. The reason became obvious, since he was busily engaged in castigating one of the canoe paddlers for allowing water to splash on a roll of silk, brought as a gift for his cousins.

"Husband," Ginny prompted quietly. "See, here is your cousin come to welcome us."

Giles turned instantly at that, his face still twisted with annoyance, but he managed to be gracious enough in responding to the welcome.

"My husband is most sorry that he was unable to be here to greet you himself," Susannah Harrington said, "but the planting in the meadow field could not be delayed. He will be back for dinner." Shooing the children in front of her, she led the way back up the hill to the house. "I hope you found the inn not too uncomfortable, Cousin?"

"Not at all," Ginny replied, "but it was monstrous crowded — four to a bed!"

" 'Tis always the way, when the ships come in," her hostess said. "Our own accommodations are somewhat limited . . ." Smiling, she indicated the brood of children, who seemed disinclined to leave the interesting company of the new arrivals, "but we have prepared a small chamber over the kitchen for you. I trust you will be comfortable there for the time being. My husband will explain further plans later."

"You are too kind, mistress," Ginny murmured, her heart sinking.

"Oh, pray let us not stand on formality. I am called Susannah, and you bear the name of our Colony, I understand."

"I am generally known as Ginny," Ginny replied, returning the smile. Except by Alexander Marshall when he is vexed, she thought irrelevantly. Such devastating irrelevancies had become less frequent since they had left Southampton, but their power had not diminished one iota, she discovered, as the lump filled her throat and the bright day dimmed.

"My dear, are you unwell?" Susannah laid a hand on her arm anxiously.

"No . . . no, not at all, I am quite well," Ginny replied firmly. "I am just a little overwhelmed, Susannah, at reaching journey's end after such a time, and at finding such warm and gracious hospitality."

Chapter Twenty-five

"There now, my pretties, enjoy that while you may, another week and you'll come to the table in a most delectable fricassee." Nodding with satisfaction, Ginny set down before a half-dozen exceedingly fat young chickens the size of blackbirds a porringer of dried raisins pounded in a mortar and mixed with milk and stale bread. Robert and Susannah Harrington were to dine with them the following Wednesday, and these plump babies, at the height of their fat, fried in butter and served with a sauce of white wine and savory herbs were destined to be the meal's crowning glory.

Closing the coops, she went out of the fowl house into the crisp air of a late October morn. The chicken house was set in a small plot where already her newly planted herb garden flourished behind the small frame house that had been her home for almost two months. The creek of Piper's Cut flowed alongside, providing the Courtneys with access to the main thoroughfare of the James River.

"Virginia!" The irascible bellow preceded the appearance of her husband in the kitchen door, tucking his shirt into his britches, blinking at the morning light.

Ginny sighed and came up the garden toward him. "Will and Rob have been gone this last hour to clear the ground about seven-acre field, Giles. They await you."

"Then they may wait," he grunted. "Fetch me ale."

"You'll at least take some breakfast with it," Ginny said, moving past him into the kitchen. "Lizzy has prepared batter for griddlecakes. It will take me but a moment to make some." Taking his grunt for assent, she stirred up the batter in the bowl, setting the skillet to heat over the range. It would not really matter whether or not Giles went to help the laborers clearing his land. He was quite incapable of doing any work himself and would probably only hinder them with an ineffectual but annoying supervision. If it weren't for the efficiency of Tom Brigham and the kindness of the Harringtons, who had put at their disposal this simple abode until the Courtneys could clear sufficient land and build for themselves, they would still be lodged above the kitchen at Harrington Hundred and their own acres would remain virgin woodland. As it was, thanks to the labor lent to them by Robert Harrington, they could put in their first crops of tobacco, corn, and wheat, and there was sufficient pasture along the creek for the two milk cows and the goat.

Giles appeared sublimely indifferent to these signs of their establishment in the New World and refused to listen to Ginny's anxieties as to how long they could rely on the assistance of his cousin and his cousin's labor. Soon, they must employ their own men about the land. Lizzy, the daughter of the Harringtons' nursemaid, provided Ginny with all the help she needed about the house in exchange for a meagerly wage and her keep, but Giles seemed to consider one house servant woefully inadequate to his consequence, and the contrast between his situation and that of neighboring planters was frequently brought home to him when they received hospitality from these welcoming families.

Ginny set a plate of griddlecakes on the table in front of him, poured ale from the pitcher by the door, and went upstairs to the single chamber it contained. She had given up racking her brains as to how one persuaded a man who had never been expected to work for his bread and his position that circumstances had changed, and that if he wanted to achieve the degree of comfort and prosperity of his neighbors he was going to have to stop relying on others and do something for himself. When she had attempted to point out that the hand of friendship would eventually be withdrawn, once their neighbors realized that their offerings of assistance, intended as temporary measures to help the newcomers settle in, were accepted as permanent fixtures, Giles had raged at her in a terrible temper, heaping vilifications upon her head until she had thought she could bear it no longer. Then, as usual, he had sought and found solace in the whiskey bottle, and matters had continued as before.

Ginny opened the chest they used as a linen press, drawing out some garments that required mending. She touched the soft folds of the turquoise gown Alex had bought her in London. Somehow, she could never bring herself to wear it, however scanty her wardrobe. She looked with distaste at the bed, its frame laced with ropes, the mattress stuffed with horsehair and rags. Before winter, she was determined to replace the stuffing with feathers, although they would not make her nights any the more restful. . . .

Another bellow from below brought her to her feet, cutting off the inevitable progression of her thoughts. She went down the rickety staircase to the main room where Giles was struggling to pull on his boots. "Is my horse saddled?" he demanded.

"There is no one to saddle it," Ginny told him, collecting his dirty dishes and dumping them into the wooden tub. "This is not Courtney Manor, husband, and we have no stable lads."

"Tell that lazy, good-for-nothing girl to do it." He went to the door and yelled for Lizzy.

"She's collecting honey at the hives," Ginny told him, waiting for him to tell her to saddle Major herself. It was the next logical step, and she supposed, in the interests of peace, that she would comply. It was certainly simpler in the long run, although her spirit rebelled. But surprisingly, he didn't, merely muttered a string of oaths and limped pointedly out of the house and round to the lean-to that sheltered their riding horses.

Ginny took a wooden pail down to the creek for water to clean the earthenware dishes. She did not mind the hard work, welcomed it in fact, since it kept her healthily occupied and she need not think too much. Unpleasant though Giles was, at least she had only him to contend with and was spared the spite of his womenfolk, and at least she was mistress of her own house and not required to play subservient daughter-in-law. It was hardly a great house, but it was not uncomfortable, and it was furnished with their own things brought from England, the decorated cherub head andirons, the pewter mugs and spoons, and the china dinnerware brought out of the chest only for special occasions. And she still had her simpling and physicking to keep her interest. It was a skill that had won her many friends in the last two months, and one that she was relying upon to keep those friends even though their disillusion with her husband might lead them to withdraw their help and support.

No, life could be, indeed had been, much worse. Even the pain of loss these days had retreated to a dull ache, that only flared and throbbed late at night after Giles, stupified with whiskey, had failed to exercise his marital rights, and her fear that this time he might succeed was slow in receding.

This Virginia legislature was an impressive body, Alex thought, shifting on the hard wooden visitors' bench in the House of Burgesses in Jamestown. For the last two days, they had been discussing the governor's right to levy taxes without legislative authority, and it looked as if the governor of this royal Colony was going to be left with dramatically curtailed powers. All of which was of great interest to the Parliamentarian, who had fought so hard and so bitterly for the curtailment of royal powers in the mother country, and it would certainly be of interest to those at home, when he eventually returned. Although, for all the good he was doing here, he might as well take ship in the morning, he reflected dismally.

For three weeks he had been cooling his heels in Jamestown, trying by casual questions to elicit some information about Ginny. So far, he had discovered that she was alive, and so was her husband. Now he did not know what to do.

He could not allow even a shadow of suspicion to fall upon her, not when the punishment for a woman accused of adultery was thirty lashes. If he surprised her, heaven only knew how she would react, but how could he get an uncompromising message to her? And why did he assume that she would be as desperate to see him as he was to see her? She must surely have settled down in her new life with her husband. The last thing she would want would be to stir up the old troubles and longings. But having come this far, he could not simply turn away again. He had hoped to find her free of her husband, that something had happened to change things. Instead, she was still as securely married to Giles Courtney as ever, and all Alex could do was pace the streets of Jamestown, hoping that by some miracle he could catch a glimpse of her if she came to town on household business. Although what he would do in such a case, he could not begin to imagine.

"General Marshall, what is your opinion of our home-grown troops? Nothing to touch the New Model, I'll be bound?" Burgess Robert Harrington came over to him as the session broke up, walking with him out of the state-house, voice and expression genial.

"They've not had a war to fight, Harrington," Alex commented. "It's not easy to be part-time soldier, when there are fields to plow and trades to pursue."

"Aye, right enough," Robert agreed as they walked to the inn. "And we'd rather be farmers than soldiers. 'Tis a matter for rejoicing that there's been no need to take up arms in recent years. Nevertheless, there's been some anxiety expressed among the burgesses about our lack of readiness, should troubles come again. Peace makes us careless."

Alex nodded encouragingly but said nothing else, having the firm conviction that this was no idle talk on the part of Robert Harrington. Harrington was putting up at the King James during the monthly meeting of the House of Burgesses and during dinner reopened the subject in the company of his fellow planters who made up the legislature.

"How long d'ye plan to stay in these parts, General Marshall? Are ye thinking, perhaps, of buying some land?"

"Perhaps," Alex said vaguely, "but my main purpose, gentlemen, is to observe your government for Parliament and to discover from you how you would have England treat its Colonies, now that the royal charter is meaningless."

This reminder of the king's execution and the abolition of the monarch's office produced a silence. The colonists were sufficiently removed from the politics in the home country to be objective about the happenings there, but they were far from indifferent as to the possible effects the new state would have upon them. Alexander Marshall was the first representative from the new government to come to the New World, and they sensed that he carried some considerable power.

"If ye're truly interested in understanding how matters are conducted here, General, ye could not do better than to spend some time on the plantations," Harrington said slowly. "We'd be glad to offer you hospitality for as long as ye wish. And, perhaps . . ." He paused, looking down the long table at his fellow burgesses. Receiving a nod from them, he continued. "If ye'd be willing to cast an eye over our defenses, our reserve troops, what preparations we can make in the event of further Indian attacks, ye'd be doing us all an uncommon favor."

Alex helped himself to another veal pasty, refilled his tankard with Spanish wine, and contemplated the question. It would give him a purpose beyond his vague instructions from Parliament and the driving need to see Ginny, and it would provide him with the opportunity to wander freely about the countryside where surely he would meet up with her at some point, and he would have a perfectly innocent reason both for his presence in the country and for their introduction.

"I am at your service, gentlemen."

"Splendid, splendid!" declared Robert Harrington, refilling his own tankard. "We'd be most honored if ye'd visit first with us at Harrington Hundred. Mistress Harrington will be overjoyed at the excuse to have a gathering before the onset of winter. Quite melancholy does she become at the prospect of a few months without company."

And so it was agreed. By the end of the week, Alex, in the company of his host, landed at Harrington Hundred, noting, as had Ginny some two months earlier, the evidence of prosperity and good husbandry. Susannah was indeed delighted to receive him and immediately set about making plans for a large gathering of neighbors to meet their guest and give him the opportunity to glean such information as would be useful to him. In the meantime, he had agreed to travel around with Robert Harrington, surveying the various defenses individual planters had prepared and offering what advice he deemed appropriate. Throughout, Alex had no idea of the kinship between the Courtneys and the Harringtons, or that Ginny lived on the Harrington plantation some five miles from the main house.

Until one morning when, returning with his host from a ride along the bridle paths cut into the backside of the plantation, he entered the stables and overheard an altercation between a little maidservant and a young stable lad. "Mistress Courtney says I'm to take the flour back in the canoe," the girl was saying fiercely. "The master can't come 'n fetch it in the cart 'cause his leg's painin' him."

"Drunk, y'mean," the lad said scornfully. "Well, I'm not carryin' that to the creek. If it's not to go in the cart, ye can carry it yerself."

"What the devil's going on here?" Robert Harrington exclaimed, swinging from his mount to stride across to the two youngsters who cowered against the wall of the stable at his approach. Alex, pretending indifference, nevertheless managed to edge his horse closer.

"Please, sir," the maidservant stammered, "my mistress says I'm to fetch the flour in the canoe because the master can't bring the cart. She would've brought it herself, sir, but Mistress Bradley needed her for a birthing and—"

"All right, Lizzy, I understand," Harrington said soothingly. "What's your problem, Jack?" He turned to the lad, a note of menace in his voice. "Did I hear you say something about Esquire Courtney?"

"No—no, sir, nuthin'," the boy said, hefting the sack of flour onto his shoulders. "I'll be takin' this to the creek." He staggered off beneath the weight, making incredible speed, Alex thought with an inner chuckle that could not be repressed in spite of the pounding of his heart at the sound of that name, at the sudden realization that she must be close, that she must have some close relationship with his host if her flour was ground at his mill.

"Problems?" he inquired nonchalantly of Robert Harrington, dismounting and handing his horse to another waiting lad.

Robert Harrington shrugged. "Servants know all too much, these days, and have scant respect for their masters."

He seemed disinclined to say more, and Alex chewed his lip in frustration before throwing caution to the winds and venturing to remark in a musing tone, "Courtney—I don't think I've heard that name hereabouts."

Harrington sighed. "Ye'll meet them at Susannah's party. 'Tis a wretched business when there's bad blood in the family. Courtney's a cousin of mine on his mother's side, came over from Dorset after the war. We've done what we could to help, but he's a drunkard and a wastrel. Never done a hand's turn in his life."

There was another silence, and Alex could bear the suspense no longer. "His wife?" he asked.

Harrington smiled suddenly. "Mistress Virginia Courtney, sir. No bad blood, there. Once that husband of hers has drunk himself into the grave, she'll not be left to mourn too long. All the womanly virtues and the most extraordinary skill with physicking."

Yes, Alex thought. You talk to the converted, Robert. But he allowed the subject to drop as if it had no further interest for him.

"I beg your pardon, Susannah, I did not quite catch the name." Ginny's hands shook as if she were in the grip of an ague, and the small knife she was using to chop endive slipped, nicking her thumb.

Susannah Harrington, who had settled down in Ginny's kitchen for a comfortable chat with her cousin by marriage, bustled over, scolding Ginny for her carelessness.

"It is nothing," Ginny said, wrapping a piece of cloth around the cut. "Fingers have a tendency to bleed considerably, that is all." Abandoning the endive, she took a flagon from the dresser. "A glass of cider, Susannah?" She had, by this time, taken control of herself again, although she felt a curious sensation as if she were filled with air, as if the space between her ribs and spine was but a void. "Pray continue about your guest."

Susannah's primary purpose in this visit had been to invite the Courtneys to her party and to enlist Ginny's help with the culinary preparations for a gathering of at least a hundred who would require feeding for probably two days. Her guest's business was definitely outside the scope of women, and she saw very little of him except at the dinner table. She had not, therefore, considered either his identity or description to be of much interest to Virginia and had mentioned his name only in passing. What was of interest to the housewife was the party for which his presence served as an excuse.

"He is come from England," she now said, looking rather vague. "He has business with the burgesses, Robert says, and, because he is a solider, has agreed to offer advice on our defenses in the event of another Indian attack. But I do not talk with them much, and he is out with Robert most of the day."

"How is he called?" Ginny asked, although she knew she had not misheard.

"Marshall," Susannah supplied cheerfully. "General Alexander Marshall. He is really quite personable, but I find him a little intimidating." She smiled as if this were only to be expected. "He is very serious, and looks stern most of the time — although the children approach him freely enough. But you will agree to come and help, will you not, Ginny? You must make the tansy, no one does it so well, and I beg you will dress up the Salamagundy."

"With pleasure, Susannah," Ginny responded through the pounding of her swift blood. Did he know she was here? If he did not and was unprepared, what would happen when they met? But they could not meet. It was impossible. But how to avoid it? For the next hour, she responded automatically to Susannah's talk, agreeing to every suggestion for the table, to every request, offering her own suggestions without thought. But at last, Susannah was seen into her canoe, which she paddled with all the expertise of the experienced, and Ginny was able to return to her quiet kitchen. She found that she could not remain within doors and, taking her simpling basket automatically, made for the woods.

One thought, so frightening that she could hardly bear to look at it, kept hammering at her confused and terrified mind. What if he had brought Jed with him? Giles would recognize the old soldier immediately and would have no trouble taking the next logical step. Confined to a locked sickroom, he had never seen Alex, except as a shape on the bed that last day, and Ginny had kept his identity a secret through all the inquisitions and accusations. But such care would go for naught once he saw Jed. And Jed went everywhere with Alex; it was inconceivable that he would have been left behind on such an expedition, and if he did not know *she* was here, why should he have had thoughts of caution? She had to find out before the party. Even if she could contrive some dread sickness that would keep herself at home, there was no way she could prevent Giles from attending.

The next morning, she set out herself in the canoe for Harrington Hundred, her excuse the need to borrow Susannah's recipe for mushroom sauce to accompany the plover Giles had contrived to shoot yesterday. Ginny had reasoned that Robert and his guest would do their traveling around the plantation in the early part of the day, since dinner was in the early afternoon, and after that there would be little time before dusk for extensive horseback journeying through the woods. It was nine o'clock when she tied up the canoe at the landing stage and went swiftly up to the house—an hour when no self-respecting man would be in evidence, when the house belonged to the women, children, and servants.

All was bustle, as she had expected, and she ran Susannah

to earth in the dairy where she was instructing the dairy-maids on the quantity of cream she would require for the party preparations. "Ginny, you are well come, indeed," Susannah declared. "I cannot recall how much cream you will require for the tansy."

"A quart," Ginny supplied, "and twenty eggs. Forgive my intrusion, Cousin, but I would borrow from you the recipe for mushroom sauce that goes so well with fowl. You are not, I trust, occupied with your guest at present."

"No, indeed not, they are gone up river."

Reassured, Ginny accompanied Susannah into the house, keeping her eyes peeled for any sign of Jed. There was none; so seeing little option, she asked the question directly. "Does your guest bring his own servants with him, Susannah? Or are you obliged to provide for him yourself?"

"No, he is quite alone, but he seems well able to care for himself," Susannah replied. "He is a soldier, and I think not accustomed to much coddling."

Ginny began to breathe more easily and took her leave soon after, hurrying down to the landing stage, anxious now to be gone. She had not told Giles where she was going but had left him abed, sleeping off the after-effects of the previous night's drinking. If he had woken and, wanting her, found her absent, his temper would not be improved.

She saw the rowboat, pulled by a sturdy oarsman, approaching the landing stage just as she reached it from the garden. The sun glinted off the auburn head of one of the boat's occupants, sitting on the thwart, his back to her. Ginny found that she could not take another step as she gazed at him, and it was as if the last fourteen months of separation had never been. Her lips formed his name, and she would have called it out, as naturally and inevitably as if there were no husband waiting for her, except that Robert Harrington called to her first.

"Ginny, well met. We have had to return early because the boat has sprung a leak." Laughing, he tossed her the painter which she caught with automatic deftness. Alex kept his back to her for a minute, knowing that he must turn and dreadfully afraid to do so. "Susannah will have told you of our guest," Robert went on, blithely unaware of the emotional devastation around him. "Here is General Alexander Marshall." An all-embracing arm was proudly outflung to include his guest and his cousin by marriage. "Mistress Virginia Courtney, of whom we spoke the other day, Alex."

Relief flooded her. He would not be unprepared then. Relief flooded Alex. She would not be unprepared then.

He turned, getting to his feet, the boat rocking beneath him. "I am honored, Mistress Courtney." She stood there, smiling up at him in the October sun, tall and graceful in her skirt of blue dimity over a white Holland petticoat, a striped dimity waistcoat molding the soft swell of those magnificent breasts, her waist banded by a dark blue apron of serviceable fustian. She curtsied politely, inclining her head where the chestnut braids coiled in the way he remembered so well.

"General," murmured Ginny. "How delightful to make your acquaintance. I am sure you have realized how newcomers are a source of great excitement and much pleasure for us."

He stepped out onto the landing stage, close enough to touch her now, almost close enough to inhale the delicate fragrance of her skin that was as pink and brown with health as it ever had been during the long days of the march. The gray eyes were as clear as ever, and there was no hiding the passion in them as she met his own. Nothing had changed, then—nothing at all. It was as it had always been between them, the magic that overcame all difficulties and differences. And it *must* do so again . . . but how?

"You flatter me, Mistress Courtney," he said, wondering how long he could stand here beside her without touching her, how long before he enveloped her, wrapped her in his arms, aching now with memory, allowed his mouth to drink of her glorious sweetness, lost himself in her.

She dropped another curtsy, then turned to Robert. "I must hurry back, Cousin. I came only to borrow a recipe from Susannah. Giles will be looking for his dinner soon." There, she had said the name, and now it lay, open between them. Turning away before she could see Alex's reaction,

437

Ginny climbed down into her canoe. A lad unfastened the painter, dropping it into the craft beside her. With a farewell wave, she dipped her paddle into the water and set off for the mouth of the creek that would take her home, back to her husband.

Alex watched her go, feeling as if he had lost her again. He knew now that just seeing her was not enough. He had persuaded himself that it would be, that he would see her, reassure himself that she was well and content, lay the ghost finally, then he could go back to England and find a wife. But it would not do. His hunger and his need, renewed, raged apace, as bad now as when she had first left him, and he knew with absolute certainty that it would be the same for her.

Ginny did not know whether the tears that poured down her cheeks were tears of joy or frustration. Both, she guessed. The sight of Alex had brought unsurpassed joy, but now all she could think was that he was as lost to her as if he had never reentered her life. The dreadful torment that had taken so many long months to abate was now rekindled, racking her like a fever.

"Where in hell have you been?" Giles yelled across the water as she appeared around the bend of the creek.

"To the Harringtons'," she called back with an attempt at cheerfulness, hoping thus to avert a storm that she did not think she had the stamina for at this point. "I wished for that recipe for mushroom sauce that you like so much, to accompany the plover." She paddled the canoe over to the bank and threw him the rope. Giles let it drop at his feet, and her heart sank. He looked worse than usual, and she was well aware that his physical ailments were quite genuine. The two wounds had weakened him significantly, and he would probably always have borne their effects, but those effects could have been lessened with a careful diet and regimen. But the dissolute life he affected only added to his debilitation. It would have ruined a well man eventually.

"You have no right to go off like that without telling me," Giles stated, making no attempt to help her as she scrambled onto the bank, catching at the neglected painter before

438

it could drift off into the water.

"You were asleep," Ginny snapped, tying up the boat. "Had I woken you, you would have cursed me up hill and down dale, husband. I know better than to disturb you from the whiskey oblivion, and if I waited for you to wake to ask your permission everytime I have to go somewhere, we would starve and the wilderness would swallow us again in no time—"

"Put a bridle on that scold's tongue, wife, else I do it for you," Giles hissed, grabbing her wrist with a vicious twist.

Ginny stood still, struggling to regain her composure. "You are hurting me," she said quietly. The pressure of his fingers increased, and tears of pain pricked behind her eyes. "Please, Giles—"

"How do I know you've been to the Harringtons'," he demanded, not slackening his grip. "Once a whore, after all . . . There's plenty around here who'd be glad of what you have to offer."

The words today struck terror into her heart, whereas before she had just shrugged them off. Now, with one man, she would have them true, and she could not keep the fearful knowledge from her eyes. She dropped her head instantly and stood in submissive silence, while Giles breathed heavily. Then he released her wrist, pushing her away from him so she stumbled. "Get up to the house. I am hungry and thirsty, and that good-for-nothing wench does not know one end of a cookpot from the other. I'll not be left here again while you're gallivanting about. Just you remember that unless you want me to take a stick to your back!"

Coward! Ginny accused under her breath. Weak, ineffectual, dissolute coward who had to take his frustrations out on her. And there was not a damn thing she could do about it. It wasn't as if he ever really hurt her, just spiteful prods, pinches, and twists. And as far as the law and the community were concerned, a man was entitled to take what measures he deemed necessary to correct a neglectful, scolding wife. She could go whining to the Harringtons and be assured of their sympathy, but they could do nothing either and would only be embarrassed.

Giles came into the kitchen and flung himself down at the table, watching morosely as she fried eggs in a whirlpool of butter. "What's to do at Harringtons'?" he asked after a while. "Tom Brigham says there's preparations for a party."

"I told you about it last night," Ginny reminded him, knowing it was incautious but unable to maintain her attitude of submissive docility. "They have a visitor from England, come to observe the House of Burgesses for Parliament." She paused, sliding the eggs onto a platter. "He was a soldier, I understand from Susannah, and is offering advice on defenses here."

"Soldier for Parliament, of course," Giles stated, taking the plate without a word of thanks.

"I should imagine so," Ginny replied. "If he's here on Parliament's business, it seems a reasonable conclusion. Anyway," she went on swiftly, "there is to be a grand gathering next week, the entire neighborhood invited from as far as twenty miles up river and down to Jamestown." She turned her attention to cleaning a basket of mushrooms, remarking, "I have promised Susannah that I will help her with the preparations. Unless you forbid it, I will need to spend the two days before the party at Harrington Hundred. I will instruct Lizzy as to how to care for you properly."

"How can I forbid it, if you've already promised?" Giles grumbled, wiping up egg with his bread.

"It is little enough to do in return for their kindness." Ginny regretted the words instantly as a dull flush mottled her husband's complexion.

"Are you accusing me of ingratitude?" he demanded.

"I was stating the plain truth." She shrugged. "We owe them a debt that I doubt we can repay except with small services of the kind I am willing to perform for Susannah. I should be glad, however, if we could see our way to managing without their assistance before the winter." She threw out the latter statement with little hope of it producing any reaction but another tirade, but at this point she found she did not care whether she annoyed him further or not. "You should go to Jamestown when the next ships come in and

440

hire labor so that we may release your cousin's men. I am sure he has need of them himself."

"I'll go when the next slave ship comes in," Giles said, his tone surprisingly moderate. "We'll do best to buy several negroes — cheaper in the long run."

"We have no quarters for them," Ginny pointed out, hiding her grimace. There was something eminently distasteful about this idea of owning men. The right to liberty was one embedded in the heart and soul of all Englishmen. How could they so easily, in the interests of expediency, suspend such a right for others?

"They'll build their own," Giles replied, as if he had thought the matter through thoroughly. Obviously, he had, Ginny realized with some surprise.

"It will be winter soon, Giles. They cannot come here without shelter."

"The colder it is, the quicker they'll work."

Ginny tossed mace and nutmeg into the saucepan containing the mushrooms and bit her lip on the retort. There was little point fighting a battle in advance of the action, and, at least, the matter of her visit to Harrington Hundred was accepted, and Giles knew in principle of Alex's presence, which knowledge seemed somehow and in the strangest way to legitimize that presence.

She was planning adultery with every shake of the saucepan, preparing herself, laying the foundations for something that was as inevitable as the sunrise. And she felt not a shred of guilt; her heart sang, her blood danced, her skin rippled in wondrous anticipation. She was back in destiny's hands.

Chapter Twenty-six

Ginny wiped her streaming eyes on her apron, blinking as a stubborn easterly wind blew the smoke from the central fireplace back into the primitive cabin where the only chimney was a hole in the woven swamp reeds and marsh grass of the structure.

The old Indian woman, sitting cross-legged at the fire and stirring something in a pot, was quite oblivious to the noxious fumes. Muttering, she beckoned to Ginny, pointing at the bunch of dried grasses and forest plants. Ginny nodded, listening to the identification of each one. They all had medicinal properties, and Ginny had early learned the need to find substitutes for many of those of her homeland. She had come upon this medicine woman some weeks ago when they had both been simpling in the woods, and with a curious mixture of sign language, the few English words known by several of the men in the village, and their shared interest and skill, they managed to communicate remarkably effectively. Last month, Ginny had helped in a particularly difficult delivery of twins in the village and ever since then her visits had been received with more than tolerance.

She kept her visits secret from her own people, however. There was still considerable mistrust between Indian and settler, and with good reason, although an uneasy truce had been in operation for more than a decade. Trade between the two still flourished, but it was conducted with military caution, and the ease with which Ginny wandered in and out of this village would be viewed as criminally negligent, even by the relatively enlightened Robert Harrington.

Now, she offered the old woman a small vial of aqua-mirabilis that she had prepared with cloves and other spices that would not be available to the Indian. It was a much-relied-upon tonic and had most soothing properties. Her companion sniffed, sipped, and nodded, replacing the cork top carefully. The morning's lesson paid for, Ginny rose from her cramped position on her knees, smiled, bowed, and went out into the village.

The day was mellow and sunny, a few fallen leaves crackling beneath her feet, although the majority still clung in coppery splendor to the tall trees forming a canopy over her head. The village was set in a clearing in the woods some distance from the nearest bridle path so Ginny had covered the two miles from home on foot, enjoying the quiet and the solitude, the opportunity for peaceful reflection on this new quirk of fate, if, indeed, that was what Alex's arrival was. She presumed it must be coincidence. He would hardly pursue her, indissolubly wed to Giles Courtney, across the hazardous ocean . . . or would he?

The unmistakable rustle of crushed leaves, the sudden prickling of her scalp told her that she was not alone. Indians, perhaps, but no Indian would cause that alerting crackle of leaves. Subduing the panicky fluttering that threatened to flare as her overly vivid imagination began to run riot, she stepped out faster, calculating how far she was from the bridle path, whether running would achieve anything. The crackle came again, and she began to run, not stopping to wonder why she should have this nameless fear, her mind straining toward the bridle path as if by thinking of it, she could bring it closer. The crackling behind grew more pronounced, and then the sound of feet moving swiftly. Someone, something, was coming after her. There were boar in the woods, and bear, and the devil only knew what else. . . .

"Chicken, in the name of the good God, will you stop running!" That resoundingly familiar voice, carrying the most extraordinarily familiar note of exasperation, came

443

softly from behind her. With a little moan, Ginny stopped dead, her heart battering against her rib cage. "What is the matter with you? I could not call out for fear someone on the bridle path would hear." Alex came up with her, and she turned slowly to face him.

"I thought you were a wild boar," she said. "Or some mad ravisher."

"I am deeply flattered." Alex grinned at her. "I was riding with Harrington earlier, when we saw you leave the bridle path. He had to get out to the far fields, and I said I would be happy to ride through the woods alone. Then I followed you to that village. What do you do among the Indians?"

They had not seen each other, apart from a few minutes on the landing stage yesterday, for fourteen months, and Alex was talking to her exactly as he used to, demanding an explanation for an activity of which he did not approve.

"Their medicine woman is very skilled," Ginny explained, "and can tell me much of what grows around here. Their simples are rather different, you understand?"

"I cannot imagine why I bothered to ask the question," Alex said, sighing, although his eyes glowed and he took her hand. "Let us go deeper into the woods. We are too close to the bridle path." Drawing her beside him, he turned back the way they had come. "It will not matter if we fall foul of Indian notions of morality, and I suspect they are the only folk, apart from you, my intrepid little gypsy, who stray from the beaten track."

Ginny said nothing because she could not. Her hand seemed to be cemented to his, the light, teasing voice washing over her like moonlight. Were there to be no questions, no explanations? No fumbling, doubtful, guilty wonderings and excuses? It would seem so, and it was only right that it should be so. This wild, magical madness that gripped them was as inevitable as it had ever been.

In a small clearing, Alex stopped, placing his hands on her shoulders, looking deep into her eyes as if he would find all answers therein. "Sweet heaven," he said softly. "I do not know how I have lived without you, my own." His lips took hers, gently at first, almost hesitantly as if the reexploration

444

of familiar territory might bring some surprises. Ginny responded in the same way, her lips soft, parting for him in breathless wonder as she too rediscovered and re-created. When she closed her eyes, the scent of his skin filled the air around her, and she inhaled greedily. Her hands ran over his back, remembering every curve, knob, and muscular ripple, up to his neck where the hair curled in wisps, then to palm his scalp, her fingers twisting in the luxuriant, crisp auburn thatch.

Alex felt the soft press of her breasts against his chest as he tasted the sweetness of her tongue. His hands cupped her buttocks, firm and round beneath the cambric kirtle, and his need rose hard and urgent eclipsing the gentle wonder of this reexploration. Ginny felt it, too, and pressed herself against him, sucking on his lower lip, nipping with her teeth in a manner that bespoke imperative demand rather than play. He drew back, his breathing ragged as he loosed her hooded cloak and tossed it on the carpet of leaves at their feet. She went down under the peremptory pressure of his hand on her shoulder, sinking onto the cloak, her hands reaching up for him as he yanked off his boots, pushed off his britches, and dropped down beside her.

"I am sorry," he whispered with an almost defeated moan, drawing her skirt and petticoat up to her waist. But Ginny could wait no more than he could. Her legs parted for him, her hips lifted as he lowered himself upon her. Then he penetrated her very self, driving deep to become that indissoluble part of her as her loins filled, contracted around him, and the sunburst shattered the serenity of the forest.

A blue jay cackled at the two spent figures lying like Hansel and Gretel on the russet bed of leaves. The sound brought them both back to awareness, and Alex kissed her with a rueful little smile. "I am sorry, sweeting, but I do not remember ever having such a powerful and invincible need."

"It was the same for me," she said, brushing back his forelock that clung damply to his brow. "What shall we do?"

Alex moved out of her slowly, then caressed the length of her exposed thighs, a thoughtful little frown knitting his brow. "I do not yet know, my own. But I do know that you belong to me, that the bargain made at Grantley Manor still holds good."

She shook her head in sudden bewildered wretchedness. "How can that be? I belong to my husband."

"In law, yes," he agreed, still calmly, his fingers playing in the curly tangle at the base of her belly, moving over the mound beneath, taking his time, now that the desperate urgency of lust had been slaked. "But by every rule of love and nature you are my own." He placed his hand over the moist, pulsing warmth of her core, holding her as he kissed her belly, tickling her navel with his tongue. "Is it not so?" His breath rustled over her abdomen, and his hand seared her.

"It is so," she groaned, her body lifting and twisting on the cloak, and when his mouth replaced the hand her little sobbing cries filled the peaceful glade as the rapturous tide swept over her, carrying her beyond memory. Then Alex found that he must draw again from the well and entered her, this time with the utmost delicacy, poised on the very edge of her body before sheathing himself slowly within the silken, velvety chamber. Breathing deeply and slowly, he stroked with firm rhythm, kneeling upright between her wide-spread thighs, his hands on his hips, watching the mobile face beneath, watching for the moment when the gray eyes would cloud with that surprised wonder that always made him want to laugh with joy. Her tongue ran over her lips, and she smiled up at him, quite at peace with this wonderfully familiar fit of bodily contour and rhythm.

Slowly, he withdrew, holding them both on the very edge of delight. The gray eyes widened in expectation. "My gypsy wanton," Alex said and took her with him into the inferno.

Afterward, he dressed himself, then helped her up, straightened her skirts, shook out her cloak, and fastened it about her shoulders again. Ginny seemed numb and incapable of doing any of these things for herself, until Alex took her by the shoulders and shook her gently. "Ginny, love, pull yourself together now." He flicked the tip of her nose teasingly. "This is not my intrepid soldier girl. You have fought worse battles than this one, chicken."

In spite of the teasing smile, the light tone, she heard the seriousness of the message beneath. This was a battle they had to fight, a battle against discovery. She had to go back to her husband and behave like a virtuous, attentive wife. When she met her lover again, it would be in company, and she must behave toward him as she would to any slight acquaintance, however much her skin danced in expectation of his touch, her arms ached to reach out for him, her lips parted in readiness. She must keep her eyes downcast, her voice even and polite, her hands busy with some comforting task, her attention elsewhere.

And now, she must go back to Giles, knowing that she must lie there in docile submission if he demanded it of her, racked with the fear that petrified her, the fear that this time he might be sober enough to move beyond the first fumblings. But she could not tell Alex that. That was her own personal hell, not to be shared by one whom she sensed could not live with the torment of that knowledge.

So she smiled, shook her head in mock bemusement as if to clear away the cobwebs, stood on tiptoe to kiss him. "Better now, love. You had rendered me senseless for a few moments."

His relief showed clear in his eyes. He glanced swiftly around the clearing. "Do you go first, then, sweetheart. I will wait for fifteen minutes before I fetch my horse."

Ginny left without further speech, back to the bridle path and the walk home. The noon sun was already high and she had been away from the house since eight o'clock, but Giles had managed to rise early enough to accompany Tom Brigham into the newly cleared fields to discuss the site for the house that they would eventually build. With luck, he would not return until dinnertime, and maybe Tom could be persuaded to stay and eat with them. . . . And tomorrow, she would to go Harrington Hundred to help Susannah with the preparations for the party. She would sleep there for two nights, bundling with the older Harrington girls in the big bed in the square parlor. Alex would sleep beneath the same roof, in the boys' room, although, as Susannah had informed her, such an important guest was in sole possession of the bed, the boys sleeping on pallets on the floor.

These thoughts rattled through her mind in an almost irrelevant stream, except, of course, that it was not remotely irrelevant to reawakened passion, and it was all tied up with the fact that her husband would be sleeping a safe canoe ride away, and he would not be there to watch her at dinner, when they dined in the company of Alexander Marshall, to listen to the talk and castigate her later for what she had said and whom she had looked at and how she had looked at them. Generally the castigations and accusations ran from her like water from an oiled back. Armed with innocence, she could ignore the drunken tirade, and she knew that by ignoring it, she reassured her husband. But in the knowledge of her guilt, how would she react if Alex Marshall became the focus of her husband's jealousy? In the large gathering of the party, she could take refuge in helping Susannah with the domestic arrangements for the guests' entertainment. She need do little more than greet Alex briefly and politely. If Giles did not see them together, there was no reason why Alex should figure in his ramblings later, and if he did not, then could she react with customary innocence.

So Ginny thought and planned as she hurried home. It was all perfectly possible to arrange, so long as one kept a clear head.

"It is to be hoped we have sufficient beds for our women guests, husband," Susannah said worriedly to her husband, passing him with an armful of lavender she was intending to strew upon the sheets. "The boys must sleep in the barn, but General Marshall—"

"Will also sleep in the barn, Mistress Harrington," Alex said, coming into the square hallway. He smiled at his hostess and when she made to demur told her firmly that as a soldier he was accustomed to far worse billets than a dry barn and fresh straw.

"You may be sure the general speaks only the truth, Susannah." Ginny, laughing, came out of a bedchamber, a

448

bolster in her arms. "If you cosset him, then he will grow soft, is it not so, General?"

"Indubitably, Mistress Courtney," Alex agreed solemnly. "And I very much fear that with the hospitality I have received so far, the process is already well begun."

Susannah flushed with pleasure at the compliment. Her guest in the last two days was become most approachable, with no shortage of pretty words and compliments, the previously stern countenance generally smiling, the green-brown eyes carrying a sparkle that had hitherto been absent. Flustered, she turned her attention to her husband. "You have given orders for the slaughtering of the sheep and the steer, husband?"

"Yesterday," he reassured her. "And the pit is being dug below the orchard for the roasting."

"And the wine?"

"Ten gallons, my love, and another ten of brandy."

Susannah, looking round at the three faces, realized that her anxieties were causing some amusement. The pink of her cheeks deepened, and she muttered something and hurried off with her lavender.

"It is quite an undertaking," Ginny said. "Providing hospitality for over a hundred guests. There are many details to be considered."

"Quite so," Robert agreed. "And we stand in your debt, Cousin, for your assistance."

"No, Robert, you do not," Ginny replied firmly, hitching the bolster higher into her arms. "Excuse me, gentlemen, I must take this outside for airing."

"Allow me, mistress. It is a somewhat cumbersome burden." Alex removed the bolster from her arms, his hand brushing against her breast. Ginny felt the nipple harden instantly and could only be thankful that her face where the involuntary shock at the deliberate touch would be clearly revealed was turned away from Robert. She managed to murmur her thanks adequately, however, hurrying outside with Alex, carrying the bolster, striding along behind her.

They reached the grassy area outside the wash house where lines of clothes and linens flapped, and bolsters and

449

mattresses lay taking the air. "Thank you, sir." Ginny turned to take the bolster from Alex. Mischievously, he hung onto it. "Alex, stop it," she whispered fiercely. "You do not know whose eyes might be upon us."

"I cannot resist teasing you," he replied as softly as she, although his eyes danced still. "I have to kiss you before I go mad with the craving."

"Not here," she said helplessly, feeling the water enter her veins, her knees begin to buckle. "You were always so cautious; what has happened to you?"

"Desperation," he said, and the laughter died between them. The bolster fell to the grass. "You must walk down by the river after dinner. I will contrive to join you somehow." He left her on the instant, and Ginny wondered how she was to comply with the instruction. There was neither the time nor the opportunity for solitary strolling at Harrington Hundred these days, and wishing for solitude would be considered most odd in her. It would never occur to anyone in this large, rowdy household that a body might prefer to be alone once in a while. At the very idea, Susannah would probably rush her to bed with a hot brick at her feet and an emetic to ward off whatever sickness threatened.

Ginny returned to the house through the garden where servants were busy setting out tables beneath the trees for tomorrow's feast. The kitchen was a hive of activity with the cooks trying to prepare today's dinner, which could not be allowed to suffer simply because they were to feed a hundred people on the morrow, while stirring, mixing, and boiling for the next day. Her own task at this point was the dressing of the Salamagundy — a delicate operation where sliced chicken, anchovies, eggs, and onions must be arranged in prescribed order on a bed of lettuce leaves. The skinning and carving of the chicken was a fiddly task, and given the number of the birds required, a time-consuming one.

She was just completing this when little Lizzy burst into the kitchen. "Please, Mistress Courtney —" she began breathlessly.

"Whatever is it, Lizzy?" Ginny spun round. "You are supposed to be at home looking after Esquire Courtney."

"He sent me to fetch you 'ome," the girl said, sniffing. "Says he's not feelin' well, and you've to come and physic him."

"What is he complaining of, girl?" Susannah asked, wiping her hands on her apron, exchanging a look with Ginny.

"His hip and stomach," the girl replied. "He won't let me do anythin' for him, and shouted at me when—"

"Very well, Lizzie, that will do," Ginny broke in swiftly, conscious of the flapping ears in the kitchen. It was too humiliating to have her husband discussed in this way, even though his vagaries were well known to everyone here and she was well aware of the pity they felt for her. "You may find your dinner here, and stay to help as you may. I will not need you at home until after the party, and I am sure Mistress Harrington could use another pair of hands." With a small jerk of her head at Susannah, she walked out of the kitchen into the hall. "I am sorry, Susannah, but I must go to him. I will try to come back early in the morning."

"What's to do?" Robert Harrington came into the hall followed by Alex, the jovial question on his lips. "You both look as if you've been visited by a ghost. Has the syllabub not curdled?"

"Oh, it is no laughing matter, Robert. Giles has sent Lizzy to fetch Ginny home. He is not well, it seems, but of course there is nothing the matter that—"

"Susannah!" Robert thundered, and his wife stopped on the verge of gross indiscretion with a horrified gasp.

"I do beg your pardon," she whispered, stricken with remorse, gazing at General Marshall standing behind her husband, looking every bit as shocked as he must feel at this appalling display. She had been criticizing someone else's husband, not just in the presence of the wife, but in the presence of a stranger. "Pray forgive me, Ginny." The plea was directed as much at her husband, however, as at her cousin by marriage.

"Think nothing of it, Susannah," Ginny said briskly, hoping to avert Robert's wrath. Suannah stood in some considerable awe of her husband. "It is most inconvenient, and you cannot be blamed for finding it so. I do myself."

451

"It is your husband who needs you," Robert stated in frigid tones. He could not take his cousin to task for her lack of respect in this matter, but he could make his displeasure felt at the unseemliness, at the unwomanliness of her sentiments.

"Quite so, Robert." Ginny met his eyes directly. "And we are all aware of the facts, are we not?" Unable to stand against the candid challenge in the gray eyes, Robert coughed and turned away.

"Alex, let us continue with our discussion on those earthworks." He marched back into the parlor. Alex, after one look at Ginny, followed. "My apologies," Robert said gruffly. "I cannot imagine what you must be thinking of us that the women of the Colonies should have such unbridled tongues and show so little respect."

"I was not thinking that at all," Alex said. "You have said something to me about Mistress Courtney's husband in the past, if you recall. It would be hard for a woman to show respect for such a man—a drunkard and a wastrel, if I may use your own words."

"Maybe so," Robert sighed. "But such matters lie only between husband and wife, and Mistress Courtney should keep such sentiments to herself. As for my wife—"

"Come now, you cannot blame her," Alex cajoled. "She has so much to think of, and to lose her right hand so abruptly. . . . It would incline a saint to indiscretion."

"Ah, I suppose you are right." Robert Harrington smiled in resignation. "A glass of brandy? We had best stay immured in here if we do not wish to be swept under the carpet in all that zealous activity."

Ginny paddled back to her cottage, furious at her husband for the selfish command that she knew to be unnecessary. He had wanted to accompany her to Harrington Hundred, and only the lack of invitation had kept him away. What he saw as a deliberate slight had also made him livid, and his refusal to allow her to complete her work for Susannah was presumably the consequence. And now she would not be able to walk along the river after dinner. . . . It was that thought, rather than having had to

452

abandon her Salamagundy, that fueled her disconsolate irritation, Ginny realized without too much surprise. But she was in no conciliatory mood when she tied up her canoe and stomped up the garden into the house.

"Giles?" There was no sign of him in the kitchen and no immediate response to her call. She called again, going to the stairs. A weak moan came in reply. "Malingering hypocrite," Ginny muttered, ascending the stairs that opened directly into the upstairs chamber. Her husband lay upon the bed, fully clothed, his eyes red and angry and unfocused, the whiskey bottle beside him. "What is the matter," she asked with scant sympathy, "that you should drag me away in this peremptory fashion?"

"Your place is with me." He struggled up until he was sitting on the bed. "My damn hip is paining intolerably, and you have no right to be anywhere but here, seeing to my comfort and my needs."

"I left Lizzie to do that," Ginny retorted, anger, disappointment, and disgust putting her beyond caution. "I will prepare a poultice for your hip and bring you laudanum." She picked up the whiskey bottle, but Giles lunged for it, wrenching it out of her hand.

"Yes, you left some half-witted girl-child to look after me," he said furiously. "What is there at Harrington Hundred that is so much more appealing and important than serving your husband who is owed your loyalty and obedience?"

"Everything," Ginny muttered, then gasped with pain as he twisted her wrist.

"What did you say, soldier's whore?" he hissed. "Is that it, then? The mere sight of a soldier is sufficient to—"

"Stop it!" Ginny yelled, pulling at her wrist, heedless of the pain. With a final twist, she broke his grip. "You have no right to talk in that way." Except that he did have the right. She turned away from him, back to the stairs, rubbing her wrist. "Do you wish me to prepare a poultice for you, or would you prefer I bring you more whiskey to drown the ache?"

Giles dived for her but tripped and fell to his knees. A look of surprise crossed his face at finding himself on the floor, but he seemed to forget about following Ginny and dragged himself back to the bed, falling across it with a groan.

He would be unconscious in a short while. Ginny's lip curled in utter contempt as she went back downstairs. They would be having dinner now at Harrington Hundred, and she was very hungry. She ate a giblet pie she had left for Giles. He would be unable to stomach it now, once he came out of his stupor. Spiced gruel was about all he could take these days, and even that sometimes aggravated his stomach after a particularly heavy bout. How would he be tomorrow, at the party? Perhaps he would not be able to go, which would mean that she would not be able to attend either. They would both sit in lonely bitter enmity in their house while the revels went on . . . and Alex . . . Oh, it was all hopeless. There was no future to anything. Ginny went out of the house. She would walk herself into exhaustion; then at least she would be able to sleep.

Alex paddled slowly up Piper's Cut, looking out for the house. He did not know what he would do when he saw it, and particularly what he would do if he saw Giles Courtney. Paddle on by, presumably. There was so much bustle at Harrington Hundred that his departure after dinner had drawn no surprised comment. Indeed his host had remarked enviously that he wished he could do the same, but Susannah would not look kindly upon her husband's desertion at this juncture.

The small, square house came into view as he rounded the bend. Smoke curled from the chimney, and the garden around was neat and well tended. As he would have expected of Mistress Courtney's husbandry. The canoe and rowboat were tied up at the bank so she was not out upon the water this evening. Lifting his paddle, Alex allowed the canoe to drift, noticing the lean-to under the trees where two horses were tethered. Either she was within doors, tending her husband, or she was out and about on foot. Well, there was no reason why he should not paddle by, keeping his eyes open. The creek was a public waterway, the marshes on

454

either side alive with game fowl, and his musket rested in the bottom of the canoe as ample evidence of his hunting intentions.

He came across Ginny some hundred yards downstream from the house, sitting on the bank dabbling her toes in the water. Her face lit up when she saw him, then an expression that he had never before seen and had thought never to see on that courageous, challenging countenance, an expression that filled him with nameless rage appeared in the gray eyes as she looked nervously around. She was afraid. Then the look was gone as swiftly as it had appeared. "Round the next corner," she said. "I will race you." She was on her feet, picking up her shoes and off and running on the instant, leaving him to follow as fast as the paddle would allow him.

When he rounded the corner, there was no sign of her, and he stopped in midstream, looking around. There was nothing but the marshes, where curlews rose and called, and the wooded bank. Then he heard an unmistakable chuckle from somewhere above. Looking up, he saw her in the crotch of an oak tree, peeping impudently at him through the copper leaves. "Can you climb trees, General, or are you grown too full of consequence for such childish sport?"

"You're going to pay for that," he threatened with a mock scowl, paddling to the bank and tying the canoe. The tree was not an easy climb, particularly as Ginny tossed twigs and leaves down on him as he clambered up to where she sat astride a thick branch, her back resting against the tree trunk. "Gypsy," he declared, swinging astride the branch facing her. "Disrespectful hoyden." Putting his hands on her shoulders, imprisoning her against the trunk at her back, he kissed her, subjugation in mind. Ginny laughed and twisted against his mouth but eventually yielded, her head going back as her lips parted and her arms went around his neck.

"What brings you here, sir?" she inquired, when at length he released her.

"A promised meeting along the river bank with a gypsy," he replied. "A kiss to claim. Must we stay up here?"

"Not if you do not care for it. But it is very private."

"Yes, but devilishly uncomfortable, and I think caterpil-

455

lars are crawling down my back."

Ginny chuckled, swung her leg over the branch so that she was sitting sideways, then launched herself into the air. Alex gasped, open-mouthed, then relaxed as she caught onto a branch opposite and swung like a monkey some six feet from the ground. "You had better catch me, sir."

He jumped down, coming up in front of the swinging figure, putting his arms around her waist. "Let go then. I have you safe." She dropped into his arms, her hands on his shoulders, smiling down at him as he held her up. Then he let her slide through his arms to the ground. Ginny straightened her skirts, reached up to pluck a twig from his shoulder. Alex took her wrist with a frown. "How did you do this?"

"Do what?" she said with an assumption of carelessness, glancing idly at her wrist where an ugly bruise was purpling against the bone. "Oh, if you climb trees, you expect a few scratches." She shrugged nonchalantly, but Alex's frown deepened.

"That is not a scratch, and it did not come from tree climbing. How did you do it? And don't lie to me, Ginny."

"I do not entirely recall," she said with bland but necessary disobedience. "And it does not hurt in the slightest."

Alex's lips tightened as he remembered that look in her eyes, but there was nothing he could do if she would not confide in him. And there was little he could do if she did, he thought bleakly. The only thing he could do for her was to avoid endangering her further.

"Do not look so somber," she said suddenly, softly pleading. "We are quite safe here, and it is surely too rare an opportunity that we should waste it. It will be dark soon, and you will have to return to Harringtons', or they will send out a search party for you."

"And your husband will be looking for you," he said directly, tipping her chin, forcing her to meet his eye.

Ginny tried to evade him but could not. "I do not suppose he will be looking for me for quite some time," she said matter-of-factly. "He is in a swinish, whiskey-sodden stupor, if you wish to know the truth."

Alex sighed and asked painfully, "Has he beaten you, Ginny?"

"Not so far," she said shortly. "And you need not fear that I would stand for it if he did. You should know me better than that."

And with that, Alex had to be satisfied. He left her soon after, paddling back as dusk turned to full night. Never had he felt so helpless, so totally without a plan of action or even the possibility of forming one. She was dearer to him than life itself, and he knew that he could not possibly leave her again, now that he had found her.

But what future did they have? He could stay here, buy land, and make his life as a planter. It was a good life for those with the drive and energy to make it work. He would be close to her and they would love — hugger-mugger and in constant fear of discovery, the voice of reality chimed. The secret scramblings, the fear, would eat into them, eventually destroying what they had. And he was a soldier, not a planter, a man with a life of power waiting for him at home. He could take her with him, wrest her from her husband to live with him in disgrace, a social outcast, a declared adulteress who could not be married because she had a husband already. And his career would be destroyed utterly under the harsh moral climate presently operating in England where adultery was now a hanging offense.

Everywhere he turned, Alex saw only the thorny thicket of an impossible dilemma. There was only one sensible answer for the rational man. He must leave her and go home. But he did not think he was a rational man any longer.

Chapter Twenty-seven

Ginny woke at dawn steadfastly determined that nothing was going to keep her from the party. The birds were greeting the new day in ecstatic chorus, and she ran downstairs, out into the dewy morning, barefoot, shivering slightly in the early chill. An autumnal mist rose from the creek and marsh, but there was nothing to indicate that the mellow warmth of this October was at an end. The sun was a red, hazy ball low in the sky, promising a clear day.

She fed the chickens, watered the horses, and put them to graze. In Lizzy's absence, she had to milk the two cows, but none of these tasks seemed particularly arduous this morning, and she was humming cheerfully as she dragged the tin bathtub into the kitchen and filled it with steaming water from the cauldron hanging on the arm over the fire. Before getting into the tub, she took the bucket to the well in order to refill the cauldron, struggling beneath its filled weight as she set it upon the arm again and swung it over the fire to heat up should she need more.

There was no sound from upstairs, Giles being still deeply asleep, and Ginny pulled her shift over her head and slid into the tub, dipping backward to wet her hair before washing it. Today, for the first time since leaving Alex at Preston, she was going to wear the turquoise gown with the quilted taffeta petticoat that she had made herself last month. She would wear the tortoiseshell combs in her hair, and her prunella shoes with the rosettes.

The creak on the stairs interrupted these pleasant musings, and she sat up in the water, drawing her knees up, crossing her arms over her breasts in a defensive reflex. Giles stepped down into the kitchen, blinking blearily, then his eyes fell upon her, sitting in the tub, her wet hair hanging down her back, her creamy shoulders bare.

"Well, well," he said slowly, crossing the room toward her. "Who are you making yourself beautiful for, wife of mine?"

"I was just taking a long-overdue bath," Ginny said, trying to keep the tremor from her voice as Giles knelt down by the tub. "If you would care to bathe, there is fresh water on the fire. I will just —"

"Why so anxious?" he said, taking her hands and uncrossing them. "It is your husband, remember, who wishes to look at you. Am I not entitled to do so?"

Ginny could feel the shudders of revulsion creeping up her back. Then his hand cupped one breast, and she thought she would scream, except that his mouth came down on hers, stifling all sounds. He never kissed her, had never taken a leisurely interest in her body before. He was interested only in the act of coition, and his consistent failure to perform that act brought down vicious accusations upon her head. She twisted her head, but he caught the wet mane on her shoulders and held her head still as his tongue pushed into her mouth, rough and inexpert, his fingers squeezing her nipples hurtfully, although she sensed that he did not intend to inflict pain; he just did not think in terms of her comfort, as was usual with him.

"No . . . please . . ." she heard herself beg and knew it to be a mistake.

Giles drew back from her, his face darkening. "What is the matter? Is this not what you are accustomed to with your paramour? Will you deny your husband what you give so freely elsewhere?"

"Giles, do not talk like that," she pleaded desperately now. "It is only that you surprised me, and it is early in the morning . . . but . . . but we must make haste if we are to reach the Harringtons' before the other guests." She could hear her babble and despised herself for it, but if he was going to insist on her cooperation, here and now, she did not know how she would bear it in silence.

"There is time," he said, pulling her upright. "Dry yourself and come upstairs. I am in need."

She could not refuse him, not without making matters between them completely intolerable. She could not afford to give him yet further ammunition for his jealous accusations that her own needs were gratified elsewhere. Ginny knew that he did not believe in his accusations, that they were made simply to wound her, but it would not take much. So she lay like a stone, while drink and ill health took their invariable toll of Giles and, as always, he was left frustrated and angry, insisting that it was her fault because she was as cold as ice and enough to dampen any man's ardor.

They went to Harrington Hundred, although Giles deliberately took his time getting ready, knowing that Ginny was anxious to arrive early in order to help Susannah. If his mood had been less ugly, she would have insisted upon going ahead in the canoe, leaving him to follow either in the rowboat or by the longer land route on horseback. But in truth, she was beginning to be a little afraid of him, sensing that drink and bitterness were eroding the civilized restraints that had previously operated, however petulant and irritable he could be.

Once at Harringtons', Ginny was able to leave him immediately and without remark. Robert, stiffly welcoming, took him up to the house while Ginny went in search of Susannah and thus missed the meeting between Alexander Marshall and Giles Courtney.

Alex saw a rather thin man of middle height, with pale blue eyes and the waxen hue of ill health. He was dressed richly and with care as befitting a landed gentleman, in a doublet of dove gray with a soft ruff, gray silk stockings, and a sleeved cloak. His sombrero hat bore a lavish plume. His hands were soft and white, and Alex thought of Ginny's brown, square-nailed competent hands that would turn themselves to any task however hard or demeaning.

Giles saw a tall, broad-shouldered individual with clear green-brown eyes that regarded him with unnerving closeness. An aura of assertion, of one accustomed to authority, clung to him and he was dressed neatly, but with little regard for prevailing fashion or consequence, in plain doublet and britches. Hatless, the cropped auburn head was held high, and the cultured voice was soft with an underlying crispness that caused Giles to feel unaccountably uneasy. The feeling irritated him, and he accepted a glass of peach brandy from Robert with a degree of relief.

Excited shrieks from the children outside indicated new arrivals, and Robert, escorting his guest of honor, went down to the landing stage to greet them. Throughout the morning, boats came to the landing stage, discharged their passengers, and were tied up further along the waterfront. A few guests arrived on horseback, but they were close neighbors with easy access to the few bridle paths. Servants bustled among the guests gathered in the garden above the river, bearing trays of refreshments, threading their way through the tables laid ready for the banquet that would start at two o'clock. A group of musicians tuned their fiddles in preparation for the dancing that would take place later in the afternoon.

Ginny insisted that Susannah go among her guests while she remained in the kitchen and around the house supervising the final details. Ginny was more than happy to remain in the background, for the moment unable to contemplate with equanimity the prospect of seeing her lover and her husband together in such close quarters. The contrast would be like a hammer blow, and for some perverse reason, her pride rebelled at the thought of seeing the contempt in Alex's eyes when he saw her husband, as surely he would, at his worst. But she could not evade her social responsibilities when the gathering sat down under the trees, and Ginny was called to the Harringtons' table, obliged to sit beside her husband and opposite General Marshall.

Alex, seeing the strain in the gray eyes that she barely raised when she murmured a greeting, did his best to keep the conversation general and light so that her unusually silent manner would not be too noticeable. Giles remarked upon it, though, and demanded in a loud voice to know if the cat had got her tongue. Susannah instantly began to fuss, asking if she felt quite well, if the sun was too hot, if her head ached, saying that it would be no wonder, so hard had she been working all morning, while she, Susannah, had been making merry.

"Pray, Susannah, do not mention it," Ginny begged. "I am feeling perfectly well." She took a large mouthful of oyster stuffing as if to emphasize this fact and choked, causing an even greater disturbance that left her red-faced and mortified and absolutely the center of attention.

Alex ached for her, ached to scoop her up and take her away into the quiet. Instead he reached across the table to fill her tankard with water from the pitcher, a service her husband had conspicuously failed to perform. She thanked him with a rather fragile smile, and he fixed her with a hard look that contained none of his sympathy but told her very firmly to take a grip upon herself. It was a message for which Ginny was instantly grateful, recognizing that she had been about to lapse into a self-pitying melancholy that would only draw unwelcome comment. She drank deep of the cold water as the coughing spasm abated, then made some apologetic joke about her immoderate appetite that had led her into disgrace, and the moment was over. Conversation became general again, and she took her part, indulging freely in the claret that flowed lavishly. It took the edge off the host of disturbing emotions plaguing her which was well worth any unpleasant aftereffects on the morrow.

She was certainly not alone in this indulgence, and if her eyes became a little too bright, her laugh a little brittle, her step a little unsteady, there was no one to single her out since almost everyone was in similar condition. Except for Alex who could not stop himself from watching her and could only hope that no one noticed his attention. When the dancing began, he took advantage of the unimpeachable excuse to be close to her during a galliard.

"I do not like to tell you this, sweetheart, but you have had enough claret for one day. Promise me you will take no more. You will not be able to paddle that canoe straight."

"Then I will swim," Ginny replied with a chuckle. "It will sober me up in no time."

"If we were alone, I would sober you," he said in some exasperation, stepping back as she whirled away from him down the dance.

"Why, General, for a soldier you are a most proficient dancer," a young woman giggled, swimming into his field of vision and reminding him that he had duties other than keeping a weather eye on Virginia Courtney.

"You flatter me, madam," he replied, taking her hand as she twirled under his arm. "But the musicians have much skill and energy."

"Indeed, dancing is quite our favorite pastime, sir," his new partner said. "You do not disapprove, I trust."

"Not at all," he replied somewhat absently.

"Well, we understand that it is now frowned upon most severely at home."

"By some," he agreed, and as she disappeared down the set, he took the opportunity to leave the dance.

"How do you find our entertainments, Alex?" Robert inquired jovially. "A little unsophisticated for a Londoner, I'll be bound, but we do our best."

Alex hastened to assure him that he found the entertainment far from unsophisticated.

"Come now, General," Giles remonstrated, lifting his head from his tankard, his speech slightly slurred. "There's no need to be mealy-mouthed. We're well aware of our shortcomings, ye know."

Ginny appeared, breathless from the dance, just in time to hear this remark. She saw that telltale muscle twitch in Alex's cheek and jumped without thought into the ring. "That is hardly polite, Giles. I am sure the general meant what he said."

"I do not need *you* to take me to task, Madam Wife," Giles declared, glaring at her. "I've told you before to put a bridle on that scold's tongue."

Alex went as white as Ginny went crimson. "Come now," Robert broke in hastily. "No squabbling between man and wife. This is a party. I'm sure Giles meant no offense."

"I find him offensive," Ginny said very quietly and turned on her heel, making her way through the gathering up to the house.

Giles gave vent to a violent expletive and lurched from the bench. Robert put his hand on his shoulder, pressing him back down. "Easy now, Cousin. I'll have no trouble in my house. If you've a quarrel with your wife, take it up at home."

Alex muttered something incomprehensible and strode off, his disgust apparent in every muscle of his back. How dared that drunken sot speak to Ginny in that fashion, particularly so publicly! And of course she would not stand meekly by and accept it. It was not her way, as he knew so well. But Alex, too, sensed the fraying of the civilized constraints that bound Giles to convention, and he knew with absolute certainty that it was more than unwise of Ginny to provoke her husband as she had done. And there was not a damn thing he could do about it!

He saw her across the garden, sitting with a group of matrons quilting under a tree. It was relatively safe company, he thought, until he saw Giles make his way over to them.

"We're going home," Giles said to his wife without preamble or explanation.

"The party is barely begun," Ginny demurred in a low voice. "It would be most discourteous of us to depart this early."

"How many times do I have to tell you not to tell me how to behave?" Giles exclaimed furiously. "I say we are going home, and that should be enough for you. Or do your good manners not apply to your husband?" His lip curled in a sneer.

Ginny felt the anger inside her threatening to slip the bands of control; then she saw Alex standing within earshot, his eyes warning her, his expression stricken with the frustration of his helplessness. She bit her lip, put down her needle and patchwork, and rose. "You must excuse me, ladies. I expect my husband's old wound is paining him." With a smile, she walked away from the group. Giles grabbed her arm.

"Where are you going? The canoe is on the river, in case you have forgotten."

"I am going to make my farewells to our hosts," she snapped, pulling at her arm. "Let go of me, Giles, or I will create such a scandal right here that will go down in living memory."

She spoke with soft, determined intensity, and he released her, but the coil of his bitter rage tightened, and Ginny shivered inside, well aware that she had won a public battle at the expense of the private one that would be fought later.

"You cannot possibly leave," Susannah exclaimed in genuine distress. "The dancing has but just begun, and there will be supper soon, and I had thought we would play blindman's buffet and—"

"Giles is not feeling well," Ginny said, daring her husband with a cold-eyed stare to contradict her. If she must leave she would do so, but with a modicum of dignity, of pretense that it was not under duress.

Giles found that he could not gainsay her and even mumbled his own excuses, blaming his hip and the autumnal mists beginning to swirl in from the river. Ginny turned round in search of Robert and found herself facing Alex.

"You are leaving, Mistress Courtney," he inquired politely, bowing over her hand as she curtsied. Her fingers quivered in his, and he squeezed them hard.

"I fear so, General," she replied brightly, moving apart as he released her hand.

For the moment they were without an audience, and Alex said in a fierce whisper, "Meet me tomorrow in the glade by the Indian village—in the morning. Do not fail. I must know that you are all right."

She nodded imperceptibly before rejoining her husband, and Alex watched them walk down to the river, Ginny stiff-backed, Giles with a pronounced limp.

"Damnable business," Robert Harrington muttered at Alex's shoulder. "Cannot interfere though, not between husband and wife."

"He has the right to treat her as he pleases, then?" Alex asked, eyebrows raised.

Robert shrugged. "You know the law, my friend. Short of serious injury or murder, a man may do as he please around his own hearth. To my knowledge, Courtney goes no further than what you saw today. Virginia would be wiser not to provoke him. She does have a sharp tongue, you'll agree."

"Like a bee sting," Alex murmured almost distractedly, and his companion looked at him, startled.

"Beg pardon, Alex?"

"Nothing." Alex recollected himself. "Nothing at all, Robert. Shall we join the ladies?"

Ginny paddled the canoe with its double burden through the misty dusk. She had had enough. Her soul was cramped by the bitter, mean spiritedness of the man crouched opposite her, glowering into the gloom. The wine she had taken earlier no longer uplifted her but had left her with a sourness in her mouth and an incipient throb behind her temples. The afternoon's scenes of humiliation played constantly in her head, and John Redfern's daughter knew that she could take no more, not without losing all self-respect.

They reached home, and the house stood square and uninviting after the cheerful revelry they had left behind. Ginny tied up the canoe and followed Giles, limping morosely, inside.

"I hope you are not hungry," she said. "I had assumed we would sup at the Harringtons', so there is nothing prepared."

"Then fetch me bread and cheese." Giles reached for the whiskey flagon standing on the dresser.

"I am sorry, but you must fetch it yourself. I have a headache and am going to bed." Ginny went up the stairs as Giles bellowed at her to come back. She ignored him, then heard his step on the stair, and apprehension shivered her. She quashed it, beginning to unloose her hair, removing the tortoiseshell combs.

"Who the devil do you think you are?" Giles demanded,

filling the stairway. "I want my supper. Now go and get it, wife."

"There is bread in the barrel, cheese in the covered dish in the pantry," she said with an assumption of patience. "It should not be beyond your capabilities to get it for yourself. I am not expecting you to till a field, or milk a cow, or grind corn, or feed the chickens, or draw water from the well—"

"Be silent!" her husband roared, breaking into the catalogue of tasks that she accomplished without murmur and that he was quite incapable of tackling. "That is not work for a gentleman."

"Is it not?" She turned on him, the gray eyes bright with scorn. "There are gentlemen aplenty around here who do such things and take pride in the doing."

"And you would reward them? Is that it, traitor's whore?" He stepped up to her, the blue eyes narrowed to slits. "You don't save your charms for *my* bed, that's for sure. Lying as lumpen as unleavened bread—"

"And what would you have me do?" she cried. "It is not my fault that the drink has taken your manhood from you . . . Ah!" Ginny reeled as he struck her with his open hand. But she came back at him, her own hands flailing, all fear, all thoughts of decorum and wifely modesty vanquished by an upsurge of outrage that for a few moments gave her the advantage of surprise.

Not for an instant had it occurred to Giles that his wife would strike back, and he retreated before the onslaught. Then the red mist of fury enveloped him as he remembered that this woman was his wife, the unfaithful traitor who had betrayed his bed as she had betrayed the king's cause, who dared to instruct him and take him to task, who made his life wretched with her icy indifference and the scorn she did not attempt to hide. And now, his wife, bound to him by vows of obedience, possessed by him as he possessed his domestic chattels was daring to raise her hand to her lord. His clenched fist slammed against her cheekbone, and she fell to the floor. Ginny saw him, towering over her, arm raised, something in his hand; then, instinctively, she covered her head with her arms. . . .

467

A long time later, Ginny lay, still crouched upon the floor listening to the sounds in the room. There was a strange, low keening sound interspersed with rumbling snores and a deep, uneven breathing. It took her a minute to realize that the keening came from her, and she fell silent with a long shuddering breath. The floor was hard and unyielding against her face, and gingerly she got to her knees, expecting the return of pain with every movement. Carefully, she stood up, forced herself to straighten her burning shoulders, looked at the inert figure sprawled across the bed. Exhausted by that burst of savagery, Giles had simply collapsed, leaving her a broken, whimpering heap on the floor.

A wash of self-disgust broke over her. How had she allowed him to do that to her? And she had permitted it, had made no attempt to defend herself from the blows raining down upon her back. And she had invited the brutality, begged for it with her provocation. What was she — to invite and permit a beating of the kind a man would give his dog?

Ginny lit a taper in the dark chamber and staggered over to the mirror, one of the more precious things they had brought from England, and looked upon her face with contempt and loathing. A livid bruise stood out on her cheek, her lip was swollen and bleeding, but as she gazed at the image that was herself, yet not herself, merciful reality reasserted itself. She had done nothing to invite or deserve that, except lose the caution that normally kept her treading warily. She had lost the caution under unbearable provocation. And she had fought back for as long as she was able.

She turned back to the shadowy shape of her husband on the bed. A sharp kitchen knife at his throat, it would be so easy. . . . Except that she was incapable of doing such a thing. But never again would he raise his hand to her, *never*. Determination entered like iron into her soul. Neither would he find her cowed and defenseless. Taking the candle, she went down to the kitchen, took the dipper to the pail of water by the door and filled a bowl, which she placed on the table, and methodically fetched her medicine basket and a soft cloth.

All of these actions, Ginny performed quite calmly, as if

operating in some cool clear space of her own. She bathed her bruised face and laid a pad soaked in witch hazel against her cheekbone. Slipping her gown off her shoulders, she examined the damage there as best she could, noting almost dispassionately that while the skin was raised and red, it was not broken. She poured herself a glass of brandy and sat down at the table to think. She had promised to meet Alex in the morning, but all the skill and medicine in the world would not remove the traces of Giles's savagery by then.

Alex must not know of it. There was nothing he could do about it, and only she could prevent a repetition. He would be tormented by his helplessness. Ginny had seen the stricken look on his face that afternoon, had heard the pain in his voice when he had noticed her bruised wrist. What would the knowledge of this do to him? Besides, it was too humiliating to think of *anyone* knowing what had happened to her. It was one of those dark, shameful secrets that must be kept buried in the deepest recesses of the soul. She would keep close to the house until her face was healed and tell Alex that she had been unable to get away—that Giles had not left the house. Something of that kind would do.

Her decision made, Ginny went back upstairs, took a quilt and pillow from the chest that served as linen press, returned to the kitchen, and made up her makeshift bed on the floor before the fire where she lay awake, stiff and throbbing, until dawn lightened the sky and bird song filled the air. Then, finally reconciled, knowing and understanding her own strength, she fell into a light but peaceful sleep.

Chapter Twenty-eight

For the next three mornings, Alex waited in the glade near the Indian village, and he waited in vain, the spiral of anxiety coiling ever tighter. If there had been a disaster, news would have reached Harrington Hundred, and no one there seemed to find a few days without contact with the Courtneys a matter for remark. But even as he told himself this, he knew that something had happened to prevent Ginny from meeting him, and whatever it was, it was not trivial. She was far too resourceful to let minor problems stand in the way of achieving her goal. This was a woman who had evaded the watchful eyes of an entire brigade, for heaven's sake!

On the afternoon of the third day, Susannah bustled into the parlor where her husband was casting his accounts, his guest examining some proposals to be put before the legislature in Jamestown at its next session. "Robert, I am much concerned."

"About what, my dear?" He looked up from the desk with its twelve drawers, one for every month of the year.

"Well, there is talk in the kitchen that matters are not going well at Courtneys . . . I know you say one should not listen to kitchen talk," she went on hesitantly, seeing his frown, "but Lizzie came this morning to collect the flitch of bacon that Ginny had put to smoke in our smokehouse, and she said that her mistress had fallen, but cook says Lizzie does not really believe —"

"I do not wish to listen to servants' gossip, madam, and if

you must listen to it yourself, I will not have it repeated," her husband declared, raising his hand imperatively for silence. "What is between the Courtneys is simply that—between *them*."

"Yes, husband," Susannah said unhappily, "but if Ginny is hurt, should we not—"

"Has she asked for help?" Robert demanded.

"No, but—"

"Is she incapacitated to such a degree that she could not send Lizzie with a message? She was able to send her for the bacon, was she not?"

"Yes, husband." Susannah sighed.

"Then leave well alone," her husband commanded in the tone of voice his household recognized as permitting of no argument. His wife turned back to the door, and Alex kept his seat only by a supreme effort. Not for one minute did he doubt the gossip in the kitchen, and he felt a cold anger at his host for adopting that head-in-the-sand attitude. But it was the attitude that everyone would take, except for her women friends like Susannah who would offer the succor and sympathy of sisters in adversity, but nothing else because they had nothing else to offer. And what did *he* have to offer, Alex thought bitterly. No more than those women, probably less. She had not come to him, after all.

"I've a mind to ride, Robert," he said, getting to his feet with a leisurely stretch. "The rain appears to have stopped, and poring over books is an activity with limited appeal."

"Aye, I'll agree with you, there," his host replied. "But you'll excuse me if I don't join you? I've a meeting with the bailiff in an hour."

"Assuredly," Alex said, relieved although he had expected the response. Outside, he saw Susannah hurrying down to the river, an alpaca cloak drawn around her, a basket over her arm. There was an air of secrecy about her that instantly piqued his curiosity. If she was going to visit Ginny, then his own plans would have to be modified. He followed her, catching up with her at the landing stage. "Do you go on an errand, Mistress Harrington?" he inquired pleasantly. "Pray allow me to paddle the canoe for you. I am

471

sore restless after a morning pent up in the house."

"Oh—that is most kind, sir." Susannah looked thoroughly discomfited. "But there is no need, really."

"Surely you will not deprive me of the pleasure of performing such a small service, madam?" He smiled. "Or of your company."

"Oh, dear," Susannah said, quite at a loss.

Alex decided he had best broach the subject directly himself. "Do you perhaps intend visiting Mistress Courtney? I will not reveal your destination, I assure you."

"Oh, you are too kind, sir." Susannah flushed. "It is not that I wish to disobey my husband, you understand, but I do feel that I must—"

"I quite understand," Alex said soothingly, bending to untie the canoe. "We will go together, paying a friendly call on your near neighbor and cousin, on a fair afternoon." He handed her into the canoe and took his place behind, raising the paddle.

Ginny took the batch of mince tarts out of the round oven built into the wall beside the fireplace, placed them to cool on the table, and went to the kitchen door. The rain had left the sky washed clear, although the air was chill and filled with the desolate patter of raindrops falling onto the carpet of leaves below the trees. There was no sign of Giles; indeed, since that dreadful night he had taken himself out of the house every morning, whether working on the land or not, Ginny did not know, but he did not return until the evening when he would eat in silence and retire to the inglenook with his whiskey.

When he had woken that morning, it was clear that he had no recollection of the night's doings until he saw Ginny's face. Then he had blustered, accusing her of provoking him, of asking for and deserving his rage with her insolent taunts, her faithlessness and constant nagging. She had made no response at all, simply set his breakfast before him, and eventually he had fallen into a baffled silence. Then she had told him, very calmly and without employing threats or pleas, that she would not tolerate a repetition. When he had demanded to know how she thought she could prevent him from correcting her in whatever manner he chose, she had walked away, out of the house. Since then, they spoke only when absolutely necessary, and Ginny waited with growing impatience for the time when she would be able to bring this self-imposed isolation to an end. The bruise on her cheek was a dull, faded yellow now, and by tomorrow, or the next day at the latest, she would be fit for company again.

Except that company had decided to take the initiative. The canoe came into sight, its occupants instantly recognizable. Her heart sank, even as she felt a thrill at the sight of that auburn head. What could have brought them here except concern? There was nothing unusual about having no contact with the Harringtons for as long as a week. Susannah would surely not have thought it strange. Alex would have worried when she had not appeared in the glade, but his hands were tied; he could not possibly have prevailed upon Susannah to make this visit without giving something away.

Well, she had better greet them as cheerfully as always. The story she had told Lizzie of slipping down the stairs would explain the fading mark on her cheek, and she would come up with some tale that would explain to Alex her failure to meet him in the glade. Gathering up her skirts, she ran down to the bank.

"What a pleasant surprise, Cousin, and General Marshall. A social call, I trust. There is no bad news?"

"No, indeed not," Susannah said, climbing agilely onto the bank. "I have brought you some quince jelly. It is quite the best batch I have made." She scrutinized Ginny in a manner that told her cousin there was definitely an ulterior motive. "Whatever has happened to your face, Cousin?" Susannah asked with an assumption of nonchalance.

"Oh, it was so silly of me." Ginny waved a hand in airy dismissal. "There is a loose tread on the stair, and I slipped. I tumbled right to the bottom." She laughed. "Most undignified and very careless. Pray come within, and let me offer you some refreshment. Do you care for mince tarts, General? I have some fresh out of the oven."

Alex mumbled something vaguely pleasant and followed

473

the two women into the house. He had to be alone with her before he finally exploded with the frustration of his impotence and his ignorance. He had to know the truth, and if Ginny did not stop prattling in this inconsequential fashion, in a minute he was going to find himself saying something that would put them all at risk.

"Giles has been unwell since the party," Ginny announced, "which is why we have been so reclusive. His hip has kept him within doors, and I have been hard pressed to find ways of amusing him." She smiled and poured black-currant cordial.

And you are lying through your teeth, Alex thought, risking a hard stare as he took the glass from her. A pink tinge crept into her cheeks, a conscious flash in the gray eyes. He nodded grimly, a gesture that told Ginny that he was not deceived and that she was not going to get away with further fabrications. His opportunity came when Susannah, with a murmured excuse, disappeared outside in the direction of the house of easement.

"Why did you not come?" he demanded directly. "And do not waste time by lying to me."

"I was not well," Ginny whispered with difficulty. "Oh, do not act vexed with me, love. I have missed you so and would have come if I could."

"That whoreson hurt you, didn't he?" The green-brown eyes were pinpricks of fury, and Ginny knew she could deceive him no longer.

"Alex, it will never happen again. I beg you to believe that. It is over and—"

"How can you say that?" he exclaimed in an undertone. "What he has done once, he can do again."

Ginny shook her head determinedly. "He will not! I will know what to do if he attempts it another time."

"This has to stop. We cannot go on like this." Alex spoke swiftly, hearing Susannah's step on the path. "Tomorrow morning, in the glade, and if you fail me, I shall come for you."

"General, I think we should be returning." Susannah reappeared. "My husband will be looking for me." She reached for her cloak, then embraced Ginny. "Dine with us tomorrow, Ginny."

"It will depend upon Giles," Ginny replied, returning the hug.

"Then come without him," declared Susannah with a defiant glare.

"You had best not let Robert hear you say such a thing," Ginny said with an understanding chuckle, and Susannah smiled a little guiltily.

"No, he would not approve, and I do not know I'm sure what the general must be thinking, hearing us talk like this."

"I am certain the general will keep his reflections to himself, will you not, sir?" Ginny looked at him, and her chin lifted in the old challenging way.

"Where things don't concern him, mistress," he replied evenly. "But do not expect him to keep silence when matters touch him nearly."

Ginny saw them off, biting her lip ruefully. As she had feared, Alex was not going to allow this business to rest. And she knew from experience how hard he was to resist when his mind was set.

Just how difficult he was going to be became apparent the next morning when she reached the glade. He was pacing restlessly, kicking up the damp leaves, a deep scowl disfiguring his expression, and it did not lift when he saw her.

"Good," he said briefly, "you are come. I was about to fetch you."

"Do not be absurd," Ginny said, wondering if he was ever going to kiss her. She lifted her face imperatively. "Am I not to be greeted in appropriate fashion, sir?"

Alex pulled her into his arms, kissing her with a fierce hunger, holding her close against him as if he would make her a part of him and thus safe from the depredations of the world. When he released her mouth, he still held her, looking down at her upturned, smiling face. "You are going to be obstinate, aren't you, Virginia?" He shook his head in exasperation. "I expected it, of course."

"I shall only be obstinate if you are," returned Ginny, standing on tiptoe to kiss the corner of his mouth. "Let us not spoil this precious time in argument." Her smile deep-ened, the glow in her eyes shone luminous. "I have a great need to be loved."

"And I to love you," he replied, loosening the strings of her cloak. "It is to be hoped this mantle is thick enough to keep the damp from striking through."

Afterward, he propped himself on an elbow beside her, tracing her lips with one finger. "This is another thing that is going to have to change. Open-air loving is all very well in high summer, but it grows chilly."

Ginny frowned thoughtfully. "I wonder if I could approach the village chief. There is an empty hut that—"

"No, that will not do." Alex silenced her with a finger on her lips. "I am not creeping around Indian villages. Now, just listen to me, my obstinate little gypsy."

Ginny sighed. "I suppose I must listen."

"Yes, you must," he said firmly. "I travel to Jamestown at the end of the week with Robert, to attend the session of the legislature."

"How long will you be gone?" she asked, desolate at the thought of his absence.

"Perhaps two weeks, no longer. While I am away, I will arrange passage for us on the next ship for the Indies—"

"No!" Ginny struggled to sit up. "Do not be foolish."

"I am not being foolish. Will you just do me the courtesy of listening to me?" Alex waited until she had subsided, before continuing. "I have decided what we are to do. Clearly we cannot stay here, and things will not be much better in England. I do not know how I could keep you hidden, and there would be much unpleasantness if our relations were discovered. Therefore—"

"But Alex—"

"Therefore," he said, placing his palm over her mouth, "we shall sail to the Indies, to Barbados, where we may settle, and no one will know who or what we are. I will buy a plantation and—"

Ginny nipped his palm vigorously until he was forced to ungag her. "I listened to you; now you will listen to me. I will not agree to any such plan. You are an Englishman too strongly rooted in your country to be able to leave it and make another life with any happiness. You must have a wife and children, not an adulterous mistress. Yes, I know it is a painful truth, my love," she said more moderately, seeing the hurt in his eyes. "But I could not live with the knowledge of what I had deprived you of, and eventually you would blame me for all the things you could have had, that were your right, that you have fought for with such passionate commitment."

"You think so little of me, of my love for you, that you could believe such a thing?" Alex demanded, getting abruptly to his feet.

"Not of you, or of the love that we share, but I face the truth," whispered Ginny, rising also. "Do not think any more of this, please. We will manage as best we may, until you must return to England."

"And if I tell you that I will carry you off, whether you will or no?"

"You would have to kidnap, bind, and gag me," she said with a light laugh that should not have sounded brittle but did. "Think of the scandal on board ship when you appear—"

"Enough! You have made your point. If you find this a laughing matter, then we clearly do not share the same sense of humor." He picked up her cloak and shook it vigorously. "Put this on, and get back to your husband. I do not wish you to run any further risks."

Ginny walked to the edge of the clearing, then stopped and turned. "Must we part like this? I do not suppose we shall be able to meet again until you return from Jamestown."

"I think it would be better if I did not return," he said coldly.

She shrugged, swallowing the pain. "You must be the best judge of that."

"God damn you, Virginia, for being such a pig-headed little—Oh, come here!" He covered the distance between them in a few long strides, catching her up against him. "I am not giving up, gypsy, I give you fair warning." He kissed her soundly, all the anger disappeared suddenly from his

477

eyes and voice. "You are as unmanageable as ever, but I will find the key, I am determined."

Ginny was too relieved that they would part friends to argue with this sanguine statement, and simply smiled and hugged him. "God keep you, love, until you return."

"And you," he replied, touching the tip of her nose. "I want you to promise me something."

"What is that?" She looked at him warily.

"That you will go to the Harringtons' if that—if your husband becomes violent. They will not turn you away, for all Robert's belief in noninvolvement in the domestic affairs of others."

"I know that," she said. "I will promise you, as I did yesterday, that I will not permit it to happen again."

Alex sighed. "I do not understand what that means."

"Be satisfied, Alex. It is a promise, and you have never had cause to doubt my word."

Having no choice but to accept her statement, Alex kissed her again and waited in the clearing until she was long gone and no chance traveler on the bridle path, in the unlikely circumstances of meeting them both on his way, would make any connection.

Ginny looked with distaste at the veal collops that she was frying in the skillet. She had always enjoyed them for breakfast, particularly with eggs, but these had a most peculiar smell. Her nose wrinkled as a wave of nausea washed over her. Dropping the skillet on the table in front of the startled Giles, she fled outside to rid herself of whatever it was could be causing her irritated stomach. When she returned to the kitchen, it was to notice with relief that Giles had helped himself to the contents of the skillet.

"What's the matter with you?" he inquired. "You're as full of color as a bowl of whey."

"I must have eaten something that has disagreed with me," she replied shortly. "We need more wood. Would you take the cart and bring some back from the cleared pasture? We could ask Teddy from Harringtons' to split the logs if you do not feel able to do it yourself." Had the last statement sounded critical? She waited for the accusation of unreasonableness, of carping.

"How can I split logs?" Giles demanded. "My hip's plaguing like the devil in this damp. I suppose you are going off into the woods again?"

"When I have done what I have to here, I shall go simpling," she replied. "You do benefit, on occasion, from the results of that activity."

"I'd like to know what else you do in the woods. It's a fine place for whoring," he sneered.

Ginny's hand closed over the handle of the skillet, and the sudden silence took on a menacing quality, Giles looked at her, reading her mind. Then he laughed, pushed back the bench, and stood up, walking out of the house without a backward glance. Ginny pressed her fingertips to her lips as that feeling of self-disgust slopped over her again. She could do nothing to prevent his making those remarks, and he now knew how much they upset her. Knowing that, he would rarely lose an opportunity to taunt her although Ginny was convinced he did not believe the accusations. What frightened her was how increasingly often the temptation to tear him apart with the truth threatened to become irresistible.

She felt so tired these last few days, leaden, her usual energy dissipated almost before she rose in the morning. Her stomach would not behave itself in spite of all her physicking. Perhaps it was loneliness and deprivation, she told herself with a tiny, self-deprecating smile. Alex had been away for over two weeks, and it was quite shameless how her body ached for the joyous stimulation it had become accustomed to. Perhaps she would visit Susannah this morning. Lizzie could set the house to rights when she returned from milking the cows. Robert may well have sent a message to his wife saying when to expect them. He was always rather considerate in those matters, sending news with anyone who might be coming down the river past Harrington Hundred.

A visit to Susannah was more appealing than simpling,

and Ginny went upstairs to change her kersey working gown for a skirt and bodice of quilted calico. She winced slightly, hooking the bodice over her tender breasts. The time of the month would presumably be upon her soon. . . . The time of the month . . . Ginny sat abruptly upon the bed, wrestling with an errant memory. That inconvenience was such a matter of inevitable routine, she rarely bothered to take note of its coming . . . except inasfar as it interfered with . . . Alex. Think, she told herself, fighting down the panic. It had been upon her just before Alex had arrived at Harrington Hundred, some six weeks ago. But surely since . . . No, not since. But it was impossible. She was barren. One hand unconsciously stroked over her breasts, over her belly, her mind turned inward, and Ginny knew with absolute certainty that she was not barren, that she was with child . . . Alex's child.

There was a moment of overpowering sweetness, of indescribable joy, then the hollowness of despair. What was she to do? What could she possibly do? A child, a bastard child, was growing in her womb, and her husband had not lain with her since the renewal of their marriage. The thoughts swirled, implications that she did not dare explore hanging on the periphery of her mind. She could not bear this child and continue to live with her husband. But she could not leave him and condemn Alex to the life of an outcast in Barbados. She could go away, leave her husband, leave Alex before her pregnancy began to show, bear the child somewhere . . . where? There was nowhere to go in this new land where, in the few civilized places hacked out of the wilderness, everyone knew everyone else . . . except to the Indians. And why would they take her? And how could she live amongst them, supposing that they would receive her? And how could she bring up the child of a Redfern and a Marshall to be a painted savage?

There was only one answer—a black and dreadful answer—and she could not . . . *would* not accept it. Not yet, not until she had thought more clearly; not until the panic had receded and she could examine alternatives realistically.

Ginny got off the bed, smoothed down her skirt, went to

the mirror to tidy her hair. She examined her face carefully and was surprised to find that she did not look any different; a little paler, perhaps, but there were no other signs of the monumental thing that had happened to her, of this other life burgeoning within her own. The challenge now would be to behave as if nothing was different, to hold this secret unto herself . . . to keep it even from Alex.

She set off for Harrington Hundred five minutes later, finding a peaceful respite in the solitary paddle through the creek on this moist November morning where curlews and plovers rose above the marshes and fish rippled the smooth brown surface of the water. The crack of a musket sent the waterfowl diving among the bullrushes. Someone was out hunting for his dinner. The creek widened as it flowed into the James River, and Ginny paddled around the corner, looking ahead down river to the landing stage of Harrington Hundred.

More bustle than usual seemed in evidence, men unloading from the sailboat that had taken the master of Harrington Hundred to Jamestown some two weeks previously. So they were home, Ginny thought, pausing, her paddle raised in indecision. She could always turn back. No one would have seen her approach as yet, and it was perhaps not discreet to descend upon her relatives in the midst of a happy reunion. But if Robert had returned, then Alex would also be there. She paddled on.

"Why, Ginny, what a pleasant surprise." Susannah hastened down the garden at the sight of the figure walking up from the landing stage. "Robert is just returned. You must come in and hear all the news of Jamestown."

"I do not wish to intrude." Ginny smiled apologetically. "I would not have come had I known, but I was feeling powerfully in need of a little quiet gossip."

Susannah laughed, taking her arm, ushering her into the house. "Well, you shall hear all the gossip of the town, which will be much more interesting. Robert, look who has come to visit."

"Welcome, Cousin." Robert greeted her as warmly as his wife had done. Ginny responded, but her eyes sought Alex

481

even as she questioned her host about his journey, accepted a glass of ginger wine and a little sugar cake.

"Did your guest not return with you, Robert?" she asked, after a decent interval.

"Indeed he did," Robert reassured her heartily. "And I have prevailed upon him to spend the winter with us. He was making inquiries about ships to the Indies, but I am happy to say that I persuaded him to postpone his departure until the spring. The journey will be much less tempestuous then. Ah, there you are, Alex. The ladies have missed you, it would appear."

"I am honored, but not such a ninnyhammer as to believe such a thing." Alex bowed, a polite smile masking his intent examination of Ginny. She looked a little pale, he thought, but otherwise quite well.

"I understand you are to remain at Harrington Hundred for the winter, sir," Ginny said, curtsying.

"My host has been most kind in his insistence," he said. "Unless some matter of urgency takes me to the Indies before the spring, then I shall gladly avail myself of his hospitality."

It was very clear to Ginny that the urgent matter referred to her capitulation in his plan, and in the general turmoil of her thoughts she was hard pressed to answer him as lightly as the social circumstances required.

When she took her leave an hour later, Alex, with entirely natural ease, offered to accompany her to the landing stage. Ginny accepted with a slight inclination of her head, and they left Robert and Susannah deep in a domestic discussion concerning their brood of children.

"Has all been well?" Alex asked, once they were outside.

"Perfectly," she replied, "except that I have missed you quite dreadfully."

"And I you." He sighed. "This is the very devil, chicken. I want to hold you, and I cannot."

"I will meet you in the glade tomorrow," she offered.

"We shall catch an inflammation of the lungs," Alex grumbled. "It is November, for God's sake!"

"What is a little cold and damp to a soldier?" Ginny teased, untying the canoe. Alex would never know what an effort it was to maintain the light tone, but the total impossibility of their situation now loomed so large and undeniable that she dared not yield an inch.

"It rather depends on the activity the soldier has in mind," Alex retorted, putting his hand in the small of her back, pretending to steady her as she stepped into the canoe. For a second she leaned backward, into his palm, and the thought of what might have been had fate not chosen to intervene blanketed them for a dizzying tormented instant. Then Ginny took her place in the canoe, and Alex turned away, too full of an unfocused rage, of the absolute certainty that he must do something, of the frustrating knowledge that he had only one plan, and it was one Ginny rejected, to stay and see her off.

But do something he would. Perhaps he could provoke that husband of hers to a duel; perhaps Giles Courtney could meet with an accident in the woods. It would not be an unusual happenstance. And then he could court the widow . . . and live in peace and trust with Virginia Courtney, keeping from her, of all people, the fact that he had removed her husband in such a manner? He laughed mirthlessly. Jed had told him how she had contemplated leaving her husband to die on the battlefield, a mild sin of omission, easily explained even to an active conscience. And that humanitarian healer had been unable to do it, even knowing what it would mean. No, she would not forgive him for such a deed, even in the certain knowledge that his action had been the last resort of a desperate man. No, there had to be another way. He went back to the house, for the moment spared the fact that the impossible dilemma had taken another twist, one that involved more than an illicit love.

483

Chapter Twenty-nine

Ginny finished the explanation of the situation and what she needed, watching the old woman's reactions. It was impossible to go into the subtleties of the situation when one was reduced to a few words and plentiful gestures, but she was confident she had got the message across. Now she looked for a sign of repugnance, or at least of deep, moral disapproval, but the woman's countenance hardly changed. She nodded briefly and went to the back of the shelter, bringing out a hide flask. The contents she tipped into a small gourd, then added a little gray powder and shavings from the bark of the slippery elm.

Ginny took the final mixture when it had been replaced in the hide flask, understood that she was to take two doses, one at night, the next the following morning. She could expect pain, some bleeding within a few hours. If this did not happen, she was to come back. There were other ways.

She made her way back to the woods, the flask in the pocket of her apron. Still she did not know whether she would take the medicine woman's potion, the very thought of it filled her with revulsion; but however hard she had tossed and turned, no alternative solution had come to her in the dark reaches of the night. At least, now, she had an answer at hand, however unpalatable it might be.

"Got you!" Alex sprang out from the trees behind her, catching her round the waist and swinging her in the air.

"You have been visiting your Indians again."

"There is no reason why I should not, is there?"

"No, I suppose not." He set her down. "It is no more dangerous than being taken for a witch. But I do feel most uneasy when I have no control over your movements." He scratched his head, smiling ruefully, "That will annoy you, of course, but it is true, nevertheless."

"I have never given you the right to control my movements," Ginny told him, amused rather than annoyed.

"Maybe not, but I have assumed it often enough." Shared memories held them for a moment; then Ginny felt the flask in her pocket, and the desolation crept over her again. It showed in her eyes, and Alex took her free hand. "Something more than the usual is troubling you, chicken. It has been so for the last week."

"Nonsense, unless it be the need to contrive some trysting place other than this forest," she said, averting her head.

"That problem I have solved." Alex took her face and turned it toward him. "What is troubling you?"

"Nothing, I told you. How have you solved the problem?"

"I am not allowing you to get away with that, Ginny. I feel impotent enough at the moment as it is, without being dismissed so carelessly when I know my concern is well founded. Something is troubling you, and you will tell me what it is."

Ginny clutched the flask in her pocket as if it were a talisman. All she had to do was go home and take the potion; then there would be no need to tell Alex or anyone else. If she could just withstand the desperate need to share the problem, to bury herself in his arms and let him come up with a solution. But she had to be strong. It was so much better this way. There were no solutions, and it would not be fair to increase Alex's burden of hopeless frustration.

"What is this that you are holding?" Frowning, Alex drew her hand from her pocket, opening her fingers to take the flask from her. "You have been clinging onto it as if it were a lifeline."

"Nothing," Ginny repeated faintly. "It is just some medicine."

485

"For what? Are you unwell? Why must you go to the Indians for medicine?" The questions came fast and anxious, as if Alex somehow sensed the shape of the tragedy waiting in the wings.

"It is just some physic for my stomach," she said. "My own medicine has not alleviated it, so I thought to try —"

"It is more than that," he insisted. "Tell me the truth. Are you ill?"

"No, I am not ill. Please, I do not wish to talk of this any longer."

"Well, *I* do," he said firmly. "God forgive me, Ginny, but if you do not tell me the truth quickly, I shall shake it out of you!"

"Why? I do not understand why this is so important to you," she cried in despair, recognizing the last vestiges of restraint slipping away from her under this relentless pressure. "You do not want to know, I promise you. It is better that you do not."

Alex went white. "What could possibly be better kept from me? Quickly, Ginny, I cannot be patient for much longer." His hands were on her shoulders, gripping in forceful emphasis.

"I am carrying a child," she said quietly, and his hands left her shoulders.

"Whose?" Alex rasped, his voice barely audible, his face ghastly.

Only then did Ginny fully realize the torment Alex suffered knowing that she belonged to another man, knowing that Giles had the right and the opportunity to possess her whenever and wherever he pleased. It was a torment every bit as fierce as that her husband suffered when he thought of the months of her unfaithfulness, but Alex had never allowed her to see it, had borne it as his own private hell, just as she had borne her own.

Now she said simply, "Yours. My husband has not been capable of claiming his conjugal rights since our marriage was —" She gave a short, ironic laugh. "Was resurrected. It is that failure that causes the violence of his bitterness —" She stopped. Making excuses for Giles did not seem relevant at the moment.

Alex looked down at her for long minutes, his expression a curious mixture of amazed wonder and great joy. Ginny recognized the emotions as being the same as her own in the first moments of knowledge, and she waited for the change that would sweep through him, wiping out the joy, when he realized the full, horrendous implications of the situation. But it didn't come. Instead, he wrapped her in his arms and kissed her with fierce passion.

"You bring me such joy, sweetheart," he whispered against her mouth. "It is what I would have wished for, of all things."

"What can you mean?" Her voice was a mere thread as she stared up at him, aghast that he did not seem to understand. "My husband will know that it cannot be his child that I bear. He would not be able to live with that—"

"He will not have to," Alex said, suddenly frowning. "You will be leaving him now, long before your condition becomes obvious. I would prefer you not to take a sea voyage, but it cannot be helped, and the journey to the Indies is not too long—"

"Alex, stop, in the name of pity. You do not know what you are saying. You would live as an outcast on a plantation in Barbados while I breed you bastards? Living in fear every minute of the day that the next ship will bring someone who knows our story—who knows Giles—who . . ."

"Enough," he said, his voice very quiet. "What strategy have *you* formed then, Virginia?" She was quite unable to answer him, to look him in the eye, even as her soul rebelled at the injustice of these guilt feelings when she had attempted to spare him, to take the whole burden of pain and decision upon her own shoulders. "Well?" he asked as softly as before. "You must have a plan, my dear Virginia. Will you not share it?"

Ginny winced at the sardonic note, the harshness in the green-brown eyes, but still she could not manage to speak the truth. "I had not decided anything, yet," she whispered.

"You lie!" Alex stated, looking down at the flask that he still held. "You have been to the Indians for medicine for your stomach, is that not what you said? Well, is it not?" he

487

demanded when she kept silent. With quiet deliberation, he took the stopper off the flask and upturned it, allowing the contents to spill upon the ground.

"You do not understand —" Ginny said, her face white as milk, her eyes huge. "Can you not see that there is no other way?"

"My vision is not as blinkered as yours," he said coldly. "Understand this, Virginia Courtney. You will not destroy my child."

"Then what am I to do?" she cried. "I do not wish to do such a dreadful thing but I would not destroy *you*."

Alex wrestled with a seemingly limitless fury. He could not at this point begin to understand why she would have chosen such a desperate solution, such a lonely solution that excluded him, denied him any rights, a solution that would surely endanger her.

"I am too angry to discuss this with you in a reasonable manner," he said eventually, hardening his heart as the gray eyes swam and she turned away, her shoulders sagging. "Come with me now. I want to show you something." Without touching her, or waiting to see that she followed, he strode out of the glade. Ginny went with him because she could think of no good reason not to. She felt cold and empty, no longer able to react with any feeling to his anger. If he did not understand, then she no longer had the energy to make him.

In a small clearing, Alex stopped, and Ginny stared at the small hut made, like the Indian cabins, of woven swamp reads and marsh grass. "Where did that come from?" she asked stupidly.

"I found it a few days ago," he said, "when I was searching for an answer to this open-air existence. Presumably, it belonged to some renegade, but it has been abandoned for some time. I have made a few improvements." He held open the flap for her, and Ginny slipped inside. It was, to all intents and purposes, an Indian home, with animal furs piled on a woven frame to make a bed, and a central fireplace. The earth floor had been swept and covered with hides, and skins hung on the walls to keep the cold and wind from penetrating the cracks.

"Come here tomorrow," Alex instructed her in the even tone she had heard him use so often to one or other of his officers — the tone of voice of one who could not imagine having his orders questioned. "By that time, I should have calmed down sufficiently to talk about this rationally, and you will have had enough time to realize that my solution is the only one, and we may discuss how best to put it into operation."

"If that is what you want," Ginny said dully. "I will make no further objections." She turned and left the hut, too dispirited even to bid him farewell.

Alex swore vigorously. Capitulation he had wanted, but not in that dull, spiritless fashion. There was no pleasure, no satisfaction in such a victory. He wanted to plan with joy for a joyous future, but how could he do that, when Ginny saw only disaster ahead?

In the next days, she continued to resist all his efforts to infuse their meetings with hope. She came to the hut obediently, sat on the pile of furs, and listened when he told her that a Dutch ship would be leaving from Jamestown at the end of the month. He explained how he would leave Harringtons' a few days early, ostensibly to reach Jamestown in ample time for the sailing, but he would come back for her in secret. She would slip away from her house in the canoe, and he would meet her down river.

Ginny listened in silence, made no objections, offered no suggestions, until, one cold, gray afternoon, Alex, at the end of his patience, accused her of deliberately trying to sabotage his plan with this studied indifference. How could he trust her to perform her part when he did not even know whether she had heard a word he had said?

"I do not need to sabotage it," Ginny responded with the first flash of spirit in days. "It will not work, anyway. Do you think Giles is going to sit quietly by while his wife runs off with another man? Do you think he is not going to know whom I am with? How can we take ship together in

Jamestown without the entire colony knowing of it with the next canoe down river?"

"There is nothing we can do about that, and it does not matter in the end. We shall be long gone and far away; the scandal will not touch us."

"You live in cloud cuckoo land," Ginny retorted. "Giles will not let me leave him. You do not know what he has become. He is determined to be revenged upon me for my faithlessness when I thought he was dead. I asked him to release me at Preston, to think of me as dead, but he would not because he would have his revenge. I could not be accused of deliberate betrayal of my vows in the days of the war, because he was believed dead, but Giles sees that as no mitigation. How do you think he will react when he discovers that I have knowingly committed adultery? He grows more bitter by the hour, and he will pursue us to the Indies and beyond for as long as his health holds."

"Do you think me no match for Giles Courtney?" Alex asked, sitting beside her on the furs and drawing her against him.

"What would you do? Commit murder? What possible happiness could we have, founded on such a base?"

Alex sighed, fighting the insidious creeping realization that he was going to lose this battle. He had tried to push through her dull indifference, to impose his will by ignoring the opposition, but in the end it was not possible. "Sweetheart, you must help me," he said gently. "You will not accept my plans, and the one you have proposed I absolutely forbid, and it is something that I have the right to forbid. Is it not?" He turned her chin toward him. "Is it not, Ginny, a matter in which I have some rights?"

Slowly, she nodded her head. "There is one other possibility. I will tell Giles that I am leaving him, but not the true reason. He must know nothing of you. I will tell him that I intend to take ship for Holland and throw myself upon the mercy of my cousin Edmund whom I believe to be with Charles II in exile."

"And he will let you go?"

"Not willingly," Ginny said. "But short of imprisoning me,

490

he cannot prevent me, and I will be committing no crime. He knows I have some jewelry of my mother's that will pay my passage, so I do not need to rely upon him for funds. I cannot be certain, but I think that so long as he sees only a dismal future for me, he will not pursue me. If he thought for one minute that I was running away with a lover, he would hound me into the grave, his or mine. But the thought of my facing a lonely sea voyage, penurious exile in a hostile land, the uncertainty of finding my cousin there, even supposing he still lives . . . I think he will say good riddance. I am no good for him, after all, simply a constant reminder of failure. He will be happier with his bottle and without a scolding wife. He can put it about that ill health has taken me home, so he need not lose face."

"But again you assume the full burden," Alex protested. "You will be in danger from him, and you will allow me no opportunity to share the risk."

"I must leave with his agreement, if we are to have any chance of a life together," Ginny said with quiet insistence. "Even so, we cannot go back to England, and you must live in exile because of me—"

"You must not say that. It is not because of *you*. It is because of *us*. And it is a sacrifice I shall count for naught." He ran his flattened palm over her belly. "I love you, Virginia, and this child of ours must have the chance to grow up in that love."

"Then you will let me do this my way? For it is the only chance we have to achieve that happiness." She spoke with quiet determination, showing him a face suddenly serene in the aftermath of having made the only decision possible. It was a plan that would risk all on one throw. Once Giles knew she was intending to leave him, if he did not react as she gambled, then he could prevent her physically and with the full support of the law. A man was entitled to keep a potential runaway wife at home. But what choice was there?

"When will you talk to him?" The question signified agreement. "It would be best to wait until just before you must leave for the sailing."

"Yes." Ginny shuddered at the thought of continuing to

491

share a roof with Giles after such a confrontation. It would be utterly impossible. "Yes, I will wait until the day I intend to go."

"You will not do this thing without telling me first, though? I must have your word on that." He drew her across his lap, holding her head in the crook of his arm. "Your word, Ginny."

"My word," she said, knowing how dreadfully difficult it must be for this man of action to surrender control, to wait upon the sidelines while she risked all.

"Then I will agree because I must." Gently Alex laid her down on the furs, dropping to his knees beside her. The hut was warm from the crackling fire, safe and enclosed in the deserted glade in the midst of the forest. But they had never yet made love there. There had been too much tension in the last days, too great a sense of foreboding for the ultimate expression of love to have a part. Now, there was peace between them, the sense of inevitability wrapping them in a silken cocoon.

Ginny smiled, stretched languidly, lifting her body to help him as Alex undressed her carefully, laying her bare in the fire glow, her skin gleaming against the rich darkness of the furs. Leisurely, he kissed his way down her body, leaving scarcely an inch of skin untouched, and when he reached her feet, he turned her over and began again, moving up her back to the nape of her neck. Little prickles of pleasure danced over her skin as he stroked her bottom, slipping his hand between her thighs, chuckling with satisfaction when she began to squirm with delight, the soft fur beneath her caressing with every wriggle of her body.

Ginny cast herself adrift on the sea of sensation, following the dictates of her body and of Alex who followed his fancy and his desire that afternoon, playing with her and upon her. Kneeling behind her, he drew her up onto her hands and knees, his hands caressing her belly, holding her gently as he entered her, stroking her stomach with the same rhythm that stroked within, as if imparting his presence to the life she carried. She dropped her head and shoulders, and the silky fur rubbed against her cheek, her eyes were tight shut on a warm red darkness, her mind was emptied of all but the tranquillity of this surrender, and when his completion throbbed and filled her, the tranquillity expanded to contain her, body and soul, in the ephemeral moment that for that moment seemed to be infinite.

It was late in the afternoon when Alex stamped out the fire and they left the hut. Ginny looked up at the sky, darkening above the bare branches of the trees. She would be lucky to reach home before dusk, and Giles, if he was not already drunk, would be bellowing for his dinner, particularly if he considered that he had put in a day's work in the fields. Lizzie was spending the night at Harrington Hundred, nursing her mother who had come down with a fever, so dinner preparations would not have advanced beyond the stage Ginny had left them when she had come out to meet Alex.

Oh, well, Ginny thought with a shrug, he could always find something to scream about. It would give him inordinate satisfaction to have a genuine grievance for once. She would grovel in a thoroughly satisfactory fashion, and, while he would not appear appeased, he would retreat into the corner with only a few residual mutters. She felt far too peaceful and fulfilled to be disturbed by anything Giles could say or do tonight, and the buoyant thought that she would have to endure him for only a short time longer brought a smile to her lips as she pushed open the cottage door.

The smile died as she looked around the darkened room. The candles had not been lit, and the fire was almost out. Of Giles, there was no sign. She lit the candles, stoked up the fire, and went outside to the woodpile to replenish the empty log basket.

"Where in the name of Beelzebub have you been?" Giles reared up out of the darkness, and Ginny screamed with shock, dropping the logs.

"Giles, you startled me!" Her heart pounded uncomfortably. "You were not in the house."

"I have been searching for you," he gritted, seizing her arm. "Where have you been all this time? I have been waiting for nigh on three hours."

"Wait-Waiting three hours for your dinner?" Ginny stuttered in bewilderment, still shocked. "But it is only five o'clock. We do not eat dinner before half-past four o'clock . . ." Even as she said this, she knew that it was not the answer. Giles had not been waiting three hours for his dinner; he had been waiting for her.

"Where have you been for more than three hours?" The pale-blue eyes glinted strangely in the dark, and her heart sank. He was drunk enough to be aggressive, but not enough to grow confused by a briskly matter-of-fact tale that would imply he was behaving unreasonably to question it. He was also a long way from falling into a stupor. "How long *have* you been away from the house? You could have left any time after I did this morning. What have you been doing?"

"Let us go back inside," Ginny said in a carefully reasonable tone. "It is surely not necessary to conduct this conversation out here in the cold and the dark." She bent to gather up the dropped logs, her heart thudding again as she realized how vulnerable the movement made her, but all she could think was that she must not show her fear. "Will you carry these, husband?" She place two logs in his arms, catching him so by surprise that he hung onto them. Picking up the remainder, she marched ahead of him into the now warm and welcoming kitchen.

"Are you going to answer me?" Giles threw the logs into the basket, sending up a cloud of dust and wood chips. "I want to know where you've been."

"Am I not to be permitted to leave the house, then?" Ginny inquired, setting a pan of sweetbreads upon the fire. "I have been known to visit Susannah occasionally."

"Don't give me that insolent tongue!" Giles swung her away from the fire, his face contorted with bitter loathing. How he hated her — as much as she hated him! The thought flashed through her mind with all the force of illumination. Why had she never realized the full power of that hatred? And the answer came — because she had been too busy thinking of her own.

"You have not been at Harringtons'," he was saying,

494

"because I was there myself earlier. They all have the fever."

"All of them?" Ginny asked, trying to keep her voice calm, to steer the conversation into everyday channels. "Susannah and the children also?"

"So you have not been there, then?" The pale eyes shone with triumph.

Ginny sighed, twitching out of his hold to turn back to the fire, shaking the skillet to spread the butter beneath the sweetbreads. "I did not say that I had been. I said only that I did go there on occasion."

"Do you think to deceive me with your devious tongue, you lying jade!" Giles hissed, grabbing her again. "Who have you been with?"

"Giles, let me go, please. I am trying to cook your dinner, and the butter will burn."

"God damn the dinner! Who have you been whoring with, woman!"

Something snapped. The long months of patient endurance rose up before her, months when she had fettered the free spirit of Virginia Redfern, the fearless, challenging Virginia Courtney who had trailed the drum for love of Parliament's general, who had allowed nothing and no one to prevent her from carrying out her duty. Now, in these months she had bowed her head beneath the abuse of a man not fit to tie her shoelaces, had done all she could to placate him, had endured the public mortification of his drunken vilifications, all because he was her husband and she had meekly accepted the yoke fate had laid upon her shoulders. In the last week she had been stretched upon the rack of unbelievable tension, not knowing which way to turn to protect those she loved from this monstrous creature who called himself her husband. And quite suddenly, Virginia could take no more. The careful plan outlined that afternoon to Alex went for nothing. It was time she stood up for herself.

"I am no whore, husband, but perhaps you should know the truth."

Giles lost all his color, and his hands dropped from her as he backed away. "What truth?"

495

"You have accused me of having a lover often enough. Does it surprise you to know that it is the truth?" she said coldly. "Come now, do not look so devastated. Why would you be always accusing me, if you did not believe it to be true?"

"Who?" he said hoarsely. "I'll kill him."

Ginny shook her head. "I do not think so, Giles." She felt amazingly calm, amazingly in control. Giles was not frightening, he was pathetic, a paper goblin revealed by the truth. If she had stood up to him before, who knows how different things could have been? Ginny, in this moment of euphoria, forgot all the occasions when she *had* faced him down with a scornful tongue or an icy dignity. And she forgot what had happened on the one occasion when, feeling as bitter as she did now, she had fought him with his own weapons.

Then Giles began to speak in a low, intense voice; vile words poured from his lips twisted with venom. Ginny felt suddenly sick as she listened, unable to block out the vileness directed at her, contaminated by it just by hearing it.

"Stop, for the love of God," she cried at last, breaking the dreadful spell, pressing her hands over her ears, and turning to run for the stairs.

Her movement broke some spell for Giles, also. When she turned to run, she was no longer in control. He lunged for her, twisting her arms behind her back. Terrified by the intense hatred in the pale eyes, Ginny fought like a demon, kicking at him, butting his chest with her head. He was not greatly stronger than she, weakened as he was by dissolution and ill health, but his frenzied fury brought him dominance. When he hit her the first time, Ginny knew with sick certainty that what she had sworn would never happen to her again was going to be repeated. The second blow made her ears ring, and with a superhuman effort born of frantic desperation, she managed to twist her head round and sink her teeth into the soft fleshy upper part of the arm holding her wrists.

Giles yelled as her teeth sank deeper, and she tasted blood. Then her wrists were suddenly released, and she sprang away from him, toward the door, recognizing that there would be no safety upstairs where she would simply be trapped. With the bellow of a wounded bull, he charged at her, slamming the door over her head as she wrenched it open. Ginny ducked beneath his arm, running to the far side of the table, looking wildly around for some means of escape. There was none. Giles advanced on her, his fists clenched, the foul words still spewing from his mouth. He was quite crazed, Ginny thought with a nauseous jolt, swallowing the bitter bile as it rose in her throat. She was in the same room with a madman, one not accessible by words and reason, one who had already proved himself capable of blind savagery when his mind turned in this way.

In a kind of mesmerized horror, she saw him pick up the carving knife from his side of the table. He was going to kill her. They were alone in this little house, their nearest neighbors a mile away by canoe, no passers-by, no one to hear a scream, a whimper — it could not be happening. A scorching smell suddenly infiltrated her petrified trance. The sweetbreads were burning in the now blackened butter in the heavy iron skillet behind her. Stealthily, Ginny stepped backward, not taking her eyes off Giles as he edged round the table, the knife gripped in his fist. Stretching an arm behind her, her hand closed over the handle of the skillet. It was hot, searing her flesh, but she ignored the pain, in fact hardly felt it, as slowly she brought the pan to the front. As Giles pounced, she hurled the scalding contents of the pan in his face. The knife whistled down, slicing her forearm. Giles screamed, blinded by the burning butter dripping down his face, but he still held the knife and came at her again. She hit him, using every vestige of strength born of desperation, bringing the skillet down upon his head.

A startled look pierced the fanatical blue eyes. Giles teetered, then fell into the fireplace. His head struck the andiron with a sickening thud, and the knife dropped to the floor from his slackened grip.

An eerie silence filled the room, broken only by the incongruous, almost indecently cheerful crackle of the logs.

Ginny knelt beside the still figure, placed her fingers on the pulse point in his neck. There was nothing, not even a tremor. His face was waxen, the eyes wide open, staring at the ceiling, a purple bruised lump on his temple the only sign of injury.

Ginny crept backward, away from the dead man, and crouched against the table leg as she fought the sickness of aftermath for long minutes. Shivers went through her with invincible repetition so that even her hands shook as if palsied, and her mind was a blank void denying all reality.

But slowly life and warmth returned, the shivering ceased, and her mind cleared to look squarely at the fact that she had been responsible, directly or indirectly was merely a matter of semantics, for the death of her husband. In the eyes of the law, she had killed him. There were no witnesses to the provocation, no one had seen the sequence of events, there was only her word — and the blood dripping from her slashed arm and the marks of the two blows to her face. Now she needed Alex more than she had ever needed him. In this matter, he would know exactly what to do. It required the soldier's clear head to steer a path through this tangle.

Ginny got to her feet, bandaged her cut arm with less than her usual care, found her cloak, and went out into the night. It was now full night, a weak moon fuzzed by clouds the only light to aid her as she untied the canoe and stepped in. But the darkness was reassuring as she paddled as silently as possible, only the faintest swish as the paddle broke the surface of the creek. She must try to find Alex without alerting the Harringtons, but if she could not, then she would have to throw herself upon Robert's mercy, trusting that his knowledge of his cousin's true character would weigh sufficiently with him to allow them to cover up the truth. If not, she supposed she would have to stand trial, but at least Robert and Susannah would be witnesses to her present condition, and they would not doubt her word. Maybe her pregnancy would bring sympathy and mercy; no one was to know that it was not her dead husband's child.

These thoughts went round and round in her head, but

what really mattered at this point was to find Alex. She couldn't manage on her own any longer, and only the thought of his arms, strong and safe around her, his voice, calm and even making the decisions, gave her the fortitude to keep going.

Ginny tied up against the bank, a hundred yards before reaching the landing stage. She did not want to advertise her arrival unless there was no choice. She approached the house through the trees, her feet noiseless on the damp, mossy ground. Only one light showed in the house, from the small parlor at the rear where Robert was wont to work on his accounts. Then she remembered Giles saying the family had the fever, presumably taken from the nursemaid, Lizzie's mother. Were they all abed, then? She crept across the grass to the lighted window, crouching for a minute under the sill to catch her breath. Her heart seemed to be drumming loud enough to summon a brigade to drill. Cautiously, she stood on tiptoe, peeping into the room, and nearly sank down again with relief. Only Alex was there, perusing some documents with that intent frown she knew so well. She tapped on the glass, too softly obviously, since he did not look up. Biting her lip hard, she rapped again, sharply this time.

Alex heard the noise and in his absorption put it down to a bird. Then remembered that it was night. He looked toward the window and saw a ghastly white face, shrouded in the hood of a cloak, enormous eyes full of mute appeal. The chair fell to the floor with a clatter as he jumped to his feet, hastening to the window. But Ginny shook her head frantically, pointing at the door. Clearly, she wanted him to come outside, and secretly. But why had she not approached the house by the front door like any law-abiding, respectable citizen? He took the branched candlestick from the mantel and went out into the darkened hall, setting the candle down on the hall table as he slipped the bolts on the great door, which he pulled gently closed behind him.

He ran round the house to the back. Ginny was sitting on the ground beneath the window, curled up in her cloak, and to his dismay made no move to get up as he reached her.

499

"What has happened?" he demanded, anxiety making his voice harsh. "Are you hurt?"

"A little, but not much," she whispered back. "Let us go into the trees. No one must see me here." She held her hands up to him.

"Whyever not?" Taking her hands, he pulled her upright, feeling the sudden dead weight of her, as if she had no strength of her own. Her hands were like ice. "You must come into the house," he insisted, but she shook her head violently, with a little cry of distress. Deciding that for the moment, he must do as she wished, Alex lifted her up and carried her toward the darkness of the trees. Once there, he set her down, although keeping a supporting arm around her, and pushed back the hood from her face. What he saw brought a violent oath to his lips. "I am going to kill that whoreson," he said in a flat voice. "And to hell with the consequences."

"No . . . no." Ginny shook her head, stuttering slightly. "There is no need. . . . He is already dead."

"*What?*" Alex stared at her in the darkness. "What are you saying, Ginny?"

"I have killed him," she whispered. "Hold me, please."

Immediately, he held her tight against his chest. "You must tell me exactly what has happened, chicken. I do not understand anything yet, but unless I much mistake the matter, I had better do so without delay."

Ginny was instantly soothed, instantly confident that everything was going to be all right, that she had played her part and could abdicate the minute she laid the full burden upon the soldier's broad shoulders. She told him the whole, sparing no detail, right up to the moment when she had knocked on the parlor window.

Alex heard her out in silence, although his mouth tightened ominously, and the green-brown eyes were cold and hard as quartz chips. "You are a most untrustworthy planner, Virginia," he said when she had done. "After everything that passed between us this afternoon, after you gave me your word that you would do nothing without telling me first—"

500

"You are angry with me!" Ginny looked up at him in utter disbelief. "After—after . . ."

"Shhh, sweeting, I am sorry." Full of remorse, Alex stroked her hair, pulling her head down against his chest again. "It was only because I am so filled with horror at what has happened to you. I would have done anything to have spared you." He continued to hold her, stroking gently but now almost absently as he stared into the darkness, formulating a strategy. "Yes . . . yes, that will serve the purpose," he said with sudden decision. "Where is the canoe?"

"Over yonder." Ginny pointed through the trees. "What are we going to do?"

"*You*, my love, are going to do exactly as I tell you, for once. We have a long night ahead of us, but it will go all the quicker if you do not hinder me with objections or questions. I wish I could leave you here, tucked up in bed, but unfortunately that is not possible." All the while he was speaking, he was bundling her down to the river, helping her into the canoe where she sat huddled in her cloak while Alex paddled back to the cottage.

"Inside, in the warm," he instructed briskly, when she hung back outside the door. "There will be nothing worse in there than you have seen already." His almost callous tone was exactly what Ginny needed, stiffening her resolve so that she was able to enter the kitchen with barely a tremor. Everything was exactly as she had left it. "Go upstairs and lie down," Alex directed, but she shook her head.

"I do not wish to be alone."

He nodded. "Very well, then sit down by the fire." He picked up a flagon from the dresser. "Is this brandy?" When she nodded, he poured a tot and passed it to her. "Sip that." Ginny took it, sipped, and felt the slow warmth of relaxation creep through her.

"What are you going to do?" she asked, watching curiously as he moved around the kitchen, building up the fire to a roaring blaze, tipping over furniture, emptying out the contents of grain and corn sacks and the flour barrel.

"Preparing a funeral pyre," he replied shortly. "I need

material, sheets, linens."

"Upstairs, in the linen press. I will fetch them." She half-rose, but Alex told her sharply to stay where she was, so she resumed her seat while he took the rickety stairs three at a time.

"Why will I not be burned in the fire, also?" Ginny inquired. The question seemed of some interest, even in her state of bemused abstraction. "And how did the fire start?"

"Renegade attack," Alex told her succinctly. "There was one over by the Grove plantation three weeks ago, so it will cause no great surprise. You happened to be out of the house at the time of the attack, hid in the woods, petrified, until the attackers had gone, then you fled through the woods to Harringtons'. Your bruised face is easily explained by running into tree branches or some such." He looked down at the dead man for the first time. "There is blood on that knife."

"My arm. But it is not a severe cut." Ginny moved her bandaged arm out of the covering cloak. A bleak look shivered in Alex's eyes, but he said nothing, merely continued with his task.

"I am going outside now, to release the ducks and chickens, and turn the horses loose."

"I cannot stay in here alone with—"

"Come along, then." He had no need of further expansion and took her hand, leading her outside. "Release the fowl. I will drive the cows and horses across the garden; that should leave it convincingly trampled."

Ginny did as he said, and wondered at the perversity of human nature that she should feel a sorrowing reluctance at this systematic destruction of everything she had worked for in the last few months, when that destruction was going to repaint the picture of her life.

At last, it was finished to Alex's satisfaction. The herb and vegetable garden was a churned mess of mud, the fowl house was ready for the tinder box, the lean-to emptied of hay that was now piled into the center of the kitchen. "If there are any small things you would save, Ginny, do so quickly," Alex said quietly. "You cannot have escaped with much, but

502

things about your person will go unremarked."

"Only my mother's combs and jewelry," Ginny said. "All else but my clothes are Courtney possessions. All my worldly goods are in a house at Alum Bay, no longer mine."

"You will come to me as you stand, then, my own?" Alex said softly. "At last truly my own, that I may love and cherish without further obstacle. Not war, nor politics, nor difference of conviction, nor the past will stand between us again. Will you wed Parliament's general, my little Cavalier?"

"I will wed the father of my child," she said softly. "I will wed the man I love with a love that has always transcended our differences. And while I may not be able to embrace your political principles, my Roundhead love, I will live in peace with them."

Alex smiled. "I do not expect to live always in peace with such an indomitable rebel. A man cannot expect miracles." Taking her face between his hands, he kissed her with lingering sweetness, then left her standing on the bank as he put to the torch the chains that had bound her.

Epilogue

Alexander Marshall stepped through the great oak door and stood for a moment on the front step of the gracious Jacobean mansion of soft, sea-weathered stone standing on the cliff top above Alum Bay. It was a bright spring afternoon, the sky pellucid, scattered with drifting, cotton-puff clouds, the waters of the Solent clear and green, flecked with white horses, stretching to the coast of England, some five miles away.

He surveyed his orderly empire with a nod of quiet satisfaction. The driveways were weeded, the lawns neat, the earth of the flowerbeds freshly turned. A gardener, skilled in topiary, was clipping the ornamental box hedges, a peacock with full fantail appearing beneath the shears. Yes, Alex thought, his late father-in-law would have approved of the neat, prosperous solidity of his estate, now gifted to his daughter by her husband. Although he had never known John Redfern, Alex had heard so much from Ginny that he felt as if they were old friends, and it gave him much pleasure to feel that his management would have earned her father's approval.

He crossed the garden, stopping to exchange a few words with the gardener, going round to the westerly side of the house facing the bay. The springy grass of the headland stretched to the cliff edge, and he glanced down at the all but invisible rectangle that formed the door to the secret passage. The elder bush still flourished, but the priest's hole and its two entrances were known only to the master and mistress of the house. The two mischievous reasons for keeping the secret so closely guarded appeared from around the back corner of the house.

Masters William and Thomas Marshall, their three-year-old legs astride a pair of Shetland ponies were in the charge of Jed, chewing reflectively on a wisp of straw as he walked steadily between them. His charges squealed and bounced at the sight of their father who, smiling, walked to meet them.

"Where are you off to, then?" he asked, ruffling the chestnut heads. "Are you pirates or bandits this afternoon?"

His own green-brown eyes twinned, sparkled back at him. "Indians," William said. " 'N Jed is a settler. We're goin' to the orchard to play, aren't we, Jed?"

"Reckon so," Jed replied, laconic as usual. "Less'n you've other orders, General?"

Alex shook his head. "Don't let them plague you to death, though."

Jed chuckled. "They're no more likely to do so than you did."

"There are two of *them*," Alex pointed out with a grin.

Jed shrugged in careless dismissal of such a minor point. "It's their mother in 'em that puts them up to mischief, if you ask me."

Alex's grin broadened. Jed was more than entitled to voice such an opinion. It was one with which he was in wholehearted agreement anyway.

"Where's Mama?" Thomas asked, looking around expectantly at the mention of her.

"Sailing," his father told him. "I am going to call her in now."

"We'll come too." William swung one chubby leg across his saddle preparatory to launching himself, in usual disregarding fashion for life and limb to the ground. His brother promptly followed suit.

506

Alex grabbed one child, Jed the other. "No, you won't come too," he said firmly. "You are going to the orchard with Jed. I am going down to the beach to fetch Mama."

Incipient mutiny hovered, but General Marshall was just about a match for his twin sons. It was a close-run thing on many occasions, but this afternoon a steely look of resolution achieved compliance, albeit a reluctant one. Laughing, Alex watched them go, their shoulders set in stiff indignation for about one minute, before the short attention span of the three year old won the day and the prospect of playing Indians and settler in the orchard again took precedence.

Alex strolled to the cliff head, to the point where the narrow trail snaked down through the colored sand to the beach. At the mouth of the bay, he could see the sailboat tacking its way back and forth as Ginny brought the dinghy in from the wide waters of the Solent. It would take her a good ten minutes, he reckoned. Long enough for him to descend to the beach by the longer, more dignified route. Even after three years in this house, he still could not adapt to the goat trail that Ginny used by preference and that his sons assumed was the only way down.

Ginny saw Alex standing on the sand, hands on hips, watching her as she made a lengthier than necessary tack just for the pleasure of it. He beckoned imperatively, and she smiled and waved, debated teasing him with another long tack, then decided against it. Much as she enjoyed scudding across this clear green water, gazing down at the flat rocks masked in seaweed embedded in the sandy bottom, feeling the tiller in her hand, the tug of the main sheet as the sail filled in response to her guidance, it bore no comparison to being in the company of her husband, particularly on the deserted beach, on a glorious spring afternoon, with no immediately compelling calls upon one's time.

She pulled up the centerboard as the dinghy entered shallow water, swung the boat into the wind, and stood up to drop the sail. "Come and help," she called to Alex, still standing watching on the shore.

"You are quite capable of managing without help," he returned, "and I like to watch my raggle-taggle gypsy."

Ginny chuckled with a prickle of pleasurable anticipation. Hitching her skirt higher into the girdle at her waist, she swung herself over the stern, her brown legs flashing in the sun as she jumped knee deep into the shallow water, wading to shore, pulling the dinghy behind her.

Solemnly, Alex helped her beach it, keeping his hands to himself with an appearace of nonchalance. But when she stood, lifting her face to the sun's warmth, reaching up to tuck an errant wisp of chestnut hair back into her braid, her bosom lifting with the movement, her slim brown legs set firmly on this land that was her own, the narrow feet curling into the sand, he could withstand temptation no longer.

"I wonder if I will ever be able to resist you," he groaned, taking her hand and running her up the beach to the cool, damp cave where the dinghy was usually stowed. "I think it must have something to do with the open air." His fingers were busy with the hooks of her bodice.

"Like appetite," Ginny chuckled. "It grows sharper out of doors."

"No, it is because in the old days we rarely made love within doors, unless it were under canvas," he said, cupping her breasts as they fell free.

Ginny's hand fumbled with his belt buckle, pushed his britches off his hips with the impatience of desire that did not know how to bide its time.

"The boots have to come off first, chicken," he teased, and Ginny bit her lip in mortification, dropping to her knees on the damp sand, lifting his feet to pull off the inconvenient obstacles.

"You are wearing so many more clothes than I am," she grumbled, raising her face, pink with her exertions.

Alex gave a shout of laughter and pulled her to her feet. "How I love you, my own. Do you know how wonderfully funny you are, how delicious — how . . ." The laughter died from his face as he touched her lips with an almost reverential tenderness. "How there would be no meaning to my life

508

without you?"

"You are every breath I breathe," she whispered.

The sea crept softly up the beach, little waves licking the shore as the tide rose. The cave was redolent with the elemental scents of seaweed and damp sand, mingling with the rich fragrance of their loving, and the world disappeared, toppling slowly about them as infinity beckoned.

YOU WON'T WANT TO READ
JUST ONE—KATHERINE STONE

ROOMMATES   (0-8217-5206-5, $6.99/$7.99)
No one could have prepared Carrie for the monumental
changes she would face when she met her new circle of friends
at Stanford University. Once their lives intertwined and became
woven into the tapestry of the times, they would never be the
same.

TWINS   (0-8217-5207-3, $6.99/$7.99)
Brook and Melanie Chandler were so different, it was hard to
believe they were sisters. One was a dark, serious, ambitious
New York attorney; the other, a golden, glamourous, sophisti-
cated supermodel. But they were more than sisters—they were
twins and more alike than even they knew . . .

THE CARLTON CLUB   (0-8217-5204-9, $6.99/$7.99)
It was the place to see and be seen, the only place to be. And
for those who frequented the playground of the very rich, it
was a way of life. Mark, Kathleen, Leslie and Janet—they
worked together, played together, and loved together, all behind
exclusive gates of the *Carlton Club*.

Available wherever paperbacks are sold, or order direct from the
Publisher. Send cover price plus 50¢ per copy for mailing and
handling to Penguin USA, P.O. Box 999, c/o Dept. 17109,
Bergenfield, NJ 07621. Residents of New York and Tennessee
must include sales tax. DO NOT SEND CASH.

DANGEROUS GAMES   (0-7860-0270-0, $4.99)
by Amanda Scott

When Nicholas Barrington, eldest son of the Earl of Ul-combe, first met Melissa Seacort, the desperation he sensed beneath her well-bred beauty haunted him. He didn't realize how desperate Melissa really was . . . until he found her again at a Newmarket gambling club—being auctioned off by her father to the highest bidder. So, Nick bought himself a wife. With a villain hot on their heels, and a fortune and their lives at stake, they would gamble everything on the most dangerous game of all: love.

A TOUCH OF PARADISE   (0-7860-0271-9, $4.99)
by Alexa Smart

As a confidence man and scam runner in 1880s America, Malcolm Northrup has amassed a fortune. Now, posing as the eminent Sir John Abbot—scholar, and possible discoverer of the lost continent of Atlantis—he's taking his act on the road with a lecture tour, seeking funds for a scientific experiment he has no intention of making. But scholar Halia Davenport is determined to accompany Malcolm on his "expedition" . . . even if she must kidnap him!